"What are you doing?" Kim demanded, halting her in her tracks.

"The field does not emit an electromagnetic charge. It is safe to make physical contact."

"You don't know that," Kim insisted, his voice rising. "Maybe it only remains stable as long as no one touches it."

"Unlikely."

"But you can't know for sure."

"Lieutenant Kim . . ."

"Stop it, Seven."

Seven lowered her hand.

"Calm yourself, Lieutenant."

Kim involuntarily released an erratic breath.

Seven returned to his side and studied him with concern. "What are you afraid of?"

"I'm not afraid," Kim replied. "I'm just not comfortable with the thought that in a fraction of a second, our lives could end."

"One day they will. Given our choice of professions, the odds that our lives will end abruptly and under violent circumstances are increased exponentially. You know this and have never before expressed undue anxiety at the prospect."

Kim stared at her, unable to form a coherent response.

"I know," Seven said gently. "It's complicated."

SEVEN STEPPED CLOSER TO THE FIRE
AND EXTENDED HER HAND.

STAR TREK VOYAGER®

ARCHITECTS OF INFINITY

KIRSTEN BEYER

Based on *Star Trek*®
created by Gene Roddenberry
and
Star Trek: Voyager
created by
Rick Berman & Michael Piller & Jeri Taylor

POCKET BOOKS

New York   London   Toronto   Sydney   New Delhi

Pocket Books
An Imprint of Simon & Schuster, Inc.
1230 Avenue of the Americas
New York, NY 10020

This book is a work of fiction. Any references to historical events, real people, or real places are used fictitiously. Other names, characters, places, and events are products of the author's imagination, and any resemblance to actual events or places or persons, living or dead, is entirely coincidental.

First Pocket Books paperback edition April 2018

POCKET and colophon are registered trademarks of Simon & Schuster, Inc.

For information about special discounts for bulk purchases, please contact Simon & Schuster Special Sales at 1-866-506-1949 or business@simonandschuster.com.

The Simon & Schuster Speakers Bureau can bring authors to your live event. For more information or to book an event, contact the Simon & Schuster Speakers Bureau at 1-866-248-3049 or visit our website at www.simonspeakers.com.

Manufactured in the United States of America

10 9 8 7 6 5 4 3 2 1

ISBN 978-1-5011-3876-8
ISBN 978-1-5011-3882-9 (ebook)

For Margaret

HISTORIAN'S NOTE

Admiral Kathryn Janeway leads the Full Circle Fleet—*Voyager*, *Vesta*, *Galen*, and *Demeter*—on a mission of exploration in the Delta Quadrant. Many things have changed since a lone, lost Starship *Voyager* was trying to find her way home. The fleet is charged with discovering what has changed since *Voyager* was last here and the ultimate power in the quadrant, the Borg, departed.

This story takes place in August 2382 CE.

"All things done before the naked stars are remembered."

—*John M. Ford*

Prologue

Well?" Admiral Kathryn Janeway asked as she stared into the placid, orange-and-golden eyes of the Department of Temporal Investigations' current director, Laarin Andos. Despite the disconcerting report Janeway had just given the director regarding her fleet's recent encounter with the Krenim, the Rilnar, and the Zahl, and the multiple violations of the Temporal Prime Directive that had occurred during their mission to retrieve a temporally displaced version of Kathryn Janeway, Andos remained completely composed. She was a Rhaandarite and, rumor had it, over two hundred years old. Janeway was well aware that during her service to the Federation, Andos had seen or studied a number of incredibly complicated temporal disturbances. If the equanimity with which she seemed to accept the admiral's report was any indication, there must be little by now that could faze the woman.

"Are you still in possession of the temporal synchronization disruptors this Agent Dayne distributed among your crew members during the first temporal incursion in which you knowingly participated?" Andos asked evenly.

"We are," Janeway replied. "They don't work anymore."

"You attempted to use them again?" Andos asked, her voice rising a fraction of a hair.

"Of course not, Director. By the time we returned to *Vesta* and removed them, they were dead. Our scanners won't detect their presence, and we didn't think it was a good idea to take one apart and go digging around for its power source. We simply catalogued them and stored them in our new temporally shielded hold."

"I thought you said you had integrated temporal shielding into all of your fleet vessels once you realized the threat posed by the Krenim and their ability to manipulate the timeline."

"We did. The temporal shields draw a great deal of power from our other systems. It's not practical to operate them around the clock. No pun intended."

"I see."

"We have isolated a few crucial artifacts as well as copies of all of our logs. Those are always shielded. We are looking for ways to expand this defensive capability without disrupting other vital operations. It's likely that within the next few months we will have found another solution. My hope is that you will be able to assess the ongoing nature of the Krenim threat better than I can."

"That shouldn't be a challenge," Andos said lightly. *"But to be clear, you have no idea what became of the other Kathryn Janeway?"*

"No," Janeway replied. "Based on the image of the child we believe to be hers left behind by Agent Dayne and our personal contact with the woman called Mollah we encountered in the future version of Batibeh—"

"The alternate timeline, *Admiral,"* Andos corrected her gently.

"Director?"

"It will be incredibly important as we proceed to call things by their proper names, Admiral Janeway. I realized you are not, nor should you be, as well versed in temporal mechanics as I, but if we are to have any hope of minimizing the potential

for future temporal violations, it will be necessary for you to reacquaint yourself with the proper terms."

An unpleasant and entirely predictable band of tension tightened itself across the admiral's forehead. She had prided herself, for most of her career, on her ability to avoid the sorts of temporal shenanigans in which many other Starfleet officers seemed to constantly embroil themselves. She understood the dangers inherent in the manipulation of time, but more than that, she despised with the heat of a supernova *reporting* the incidents. Temporal mechanics, like all areas of scientific inquiry, was a constantly evolving field. Those immersed in it, like the director of the DTI and the field agents that served under her, added daily to their knowledge of the many ways in which space-time's dimensional boundaries could be altered. They lived on the cutting edge of temporal anomalies. Janeway had been happy to survive the course work on the topic at the Academy. That in the last several years she had so frequently found herself in a position where violating the Temporal Prime Directive was the best of many bad options was more than annoying to Janeway. It felt like a deeply personal failure.

Choosing her words with great care, the admiral said, "We cannot state to any degree of certainty that the alternate Kathryn Janeway who was created when the Krenim targeted *Voyager* with a chroniton torpedo in 2377 is still alive and occupying our current timeline. We believe Agent Dayne may have taken her with the intention of reuniting her with their daughter, Mollah. The existence of the elderly Mollah we encountered in the alternate timeline we visited, using the Zahl's temporal portal, suggests the possibility that the child had been raised in that alternate timeline. The statues present in the grove there of the two brothers tie

Dayne directly to that timeline and if his words to me can be believed—a dubious proposition at best, I know—the Krenim were responsible for its creation."

"But this Mollah did not recognize you or the alternate Kathryn Janeway when she met you, did she?" Andos asked.

"She did not appear to," Janeway admitted. "And any connection between her and the child in the portrait might be nothing more than wishful thinking. But if she spent any amount of time with her father prior to our arrival, she would no doubt have been informed of the necessity of not indicating that she knew us to avoid creating a temporal paradox."

"It was much too late by then to avoid any such thing," Andos cautioned her.

"Be that as it may, I like to believe she was Kathryn's daughter and somehow Dayne managed to return her to her mother."

Andos shook her head slightly. *"I understand that desire, Admiral. But in the absence of concrete evidence, I am afraid we must consider the fate of the alternate Kathryn Janeway an issue as yet unresolved."*

"I understand, Director."

"And one you will under no circumstances attempt to investigate further."

"If it's something you feel strongly about."

"It is. The artifacts you mentioned that remain shielded—do they include the logs from Voyager's *contact with the Krenim in the alternate timeline in which you encountered this Annorax?"* Andos asked.

"Yes. The temporal buoys that housed them disintegrated after only a few hours once they were removed from subspace but we had copied all of the logs by then."

"I am impressed with the resourcefulness of whichever version of you it was that decided to create those temporally shielded records. We utilize a similar protocol here, and my first order of business will be to have the agent I intend to assign to your case forward you the latest technological specifications for replicating the least invasive sustainable temporal shielding currently used by the DTI. I congratulate your mission specialist, Seven, on her industriousness, but I would prefer that Starfleet refrain from dabbling with Borg-inspired technology, especially when it comes to temporal disturbances."

Janeway's spine stiffened involuntarily. Seven was the only reason any trace of *Voyager*'s previous encounter with the Krenim existed. "Out here, in the wilds of unexplored space, I am not inclined to dismiss a good idea, no matter where it comes from, Director."

"That's because you cannot properly contextualize, as I can, the manner in which certain ideas have the potential to do much more harm than good. In every instance of which we are aware that the words 'Borg' and 'temporal manipulation' were used in proximity to one another, a cataclysmic end result was narrowly avoided. I must insist that you adhere to our regulations going forward, Admiral. Therein lies our best hope of untangling any future temporal disturbances you may unintentionally cause."

Thus far, the director hadn't hinted at disciplinary action as a result of the many violations of the Temporal Prime Directive this latest incident might have indicated, but the warning was clear and Janeway hastened to defend herself and her crew.

"Director, we didn't go looking for this fight. We learned of the existence of the alternate Kathryn Janeway while attempting to open diplomatic relations with an unrelated species. This is the definition of my fleet's mission out here. Would the Department of Temporal Investigations have preferred that we not have investigated this anomaly? By doing so, haven't we revealed a potential threat to the Federation and made it more difficult for the Krenim, should they so desire, to act against us unawares?"

"A threat you caused, Admiral."

Check and mate. Janeway could not argue with the fact that it was *Voyager*'s first encounter with the Krenim several years prior that had begun the series of tragic events that followed, nor could she shift responsibility for the Krenim's current interest in her and other "chaotic variables" elsewhere. Her review of the shielded logs detailing that initial encounter had revealed in nauseating detail the depths to which her desire to end Annorax's reign of temporal terror had led her: the loss of much of her crew and the destruction of *Voyager*. It had been a harsh realization, one for which she was now grateful. Until she had heard her own voice detailing the devastation in bleak detail, she would never have believed it possible for her to miscalculate a situation so thoroughly. But she also knew that for the fleet to move forward, she had to face her fears about the Krenim's capabilities head-on. She needed to know how bad the current situation could get and begin to prepare appropriate countermeasures.

She wanted to believe that the détente she had apparently reached with Agent Dayne would remain in effect indefinitely. But every other word Dayne had spoken had been a lie, so it was hard to take comfort in the substance of their final conversation.

"Is there any way for you to calculate the odds that any future incursions the Krenim might make could adversely impact the Federation?" the admiral asked.

"The Federation or your fleet?"

"Wouldn't one affect the other?"

"Yes, but depending upon the penetration of the technology used, the greater impacts of an initial attack on your fleet in the Delta Quadrant might not register in Federation space for quite some time."

"Doesn't your department possess technology that alerts you to instances of temporal tampering?"

"In a manner of speaking," Andos replied. "We have temporally shielded records that can alert us to alterations of the timeline. But as you yourself have recently discovered, the Krenim have been making adjustments, small and large, to their corner of the Delta Quadrant for some time. We have no way to monitor that history. The Krenim are therefore free to continue to make alterations we would have no way to know occurred."

"This conversation was supposed to make me feel better," Janeway mused.

"I apologize for my inability to oblige you, Admiral. The only comfort I can offer you going forward will be the constant vigilance of one of my most experienced agents. By monitoring all of your activities and adding the records to our temporally shielded logs, any temporal anomaly should be captured almost as soon as it occurs. We will then seek out the quickest and most efficient way to deal with any such eventuality."

"Have you already selected the agent you intend to assign to our case?"

"I have. His name is Gariff Lucsly."

Janeway tried and failed to hide her dismay.

"Are you certain he is the best choice for this assignment?"

"As far as I am concerned, Admiral, Lucsly is the only agent currently in our ranks equipped to handle a case of this magnitude."

The admiral couldn't argue with the director's right to assign her staff as she saw fit. She also couldn't take any solace in Andos's choice. The most thorough debriefing she had endured when *Voyager* had first returned to the Alpha Quadrant had been at Lucsly's hands, and she had left their session certain of two things: Lucsly held her in the lowest possible esteem and intended to bring charges against her that would end her career. The fact that no such thing had occurred led her to believe that at least one of his superiors disagreed with his assessment. His inability to act on his convictions had likely only deepened his disdain for her. Briefly Janeway wondered if allowing the Krenim to continue altering the timeline to suit their whims was a better fate than submitting herself to the will of the officious temporal bureaucrat.

As was so often the case, none of the options before the admiral were good. Her only choice was among variations on a bad theme.

"I will transmit your report and logs to Lucsly now, Admiral. You will hear from him shortly."

"I look forward to it, Director," Janeway lied.

1

"You don't believe in lying?"

"Waste of time."

"Even to spare someone's feelings?"

Ensign Aytar Gwyn shrugged. "How is that helpful? If you don't respect someone enough to be honest with them, why say anything?"

Lieutenant Devi Patel paused momentarily over the samples she was analyzing at the shuttle's small science station. "Last week you told Gaines Aubrey to his face that you were celibate. *That* was a lie."

"Not right then, it wasn't."

"You've bunked it with half the fleet in the last year. What was so objectionable about poor Gaines?"

"If you don't know, then you should give it a go, Devi. Clearly he's lonely."

"Awa—tea- to Va— *-ise."*

Gwyn, who had brought the shuttle into orbit around this uninhabited rock on Lieutenant Harry Kim's orders was now maintaining orbit, while monitoring his and Seven's life signs. She tweaked the automated gain control in the comm system's signal quantizer to clear up Kim's transmission. "What can we do for you, Lieutenant Kim?"

"You can start by observing proper comm protocol, Ensign," Kim replied abruptly.

Gwyn turned to Patel, hoping to find a kindred spirit in her annoyance. The science officer's tight lips and wide eyes implored Gwyn to take Kim's admonishment seriously and adjust her attitude accordingly. Gwyn rolled her eyes before responding. "Of course, sir. I apologize. Lieutenant Patel has almost completed her analysis of samples . . ."

"Sixteen through twenty," Patel interjected quickly.

"And?" Kim demanded.

"All five samples confirm prior readings and Seven's hypothesis, Lieutenant," Patel continued. "There are two distinct isotopes present, but the atomic weight indicates a previously undetected, super-heavy—"

"I'll be damned," Kim cut her off, clearly pleased.

"We've also noted the unexpected molecular structure and the presence of several other more common elements and isotopes."

"Any idea if they are simply the product of decay?"

"Not yet, sir. We're going to have to analyze them further when we get back to *Voyager.*" After a moment Patel asked, "Do you know what you're going to call it?"

"We should give that some serious thought," Kim replied. *"It's a brand-new element, after all."*

Gwyn tapped the comm channel to momentarily silence the shuttle's transmitter and said to Patel, "A week of holodeck privileges says it ends up being named *Sevenofninonium.*"

Patel stifled a laugh. Gwyn was moving to restore the open comm channel when Seven's voice echoed throughout the shuttle. *"Unlikely, Ensign Gwyn, but we will pass your recommendation along to the Federation Division of Applied Chemistry."*

Panic struck the pilot's gut. Double-checking the controls, she realized that she hadn't actually closed the channel from her end. She had unintentionally increased the signal strength. *So Seven had heard the joke.*

Gwyn shook her head in frustration at her mistake. She'd felt a little off her game for days now; ever since the fleet had departed the system containing the planet Sormana. Apparently this afternoon was not going to be a significant improvement in that department.

To Gwyn's surprise, Kim refrained from chastising her further. *"We'll be ready to transport back shortly. Away team out."*

Only then did Patel say, "Thanks, Gwyn. You almost got both of us on report. Push it much?"

Gwyn sighed. "I don't think Seven was offended. I'm not sure it's even *possible* to offend her. And Kim has been in a crap mood for weeks. Nothing I do or say is going to change that. It's not my fault, or yours. But just because his life is hard right now doesn't mean the rest of us have to cover our faces with *chiicsel*, rub *sorgh* in our hair, and wear black *mealtisa* wraps."

"Yes, observing full Kriosian mourning might be taking things too far. But common courtesy, not going out of your way to tick him off would be a good idea."

"The *Sevenofninonium* thing was not out of the way. It was right there in front of both of us. *Somebody* had to say it."

Patel smirked in spite of herself. "Of course a former Borg, now Caeliar-catomic enhanced mission specialist who just happens to look like a cross between a Grecian, Thettin, and Hyliat goddess would be the one to discover a brand-new element."

"Naturally," Gwyn agreed.

"How many times has she single-handedly saved the universe?" Patel asked.

"I stopped counting after the fifth . . . or was it sixth time?" Gwyn asked. "Just don't be bitter because she's beautiful, Devi. *That's* beneath you."

"Oh, I'm not. I'm bitter because despite the fact that she never even attended Starfleet Academy, has never accepted a Starfleet commission, has no official rank or the attendant privileges, she is and will always be the first person on *Voyager* that Captain Chakotay looks to whenever the solution to any science issue isn't already displayed on his terminal."

"As opposed to?" Gwyn asked.

"His actual senior science officer," Patel replied, punching Gwyn in the upper arm.

"Ow. I know. I was just teasing," Gwyn said, automatically applying pressure with her free hand. "That hurt."

"Sorry," Patel said, but clearly wasn't.

"You know, if you get your ass out there and discover a brand-new element yourself, maybe that'll change," Gwynn suggested.

Patel finished stowing the portable magnetic particle imager and flopped down in the navigator's chair beside Gwyn. "No, it won't," she said seriously.

Gwyn's eyes met Devi's in silent commiseration. Several of *Voyager*'s senior officers, including Captain Chakotay, Commanders Tom Paris and B'Elanna Torres, and Lieutenant Harry Kim, had spent years together traveling through the Delta Quadrant in a valiant attempt to return home after an alien technology had flung them to the far end of the galaxy on their maiden trek. Seven of Nine (Tertiary Adjunct to Unimatrix 01), née Annika Hansen, now simply Seven, had joined them roughly halfway through during one of many terrifying encounters between *Voyager* and the Borg. Those years had forged a unique bond between the men and women who had shared them.

Gwyn wasn't sure she would have sacrificed seven years

cut off from the Federation and Starfleet's resources, braving unknown space and hostile species, in order to join that exclusive club. But she couldn't deny the power of it, or the fact that it made life and duty harder for those who transferred to *Voyager* any time after they returned to the Alpha Quadrant.

Patel had been on board since their first refit as Captain Chakotay's science officer for almost three years before Seven rejoined the crew as a mission specialist, but as soon as the former Borg had returned, she had become Chakotay's go-to resource the minute things got tricky. Gwyn didn't believe the captain doubted Devi or her abilities. But Seven was, and always would be, *Seven.* She was one of the captain's oldest and closest friends, and she was inarguably brilliant. Neither Devi nor anyone else would ever be able to compete with that, and they shouldn't try. Like Gwyn, she should just keep her head down and her record clean and look forward to the day when she would find herself aboard a more traditional Starfleet vessel where rank and experience mattered more than personal relationships. No matter how much she, or Patel, or any of the other new faces among the Full Circle Fleet might wish otherwise, they were never going to join the ranks of *Voyager*'s inner circle and it was "effort after folly," as Gwyn's mother used to say, to wish otherwise.

"You've got a little less than two years left on this mission, Devi," Gwyn said. "That's plenty of time to prove to the captain that you are every bit as brilliant, resourceful, and necessary as Seven."

Patel studied Gwyn's face for a long moment. "That's why you don't lie," she finally said. "You're terrible at it."

"I really am," Gwyn acknowledged. "My mother used to

know the split second she saw my face. I never even had to say a word."

The young science officer shifted her gaze to the shuttle's-eye view of the planet beneath them. From orbit, most of the surface was reddish brown and decidedly inhospitable at first glance.

"What do you think is wrong with Kim?" Patel finally asked.

"Hard to say. But if I had to place latinum on it, I'd bet it has something to do with Lieutenant Conlon's transfer to *Galen*."

"I don't know. I could never really tell if they were serious about each other."

Gwyn tossed a dubious glance in Patel's direction. "No?"

Patel shook her head in response.

"Come to think of it, Devi, you and Aubrey should definitely have dinner. You're perfect for each other."

"Why?"

"You're both absolutely clueless when the subject is anything we weren't tested on at the Academy."

After a stunned moment, Patel said, "Should I take your honesty as evidence of how much you respect me?"

"Yes."

"I'm done talking to you now."

"For how long?"

"At least until we get back to *Voyager*."

"That's going to be a whole day."

"Yes, it is."

"Starting when?"

Patel busied herself making notations on her padd.

"Now?"

Silence.

"Really?"

Longer silence.

Gwyn sighed. *Definitely still off my game.*

SURFACE, UNNAMED CIRCUMBINARY PLANET

Lieutenant Harry Kim stood waist-deep in fine, grasslike blades that covered the ground as far as the eye could see. The delicate stalks were a fluffy white, and sticky bits were deposited in generous amounts on his black uniform pants everywhere they had touched the alien flora.

The unending field was an illusion. Kim was actually fifty-one kilometers from dead center of a biodome, a spherical energy field constructed by unknown hands and sustained by awfully impressive alien technology. This biodome and forty-six others like it were the only habitable regions on this unnamed planet located in one of many sectors of the Delta Quadrant that used to belong to the Borg.

Despite the extraordinary characteristics of the biodome, Kim had spent the better part of this day studying the construct before him. Almost eight meters tall, and fourteen deep in certain sections, it resembled dozens of discrete interwoven tendrils bursting forth from the ground. Each one varied in length and thickness and there was no pattern to their plaiting. But, like many transcendent sculptural pieces, there was a sense of motion to it, an undulating quality even in its absolute stillness that was mesmerizing.

It was also no longer intact. Some of the "vines" had been broken off haphazardly. There were large chunks missing from others. What might have once been an upper section lay on its side several dozen meters away, all but buried in the white grass.

Neither the dome nor the magnificent sculptural properties of the construct interested Seven in the least. She had come with one goal; to remove samples of what Patel had just identified as a previously unknown element. Now that the heavy lifting was done and Lieutenant Patel had confirmed what Seven had believed to be true since her astrometric sensors had completed deep scans on the unusual planet located just outside the binary system's habitable zone, Kim should have been more than ready to return to the shuttle.

He wasn't.

Captain Chakotay was going to be thrilled with their report. Eliciting this reaction from the captain as often as possible was very near the top of Kim's priorities these days. Chakotay said he had forgiven his security and tactical chief for the lapses in judgment that occurred during their last mission, especially now that the causes of those transgressions were clearly understood.

Kim could not say the same for himself.

Days like this one, filled with purpose and discovery, were the only things standing between Kim and the abyss. He was grateful for it and not at all looking forward to its conclusion or the shuttle journey to rendezvous with *Voyager* that lay ahead of his team. Gwyn would remain just this side of professional, but only *just*. She had been the greenest of ensigns when the fleet launched a little over a year ago, and while proving herself time and again to be a fantastic pilot—worthy of filling Tom Paris's seat at *Voyager*'s helm—her sense of decorum still needed work.

Patel could be professional to a fault. Sometimes Kim found it hard to believe she wasn't Vulcan. Her sense of propriety and stoic demeanor, even her fine black hair and severe cut, reminded him of several Vulcan officers with whom Kim had served. Patel was human. She just didn't seem to want anyone to notice it.

And Seven would be . . . Seven. She would spend her time running calculations and planning experiments to run with her *Sevenofninonium*. Thanks to Ensign Gwyn, Kim was never going to be able to think of the new element as anything else now, no matter what the Federation officials tasked with naming such discoveries eventually decided to designate it.

Which would leave Kim alone with his thoughts; literally the last place he wanted to be right now.

His musings were interrupted by Seven. "I have completed my final scans, Lieutenant. Shall we signal the shuttle for transport?"

"Are you sure you don't want to check out any of the other biodomes?" Kim asked, even though he knew what her answer would likely be.

"The odds are extremely low that you and I have seen the last of this world. Captain Chakotay will most certainly wish to investigate further."

"So that's a no?" Kim asked, half teasing.

In her early years as part of *Voyager*'s crew, Seven would have let the comment pass and simply signaled the shuttle. Now, she affixed her tricorder to her belt and said, "We have not, however, taken any visual readings of the edges of this biodome. The nearest one is less than a kilometer south-southeast of this position."

Kim was oddly touched by her simple gesture. There was no need to visually inspect the edge of the dome. There was little to be learned that their shuttle's sensors couldn't tell them. Seven knew that. She was reaching, for his sake. Sometime in the last few years Seven had become a great

deal more sensitive to the emotions of her friends and infinitely more patient with them than she had been when she
was first reintroduced to her humanity.

"Sounds good," Kim said.

They walked in comfortable silence for a few minutes.
Seven checked her tricorder occasionally to confirm their
heading. The configuration of the invisible energy field that
was responsible for sustaining this biodome was similar to
the others found on the surface. This one was only a little over a hundred kilometers in diameter, comparatively
speaking rather small. Contained in most of the domes was
a version of a nitrogen-oxygen atmosphere, a vast array of
plants, water sources, and other examples of structures like
the one Seven had just identified as partially composed of
her new element. The domes also regulated exposure to
light and radiation, eradicating the dangers posed when the
planet's rotation was turned toward the binary stars. There
were no other life-forms present and no immediate indication of who might have placed the domes here. This was
the very definition of the "strange new worlds" Starfleet had
been created to discover.

"I would have thought you would be anxious to return
to the fleet as soon as possible," Seven finally said in an obvious attempt to draw him out.

"I don't expect anything will have changed in the last
few days."

The tall grass had begun to thin out a bit and Seven
paused her steps to brush some of the heavy white particles
from her black uniform pants.

"While I understand your desire to avoid confrontation,
I do not believe it to be a viable long-term strategy," Seven
said.

"I'm not expecting a confrontation when we return."

Seven lowered her eyes to meet Kim's. Her newfound patience was clearly beginning to wear thin.

The back of Kim's neck began to burn intensely. For a few seconds he was incapable of rational thought. After a deep breath, the sensation passed, leaving the lieutenant shaken. "So much for doctor-patient confidentiality," Kim said.

"I was not advised of Lieutenant Conlon's condition by Counselor Cambridge," Seven said. "I was briefed by Doctor Sharak, who did not violate her privacy intentionally. He inquired about several hypothetical uses for my catoms, including their ability to aid in gene regulation and any complications that might occur when an individual is pregnant. I advised him that following my work with the small gestalt created by Doctor Frazier's people, I intentionally severed my conscious ability to interact with my catoms. Even had Commander Briggs's experiments not demonstrated the folly of rushing catomic research at this time, I am in no position to attempt to use my catoms as Doctor Sharak requested. Only once our discussion had concluded did I intuit the true nature of his *hypothetical* inquiries."

"Fair enough," Kim said. Seven was one of the brightest people he'd ever known, and he couldn't fault Sharak for exploiting every possible resource available to cure the degenerative genetic condition now plaguing Nancy Conlon. That *Voyager*'s CMO was already looking for wildly speculative options like catomic intervention didn't bode well. "The last time Nancy and I discussed it, she indicated that she did not intend to carry the child to term. She also made it absolutely clear that it was *her* decision. I don't get a vote."

Seven silently held his gaze.

"What?"

"Did you or did you not contribute fifty percent of the child's genetic material?" Seven asked.

"I did."

"And I assume you did not force this material on Lieutenant Conlon against her will."

"Of course not."

"The child in question is then *yours* as much as it is hers, is it not?"

"Yes, but . . ."

"But because you are not required to carry it within your body while it gestates you have no rights where it is concerned?"

"Something like that."

"That is absurd."

Kim paused, wondering if it was possible that Seven could be more frustrated by Nancy's choice than he was. He doubted it, but he had rarely seen her take a position this strong on a subject that did not impact her directly.

"It's complicated, Seven."

"Do you want the child?" she persisted.

Kim sighed. Suddenly, being left alone to his thoughts in the shuttle seemed infinitely preferable to continuing this conversation.

"I don't know," he finally admitted. "I just know what I want isn't going to matter."

Seven considered him for a few moments before resuming their course toward the edge of the biodome. Upon reaching the top of a gentle incline, it came into view: a disorienting sight.

The grass gave way to reddish-brown dirt, punctuated here and there by small clumps of indigo weeds. The soil came to an abrupt end at an invisible barrier whose curve was impossible to see this close. Beyond that barrier a hellish, uneven, rocky red plain extended as far as Kim could see. On this side of the energy field, he and Seven could stand until they grew old in a breathable atmosphere. Should the field fail now, they would be burnt to a crisp in seconds by the intense radiation kicked off by the twin stars this lonely planet orbited.

For the first time since they had arrived, anxiety not directly related to the mess his personal life had become threatened to overwhelm Kim. He knew, based on the age of the construct and the scans of the planet, that this biodome had stood continuously for thousands of years. There was no reason to believe it was going to cease functioning simply because at this moment he was imagining the potential consequences of such a failure.

But Kim couldn't shake the thought. His breath grew shallow.

Seven stepped closer to the field and extended her hand.

"What are you doing?" he demanded, halting her in her tracks.

"The field does not emit an electromagnetic charge. It is safe to make physical contact."

"You don't know that," Kim insisted, his voice rising. "Maybe it only remains stable as long as no one touches it."

"Unlikely."

"But you can't know for sure."

"Lieutenant Kim . . ."

"Stop it, Seven."

Seven lowered her hand.

"Calm yourself, Lieutenant."

Kim involuntarily released an erratic breath.

Seven returned to his side and studied him with concern. "What are you afraid of?"

"I'm not afraid," Kim replied. "I'm just not comfortable with the thought that in a fraction of a second our lives could end."

"One day they will. Given our choice of professions, the odds that our lives will end abruptly and under violent circumstances are increased exponentially. You know this and have never before expressed undue anxiety at the prospect."

Kim stared at her, unable to form a coherent response.

"I know," Seven said gently. "It's complicated."

Kim stepped back and turned away from the edge of the biodome. Staring out at the calm sea of pale grass before him restored his sense of equilibrium.

Seven reached his side and placed her hand on his shoulder. They stood like that for several moments before Seven activated her combadge and requested transport back to the shuttle.

U.S.S. GALEN

Lieutenant Nancy Conlon stood on a ridgeline, marveling at the forest below. It wasn't the riotous golden shades of the leaves that held her enthralled, although they were spectacular. It was another mind-boggling feature of this particular holographic vista.

As far as the eye could see, for acres in every direction, a canopy of autumnal glory topped tall, slender, white-barked trees that numbered in the thousands. She had spent most of the morning walking among them, struck by the regularity in the twenty-meter-high trunks, peering closely at the black scarring that looked like self-inflicted wounds, and pausing from time to time as a crisp breeze wafted through, setting the leaves aquiver.

Gorgeous as they were up close, however, they were best appreciated en masse from above. It was from this perspective that the quaking aspen really knocked one's socks off.

Because all of them, *every single trunk*, belonged to one tree. Technically, they were clones of one another, but the vast interconnected and invisible root system created what was, essentially, a single living organism. The vast deciduous masterpiece of nature had grown from a single seed, and a few hundred years later had spread itself out, mile after mile, daring anyone who witnessed it to deny its power.

Conlon had spent a great deal of time lately wondering at and cursing the mysteries of genetic biology, and when she'd come across this holodeck program's description in *Galen's* library—a file placed there by the ship's captain, Commander Clarissa Glenn—she hadn't been able to resist a peek.

A brief walk meant to clear her head had given way to hours of exploration. But the exertion had cost her dearly. Her heart rate refused to slow, even after several minutes of stillness. A dull throb in her head was ratcheting itself up toward pounding. She fervently hoped that the headaches that had followed on the heels of Xolani's attack several months prior weren't about to return. Her empty stomach churned mercilessly. A few sips of water only made it worse and threatened to come right back up her esophagus.

Keep it together, she chided herself, trying to take long, deep breaths. She had come a long way in the last few weeks. She had been taken off "suicide watch" within days of its imposition, and her use of *Galen's* holodecks had become unrestricted. She had submitted dutifully to her daily sessions with Counselor Hugh Cambridge and their talks had done much to help put her current condition in perspective. Now that she was no longer considered a danger to herself, she had asked and been granted the right to return to light duty aboard *Voyager*. Tomorrow would be her first day back, and she was truly looking forward to it, as was Commander Torres, the fleet's chief engineer who had been filling in for Conlon since she was first diagnosed with the DNA damage repair syndrome that was likely going to kill her.

She had also made peace with the pending termination of her pregnancy. It was not a choice she took lightly, but she knew in her bones that it was the right decision. She and Harry loved each other, but they were not ready to be parents. Even if they had been married, she might have made the same call given her current life expectancy. Without a miracle she was going to be lucky to see the next three years, and it was likely she would be moderately to severely disabled for much of that time. She had agreed to continue the pregnancy thus far while wrestling with the decision Doctor Sal had pressed upon her. Sal wanted to extract embryonic stem cells to determine whether or not they could be used to help repair the damage to her DNA. Conlon had resisted until now. Finally, that choice, too, had been made.

All that remained was to inform Harry and her doctors and to get back to the life she had worked so hard to create for herself as *Voyager*'s chief engineer. She had no idea how long she would have to enjoy it, but she was determined to make the most of it until that was no longer possible.

These thoughts had cheered her as she walked among the quaking aspens. They should have calmed her as she stood above them, awash in their vast beauty.

The distant sun suddenly began growing, its light blinding as it expanded, absorbing the golden foliage below. Conlon turned her head away and closed her eyes as a sharp pain shot through her skull. The last thing of which she was aware was the odd momentary sensation of floating above the earth.

She lost consciousness before her body impacted the soft soil of the holodeck.

2

don't want you to violate Lieutenant Conlon's privacy, Counselor," Captain Chakotay insisted.

Voyager's counselor, Lieutenant Hugh Cambridge, a lanky, middle-aged Brit who was sporting a few days' nonregulation stubble on his cheeks, continued to meet his captain's eyes defiantly. In an officer Chakotay didn't know as well, the counselor's expression might have risen to insubordination, but for Cambridge this was pretty much his default setting.

"Then stop asking me questions you know I can't answer," Cambridge suggested.

"Is she going to die?"

"Someday."

"Hugh."

"She's probably already in surgery. As of this moment, you know as much as I do about her prognosis. All I can tell you for certain is that she will be unable to resume her duties for the foreseeable future. Her medical leave aboard *Galen* has once again been categorized as *indefinite* by her physicians."

"Why indefinite?"

"None of us can say how long it's going to take to crack this thing."

"And her entire medical team is in agreement?"

"Is that so hard to believe?"

Chakotay shrugged. "I imagine everyone gets along well enough with Doctor Sharak."

"Indeed," Cambridge agreed. "The man is utterly delightful."

"And Doctor Sal certainly seems competent."

"She's the only one among us with any experience treating a condition similar to Conlon's. Her expertise is invaluable even if her bedside manner tends toward the bracing end of the spectrum."

Chakotay smiled in spite of himself. He could well imagine how little patience *Vesta*'s octogenarian chief medical officer had for anyone's nonsense. Personally, he liked her directness. Then again, he'd never been her patient.

Although both Sharak and Sal were consulting physicians and Cambridge had chosen to continue on as Conlon's psychological counselor, *Voyager*'s former Emergency Medical Hologram, known only as "the Doctor," was taking the lead on the case. He was one of a handful of crew members Chakotay thought of as family, and the captain's confidence in him was absolute. He was well aware however, that Cambridge had not always felt the same.

"How are you and the Doctor getting along? You've had your challenges in the past," Chakotay said, cutting right to the chase.

"I can't speak for the Doctor, but as far as I am concerned, that is where they will remain: in the past," Cambridge assured him. "When it comes to Lieutenant Conlon's health, we all want the same thing. If anything, I'm concerned about the Doctor. You know how he is when he's got something stuck in his teeth. His program has been running constantly since she was first diagnosed, and his tolerance for failure is even smaller than mine. He will leave no avenue that might lead to a cure unexplored."

Chakotay expected no less. Conlon was in the best possible hands. But she was also a critical member of *Voyager*'s crew, and her temporary loss was proving difficult to manage.

"B'Elanna is swamped balancing her responsibilities as both the fleet and *Voyager*'s chief engineer. Her son is barely two months old and Miral is a handful. I'd like to offer her some relief, or at least certainty that there's an end in sight."

"When there is, I'll tell you."

"Fair enough," Chakotay said, stepping back toward the desk in his ready room and picking up a padd containing the day's duty roster. Despite the fact that his ship was currently holding position with the rest of the Full Circle Fleet several light-years from the nearest star system in a pocket of unexplored space, the number of issues requiring his immediate attention was daunting. The status of his chief engineer wasn't the least of his worries, but there were several other matters that currently took priority. Every morning since her diagnosis when Cambridge had briefed him, Chakotay had expected to hear that Lieutenant Conlon had been cured. He understood that her medical condition was serious and complicated, but he was also accustomed to the Doctor making short work of the most challenging medical mysteries. That he had been assisted by Doctors Sharak and Sal and still made no discernable progress was discouraging.

"Should I take this development as a sign that I need to make other arrangements?" the captain asked.

"We're not there yet, Chakotay. We are exploring a number of promising therapies. And given the rigors of her normal duties and the sheer tonnage of devastation she and the other officers and crewmen in the fleet have faced in the last year, a few weeks of complete relaxation hardly seems too much to ask."

"I'm starting to wonder if a little rest and relaxation wouldn't do all of us good," Chakotay mused.

Cambridge shrugged. "Our efficiency reports have been

lackluster lately, and a fair number of my other patients are clearly struggling. I've searched your logs but found no mention of any previously discovered worlds you could classify as the Delta Quadrant's version of Risa, but if one existed, I'd be willing to declare a shipwide medical emergency, assume command, and set a course."

"It won't come to that," Chakotay said.

"Pity. I look rather striking in red," Cambridge quipped.

"Commander Paris to Captain Chakotay," the first officer's voice sounded over the comm.

Chakotay tapped his combadge. "Go ahead, Tom."

"The Van Cise *just made contact. Seven's preliminary report is promising."*

"She was right?" Chakotay asked, a smile breaking over his face.

"Yes, sir. For the one million, six hundred and ninety-two thousandth time."

Cambridge chuckled as Chakotay said, "Forward her report to me. Set an intercept course. Advise Admiral Janeway that we'll be breaking formation but should return in a few hours."

"Aye, sir."

"Why the rush?" Cambridge asked.

"Seven didn't tell you anything about the planet she and Lieutenant Kim just went to investigate?"

"She might have." When Chakotay's eyes narrowed, he added, "Had I known there was going to be a quiz, I would have given her my full attention. As it stands, I recall something about an unusual mineral deposit."

"Element. She thought she had discovered a new element."

"Oh, well done," Cambridge said.

"Yes. And the planet in question has several habitable

areas free of hostile life-forms, or *any* life-forms if her initial scans are to be believed."

"Indeed?"

"It's not Risa."

"These days, even Risa isn't Risa anymore."

"But it might do."

"What percentage of our resources do you think Admiral Janeway will consider allocating toward further exploration of this new element and the planet it calls home?" Cambridge asked.

"Forward me the most recent efficiency evaluations and request copies of the same from *Vesta, Galen,* and *Demeter*," Chakotay replied. "I'm going to suggest a fleet-wide break."

"Ambitious."

"Necessary."

"Care to wager on her response?"

"Wouldn't be fair."

"No? I'm not sure the words 'rest' or 'relaxation' are even in the admiral's vocabulary. Not with so much of the Delta Quadrant still to be explored and only two more years in which to do it."

"True. But we don't have to describe it that way."

"How would *we* describe it?"

Chakotay grinned. "Leave that to me."

"Just don't get your hopes up, Captain."

"Shouldn't one of us?"

GALEN

Surgery wasn't often a team effort. Most procedures performed aboard a starship could be completed quite safely with one attending surgeon guiding the medical scalpels and cellular repair sutures. The computer could also notify the surgeon if common medications might be required during surgery and inject them upon verbal authorization.

The unique sickbay aboard the Federation *Starship Galen* had been designed by the Doctor, his creator, Lewis Zimmerman, and the holographic specialist Lieutenant Reginald Barclay to make reliance on other organic medics or doctors unnecessary in almost all cases. This wasn't only because the Doctor preferred to work alone. The entire experimental vessel was a testbed for the Federation's latest holographic technology and, as such, meant to collect data on the viability of staffing any ship's sickbay with a minimum number of organic doctors and a plethora of specialized medical holograms.

The procedure the Doctor was performing to repair a rupture in Lieutenant Nancy Conlon's anterior cerebral artery was an exception to this rule for two reasons.

The first was that Nancy Conlon wasn't the only patient on the biobed. The embryo she carried was developing normally despite the genetic damage that had caused the bleeding in Conlon's brain. It was also in danger of spontaneously aborting if Conlon's blood pressure fell too low or her other organs began to fail during the surgical procedure. *Voyager's* current CMO, Doctor Sharak, was on hand to monitor the embryo's vitals and advise the Doctor should its biosigns indicate distress.

The second was the other urgent issue at hand— determining whether or not the arterial rupture was an isolated incident or a systemic failure brought about by the inability of Conlon's DNA to repair itself as all cells did in the normal course of their lives. As the Doctor worked carefully to repair the damaged artery, Doctor El'nor Sal, the

CMO of the *Vesta*, completed a thorough neural scan, hunting for any other damage that had not yet presented itself.

The Doctor's internal chronometer indicated the procedure was at the five hour, eighteen minute mark when Sal asked, "What is your count, Doctor?"

"Estimate seventy-nine more points of closure along the arterial wall. We've got at least another hour to go."

"Once you're done, we're going to need to reinforce two other arterial lines," Sal advised. "And just so you know, I've decided here and now that your creators were wise beyond their ken. You could do this for the next three days without growing weary if you had to, couldn't you?"

The Doctor registered satisfaction at Sal's remark. There were still numerous physicians who distrusted the use of medical holograms on principle. The Doctor didn't know how long it would take, but he firmly believed that eventually, petty prejudices would be overcome and that he and others like him would regularly stand shoulder to shoulder beside their organic brethren in healing.

"I could," he replied, "but I don't think our patient could survive that. Assuming there are only two other detectable weaknesses, we should be able to close in the next three hours."

"You'll be inducing a coma at that point, yes?"

"Absolutely. We'll monitor any residual swelling for at least a week, perhaps more," the Doctor agreed.

A small bleat of alarm came from Doctor Sharak. "Doctor?"

"Yes?"

"The embryo's heartbeat is slowing. It has averaged a little over one hundred beats per minute but in the last three minutes has fallen to ninety-three."

The Doctor couldn't tear his eyes from the microsurgical monitor through which he observed the repairs to Conlon's brain. He could imagine, however, the concern on the Tamarian doctor's wide, mottled brown face.

"Let's give it another minute to stabilize," the Doctor suggested.

"Is the gestational incubator prepped and ready for emergency transport?" Sal asked.

"It is standing by," Sharak replied.

"We will not remove the embryo unless the heart rate falls below eighty beats per minute," the Doctor said.

"Do you want our patient to live?" Sal asked, exasperation creeping into her voice. It could also have been exhaustion, the Doctor realized. She was, after all, only human, and in her early eighties.

"I would think the answer to that question would be obvious," the Doctor said. "I also want the embryo to survive and while it can be stabilized within the incubator, its chance for a normal gestation when transport is induced at only five and a half weeks is reduced by almost thirty percent."

"Has Lieutenant Conlon made a determination about terminating the pregnancy?" Sharak asked. "Her most recent chart entries do not contain current orders."

"We all heard her say that she did not intend to carry the child to term when we advised her she was pregnant," the Doctor reminded them.

"And you all read the notes that indicated she had agreed to postpone termination until she had decided whether or not to allow me to remove the embryonic stem cells her therapy is going to require," Sal said. "As of this morning, she had not given me an answer, and while this surgery is going to save our patient in the short term, her long-term prognosis depends entirely on the survival of the few undifferentiated stem cells still present in the embryo. We need to save the embryo, if only to harvest those cells. I recommend embryonic transport at eighty-five beats per minute."

"We are now at eighty-seven beats per minute," Sharak reported.

The Doctor was conscious of competing ethical subroutines running through multiple consequence vectors creating a point zero-zero-two percent diminishment of his primary program efficiencies. It wasn't enough to compromise his ability to perform the surgery, but the sooner it was reconciled, the better.

"Once we remove the embryo, it cannot be safely implanted again," the Doctor noted, knowing full well that both Sharak and Sal were aware of this.

"Nor can the lieutenant elect termination," Sharak said. "Once the embryo is no longer gestating within her body, it becomes an individual, enjoying the same rights to exist as every other person."

"If the lieutenant intended to terminate the pregnancy, that would complicate her situation considerably," the Doctor said.

"The frustrating reality of our situation, gentlemen, is that our patient did not officially make that determination before she began to bleed into her brain. There is no ethical dilemma present. We have no choice but to do everything in our power to save both her and the embryo. After embryonic transport, her pregnancy is effectively terminated. Any concerns she had that its development would be affected by her illness will no longer exist. She could waive her rights to custody in favor of the father, or to the Federation until an individual willing to raise the child can be found. She would still have to give permission for us to use the embryonic stem cells, however."

"She's not going to regain consciousness in time to do that, Doctor Sal," the Doctor said. "Right now, only ten percent of the embryonic cells remain undifferentiated. That number is going to fall to zero within the next thirty-six hours at most. I'm afraid no matter what happens to the embryo, you are not going to be able to pursue your stem-cell therapy."

"Eighty-five beats per minute," Sharak advised.

Sal stepped away from her neural monitor and double-checked the readiness of the gestational incubator. "Make the call, Doctor," she said. "I advise initiating transport immediately."

After a delay of two point six seconds, during which his ethical programming reconciled the dilemma before him, the Doctor said, "Agreed. Computer, initiate embryonic transport to gestational incubator." This order added a visual feed of the incubator to the statistical display running alongside the image of Conlon's neural cells visible through the microsurgery monitor.

In a swirl of what looked like stardust, an object the size of a sesame seed appeared in the incubator. It floated in synthetic amniotic fluid that had been created from samples of Conlon's own, and the tubes that would provide its nourishment and elimination of waste attached themselves immediately to the portion of the gestational sac that had once been connected to Conlon's uterus.

"Transport complete," Sharak said. "Embryonic heartbeat rising. Ninety beats per minute."

"Come on, little one," Sal said softly.

"Ninety-three."

"Lieutenant Conlon's blood pressure is falling," the Doctor advised.

"Prepping immunogen hypo," Sal said. "It will restore

her hormonal balance shortly and minimize the uterine bleeding for now."

"One hundred beats per minute," Sharak said, the relief clear in his voice.

"Well done," Sal said.

The Doctor was not at all certain this turn of events was going to please Conlon when she learned of it. He suspected the opposite was true. But he also knew that they'd had no choice in the matter, and in time, she would come to accept that. What he did not understand was Sal's equanimity. She was the only one of the three doctors present who had first-hand experience treating complicated DNA damage repair syndromes, and she had insisted from day one that the embryonic stem cells were the best available treatment option. She had just lost them and did not seem fazed in the least.

He admired her professionalism as he returned his complete focus to the surgery he was performing.

VESTA

Admiral Janeway's personal aide, Lieutenant Decan, approached her desk briskly. The tall, officious man who had been in Janeway's service off and on for the last five years was, among many other things, a gifted telepath and chose this moment to once again put that special talent to use.

"Captain Chakotay wishes to speak with you."

Janeway checked her comm queue but saw no incoming requests. She then looked automatically toward the door to her combined office and personal quarters despite the fact that no one had requested access in the last few moments.

"It's not nice to read people's thoughts without their permission," Janeway said.

"I would never presume," Decan assured her. "The captain's transport to *Vesta* four minutes ago was reported in the logs. I simply noted the fact and intuited his most likely destination."

"And then you double-checked telepathically."

"That didn't require reading his thoughts, merely confirming his location and direction of movement."

"Decan, you are an outstanding aide. I would be truly lost without you."

There was a brief pause until Decan said, "I hope you do not expect me to disagree with that assessment."

"Anticipating my needs is helpful. Using telepathy to do it is creepy."

Decan's face betrayed nothing. He was Vulcan. Her desk could have been on fire and his face would have worn the same placid expression.

"Would you prefer that in the future I become slightly less helpful?"

"I really would."

"Your wish is, as ever, my command, Admiral."

The door's chime sounded softly.

"Enter," Janeway said, rising, then added to Decan, "Dismissed. And by that I mean: well out of range."

"That would require me to board a shuttle and set course several million kilometers from our present position."

"You did say when you accepted this post with the fleet that you had always longed to travel."

Decan didn't smile, but it was nonetheless clear that he appreciated her dry wit.

"Or you could simply wait until I summon you to report back here."

Decan turned to Chakotay and considered him silently for a moment.

"Admiral, Lieutenant," Chakotay greeted them.

"Perhaps the mess hall," Decan said. "Can I bring you anything? Coffee?"

"No," Janeway replied.

Decan nodded discreetly and departed.

When the door closed behind him, Janeway turned her full attention to Chakotay. Normally, his presence was enough to set her at ease. But there was an anxious tension in him—lips set tight, shoulders squared—and if she wasn't mistaken, he was holding something behind his back.

A gift? She wondered silently.

For a brief moment their roles were reversed in her memory. She had stood before him, on the occasion of his birthday several years prior, ready to present him with a gift whose design she had labored over intently only to subsequently discover that it did not mean at all what she thought it meant. Chakotay had believed she was proposing altering the dynamic of their relationship, taking it to a more intimate level. She had merely intended to memorialize the significance of their friendship. Looking back, it seemed to Kathryn that that moment and the conversation that followed had really been the first steps on their road toward the deeply fulfilling, if occasionally fraught, relationship they now enjoyed.

Not that she would have had it any other way.

A light smile played over her lips. She was being ridiculous and she knew it. They had only been back in each other's lives for a year and there were almost two more in front of them where they would both be devoted to the fleet's service. The idea of formalizing their relationship in any way hadn't come up often and usually only in passing, playful exchanges. But she couldn't deny the anticipatory trepidation she read in his countenance.

"Good morning, Kathryn," he greeted her, moving in to kiss her lightly on the cheek before taking her hand and leading her to sit in the nearest chair.

"What's all this?" she asked.

"I come bearing gifts," he replied, "and a proposal."

Janeway rose instantly and involuntarily to her feet. Rather than wounding Chakotay, her reflexive resistance seemed to amuse him.

"What sort of proposal?" she asked calmly, despite the fact that her heart suddenly felt as if she had just completed a wind sprint.

Chakotay brought the hand he had been hiding behind his back forward. In its palm rested a small black box.

"Trust me," he suggested in a tone with which she was all too familiar. It invariably promised good things.

She tore her eyes away from the box and lifted them to his. He was enjoying the hell out of this at her expense. It was equal parts infuriating and tantalizing. Despite the fact that her gut reaction was going to require some deeper thought at a later date, she decided to play along.

Taking the box and wondering silently for a moment at its weight, she gently opened the lid.

Her face fell into confused lines.

Inside the box was an odd-shaped black rock.

"You shouldn't have," she said dryly. "Really."

Chakotay forced his face into serious lines, though his eyes were still smiling. "Don't tell me you already have one."

"I don't think so. What is it?"

"We don't actually have a name for it yet," he replied. "Well, most of it is an osmium isotope but buried inside are a few atoms of a brand-new element."

The scientist Janeway had been long before she chose to

pursue a career in command was almost moved to tears as she released a slight gasp.

"Where did it come from?"

"A single planet orbiting a binary star configuration approximately two light-years from our present position. For the moment we have designated it DK-1116."

Janeway palmed the small stone and tossed it gently up and down. "Super-heavy?"

"And surprisingly stable."

"How much of it is there?"

"We don't know yet. Thus far we have detected more than ten sites containing the element."

"In natural formations?"

"Seven doesn't know."

Janeway again met Chakotay's eyes. "You want to take *Voyager* and go find out," she guessed.

"No. I want you to order the entire fleet to set course and make orbit for the next two weeks."

The admiral shook her head in surprise. "We don't need all four ships to analyze this. All you need is Seven and a high-powered portable microspectrometer."

"Would you believe me if I told you that this element is by far the *least interesting* attribute of DK-1116?"

The admiral moved back to the seat she had inhabited briefly and made herself comfortable. "I'm listening."

Chakotay settled himself in the chair across from her. "The planet is too close to the binaries to sustain life. But several thousand years ago, if our scans are to be believed, someone established almost four dozen biodomes on the surface. Most of them contain water, breathable nitrogen-oxygen atmosphere, a variety of plants, but no other living things. No bugs, no small animals, no higher life-forms and no trace of who they were, where they came from, or where they went apart from several odd, sculptural constructs containing this element."

Janeway turned these facts over in her mind a few times before she said, "Two light-years in what direction?"

"Deeper into former Borg space," he confirmed, answering her unspoken question. The Borg tended to pillage any world they came across in the Delta Quadrant that had plentiful, useful resources. It was hard to believe they hadn't gotten around to this one, although technically possible.

"So you want multiple teams to take this on? Maybe *Vesta* should take the lead."

Chakotay shook his head. "I'm suggesting more than a few days of research. This is exactly the kind of mission the entire fleet needs right now—a combination of scientific exploration and several days of shore leave."

"Chakotay, we've got less than two years and lots of Delta Quadrant yet to see," she reminded him.

"I know. I also know that the crews of *Voyager*, *Galen*, and *Demeter*, who have been at this nonstop since the fleet launched, are overdue for a little R&R. And I doubt Captain Farkas would scoff at the idea of treating *Vesta*'s crew to a short working break. Many of them were part of *Quirinal*'s original complement."

He had a point.

"Our efficiency evaluations are dismal. We've seen more than our fair share of battle out here in the last year, whether it was testy aliens or multiverse-altering anomalies. Everywhere we turn, we seem to be picking fights. We know how to handle that, but over time, it takes its toll. Every once in a while, we need to allow our people to focus on more inspirational endeavors, the good, old-fashioned mysteries that made most of us decide to join Starfleet in the first place."

Janeway couldn't argue with this, or the fact that the timing was near perfect for Chakotay's proposal. That was, of course, assuming the Krenim didn't have any immediate plans to alter everyone's priorities.

"You're worried about the Krenim?" Chakotay asked.

She nodded. "I've already had a lengthy discussion with the Department of Temporal Investigations' director about the many ways in which our mission just got a lot harder now that we're back on the Krenim's sensors."

"Did she have any suggestions?"

"Keep our heads down and our scanners at full power, at least until her analysts have a chance to thoroughly digest my reports."

Chakotay shrugged. "Doesn't this sound exactly like what the director ordered?"

"Maybe," Janeway agreed. "I want you to prepare a full briefing for the senior staffs of all fleet vessels. I'm going to let everyone weigh in on this before I make a final determination."

"Okay," Chakotay said, clearly a little disappointed. "But can I assume you're leaning toward saying yes?"

"Honestly, you had me at 'no bugs.'"

GALEN

Doctor El'nor Sal, *Vesta*'s chief medical officer, knew herself to be in remarkable shape for a human female of her age. The height she had inherited from her mother. A tendency toward lean, long muscles had been a gift from her father.

Her longevity could have come from either. Her parents had both been well into their twelfth decade of life when they died. When in motion she still enjoyed a sense of vigor and strength. Her mind was as sharp as it had ever been, as was her tongue. The only thing suffering these days was her patience. She chalked that up to her new regimen of sleeping only three to four hours per night. Like her fellow physicians intent on curing Lieutenant Nancy Conlon, she understood that time was of the essence. Unlike her compatriots, she knew intimately how long and dark the road ahead of all of them really was.

Thirty years prior, Sal had been the CMO of the *U.S.S. Thetis*. Then, as now, Regina Farkas had been her captain. They'd lost twenty-three of their crew to a similar syndrome caused by a rare insect bite. The culprit would eventually come to be known as Vega Nine.

The cause of Conlon's illness remained stubbornly obscured, and clearly it was moving more quickly than its deadly cousin. Sal had hoped that she'd have considerably more time before damage to Conlon's DNA started to manifest itself in frightening and potent ways.

She should have known better. Systemic damage like this left no room for hope. That nicety—along with sleep, exercise, and healthy interpersonal relationships—was forced by the wayside in battles like this one, replaced by singular focus and determination. The only way to beat this was to locate it and correct it. Somewhere in the three billion base pairs that made up Nancy Conlon's genetic code was a transcription error that had rendered her DNA incapable of repairing itself. Sal was nowhere near finding it, nor was she certain that she would have the opportunity to do so. But she'd be damned if she didn't at least lose a little sleep trying.

Sal's dark gray eyes were glued to the screen displaying Conlon's vitals. The surgery to repair the weakness in the wall of the anterior cerebral artery and reinforce similar degradations of the middle cerebral artery had taken Sharak and the Doctor almost nine hours to complete. Sharak had departed for his ship immediately following the procedure for some well-earned rest. The Doctor had excused himself for the holodeck. He had a new premise he was testing, one that might stabilize their patient indefinitely while they searched for a cure. He had indicated it was too soon to share the specifics. Sal wished him well. Any port in this storm would be welcome.

Conlon would remain in an induced comatose state for the next week at least as her intracranial pressure was carefully monitored. That she had survived the sudden arterial hemorrhage at all was a miracle, and testament to the brilliance of the men who had designed the *Galen*. Conlon had been monitored constantly by a uniquely modified medical computer no matter where she was on board the experimental ship. A sister to the standard processor that was the heart of all starships, this system had been created to report a patient's vital signs continuously. It had detected her loss of consciousness on the holodeck and immediately transported her to sickbay, where she was quickly stabilized and diagnosed. Had Conlon been sleeping peacefully in her quarters aboard *Voyager* when the artery ruptured, she would never have awakened and Sal would only have understood the cause of death following autopsy.

"Doctor Sal?"

Turning, Sal saw the haggard face of Lieutenant Harry Kim, the father of Conlon's child.

"What the hell happened?" Kim demanded without

preamble. "I was only gone for two days. Counselor Cambridge said Nancy almost died."

"Pull up a chair, Harry," Sal replied.

As Kim did so, Sal sipped from a mug of *raktajino* that had gone cold an hour ago. It was disgusting. She hardly noticed.

Once Kim had settled himself across from her with his elbows planted on the tops of his thighs and his hands clasped tightly before him, Sal began. "Weakness in the wall of one of the arteries of Lieutenant Conlon's brain caused a rupture. Within seconds, this medical marvel we're sitting in initiated an emergency site-to-site transport and the Doctor began treatment. We were able to stabilize her and perform surgery to repair the damage. We're going to keep her unconscious for the next several days while the swelling goes down. In the event any other nearby arteries are affected, we'll catch them before they can cause any more trouble."

"And this was caused by the problem with her DNA?" Kim asked.

Sal nodded.

Kim dropped his face into his hands and shook his head slowly back and forth. When he lifted it again, his eyes were glistening. "I thought you said we had months, maybe longer, before her body would start breaking down."

"That's what I believed at the time. Clearly, I was wrong," Sale said simply.

Kim rose from the chair and began to pace restlessly. "So what does this mean?"

"My best guess?"

"Please."

"It means if we don't start making progress in the next few months, she's probably going to die. The only upside I can offer is that her demise probably won't be as slow and painful as we first feared."

Kim stopped, crossed his arms over his chest, and turned his head, peering into the dimness of the private room where Conlon rested. He looked like he was holding himself together with both hands. Finally he turned back and asked, "Have you made any progress?"

Sal sighed deeply. There were two different protocols she could implement immediately, both of which stood a fair to good chance of slowing the progress of the disease, if not curing it outright. But one depended on the embryonic cells she could no longer access and the other upon consents she was not likely to receive.

Sal had advised Conlon from day one that her best hope were the undifferentiated stem cells of the embryo growing in her uterus. Although her umbilical cord would eventually contain billions of stem cells, they were blood cells and not likely to be as useful as the incredibly malleable embryonic cells. For reasons she had refused to share with her physicians, Conlon had been unwilling to agree to the embryonic harvesting and had pressed them to find an alternative. Sal had assured her that the process would not harm the embryo, although she wasn't sure why it mattered, as Conlon had also indicated early on that she did not intend to carry the pregnancy to term.

Following some intense wheedling by her counselor, Hugh Cambridge, Conlon had agreed to postpone a final decision on the stem cell extraction and the abortion until she'd had more time to come to grips with the reality of her condition. The last few weeks had been a slow hell for Sal. With each day that passed, the possibility that enough embryonic stem cells would remain diminished exponentially. Even now, it might be too late.

The second option was going to be an even harder sell. In the last few days, however, Sal had turned her attention almost exclusively to researching the possibility. The first person she was going to have to convince was her captain. Farkas's permission was going to be significantly harder to come by than Conlon's had been.

"There are always possibilities," Sal finally advised Kim.

Kim nodded somberly.

"By the way," Sal added, "there's someone you should meet."

The utter confusion on Kim's face was painful to witness.

Sal rose and directed him out of the office to the private treatment room, where the gestational incubator would remain for the next thirty-four weeks. As she did so, she explained. "During the surgery to repair Nancy's brain, the embryo went into distress. In order to save it we were forced to transport it outside Nancy's body."

"I don't . . . I don't understand," Kim said. "I thought she was going to . . ."

"She did not make a final decision prior to falling ill," Sal advised. "We were required to save both of them if possible, and that's what we did."

Kim paused at the doorway to the room containing his child. It seemed like he might pass out at any moment.

"Are you all right, Lieutenant?"

He nodded, but his breath was coming in shallow bursts and his cheeks were flushed. He took a few more steps until his gaze locked on the tiny being suspended within the incubator.

"That's it?" he whispered.

"That's your daughter, Harry."

Tears began to flow freely down Kim's face. Sal excused

herself for a moment and returned with a tissue dispenser and offered him a handful.

He smiled even as he shook his head rapidly in disbelief.

"Will she . . . I mean, can she survive?" he asked.

Sal nodded. "The odds are very good that she will. There are complications that can arise from external gestation but medicine has come a long way over the last few hundred years."

Kim began to study the monitors on the side of the incubator. Indicating a small wavy line, he asked, "Is that her heart?"

"It is."

More tears followed this.

"Why don't I give you some time," Sal suggested.

She left the room and several minutes later, Kim emerged. He looked exhausted and elated at the same time. He had regained most of his emotional equilibrium.

He seemed to struggle with himself for a few moments, then asked, "Can I see Nancy?"

"Of course," Sal said. As they moved toward Conlon's private room, she followed Kim's eyes to one of the monitors in the main bay that charted Conlon's vitals. Kim paused over it and with a finger, traced the line of Conlon's heartbeat.

"The last time we spoke, Nancy said she was going to terminate the pregnancy," Kim said. "I figured she had done it already."

"She hadn't come to a final decision," Sal said, then continued gently, "Did you and she discuss why she was waiting?"

"She said you wanted to use some of the baby's stem cells to try and reverse her condition. She didn't want to do it. I begged her to give it a try. She said she'd consider it, but I didn't think she'd agree."

"Did she tell you why?"

Kim lifted his eyes again to Nancy's still form visible behind the transparent wall of her room. "She didn't feel right about using the baby's cells to cure her and then terminating the pregnancy. She said whether it worked or not, she would feel obligated to continue the pregnancy if she allowed you to harvest those cells. She just didn't want to do that."

"Well, part of that decision has been made for her by circumstance," Sal said. "The embryo is no longer gestating inside her. For now Lieutenant Conlon retains shared custody of her, but neither of you can order us to terminate her. She's an individual and protected under Federation law."

Relief spread over Kim's face.

The part of Sal that was required to defer to Conlon's wishes had been at war for weeks with the doctor that wanted to cure her patient. The moment the embryo had gone into distress during the surgery she had realized that another door might be opening to her. She had not known until now whether or not she would avail herself of it.

"Lieutenant Kim," Sal began, "the calculus has now changed considerably. I understand Nancy not wanting to use the embryonic cells and then terminate the pregnancy. Termination is no longer an option, but the embryonic stem-cell therapy still might be. The cells I require to attempt to reprogram Nancy's DNA aren't going to exist for very much longer. Last night's scans showed a ninety percent differentiation rate. My guess is that will be closer to ninety-three percent this morning. By the time we're able to wake her, it will be much too late."

Kim's eyes turned back to Sal. He blinked rapidly, considering the statement, and his brow furrowed.

"Do you think there's any chance she might change her mind?" Sal asked.

"I don't know."

"Do you think if she understood how much more quickly than we had anticipated her condition is advancing, she might reconsider?"

"It's possible, I guess."

"Once the cells are extracted, it will still take me several days if not more to modify the appropriate vector and begin treatment. With your permission, I could harvest them now, while they retain their multipotentiality, and still allow Nancy to accept or refuse the procedure when she wakes up."

"My permission?"

"You're not her designated representative, so you can't approve treatments on her behalf," Sal said. "I believe that responsibility still rests with her sister back on Earth. But you are currently the only individual able to grant me permission to harvest the cells I need. If you agree to the procedure, I can perform it now."

"But I'm not . . ."

"You're the child's father," Sal reminded him. "You share full custody of the child. With Nancy incapacitated, the right to make medical decisions on the child's behalf falls to you."

Kim paled as a penny the size of a small moon dropped.

"I could decide?"

"Just to allow me to extract the cells. Nothing else."

"But if she didn't want that, she'd never forgive me."

"You said her primary concern was *using* the embryonic

cells. That won't happen unless she consents. All you are doing is allowing the potential for treatment to continue to exist. *Nothing more*. She still gets to make the final decision when she wakes up."

"I don't know."

"Take all the time you need to think about it," Sal said. "As long as all the time you need is less than twenty hours. After that, there won't be any point. I understand that what I'm asking you to do might feel like a betrayal. And I understand that you are being as supportive as you possibly can in these circumstances. But this door is closing, and when it does, my chances of curing Nancy go way down. Faced with her imminent demise, she might be more willing to consider the stem-cell therapy. You're just keeping her options open. For all we know, she'll thank you for it."

Kim was clearly struggling. Sal hated to see that. But she also knew better than he what they were up against. She would not voluntarily tie her own hands.

"You'll just extract the cells for now?"

"With your permission."

"And if Nancy still doesn't want to go through with it when she wakes up . . ."

"There's nothing more to discuss. I get busy working other alternatives."

Silence hung heavy between them for several moments. Finally Kim said, "Do it."

3

The Full Circle Fleet's chief engineer, Commander B'Elanna Torres, had three children. Her daughter and newborn son she shared with her husband, *Voyager*'s first officer, Commander Tom Paris. Her first child, however, would always be the countless interconnected assemblies, circuits, chips, ODNs, conduits, and panels collectively known as *Voyager*'s engine room.

Torres hadn't fully appreciated this fact when she had been given command of the engineering department as a field lieutenant and new member of the combined Starfleet and Maquis crew that would spend seven years together struggling to leave the Delta Quadrant behind them and return to Earth. She hadn't given it a thought when she had left *Voyager* upon their return, so engrossed had she been in the birth of her daughter, introductions to her new in-laws, and a cryptic message left by her mother.

Only once she had been made the fleet's chief engineer and found herself overseeing *Voyager*'s engineering department, along with *Vesta*'s, *Galen*'s, and *Demeter*'s, had she understood the hold this place would always have on her heart. Despite her appreciation for how small it made the galaxy, she found the addition of the quantum slipstream drive that now occupied the lower half of what had once been the solid warp-core assembly unsightly, but only because it was a change. Torres had never been a fan of change. There were also a few dozen new faces tending to her engines. A number of *Voyager*'s original crew had requested reassignment after their initial journey through the Delta Quadrant had ended. But there was something joyful about introducing a new crop of young, fresh-faced engineers to her favorite technological child's idiosyncrasies and moods.

Even so, she would bid *Voyager*'s engines farewell forever without regret if she could have given them back to Nancy Conlon.

Torres had been the first person Conlon had confided in about her declining stability and her belief that she was dying. When that belief had been confirmed, no one had been more surprised than B'Elanna. She had hoped until the last possible moment that Conlon's condition was some horrible unforeseen aftereffect of the ravaging of her mind and body by an alien trespasser. It had been the harshest of gut punches to learn that Conlon had been right, and now it seemed that a massive ticking clock hung over everyone's head as they waited for the fleet's medical staff to pull just one more miracle out of their bag of tricks.

Torres had visited Conlon regularly over the last few weeks, determined to help lift her spirits. When her doctors had agreed to allow Nancy to resume an abbreviated duty schedule, both of them had been elated. Torres hadn't learned until a few hours ago that Conlon's return was, once again, postponed.

Few things roused B'Elanna's Klingon half anymore. The events of the last few years had shifted her perspective in a positive way. They had been filled with challenges, but each of them had been faced and overcome. To stare down Conlon's fate now and be entirely powerless to affect the outcome was becoming a daily test of her self-control. Once, long ago, her former crewmate Commander Tuvok had tried to teach her Vulcan meditation techniques to help her calm her inner Klingon. She could have used his help and regretted not asking him for a refresher course when he'd recently joined the fleet for their mission on Sormana.

But Tuvok was gone. Nancy was sick and getting sicker by the day. *Voyager* was once again hers for the foreseeable future.

She was already running late for a briefing in astrometrics when she arrived in engineering. Miral had been extra fussy that morning. Sharing her parents with her new baby brother was bringing out the one-quarter Klingon in Miral Paris. When she wasn't sleeping or on duty, B'Elanna tried to carve out time for just the two of them to engage in their favorite activities on the holodeck or dig into the educational curriculum created for Miral by the Doctor. Some days it was enough to soothe the little warrior. Today had not been one of those days.

Her plan had been to quickly run down the day's maintenance schedule with Ensign Icheb and assure herself that there were no pressing issues before joining the senior staff for Chakotay's briefing. That plan was scuttled the moment she entered and found Icheb standing over what looked like a replicator module that had been hefted onto one of the engineering diagnostic stations. Beside him stood a slightly shorter young man who should have been running *Vesta*'s engineering section right now, Lieutenant Phinnegan Bryce.

"What do we have here, gentlemen?" Torres said as she joined them and glanced quickly at the numbers and symbols flowing over the nearest screen.

"Good morning, Commander," Icheb greeted her. The young man had recently graduated early from Starfleet Academy, but given that he had been found as a child in the

Delta Quadrant by *Voyager* when the Borg had abandoned him and spent his early years regaining his individuality, he was as much the younger brother Torres never had as her right hand in engineering these days.

"Hi, B'Elanna," Bryce said cheerfully. "Don't worry, this isn't yours. It's mine."

Bryce was *Vesta*'s chief engineer, and thus far, he had impressed Torres every time they'd worked together. She genuinely liked him, and the frequency with which Icheb mentioned him—*Lieutenant Bryce believes an excess of free hydrogen particles purged by the coolant assembly are responsible for the point zero four percent degradation in the adjacent optronic relay housing* or *Phinn says if we perform more frequent ionic sweeps of our bioneural gel packs, we will extend their functionality by several months*—suggested a developing friendship between the two. Torres would normally have gone out of her way to encourage this. Icheb had faltered in his early days as her aide, especially with *Voyager*'s engineers. Course corrections in his attitude and deference had helped to right that situation, but it was slow going, not to mention the fact that as a former Borg, there was an ingrained haughtiness with which Icheb could not help but carry himself. Bryce didn't seem the least bit intimidated.

This morning, however, Torres had neither the time nor the patience for whatever this was. "If it's not mine, why is it in my engine room, Bryce?"

"I asked him to bring it over," Icheb replied for him. "This is the processor matrix for *Vesta*'s primary industrial replicator assembly, and we've been trying to track down a circuiting glitch for days."

"It keeps randomly inverting certain integers, but there's no rhyme or reason to the errors," Bryce added.

"I hypothesized that the problem might lie with the gel packs and wanted to test my theory with one of ours."

"Our gel packs are better than *Vesta*'s?" Torres asked.

"Ours are *older*. This particular lot might have been corrupted when they were first installed."

"Is there some reason you didn't just send him a few of ours to test on *Vesta*?" Torres asked.

"I . . ." Icheb began, but faltered.

Bryce picked up for him. "It was Icheb's theory, and I thought he should have the chance to test it. Since he can't really get away from *Voyager*, I thought I'd bring the mountain to him."

Torres considered both of them silently as her inner Klingon offered dozens of potential responses, none of which were particularly helpful but all of which would have been briefly satisfying to utter.

"And have you successfully tested your theory, Ensign?"

"We were just about to."

Torres nodded slowly. This wasn't about a fritzing replicator. This was about Icheb and Bryce. Their growing interest in each other had been obvious to B'Elanna for weeks. And much as she wanted to encourage their friendship, especially for Icheb's sake, there was a time and a place for that, and engineering was not it.

"I have a briefing," she said curtly. "I want Bryce and his replicator back on *Vesta* before I return. Understood?"

"Yes, Commander," they replied in near unison.

Torres started to turn away when Icheb asked, "When will Lieutenant Conlon be reporting for duty?"

Torres looked back at Icheb. It was instantly clear that he read the disappointment in her face and shared it.

"Not today."

VESTA

"What did you do?"

Doctor Sal did not look up from the display panel of her microscope. She had spent the last several hours analyzing the embryonic stem cells she had extracted from Nancy Conlon and Harry Kim's child. The results were far from what she'd hoped to find when she performed the procedure.

"Good morning to you, too, Counselor Cambridge," she replied.

"Our patient's medical log shows a procedure done in the wee hours of last night to harvest stem cells from her embryo."

Despite the fact that Sal didn't have time for his displeasure at the moment, she marked the current slide as unfinished and gave the counselor her full attention.

"That's right."

"The timing of the procedure coupled with the approval from Lieutenant Harry Kim suggests that you did not receive Lieutenant Conlon's permission."

"I didn't need it. The father is well within his rights under these circumstances to authorize the removal of the cells from *his* child."

"You know damn well that our patient would never have allowed you to remove those cells."

"And you know damn well that her approval was made irrelevant by the progression of her illness. At least she got part of what she wanted. Her pregnancy was effectively terminated during the surgery."

"Do you honestly believe that when she is revived and sees the child gestating in that incubator, she is going to feel relief?"

"I don't know. And at this point, it's not really high on my list of things to worry about. The embryo was in distress. We had to transport it in order to save it. In the absence of a prior authorization to terminate the pregnancy, we had no other option."

"But you did have an option when it came to convincing Lieutenant Kim to go against Conlon's expressed wishes."

"Save your indignation, Counselor. I was too late. I didn't get a tenth of the number of cells I needed to create a therapeutic regimen. The cells I extracted will have to be discarded. They're of no use to us now."

Cambridge actually paled slightly at this revelation. "Oh," he said softly.

"As far as I'm concerned, she never even has to know we performed the procedure. When she wakes up . . . if she wakes up, we will simply advise her that stem-cell therapy is no longer an option."

"Is there an alternative?"

Sal smiled wanly. "Not a good one."

Cambridge sighed. "How bad?"

All I have to do is risk pissing off the entire scientific community of one of the Federation's most venerated members, lie to my best friend and captain, and quite possibly coerce an unsuspecting ensign to betray her people's oldest cultural taboo, Sal thought. Aloud she said, "Just this side of impossible."

"That sounds like a tall order, even for you," Cambridge observed.

"I'll make sure I get plenty of rest tonight," Sal said.

"Do I want to know the details of this prospective cure?"

"I doubt it. The less any of you know going forward, the better for your careers."

"El'nor, speaking as a counselor now, and not just part of Conlon's team, have you considered the possibility that you will fail to cure Nancy?"

Sal's face hardened. "Of course I have. It's not something I'm accustomed to. It's not something I take lightly. But it's always there. I can tell you this: In the few instances in the past where I have failed, I have done so spectacularly. I have done so in fantastic fashion. It was truly a sight to behold. I don't expect this one to be any different. If I fail, it's going to be for the right reasons. It's going to be because I exhausted every single possibility available to me, and it won't be without a fight, Counselor."

"That's how you live with it?"

"It's the only way I know to keep the ghosts quiet."

Cambridge nodded slowly and turned to go. Just before he reached the door's sensor, he said, "I'm not comfortable with the idea of lying to Nancy about the procedure."

"Given that you know how she will likely respond and that the emotional distress could further exacerbate her condition, you might consider it a small sin of omission. Before she collapsed on that holodeck, she had one vision of her future in mind. Whatever it was, the reality of her future when she wakes will be quite different. She will have to decide whether or not to participate in the life of the child she inadvertently created or to give up custody. I'm guessing those are going to be some long counseling sessions between you two and Lieutenant Kim. There is no reason to add information that will only create acrimony between them. Especially since the results of the extraction were useless."

"You don't think she has a right to know that the man with whom she will be considering raising this child made a choice that went explicitly against her stated wishes?"

"I was pretty convincing. Without my interference, he never would have done it. Tell them they can blame me. Or don't. Personally, I think where matters of the heart are concerned, ignorance is often underrated."

"You never married, did you?"

"I did not."

"That's almost hard to believe," Cambridge said lightly.

"It wasn't for lack of desire, I assure you. We all have two lives, Counselor: the one we want and the one we learn to live with. I'm content with both of mine."

"I think it would be quite something to know the man who would have tempted you."

"The man?"

"Ah. My mistake. The woman?"

"Honestly, the few times I was *tempted*, the last thing I cared about was the arrangement of either of our reproductive organs."

Cambridge smiled. "Forgive me for underestimating you. It's not a mistake I will make twice."

"Now, unless there's anything else, I have some ethical boundaries to test."

"I and my ignorance will leave you to it. I wish you luck."

Sal nodded. She was going to need it.

VOYAGER

"Good morning," Chakotay greeted his fellow captains, Regina Farkas, Clarissa Glenn, and Liam O'Donnell. Seven stood beside him at the astrometric lab's main control panel. Commander B'Elanna Torres hurried in with her head down and situated herself beside Admiral Janeway on the staging area between the controls and the massive display screen that dominated the lab. Knowing full well how much she had on her plate these days, the captain gave her a quick nod and tight smile to indicate that her tardiness was not an issue.

Chakotay could have held this briefing in *Vesta*'s large conference room. The holographic rendering technology embedded in the conference tables would have provided the same data. But the effect of the larger display combined with Seven's ability to manipulate it—zooming in on several of the notable features the shuttle's sensors had captured in transit—was significantly more impressive.

The screen showed a small, reddish-brown planet orbiting two stars of unequal mass. Several hundred million kilometers outside the system lay a massive and likely ancient spherical asteroid field, a common enough phenomena given the extreme stresses of binary system formation. The stars were engaged in a graceful dance around their barycenter, which was located closer to the A star. A smaller debris field was also present around the pair's B star.

The planet's orbit was circumbinary: its course followed a stable path around both stars, approximately eighty-three million kilometers distant from the B star at its closest approach. The planet appeared to be nothing more than a dead terrestrial world.

Glenn stepped past Chakotay and placed herself next to Commander Torres. Farkas and O'Donnell followed as Chakotay said, "Permit me to introduce you to DK-1116."

"If I had my way," *Vesta*'s captain mused, "only poets would be permitted to name planets and stars."

"Regina, there are three hundred billion stars in our galaxy alone, and our galaxy is one of two trillion," Janeway observed. "The last time I checked, the number of planets in our universe topped one septillion. If they did nothing else with their lives, all the poets who have ever lived could spend all day every day naming astrometric phenomena and we'd still be short by at least a couple hundred sextillion, give or take."

"Did you just do that math in your head?" Farkas asked the admiral.

Janeway nodded. "I've already had my coffee."

O'Donnell, who was reading the data stream running along the side of the screen, said, "There's something wrong with your display. That planet falls outside the Goldilocks zone. It can't sustain life."

Seven turned to O'Donnell. "I assure you, the display is accurate."

"Did somebody change the laws of physics while I was asleep?"

"Seven," Chakotay said.

With no further prompting, Seven enlarged the view of the planet and the binaries vanished. Several gasps sounded as the surface's patchwork of red rocks interspersed with vibrant green and blue swaths became clearly visible.

"Apparently they did," *Demeter*'s captain conceded.

Commander Torres interrupted. "Can I see the biodome-field readings, please?"

A new chart appeared beside the graphic of the planet.

"Geothermal?" Torres asked.

"At least partially solar," Seven replied.

"Huh," Torres said, clearly impressed. "No discernable degradation. Those things are going to last as long as the stars do."

"That is my belief as well," Seven agreed.

"Here's what we know," Chakotay said, taking control of

the briefing. "Based on the scans done by Lieutenant Kim and Seven when they were on the planet, the biodomes you see on the surface have been operational for roughly four thousand years. That's the blink of an eye in the life of the binaries and the planet, but apart from the Borg, we don't even know of any other alien species that have been around these parts long enough to have created this. All of the biodomes contain water and most contain atmosphere we can breathe. A few have different atmospheric mixes, so we'd have to study them in EV suits. All of them also contain these odd sculptural growths. The biodomes appear to have been designed to sustain themselves and their particular ecosystems indefinitely."

"Growths?" O'Donnell, the resident botanical geneticist, interrupted.

"They're not living now by any definition we use," Seven said. "But their molecular structure is unique. It is theoretically possible that they are some sort of fossilized remains."

"Some of these structures also contain molecules of a heretofore undiscovered element that in theory shouldn't be stable," Chakotay continued.

"And yet it is," Janeway noted.

"I, for one, would like to know more about this element and the planet it calls home," Chakotay said. "But beyond that, I'd like to see us take a few weeks for a combined exploratory mission and recreational retreat."

"How would that work?" Farkas asked.

Chakotay handed out padds to each of the captains and continued, "If we send small teams to each biodome on six-hour rotations, each crew member could look forward to a minimum of fifty hours planetside over the next two weeks and maybe twice that much for personal recreational pursuits. One of the larger domes contains a body of water so massive it's basically a freshwater lake. I'd like to establish a central camp there for any and all off-duty crew members to enjoy outdoor activities. Other domes offer opportunities for rock-climbing, hiking, or just enjoying the alien flora.

"I would also suggest that we use this time as an extended exercise in intrafleet cooperation. Rather than assign away teams in familiar groups by ship, we could select them by specialty. Obviously, *Vesta*'s crew is much larger than any other fleet ship, but as many as possible could be assigned to groups made up of individuals from their sister ships in the same specialty. By assigning our science, security, tactical, flight control, engineering, operations, and command officers from each ship to joint task forces, we can give them a rare opportunity to work side by side and really get to know one another. I believe that the knowledge gained through such an exchange could go a long way toward improving performance and cohesion in the future. And I think a few weeks spent in constructive exploration would significantly improve morale."

"This system also presents a unique opportunity for those remaining on board to expand our knowledge of binary star formation due to gravitational capture," the admiral added.

"They're almost the same age, aren't they?" Glenn asked. "Why wouldn't you assume that they have always orbited each other?"

"The debris field around the secondary star," Janeway replied. "Something cataclysmic happened here and fairly recently in astronomical terms. The amount of mass present in that field and the size of the fragments suggest that there might once have been other planets in this system. That in conjunction with the ancient terraforming efforts on the surface of the one otherwise uninhabitable planet is awfully intriguing. Is this a case of an advanced civilization attempting to colonize another planet in their system when the death of their own became inevitable? And if so, where did they go? Any evidence we could find of the civilization that established those biodomes might lead to one of the most interesting first contacts in the history of our Federation."

"Then we are agreed?" Chakotay asked.

"Are there any objections?" Janeway asked of the other fleet captains.

"Have all of the domes been scanned for biotoxins and hostile life-forms?" O'Donnell asked.

"There are no higher life-forms present," Seven noted.

"But those ecosystems contain a variety of plant life that could be every bit as hostile as any animal," O'Donnell cautioned. "Never mind the potential for alien bacteria, viruses, and extremophiles that might inhabit the unprotected areas of the surface."

"Prior to beginning the shipwide rotations, small teams will conduct safety surveys," Chakotay said. "We don't want any unpleasant surprises."

"We should hold off announcing the planned retreat until those surveys are complete," Farkas suggested. "The only thing worse for morale than skipping an opportunity like this would be getting everyone prepped and then disappointing them."

"Agreed," Janeway said. "I'd like Commanders Paris and Roach to take point with personnel assignments."

"Will participation in the planetside explorations be voluntary?" O'Donnell asked. Off Janeway's raised eyebrows, he added, "In the event anyone has experiments currently under way that might be disadvantageously affected by a prolonged absence?"

"I'd be willing to entertain requests," Janeway conceded, "but not from you, Commander."

O'Donnell's shoulders drooped visibly.

"This is truly a rare opportunity for us to work together without the concurrent pressure of establishing diplomatic relations or fending off hostile aliens. I, for one, am looking forward to it, aren't you?"

"I wouldn't miss it," O'Donnell said, clearly unwilling to court the admiral's displeasure. "Seven, would you mind forwarding copies of your scans and any samples you can spare of this new element to *Demeter*? I'd like to review them en route."

"Of course, Commander O'Donnell."

Turning back to the viewscreen, the admiral smiled. "Let's set course and see what this strange new world holds."

GALEN

It wasn't unusual for Lieutenant Reginald Barclay to find himself summoned to the Doctor's presence at all hours of the day. The Doctor never slept, and Barclay kept odd hours when he was engrossed in his own projects, so when the Doctor requested Reg meet him on *Galen*'s main holodeck in the middle of gamma shift, the holographic specialist thought nothing of it. The moment he entered the holodeck, however, he immediately questioned his sanity.

Seated on the biobed before him, wearing a familiar crimson velvet smoking jacket, was Commander Data. His left scalp access panel had been opened and *Galen*'s CMO, the photonic being that had begun his existence as

Voyager's Emergency Medical Hologram and was now one of Barclay's closest friends, peered intently at Data's neural network.

"Hello, Reg," the android said congenially.

"Ah, Reg," the Doctor echoed, "thank you for coming so promptly."

"What the . . ." Barclay began, but a stammer that hadn't bedeviled him in years locked the rest of the question securely behind his lips.

"Reg?" His obvious distress earned the Doctor's full attention. "Are you all right?"

Barclay tried desperately to force his mouth past the words it would not form. "Wha . . . wha . . . *what* have you done?" he managed.

The Doctor appeared to be at a loss.

Barclay stepped forward, placing himself between the Doctor and Data. Turning to face the android, he was momentarily overwhelmed. A thousand thoughts unspoken and words unsaid fought for release. All he could do was gently close the panel that had exposed Data's delicate cranial innards and smile sadly at his beloved friend.

"Data?" he finally managed.

"It is good to see you again," Data said.

Barclay couldn't respond to this most basic pleasantry. Commander Data, former first officer aboard the *Enterprise* and one of the most extraordinary beings Reg had ever known, had sacrificed his life in the line of duty three years prior. His existence had been unique and his loss exquisitely painful. By all rights, Data should have lived forever. Even now, his absence was most keenly felt by those who had served with him, including Barclay. There was no way *this* . . . whatever it was . . . was Data.

That didn't make the illusion any less compelling.

"The Doctor and I have been discussing the ways in which a positronic neural network could be made to temporarily house the neural pattern of a living individual," Data said with the light timbre Barclay thought of as cheerful.

Briefly wondering if he might have wandered into a nightmare, Barclay gathered his courage and said, "Computer, end program."

To his relief, Data immediately shimmered out of existence.

Fresh tears rose to Barclay's eyes. When he turned back to the Doctor, he could barely contain his rage.

The Doctor clearly sensed the depth of his transgression but remained bewildered. "Reg . . ." he began.

"Where did you get that file?" Barclay demanded.

"I found it in our database."

"You found it in *my* personal database," Barclay corrected him.

"I found the template in your personal database. I extracted Data's files to re-create them here so I could study them. I asked you to join me because I have a number of questions I believe you might be able to help me answer."

"Questions?" Barclay shook his head in rapid disbelief. "I didn't create the holodeck program from which you surgically removed this file for *you* or anyone else. I wasn't aboard the *Enterprise* when they encountered Shinzon at Romulus. I never had the opportunity to say good-bye to him. *This* program exists because I needed to do that. I needed closure, and this was the only way for me to get it."

"Reg, I'm so sorry."

"I know I should have deleted it, but I couldn't. It was too hard. It was like killing him again. But I haven't run this program in almost three years. It was never meant to keep him alive and certainly not for anyone to use it to study him.

"Countless analyses of Data exist in Starfleet's records. Commander Bruce Maddox has done the most extensive work to date. If you have questions, you should contact him to satisfy your curiosity."

"Please, Reg. I had no idea you would react this way," the Doctor said softly. "I've been consumed by a new case for the last few weeks. One of our officers is suffering from a debilitating terminal illness. We had hoped the cure might lie in stem-cell therapy. As of now, that door is closed to us, and her condition is deteriorating rapidly. It occurred to me that if we aren't able to reverse it quite soon that, when the time comes, we might be able to temporarily transfer her neural pattern to a holographic buffer. When I was going through the files I found your program and inspiration struck. Perhaps a neural pattern could be stored indefinitely in a positronic brain. *Enterprise*'s logs indicate that a Doctor Graves once transferred his consciousness into Data, so it *is* possible."

Barclay couldn't help it. An incredulous laugh escaped his lips before he could think better of it.

The Doctor blanched, clearly offended.

"I wouldn't use that lunatic's work as the basis for any serious inquiry. I have no idea how Graves did what he did and no intention of helping you figure it out."

"But . . ."

"And even were I so inclined, you're forgetting the much harder preliminary step—*creating a new, functional positronic brain*. That's something even Data could never perfectly reproduce and he was *Data*. Watching him try and fail with his daughter, Lal, was excruciating."

"I understand it might be challenging, Reg, but this is what we do. Past failures are not certain indication of future possibilities. If we worked together, imagine what we might learn and achieve in the process."

"I would never," Barclay insisted.

"Why not?" the Doctor demanded.

"It's disrespectful."

The Doctor did Barclay the credit of seriously considering the notion. "Is it disrespectful to re-create Socrates and ask him to demonstrate his method, or to re-create Shakespeare to discuss the pitfalls of iambic pentameter?"

Barclay stepped back. The shock was wearing off slowly, giving way to the same dull misery he remembered experiencing so frequently in the first few months after he had learned of Data's death. "No, but . . ."

"But what? I am trying to solve one of the most difficult medical issues I have ever faced, and Commander Data might hold the key to saving a life."

"If re-creating a functional positronic brain is the only solution, your patient is going to die."

"But if I can prevent that . . ."

"Who are you?" Barclay bellowed. "I understand doing everything within your power to cure an illness or prolong a life. But sometimes you can't. Sometimes people die. Is it your intention to create positronic brains for all of the fleet's crew? Who decides who might get to use one of these medical marvels and who doesn't? Never mind the fact that you would be damning them to an existence I'm not sure any of them would appreciate. They might live longer. They might live forever. But you cannot possibly believe that the life of an individual stored in an android's body, no matter how advanced, can compare favorably to human existence.

"I knew Data. Data was my friend. He wanted to be human. In some of the most important ways, he was, even though he would probably deny that statement. But I guarantee you that if he were here right now, he'd tell you to stop. And since he can't, I'm telling you to stop. Don't do this."

The Doctor shook his head slowly, his disappointment clear. "I assumed you of all people would understand the need, would see what I'm trying to do here."

"I don't know what that means, me *of all people*. We've known each other for many years, and in all that time you've never intentionally insulted me. I know that wasn't your goal, but you just did."

The Doctor rested his back against the biobed and crossed his arms. "I apologize."

"There has to be another way, Doctor. And if you need me, of course I'll try to help you find it. But you and I aren't going to create a new positronic brain out here with the limited resources at our disposal. What was wrong with your initial thought . . . a temporary holomatrix?"

The Doctor shrugged. "Processing power," he replied. "The last time we did it, we had to pull space from the main computer. We can't do that safely on *Galen*. She's too small."

"Yet," Barclay said. "We can't do it yet. Give me some time?"

The Doctor nodded.

4

. . . e ighty-one, eighty-two . . .

The proximity sensor outside Commander Malcolm Roach's door chimed.

. . . eighty-three . . . eighty-four . . .

"Come in," Roach called between sit-ups.

Lying on the deck at the foot of his bed, Roach attacked the remainder of the set with extra vigor as a pair of black boots beneath black uniform pants stepped into view.

"Oh, I'm sorry to disturb you, Commander," the voice of *Vesta's* young chief engineer, Lieutenant Phinnegan Bryce, said.

. . . ninety-six . . . ninety-seven . . .

"You're not," Roach insisted, quickly finishing the last three before taking a moment to catch his breath.

"No, we can discuss this another . . . in the morning . . . or whenever you have a minute," Bryce said.

Roach rolled quickly to his side and pushed himself up. As soon as he'd regained his feet, he grabbed a tall glass of water he always kept near at hand and took a generous swig. "What's on your mind, Bryce?"

"Don't worry about it, Commander."

Roach considered the lanky young man. His sandy blond hair fell just over his ears, too long for the commander's taste. He preferred to keep the sides of his jet-black hair almost buzzed and the top around half an inch in length. Bryce had striking blue eyes. They were one of the first things you noticed about him, as they tended toward the intense end of the spectrum.

Reticent, reluctant, and ill at ease were not words that usually came to mind in Bryce's presence. As a lieutenant junior grade he had nearly single-handedly saved the first vessel attached to the Full Circle Fleet that Captain Farkas had commanded, the *Quirinal*, and that minor miracle followed by a few major ones had caused Farkas to ask Bryce to serve as chief engineer when it became clear Preston Ganley wasn't going to recover from the injuries he sustained when a group of noncorporeal aliens invaded and nearly destroyed the ship. This was an extraordinary leap for such a young engineer, even a gifted one, but Bryce tended to shrug off any attempt to remind him that his promotion was well earned. He moved through his duties with assurance, attacked problems with vigor, and maintained a healthy spirit of optimism, even in the darkest of times, while simultaneously remaining low-key and approachable. Roach knew that Bryce was bright as the day was long and rarely at a loss for words. A few seconds of sizing up his obvious discomfort, combined with the realization that Bryce had never requested access to Roach's personal quarters after hours, left the commander intrigued.

Dropping onto the edge of his rack, Roach motioned for Bryce to take the room's only chair opposite him. "Park it, Lieutenant."

Roach had served for more than two years as Captain Farkas's first officer and, as was required by his position, knew every single member of their crew by name and billet. But he tended to keep people at a distance, more than arm's length whenever possible. He had found as he'd risen through the ranks that this arrangement suited him and the demands of his job. It wasn't that he didn't like people. He just lacked the patience to get to know them well and rarely found cause to.

For a second, Bryce looked ready to bolt. He stepped toward the chair, then reconsidered and assumed a stance somewhere between attention and at ease.

"I'm really sorry to bother you, Commander, but I wanted to make a request regarding our upcoming team assignments."

Roach was taken aback. He and Commander Paris had spent the better part of this day beginning to divide the fleet's crews into small exploratory teams that *no one* was supposed to know about yet. *Vesta* wouldn't assume orbit around DK-1116 for another thirty-six hours, and it would be another day at least before the security teams determined whether or not this massive waste of time—at least in Roach's estimation—was going to go forward.

But if Bryce was already in a loop of which Roach was unaware, he was also likely aware that as chief engineer of *Vesta,* he would be assigned to work with the other available chiefs, *Galen*'s Cress Benoit, *Demeter*'s Garvin Elkins, and the fleet chief, B'Elanna Torres.

"Which team are we talking about?" Roach asked.

"The group of engineers I'll be assigned to once we reach the planet where Seven found that new element."

"Those assignments aren't final yet and more important, *no one is supposed to know about them,*" Roach said, rising and squaring his shoulders.

Roach wasn't the tallest officer in the fleet. Neither was Bryce. Roach compensated by maintaining an exceptional level of physical fitness. Bryce apparently felt no need to do the same. He looked as if a strong wind might take him off his feet. Only his record and a clear inner strength belied that impression.

"I know, Commander," Bryce said. "But you know as well as I do that a rumor of two weeks of upcoming shore leave makes its way through the fleet at maximum warp."

"If that's the case you'd better hope the advance survey teams don't find anything hostile down there."

"The last sensor scans I saw showed a bunch of plants, Commander. I think we can take 'em, should the need arise."

"So, what's your request?"

"I'd like you to consider assigning Ensign Icheb to our group," Bryce said.

Ensign Icheb was new to the fleet and over the last few months had been serving as Commander Torres's personal aide. *Voyager*'s chief, Nancy Conlon, had been taken off duty indefinitely. Roach knew that Torres was leaning heavily on the ensign, much to the dismay of the rest of *Voyager*'s engineering staff. Icheb was actually one of the crew members that Paris was considering leaving off the rotation for now.

"I'm not sure that's going to be possible. A handful of critical officers will remain on board each of the fleet ships to maintain operational efficiency, and given that Icheb hasn't been with us that long, Commander Paris thinks he'd be an excellent choice for *Voyager*'s engine room."

Bryce's face fell, but he soldiered on. Roach liked that in a fellow officer. "I get that. I really do. And if I were Commander Paris, I might come to the same conclusion. I've spent a great deal of time with Icheb over the last few months. His assistance was critical in determining potential flight paths following *Voyager*'s initial encounter with the Krenim and locating the message buoy she dropped. He was the one who figured out the temporal displacement ratios that allowed us to reintegrate the buoy into our time period, and he gave us the down-and-dirty specs on integrating Borg-inspired temporal shielding into our defense grid in a tenth the time it would have taken me to complete. I'm good at what I do, Commander. Part of what I do now is identify potential and make sure it is utilized to the greatest possible advantage. I know two weeks sounds like a lot of time to spend on a single planet, but the advance specs I've seen of those biodomes are intimidating as hell. Can you imagine building a starship that could last a thousand years? Forget that, what about a hull plate that could last half that long? Those biodome fields are energy based and they've been holding steady for four thousand years. Do you have any idea how many things can happen on a planet or near a planet to alter conditions enough over four thousand years and make technology like that collapse? There's a regenerative component to those fields, I'd bet my life on it, and no one in our fleet except for Seven knows as much about regenerative systems as Icheb. He's critical to the work our team will be undertaking."

"Benoit and Elkins aren't exactly slackers, Bryce," Roach noted.

"No, they aren't. In fact, Elkins scares the pants off me. But he's also been working closely with Icheb over the last few weeks, and I bet if you asked him, he'd second this motion."

"It's not going to be up to me. It's going to be up to Commander Paris," Roach said.

"I understand."

"I'd suggest requesting Seven spend some time with you on the surface, but she has already asked to remain on *Voyager* to study the binaries and the debris fields."

"There's more than enough work to go around," Bryce agreed.

A new thought struck Roach. "Is this a professional request, Lieutenant, or a personal one?"

Bryce responded immediately, "Professional, sir. I would never . . . I mean . . ."

As he considered the question more fully, the lieutenant's cheeks reddened ever so slightly.

"I don't mean that he's not . . . but he wouldn't . . . I mean I don't know if . . . why? Has he said something?"

"Shit, Bryce."

"Forget I asked. I think our team would benefit from his presence. That's all. And if he thought for one second I was making this request for any reason other than his obvious abilities . . ."

Roach had heard enough. "I can't make any promises. But I will take this under advisement and raise the issue with Commander Paris."

"Do you have to tell him I was the one who asked?"

"I tend toward honesty in all of my interactions with fellow officers, Bryce, if only because the truth is the easiest thing to remember."

"I understand, sir."

"But if it makes you feel better, you make a good case. We'll consider it on its merits."

"Thank you, sir."

Bryce looked just this side of miserable as he left. Roach remembered being that young. He didn't miss it.

VOYAGER

Lieutenant Kenth Lasren was sitting alone in the mess hall, halfway into a bowl of gazpacho, when he suddenly realized someone was sitting to his left. A young boy, his jet-black hair hiding most of his face, was bent low over a padd, furiously keying a calculation.

More troubling, this boy wasn't seated in *Voyager*'s mess hall. He was seated in a classroom.

Lasren looked to his right. Another young student, this one a girl, her silvery dark hair pulled back into a tight bun. Around her neck was a string of beads, and as she worked her padd with one hand, she absentmindedly counted each individual bead with the other. Her lips moved without any sound escaping as she talked herself through whatever problem she was attempting to solve.

Beyond her, the row continued as far as Lasren could see. The same was true on the left. Countless rows stood in perfect order in front of him, a sea of standardized desks filled with students engrossed in a complicated mathematical calculation. He didn't need to look behind to know that there was a battalion of children there, too, all of them striving to do more than complete the problem.

All of them were united in and defined by the absolute need to find the answer *first*.

The anxiety of that room was nothing Lasren had ever known. He closed his eyes and tried to visualize the mess hall, the small table at which he had seated himself, and his bowl of soup. When he opened them, Lieutenant Devi Patel had taken the seat across from him.

Instantly he understood the source of the strange vision. It was unusual, but not a huge mystery.

Lasren was tired. He had pulled a double operations shift at Chakotay's request, enhancing long-range scans of the system the fleet was now approaching. His guard was down. Otherwise this odd, deeply personal moment could not have forced its way into his mind. As one of the few Betazoids in the fleet, Lasren was called upon from time to time to utilize his psionic abilities in first-contact situations, but as a rule, he didn't train it on fellow officers, believing that to be a violation of their privacy.

The sheer tonnage of expectant anxiety currently animating Patel was rolling off her in waves. In an attempt to clearly identify the emotions overwhelming him, his mind had automatically reached into hers and plucked out a context. He wanted to apologize but odds were she wasn't even aware he had done it. It certainly hadn't been intentional.

"Hi, Devi."

"Hi, Kenth. Would you take a look at this for me?"

She turned the padd she was holding to face him and slid it across the table until it rested by his free hand. It contained an open file consisting of detailed sensor scans of a large pool of water located on the surface of DK-1116. Despite the official attempts at secrecy, like everyone else on board, Lasren was well aware of the fleet's new mission and was thrilled with the prospect of a brief respite from the chaos that usually seemed to characterize the Delta Quadrant. He recognized the data as he had compiled it during alpha shift. What he did not understand was Patel's interest in the site or the intensity it provoked in her.

"Do you see it?" Patel asked.

"I'm not sure. See what?"

"The unique carved stones beneath the surface?"

As soon as she had pointed it out, he did.

"Oh. Yeah."

"This pool is actually a stepwell."

"I don't know what that is."

"It's a kind of large well carved into deep canyons. But there are no other similar formations in any of the other biodomes. This site is unique, and the formation suggests it might have been created for a special purpose."

"How do you know that?"

"I've been analyzing the sensor feeds all day," Patel said quickly, as if that were a normal thing for her to have done. "This is going to be *our* team's research site, and I want to get a jump on our analysis."

"So we can spend most of our time when we arrive on the beach relaxing beside that massive freshwater lake in Biodome 10?" Lasren asked hopefully.

"Of course not. What's wrong with you?"

"Nothing, Devi. I just spent two shifts compiling data as fast as our sensors could spit it out. Personally I'm looking forward to the rest-and-relaxation portion of our mission more than the work. You might want to think about fun ways to reduce stress yourself."

"I'm not stressed," she insisted.

"Right now, Commander Torres could use you to power the warp reactor."

Devi sat back in her chair, crossing her arms over her chest. "Forgive me for wanting to be prepared."

"Prepared for what?"

"We can't screw this up, Lasren," Patel insisted.

"We haven't even arrived at the planet and already we're screwing something up?"

"We're only going to have a few days to sort this out. This is the strongest potential evidence I've seen of the species that constructed these biodomes. Wells like this sometimes contain water displacement mechanisms. If we can find it, we can drain the well and see what else is down there. Otherwise we'll be forced to dive in order to search for underground access to the caverns connected to this well. We have to be ready."

"Can't we just use EV suits?"

"They're not the greatest under water. Regulation dive gear will be easier and quicker and everyone on our team is certified."

Lasren set his spoon down beside his soup, pushed the padd back toward Devi, and leaned back. He had known Devi for four years. They weren't particularly close but shared a healthy respect for each other's abilities. It was flattering, in a way, that she was seeking out his counsel. But he couldn't shake the sense that she was seeking to exert control over something rapidly slipping through her fingers.

Patel's short black hair framed her face closely, giving it the illusion of greater length than width. With her chin tilted down and her eyebrows lifted, her head almost seemed to come to an unnatural point.

"I have to be honest with you, Devi. You're freaking me out a little."

"I'm sorry. I don't mean to. It's just . . . I spoke with Commander Paris earlier today. I asked specifically to be assigned to the same away team as you and Ensigns Jepel and Vincent."

"Why does it matter what away team you're on?"

"I don't care about the team as much as our research site. I've looked at most of the others, and while there are some intriguing formations, this is the one with the greatest potential for discovery. Every single biodome contains at least one water source, but none of them look like this one. The water lines vary between half a meter and two meters below the surface of the pools, but this one is almost twenty meters down."

"Maybe it has receded slowly over time."

"If it could recede, whatever atmospheric process evaporating it would long ago have rendered it dry without a natural underground source replenishing it. We'll have to wait until we reach the surface to scan for those, but I don't think we're going to find them. I believe *this* is the well's natural level."

"What exactly do you think is down there?"

"Look at the compositional scans," Patel suggested.

Lasren did so and immediately saw what had likely piqued her interest.

"There's more *Sevenofninonium* beneath the surface of that well than in any other biodome. The water is hiding it. We have to figure out how to get to it," Patel insisted.

"First of all, we're not calling it that."

"You prefer UI791116PJ4702700001?"

"No, but . . ."

"We have to call it something. Just tell me what you want to call it, and I'll add it to our mission schedule."

"The thing is, a new element is interesting, but this one isn't of any practical use to us. We're probably going to collect as many samples as we can closer to the surface and call it a day, right?"

"Don't you see that this is our chance?" Patel insisted, raising her voice enough to attract a few curious stares from the other officers hurrying through their own dinners.

Lasren liked Patel. She was a devoted scientist and usually quite pleasant to work with. She took her job seriously and was quick to provide expert analysis. But in the four years they had served together, he had never seen her like this.

"Devi, talk to me. Forget the planet and the biodome and the water levels for a second. Where is this sudden sense of urgency coming from? This isn't a test. You can't fail."

Patel looked away for a moment, then shook her head quickly, as if she had fought and lost a battle with herself.

"We're never going to have another opportunity like this,"

she finally said. "If this were any other away mission, Kim, Seven, and maybe Commander Torres would be heading down to the surface to analyze the area. Gwyn might get lucky and get to go along if they wanted to use shuttles rather than the transporters. And if there was a new intelligent life-form there, you might be asked to use your psionic abilities to add to the data collected. But *I* would be stuck on the bridge collating Seven's data, and whatever we eventually learned would be added to her already brilliant service record.

"I don't think anyone else has seen this yet. And I'll bet you anything that if they do, we'll be pulled off this site so more senior officers can investigate it. I don't want that to happen. If we do a thorough enough evaluation now, by the time the captain figures out what's really there, we'll still be the best team to do the work."

Lasren leaned forward. He understood. The complex cocktail of emotions he was sensing from Devi had more to do with fear than stress. She was afraid of being overlooked. She knew she could find the right answer, but in a sea of a thousand students it didn't matter unless she found it first.

In a way it made sense. Her work on *Voyager* had been a great deal more interesting and her responsibilities more defined before Seven had joined the fleet. Lasren didn't give much thought to personal advancement. It was enough for him to be a member of the alpha-shift bridge crew. He'd had a few really interesting and terrifying encounters already on this mission, and that was more than enough excitement for the adventurer in him. He'd also been one of the few officers singled out for promotion since the fleet had launched. Until now, he'd never imagined that Devi resented her status, or was withering away as her skills went unnoticed or underutilized.

Tired as he was, he wanted to help her, if only to banish the specter of that sea of unhappy children and their math problems.

"You're probably right," he finally conceded. "This is a rare moment for us. And I promise you, as soon as I've had a few hours of sleep, I'll make sure that our scans tomorrow give us better resolution of this, what did you call it?"

"Stepwell."

"Okay. Got it."

"A number of ancient Earth civilizations utilized them. It's weird to see something so similar here. Many of the ones we know about conceal vast networks of tunnels carved into the surrounding rocks. Their purpose was often ceremonial, but I have no idea if that's what we're seeing here."

Lasren smiled gently. "Don't worry. We'll find out together."

After a moment, Patel returned his smile ever so faintly. "Good."

Michael Owen Paris slept soundly in his mother's arms, despite the scene currently under way in his family's living room. B'Elanna Torres had once replicated an antique television set for her husband, Tom Paris. Most evenings, the entire Paris family could be found seated before it sharing popcorn and marveling at what passed for entertainment a few hundred years ago.

Not tonight.

The television and the rest of the room's furnishings had all been shoved unceremoniously against the bulkheads to make room for a Starfleet-issue, self-constructing domical surface shelter.

When B'Elanna and her father had gone camping with

her cousins in summers long past, their tents had been smaller and harder to build. Tom had decided this should be a learning experience for their four-year-old daughter, Miral, so he had deactivated the autonomous set-up protocol, removed the spring poles and guide ropes, and was attempting to show his daughter how to construct a tent without the aid of modern technology.

Torres wanted to take Michael to his crib and join Tom and Miral on the floor. But she was enjoying watching Tom too much as he tried to extricate himself from the mess he'd made.

Miral was proving to be a quick study with the spring-loaded poles.

"Look out, Daddy," she warned as she pressed the small release at the base of a pole and watched it double in length with a loud, satisfying snap. The first time she had discovered this capability, the pole had snapped open into Tom's midsection. Miral had appeared momentarily stricken at the sight of her father's pain, but her concern quickly morphed into peals of delighted laughter.

Tom was underneath the silver fabric, careening about as he searched for the slits from which he had removed the poles. His mumbled, frustrated monologue was only half-audible. The half Torres couldn't hear was probably unsuitable for their children's ears.

"Now where the . . . I just had it . . . hang on, hang on, okay, Miral, call off the dogs, I found it, honey . . ."

Tom's head poked out through the entrance flap.

"Hand me that pole, sweetie, and come here."

Miral did as she had been instructed, disappearing underneath the tent with her father.

"Where are the dogs, Daddy?"

"What?"

"You said there were dogs in here."

"No, that was just an expression. Here you go. Put that pole in this opening and . . ."

A distinct ripping sound paused his instructions.

"Oh, come on," Paris said, clearly frustrated.

Torres stifled her laughter, placing a hand firmly over her mouth.

"What happened, Daddy? Are you okay?"

The moment Tom had laid eyes on Biodome 10, he had decided that as much time as duty would allow was going to be spent with his family, camping beside that large lake. The water was unusually still, excellent for giving Miral her first swimming lessons. A *forest*—for want of a better word—wrapped around the northern edge of the lake and continued for several miles. The growths weren't made of wood, they were soft metal. Numerous bands were braided together in thick trunks and some of them extended as high as twenty meters in the air. Thinner branch-like extensions burst from the tops, bending gracefully and providing minimal shade. The place beckoned to the explorer in both of them, and Miral was over the moon at the thought of the days to come.

The nights were going to get pretty cold, however, if Tom insisted on building their tent rather than relying on the genius of the Starfleet officers who had gone before him.

"I'm going to replicate sleeping bags for all of us," Torres said.

"Make mine purple, Mommy," Miral commanded from beneath the tent.

"I can do that."

"And make Michael's yellow."

"But you hate yellow. What makes you think he will like it?" Tom asked.

"He can have the yellow so I don't have to."

"Do you think he likes yellow?"

"He likes bananas."

At this, Torres's heart broke a little. For most of Miral's young life she had been unable to properly pronounce "banana," instead calling them *gunana* or *bugunana*. That little Miral-ism, along with a hundred others, was vanishing as her language skills increased daily.

"He's not old enough to like bananas, honey."

"He will like them. Can I give him a banana?"

"Not for another few months," Torres said. "For now, he just needs milk. And he doesn't need his own sleeping bag."

"Hang on, is this the groundsheet?" Tom asked.

The door chime sounded, and Torres rose from the sofa and moved to open the door manually. Miral had recently discovered the floor sensors inside and outside the door and had almost broken the mechanism standing with one foot on each side, so Torres had deactivated it, hoping her daughter would soon lose interest in the game.

Icheb stood in the hallway, and Torres greeted him cheerfully, hoping to make up a little for her testiness that morning. While reviewing his reports she had learned that, to his credit, his theory about *Vesta*'s replicator had been proven right.

"Good evening, Commander."

"Come on in, Icheb. Good catch, by the way, with that lot of gel packs."

"Thank you, Commander." After a pause that threatened to become uncomfortable, he asked, "I don't wish to upset you, but many of our engineers are wondering if there is any word on Lieutenant Conlon's status?"

Torres bowed her head and inhaled deeply. For a few brief hours, she's managed to forget that one of her closest friends had almost died the previous day. At least she *knew*. How frustrating must it be for those who cared about Conlon but weren't part of the small group that received regular updates.

"Yesterday was a bad day," Torres finally said. "She pulled through, but it's going to be several weeks at least before we have a new prognosis."

"And before we see her again?"

"Most likely."

Icheb nodded. "I understand. Thank you for telling me."

"Of course. I'll make an announcement tomorrow. And the next time I see her, I'll make sure she knows that everyone is pulling for her."

Despite the implied dismissal, Icheb remained rooted where he stood.

"Was there something else?"

"Um . . . Commander Paris wished to see me."

"Oh. Sure. Tom, Icheb is here."

A loud rustling was followed by the emergence of her husband from the folds of silver fabric.

"Hey, Icheb."

"Sir."

Several minutes of fabric friction had left Tom's fine, light-brown hair standing on end. Icheb pretended not to notice.

"That's a good look for you, honey," Torres said before heading toward Michael's bedroom.

"Can I be of any assistance?" she heard Icheb ask.

Miral clearly remained under the silver mess of the tent and could be heard, lurching around, randomly calling out, *"Here, puppy. Here, puppy, puppy."*

"No, thanks. I've got it," Paris said, though nothing could have been further from the truth in his wife's opinion. Torres returned, her arms empty, and set about retrieving the poles Miral had stacked in a small cord and carried them under the fabric.

Tom and Icheb's conversation was muffled as Torres set to work. After convincing Miral to sit in the center of the ground sheet holding the poles, she spread the rest of the fabric out, quickly located the pole slits, and threaded the poles back into them. She untangled the guide ropes and had Miral carry them out the front opening, which was now discernable, if not fully extended. Finally she located the autoconstruct mechanism over the door flap and reactivated it. Instructing Miral to stand back, Torres allowed her to depress the remote activator and, with a crack, the domical tent snapped to full extension.

Miral gave her mother an enthusiastic round of applause and a tight squeeze around the knees before rushing into what would likely be her quarters until they reached DK-1116.

"What the . . . ?" Paris asked.

He stood before the perfect tent, hands on his hips.

"You're welcome," his wife said.

"I was going to finish that."

"And now you don't have to. You can get right to the playing in it. Just promise me, no campfires until we're on the surface."

"*Daddy, can we pull the TV in here?*" Miral asked from inside.

Paris shrugged. "Can we?"

"Sure. Hey, what did you need with Icheb?"

"Nothing. Roach advised me that one of his officers requested Icheb for their exploratory team, but I confirmed he's going to have the majority of alpha shifts in *Voyager*'s engine room while we're in orbit."

Torres nodded. She had privately planned to make sure Icheb got a few days rest on the surface, but without Nancy that was going to be hard to do.

Hard, but not impossible.

"Honey, did Roach mention who made the request?"

"Uh, Bryce, I think? He wanted Icheb to join the team of engineers studying the biodome field generators."

"Bryce?"

"Yeah."

Torres playfully smacked the side of Tom's head.

"Hey!"

"Why didn't you tell me it was Bryce?"

"Because, who cares?"

"First thing in the morning, you let Roach know that Icheb will be assigned to that team. I'll cover the engine room while you're on rotation, and we'll still spend the evenings and off-shifts camping with the kids."

"Why in the world would you do that? You need a break as much as any of us."

"I'm going to get plenty of time off. But this is a big deal for Icheb. I should have thought of it myself."

Paris pondered his wife for a few silent moments.

"You're not playing matchmaker again, are you?"

"Bryce asked. I'm just approving the request."

"That's my job."

"What's yours is mine, my love. It was in the fine print when we got married."

Paris opted not to argue with that.

5

Captain Regina Farkas paused briefly at the entrance to *Vesta*'s medical bay. Gamma shift was well under way, and both she and her CMO, Doctor El'nor Sal, should have been sleeping. That El'nor wasn't meant trouble, and while Farkas would gladly travel from one end of the galaxy to the other in an EV suit for her oldest and dearest friend, the captain had absorbed more than her own fair share of awful since assuming command of *Vesta* and her short-lived predecessor, *Quirinal.* She wasn't sure she was up for one of El'nor's moods tonight.

Not that she had a choice. Sal would have traveled from one end of the galaxy to the other for her in an EV suit filled with fire ants. And according to her duty logs, Sal was currently getting by on less than three hours sleep per day. In Farkas's experience, this was a recipe for disaster.

The captain found Sal hunched over one of the lab's data terminals. The other gamma-shift medics were clearly giving her a wide berth and conducted their work in hushed tones despite the fact that there were no patients present.

Taking the bull by the horns, Farkas moved to Sal's side. "Last call was a few hours ago," she said softly.

Sal didn't tear her eyes away from the display, but replied, "It's okay. The owner is an old friend of mine."

"You know, the only person on this ship who needs her beauty sleep more than I do is you."

Sal chuckled grimly and rubbed her eyes. "I'm afraid that ship has sailed for both of us, Regina."

A genetic analysis ran down the screen Sal was studying. A single word caught Farkas's eye.

Kriosian.

The captain's stomach lurched.

It might mean nothing.

Or it might mean that the doctor was inexplicably courting demons laid to rest thirty years ago.

"I've got a sciences briefing on the planet we're about to explore at oh-seven-hundred," Farkas said. "I have reason to believe that some fairly challenging math will be involved, and I really want to be at my best."

Sal turned toward Farkas. "I have a patient I'm not going to be able to save."

Farkas placed a hand on Sal's shoulder. "I'm so sorry, El'nor."

"I hate my job," the doctor said.

"It's still not too late to throw sixty-some-odd years of experience out the window and enter the command track. You could have my job."

"Your job is the only one on this ship that is worse than mine."

"Yeah, but think of the perks. For instance, I get to order you to take better care of yourself. Get some rest. Now."

Sal looked at her data screen and reached over to shut off the display. Turning back to Farkas she said, "In the last few weeks, I've bent, spindled, and done everything short of mutilating my Hippocratic oath to get my patient to agree to the one procedure that might help her, but for a lot of reasons I can't go into, that door is closed. I have to find another option, and I have. But you're not going to like it."

Farkas knew what was coming next.

"Did you know there is a half-Kriosian female on *Voyager*?" Sal asked.

"I didn't. I suppose the odds were pretty good in a fleet this size. I bet we had a few more before we lost those other five ships."

"Do you think if we asked the Kriosians one more time?" Sal began.

"No."

"It's been decades, Regina. Most of the folks who were there back then have probably retired by now. Their successors might see things differently. They might at least *talk* to me."

"We barely made it off that planet with our careers intact, El'nor. Just hand over your pips now. You stir up that hornet's nest again, that's how the story will end."

"I'm trying to save a life."

"And what, pray tell, do the good people of Krios have to do with that?"

"You and I both know at least part of the truth. We know what they hid from the Federation when they joined. We know what they are capable of."

"No, we don't," Farkas said, her voice and her ire rising. "We know the story of one troubled woman."

"She wasn't crazy, Regina."

"She was at the end."

"That wasn't her fault."

"Why are we relitigating this thirty years later in the middle of the damn night? We tried to help her. Against my better judgment and most of the words in the oath I swore to Starfleet, we gave it our best shot and we failed. I took responsibility for that because I was the senior officer. Along the way, unless my memory is faulty—*which it isn't yet*— we almost lost the Federation one of their most important members. We aren't responsible for the sins of the Kriosians' past any more than we are responsible for the merry mess our ancestors almost made of the planet we both call home. We are responsible for the choices we make tonight and tomorrow and the day after that. So help me, I won't allow you to pick up that tattered flag and start waving it around when all it will most likely do is bring the full weight of the uniform code down on both our heads."

"I just need a few thousand cells."

"You said she's only half Kriosian."

"They're there."

"Not according to Starfleet Medical, or the Kriosian Science Ward."

"You can't stop me from asking her."

"No, but I can stop you from repeating rumors that have no basis in fact in order to convince her to part with those cells, which I'm guessing she will be unwilling to do."

Sal picked up a cup of something dark and murky at her station that had long ago grown cold and took a generous sip. She grimaced as it went down, then reared back and threw the cup with all her might. It slammed into the partition separating the terminal from a biobed and bounced off the transparent aluminum, landing on the deck.

"Feel better now?" Farkas asked.

"Not really."

Farkas shook her head, dismayed. "I'm going to have to make this a direct order, aren't I?"

Sal lifted a padd from her station. She scrolled through a few documents before finding the one she wanted and handed it to Farkas.

"What is this?"

"A paper published by Doctor Dorothy Chen-Minatta fifteen months ago."

"That was going to be my first guess."

"She's not in Starfleet anymore—has her own research facility on Thrux. She cured Rinoud's syndrome in a sixty-three-year-old human female by successfully reverting a single donated blood cell to an undifferentiated state, correcting the regulatory sequence that governs C27a, making a few million copies, and delivering those copies directly to the woman's bone marrow. Once there, the cells made some friends, shared some data, and corrected an error that has killed thousands in the last fifty years. Do you know why that's amazing?"

"You know damn well I don't."

"Because it is one of a handful of occasions in the last several hundred years of gene therapy when reversion of an adult cell to an undifferentiated state resulted in a vector that was malleable enough to survive the necessary gene editing. We've been able to revert adult cells for a couple hundred years now. But they are typically useless when it comes to modifying damaged DNA. They look like embryonic stem cells, but they don't act like them. Even removing as many of the epigenetic markers as we can identify doesn't solve the problem. Do you know why it worked this time?"

"Because the donor was Kriosian?"

"Because the donor was Kriosian, the patient's sister-in-law. That got them around the cultural restrictions regarding tissue donation. Chen-Minatta doesn't come right out and say that the blood cell in question was metamorphic. The Kriosians would have silenced her had she mentioned the alterations to chromosome seventeen that I'd bet my life and yours were present. Maybe she honestly had no idea why the cell was so easy to manipulate or she had to play by their rules to get this published and save lives. Either way, it's all the cover I need."

"You believe you can do the same here?"

"I just need an ensign to give me some blood. If she's carrying the mutation, we're in business."

"Even if she were willing to overlook her people's cultural taboos, you can't genetically modify her cells and inject them into someone else."

"I can if she gives me permission. And according to her file, she is unaffiliated. For all I know, she doesn't give a damn about her people's quasi-religious bugaboos."

"El'nor."

"If there was another way, Regina, don't you think I would be using it? This mutation is already killing my patient slowly and incredibly painfully."

"All you're asking for is a blood sample?"

Sal nodded. "I'm pretty sure I can incite the necessary changes to the cells once they are extracted. From that point on, I follow Doctor Chen-Minatta's protocol to the letter."

Farkas sighed. She didn't know if she believed El'nor, or if she just *wanted* to believe her.

"No one else ever has to know," Sal insisted.

"What about the other fleet doctors?"

"Unless I point out the variation, they'd never begin to know where to look for it. We're trying to cure a unique mutation. This therapy isn't going to have widespread applications beyond curing this one patient."

"Promise me."

"I promise."

Farkas suddenly realized she had lost the argument before it started. By the time she had returned to her quarters and settled herself into her rack, sleep was a lost cause.

U.S.S. DEMETER

During the first year of the Full Circle Fleet's exploration of the Delta Quadrant, Seven had never had cause to board *Demeter*. She was the smallest of the fleet's experimental mission ships, and the chain of command was unusual for a Starfleet vessel. Commander Liam O'Donnell was the ship's captain, but given that his expertise was botanical genetics, the ship's XO, Lieutenant Commander Atlee Fife, functioned as O'Donnell's *de facto* captain during tactical engagements. For the first several months of their journey, it was an open question as to whether or not this command structure would work. After a near mutiny by Fife when the ship was captured by the Children of the Storm, that question was answered, just not in the way anyone expected.

Rather than ship Fife back to the Alpha Quadrant to stand court-martial, O'Donnell had offered him a second chance. By all accounts, the partnership that now existed between them was stable and incredibly productive.

Fife greeted her when she transported aboard at O'Donnell's request. A tall, gangly human male in his late thirties with sandy-blond hair and unusually large brown eyes, he had escorted her to O'Donnell's private lab in companionable silence.

While guiding her through a long hall containing a transparent canopy, he noted that this feature unique to *Demeter* was capable of absorbing and storing several different kinds of radiant energy for use in the ship's ongoing botanical experiments.

"Will it be programmed to collect exotic waves created by the binaries?" Seven asked.

"Of course. Commander O'Donnell has already given us a lengthy to-do list pending our arrival. There are a number of experiments he intends to run while we're in orbit."

"I see."

"Will you continue your analysis of the biodome where you made your initial discovery when we return?"

"I have asked to remain aboard *Voyager* for the duration of our mission."

"Why?" Fife asked, clearly surprised.

"There are a number of interesting features in the binary system I wish to analyze further, and they can best be studied from our astrometrics lab."

"Why don't you tell him the truth, Seven?" a familiar voice called.

At the end of the hall a stout man in his late fifties stood just outside an open door. Wiry tufts of dark curls, generously flecked with gray, began at his temples and circled the lower third of his otherwise bald pate. His eyes met hers merrily as she approached.

"What truth is that, Commander O'Donnell?" she asked.

"You have even less patience than I do with the idea of these forced team-building exercises," O'Donnell clarified.

Seven could feel Fife's eyes bulging in her direction. She didn't want to admit to this, but she couldn't deny it either. Chakotay's suggestion of intership cooperation was fine, in theory. She, however, preferred to work alone and was looking forward to several days of uninterrupted analyses. Rather than run the risk of insulting Fife, she settled for replying, "How can I assist you, Commander O'Donnell?"

"Thank you, Atlee," O'Donnell said with a knowing smile as he gestured for Seven to precede him into the lab.

The space was large for any single officer aboard a ship *Demeter*'s size. Three long diagnostic stations occupied the center of the lab. Their contents were meticulously arranged and banked by operations panels. At the far end of the lab a large workstation stood beneath a long port with a stunning forward view. Seven guessed the lab was situated just below the ship's bridge.

Without further preamble, O'Donnell invited her to the nearest diagnostic station and called up an analysis of a sample of the construct she had taken while on the surface of DK-1116.

"I thought you might want to take a look at this before I go any further, Seven."

At first blush, there was nothing surprising in the data. A handful of atoms of the new element were present, reinforced by several more common stable elements and isotopes. Whether or not these elements were responsible for the unexpected stability of the *Sevenofninonium* was, as yet, unclear. Chemists had discovered a few unexpected islands of stability as they had added to the periodic table over the centuries, but Seven's discovery was well outside any previous theoretical bounds.

It was the final data set that caught her eye, however.

"A fossilized helix?" she asked.

"A partial fossilized double helix," he confirmed.

"But not DNA."

"Strictly speaking, no," he agreed. "Until I'm on-site and can be certain this isn't simply a case of cross-contamination by a nearby life-form, I can't be certain of the significance of this finding. But the gross structure of this find is incredibly provocative."

"Four thousand years, give or take, should not be sufficient time for genetic material to have decayed this much," she noted.

"Were we looking at a living thing, I would agree with you. But we aren't, are we?"

"I don't believe so."

"Look at this," he said, magnifying a section of the sample shaped similarly to a brick wall.

"What are these?" Seven asked.

"I don't know. I just know what they resemble most other places we find them in nature."

"Cell walls."

"I'd say so."

"Is this where you found your fossil?"

"It is."

"It is your hypothesis, then, that we are looking at a life-form?"

"I'm not sure I'd go that far."

Seven turned to face O'Donnell. "Explain."

"Whatever this is, I don't believe for one second that it is a naturally occurring organic life-form. But every single one of those biodomes is lacking evidence, at least on the surface, of any technology that could have created the structures containing your new element. And there is almost no way it simply arose on this planet."

"As far as we know," she insisted.

"Granted, but you have to admit we would have been far more likely to have discovered it in a black hole or subspace permutation than here, sitting on this uninhabitable planet, and *stable*. This and the constructs that contain it have to be as synthetic as the biodomes."

"These structures could have been created on starships and brought to the surface."

"Also possible, but not likely. Biodome 10 contains acres of constructs surrounding that water source. That's a lot of weight for a starship to carry. And even if it did, why just leave it here?"

"I'm not sure what you're getting at."

"I'm trying to understand the purpose of these constructs as suggested by their design and how they ended up where they are."

"They might be merely ornamental," Seven suggested.

"Their subjectively pleasant physical arrangement aside," O'Donnell said, "vast sections of them are composed of this boxlike structure similar to a plant cell. They're relatively large, and it's possible they *grow* by expanding rather than multiplying."

"Plant cells that grow in this fashion absorb nutrients. Do you have any theories as to what might serve as a food source?"

"There's plenty of exotic radiant energy hitting that planet from the binaries."

"Have you considered the possibility, Commander, that as this is your particular area of expertise, you are simply seeing what you want to see in this sample?" Seven asked.

"To a hammer, everything looks like a nail?" he asked, smiling.

"Something like that."

"I don't particularly care which conclusions the evidence points to, as long as it is supportable and can be reproduced under multiple discrete experiments."

"Nor do I."

"What I see here, however, scares me a little."

"Why?"

"In nature, this structure is associated with one thing—the most efficient absorption and conversion of energy possible."

"Which would make these what, exactly?" Seven asked.

"Some sort of incredibly advanced matter-energy storage and conversion device. Plants absorb energy in order to grow. They store excess energy until it is needed, at which point it is released. A structure like this could have been designed to store vast amounts of energy for release by growth or all at once."

"As in, explosive? You believe these things might be living bombs?"

"Well, not anymore. Even if these fossils were actually part of the structure and were once nucleic acids, they're dead now to all intents and purposes. But a long time ago . . . ?"

Seven considered the readings again for a few more silent moments.

"Still think there's nothing really interesting left to discover on the surface of that planet?" he finally asked.

"No. But I am willing to leave the collection of further data from the surface in your capable hands," Seven replied. "I will continue my own analyses. Perhaps between the two of us we will be able to construct a plausible hypothesis to answer some of these questions."

O'Donnell stared at Seven for a long moment, a faint smile playing over his lips. Finally he said, "Among your many attributes, I think the one I most admire is your consistency, Seven."

VOYAGER

Commander Tom Paris found his oldest and best friend, Lieutenant Harry Kim, on the holodeck, beating the living hell out of a punching bag. The sweat dripping from Kim's face suggested he'd been at this awhile.

"Hi, honey, how was your day?" Paris asked.

Kim paused briefly, acknowledged Paris with a slight nod, and continued punching. "Fine."

Paris knew a dismissal when he saw one. He'd first learned how those worked at the hands of his father, the late Admiral Owen Paris. He also knew that Kim had been in eighteen different kinds of pain since Nancy Conlon had been diagnosed and transferred to *Galen*. Paris didn't know the particulars of the illness. He didn't need to. He figured B'Elanna knew more and was probably respecting Conlon's privacy. There was nothing Conlon could have asked of him that Paris wouldn't readily have given to help her, but his focus during this crisis had been and would always be Kim's well-being.

"Got a second?"

Kim released a loud huff and grabbed the bag to still it.

"What do you need, Tom?"

"I have good news and I have bad news, so I thought I should deliver it personally. Why don't we get the bad news out of the way first?"

Kim's eyes didn't register trepidation at this pronouncement. That wasn't, in Paris's opinion, a great sign. Clearly, for Harry, whatever Tom was about to tell him couldn't make his life any worse. He had hit some relative bottom and made himself comfortable.

Paris didn't have a problem with this in theory. The depths to which he had sunk from time to time in his life were horrifying to contemplate, even now, and all of his own making. The hell Harry was moving through had been thrust upon him by circumstance, and while he was going to eventually have to take responsibility not for the hell, but for his response to it, now wasn't the time to have that conversation and Paris wasn't going to push it. Depending upon how long this lasted, he might order Kim to see Cambridge, who would do a better job of bringing Harry around. Paris knew how to be a good friend, but he would never have confused his ability to deal with issues of this magnitude with those of a trained counselor.

"What is it?" Kim finally asked.

"You must have figured out by now that your and Seven's little discovery was going to have consequences, but I'm guessing even you didn't foresee Chakotay's response."

"The whole fleet is going back to spend at least two weeks investigating the planet and taking turns at a lengthy shore leave," Kim said, deadpan.

"How do you know that?"

"Everybody in the fleet knows that, Tom."

"Well, everybody in the fleet better prepare to be disappointed if when we get there the security teams you lead down to the surface find DK-1116's version of poison oak everywhere and the shore leave gets cancelled."

"That's not going to happen."

"It might."

"It won't. So that's the bad news? I need to prep an away team?"

"No," Paris admitted. "The bad news is that once you determine that the planet is perfectly safe, you're not going on rotation for shore leave."

"Why not?"

"That's the good news. Chakotay is going to leave you in command of *Voyager* while the rest of us enjoy shore leave."

A few months ago, this revelation would have been cause for celebration. Sometime in the last year, Kim had decided to set his sights on the command track in earnest. To have Chakotay place this kind of faith in him would have been cause for celebration.

Today, it was met with a slight nod.

"Okay."

"Come on, Harry, it's not okay. It's awesome."

"I run this ship several shifts each week, Tom. It's not that big of a deal."

"Two weeks, all to yourself? It's huge."

"Fine. It's huge."

Paris sighed. "Should I tell the captain you don't want the job?"

"No. I'll do it. I've already seen the planet. It's not that great."

"Okay."

Paris couldn't deny that he'd hoped this development would at least bring a little light back into Kim's eyes. Obviously it wasn't going to change any of the underlying problems, but as a sign of Chakotay's restored respect after a rough patch during their mission to Sormana, Tom had hoped for better. Maybe it really was time to bring Cambridge in on this.

"And yes, you need to prep your away teams. We'll make orbit start of tomorrow's gamma shift."

"Consider it done."

Paris turned to go. He expected to hear the sound of punching begin again but it didn't before Kim called to him. "Tom?"

"Yeah?"

"What was the name of that JAG officer who helped you out with that thing with your mom?"

"The family law specialist?"

"Uh-huh."

Paris turned back to face his friend. He tried desperately to imagine what possible need Kim would have for the officer who had prevented Julia Paris from gaining custody of her grandchildren a few months prior but drew a disquieting blank.

"Lieutenant Garvin Shaw."

Kim nodded but offered nothing more.

"Are you finally going to sue your parents for emancipation?" Paris teased.

"Very funny," Kim conceded, though he didn't really seem to appreciate the joke. "You liked him though, right?"

"He was great."

"Okay."

"Okay? What the hell, Harry? What do you need with a lawyer?"

Kim dropped his head. He shook it back and forth a few times as if unable to find the words he sought. When he raised it again, the look in his eyes bordered briefly on feral.

"I don't want to talk about it," Harry said.

"If you think for one second I'm leaving this holodeck without a better answer than that, you're out of your mind, Harry."

"You can't tell B'Elanna."

Paris felt the words as a physical blow. Kim was deadly serious, and Paris knew that if he pushed, he was going to have to live with this promise. He also knew he was going to have to live with his wife's wrath when she inevitably learned of it. This was a dance they'd done more than once in their marriage, and Tom had no interest in taking the floor again. But whatever was slowly killing his friend demanded that he rise to this occasion. Kim would have done no less for him. In fact, Tom's failure to show that level of confidence in Harry a long time ago had been the only thing that had seriously threatened the continuation of their friendship.

"Ever?"

"For now."

"As long as *now* isn't very long."

Kim took a moment to summon something. *Courage, maybe?* Paris wondered. Finally Kim said, "I'm a father."

Paris had steeled himself for the answer. *The doctors have given up. Nancy only has a few weeks/days/hours to live. Turns out it's contagious and I have it too.* But Paris had not been at all prepared for this.

Once the shock began to abate, however, the next question was obvious. "Who is the mother?"

Kim stared at him for a moment with the same disbelief he might have summoned at the sight of a monkey lecturing on particle physics.

"Nancy, right?" Paris asked.

"Uh-huh."

"So you mean you're *going* to be a father?"

Kim shook his head. "Nancy was only about six weeks along. They had to perform emergency surgery on her brain and in order to save the embryo during the procedure they transported her to a gestational incubator. She's aboard *Galen* right now."

"Is Nancy okay?"

"She's stable. She's going to be in a coma until they're sure it's safe to wake her."

"Harry, I'm so sorry."

Kim's face set in hard lines. "Me too. But that doesn't change the fact that I've got to figure this out."

"Yeah, but you've got some time. Anything at all you need, B'Elanna and I will help. We can start setting Michael's things aside as he outgrows them."

"She's a girl, Tom."

"Whatever. With most of the baby stuff, gender doesn't matter. But I still don't understand why you need to talk to Shaw."

Kim moved back to the weight bench and sat. Grabbing a nearby bottle he took a long drink of water. Once he'd wiped his mouth with the back of his hand, he continued. "Nancy didn't want to keep the baby."

Paris considered his next words carefully as he took a seat beside Kim. This was one complicated issue he'd never had to face, and he was grateful for that. Much as he adored his children and had grown to love being a father, he also knew that if B'Elanna hadn't been on board with his desire to have a family, that would have been the end of it for him. Suddenly Harry's request to speak to Shaw took on a troubling significance.

"You said they performed an emergency embryonic transport, right?"

"Right. Technically, the baby was born last night. She's here and assuming she survives the next eight months, she's my responsibility."

"She's your and Nancy's responsibility," Paris corrected him gently.

Kim shrugged. "I don't think Nancy's going to change

her mind when she wakes up. She was very clear from day one that she didn't think either of us was ready to take this on. And she's pretty sick, Tom. Even if she wants to do this, she might not be physically able to."

"So what's your plan?"

"I want to make sure the baby is taken care of," Kim said, his voice tinged with desperation. "When I thought Nancy was going to terminate the pregnancy, I was a wreck. I promised her I would go along with whatever she wanted, but the more I thought about it, the more I felt like I was making the worst mistake of my life. You know me, so you know that's saying something," he said bitterly. "The doctors originally said it might be years before Nancy's illness caused serious problems. I figured that if I could change Nancy's mind, there was more than enough time for us to create a life for the three of us here as a family. That was the impossible version I kept turning over and over in my head without really believing for a minute it could happen. But Nancy almost died yesterday. The illness is already attacking her brain. What if she wakes up and doesn't remember me or us or the baby? Or what if she never wakes up? As much as I thought I wanted this, now that it's happened, I have no idea if I can do it at all, let alone without Nancy."

"You've got plenty of people here who will help, Harry," Tom insisted.

"Plenty of people who all have their own demanding responsibilities to attend to," Kim countered. "Starting with you and B'Elanna. You have two human beings to keep alive and nurture while serving as first officer and chief engineer of this fleet. That's more than enough on your plates." Kim paused, trying to collect thoughts that had apparently fallen to the ground in a million mixed-up tiny pieces. "I'm finally on a path that might lead to a ship of my own eventually. How am I supposed to pull all of the extra shifts required to make that happen as a single parent?"

"There are options, starting with holographic ones like Kula."

"Neither of you rely on Kula as much as you think you do. And even if she's more involved now, for the first few years of Miral's life, the really formative ones, B'Elanna was with her twenty-four/seven, right?"

"Yes," Tom admitted.

"That's what a child needs. And that's what she should have. I don't know if I can do it, and if I can't, I want to know what my options are."

"Okay, slow down," Tom said. "The future you are trying to plan doesn't exist yet. Well before you have to figure out how to care for your daughter—I can't believe I just said those words, by the way—you're going to know what Nancy wants to do and whether or not she's going to be able to be a part of this. Honestly, the best-case scenario here is that she gets better and you two figure out how to make it work."

"I hope she will, Tom. But what if she doesn't?"

"First thing I learned about being a father? You do everything one moment at a time. Forget hours, forget days. It's moment by moment. That's what makes it so exhausting."

"But worth it, right?"

Tom stared hard at his best friend. "Absolutely."

VESTA

"Ensign Gwyn?"

Doctor Sal looked up from her desk as the petite ensign

sporting short, spiked indigo hair entered her office just off the main medical bay.

"Doctor Sharak asked me to report to sickbay as soon as we made orbit. When I got there he said you had requested a sample of my blood."

"That's right."

"When I asked him why he wanted it, he said he didn't. *You did.* And there was nothing more he could tell me."

"I hope the request didn't alarm you, Ensign," Sal said, rising and gesturing for Gwyn to take the seat opposite her desk. Perching on the front edge of her desk, she continued, "Since Sharak is your CMO, it is customary for him to perform any standard medical procedures. Any other fleet doctor can step in during an emergency, but usually we keep our crew's medical needs segregated."

"Why do you want my blood?"

"I believe your blood cells might contain some unique factors that will help me develop a treatment for another patient. Think of it as donating blood to someone in need."

"Am I allowed to know who?"

"No," Sal replied. "Does it matter who?"

Gwyn sat very still, almost like a small, trapped animal.

"I'm half Kriosian."

Sal nodded. "I know that, Ensign. Your file also indicates that you have no *Degnar* affiliation."

"I've never been observant. My mom was, but I'm not. Still, we're not supposed to give blood to anyone who isn't Kriosian."

"I understand, and you are well within your rights to refuse my request. I just hope you won't."

"But if the patient was Kriosian . . ."

"I'm sorry, Ensign. I can't tell you anything about the

person I'm trying to help. They enjoy the same rights to privacy you do."

"Meaning what?"

"Meaning no one, not the patient, nor your mother, will ever know if you choose to break with your cultural traditions in this instance. What I can and will tell you, is that the patient in question is seriously ill, and your blood might very well help me cure them."

"How is that possible? How is my blood even compatible with someone who isn't Kriosian?"

"You're also half human."

"But there are hundreds of humans in our fleet. None of them can help you?"

Sal shook her head. "The kind of compatibility you're thinking of isn't the issue."

"Then what is the issue?"

"I believe your blood cells can help me save a life, Ensign. It's that simple."

Gwyn rose from the chair. "I'm sorry, Doctor. I'd like to help you, but I don't think I can. It's just something we don't do."

"Sit down, Ensign."

Gwyn started at the fierceness of Sal's tone and immediately did as she had been ordered.

"Do you know why Kriosians have this cultural taboo in place? Do you know where it comes from?"

Gwyn shook her head, refusing to meet Sal's eyes. "No, Doctor."

"It only goes back a little more than five hundred years."

"Since the Dawn?"

"That's right, since your people learned they weren't

alone in the universe and other intelligent, spacefaring races were out there."

"There must have been a good reason for it. Are you sure my blood won't hurt your patient?"

"There is a good reason, and yes, I'm sure. I wouldn't ask if I had any doubt."

"Do you know the reason?"

Sal paused. From this point on, anything she said would be well-reasoned speculation. She was already treading on the thinnest of ethical ice. If Regina were here, she would have ended this conversation the moment Gwyn refused the donation.

But Regina wasn't here, and Nancy Conlon was dying. Much as Sal understood the need to respect the traditions and social mores of every individual she encountered, in this case, the petty, arrogant, self-serving individuals who had created this restriction to cover crimes committed against countless generations of Kriosians weren't worthy of that respect. If she'd had her way, all of them would have been exposed and prosecuted for their actions. Those bridges had been burned long before Sal was born. There was no one left to blame. But allowing the fruit of an immoral tree to stand in the way of healing Nancy Conlon felt worse than unfair. Perpetrating this lie was wrong, and Sal hated that she was one of only a handful of people in the galaxy who knew it. She had no latitude when it came to sharing it. Regina had been perfectly clear on that point. *Still . . .*

"Your people have historically been reluctant to share medical knowledge with their peers in the Federation. It was actually one of the barriers to their initial entry and took a great deal of diplomatic maneuvering to overcome.

By categorizing their silence as a 'culturally specific observance' certain aspects of your traditions became exceptions to our normal rules and procedures."

"It's all because of the metamorphs, right?"

"I can't say for sure, but I'd be willing to bet that the Kriosian practice of breeding certain individuals to become perfect mates to others, normally for political alliances, was one of the larger stumbling blocks. Many cultures frown upon that kind of genetic manipulation as well as servitude, even when it is culturally acceptable."

"It's such a rare thing, Doctor. Most of us have never and will never know an empathic metamorph."

"I know."

"And I'm certainly not one."

"I know that too."

"So that's not why you want to use my blood?"

Sal paused again. The potential presence of the metamorphic gene factor was exactly why she wanted to use Gwyn's blood. Lying straight to the young woman's face wasn't an option. But her captain had also ordered her not to share her beliefs about this potential.

"Would it make a difference if I told you that I will not be directly transfusing any of your blood into the patient? My intention is to isolate a particular genetic sequence unique to your blood and transcribe that sequence into a vector that will transmit it into human cells."

"To what end?"

"I can't tell you that."

"But it will heal your patient."

"It very well could."

Gwyn shook her head slowly. "I don't know. My mom would hate it. And I'd have to tell her. She'd know even if I tried to hide it. I can't lie to her. According to Patel, I can't lie to anyone."

"I'm not asking you to lie to your mother or anyone else, Ensign. I'm asking you to consider whether or not a cultural taboo placed upon you by previous generations without your consultation or consent is more important than the possibility that you could help me save a life. I'm asking you to think bigger when you consider the question 'Who is Kriosian?' Your people have a tradition of considering aliens who marry into your families as full Kriosian. There are no restrictions concerning donating necessary blood or organs to them when they are compatible. I know you haven't married anyone within this fleet, but when you joined Starfleet, you became part of a larger family. Every individual you serve with could be considered an adopted brother or sister and in that sense, Kriosian."

Finally, Gwyn looked directly at Sal. "When you put it that way . . ."

Sal didn't wait for her change her mind. "Your arm, Ensign."

6

Lieutenant Devi Patel had slept incredibly well the previous evening. She was ready. The last time she'd prepped this thoroughly for a mission, she'd been leading her team in their final survival exercises at the Academy. She'd received the highest marks possible for that test and, comparatively speaking, this one should be much easier. She'd arrived early on the bridge to be on hand when word arrived from Lieutenant Kim that his survey teams had all reported in with the same findings: no hostile life-forms were present on the surface. She'd seen the delight on Captain Chakotay's face as he ordered the first of the away teams to report to the transporter room. She'd stopped by her quarters to pick up her personal supplies and, when she reached the main transporter bay, received confirmation that her cargo crates had already been sent to the surface. *Demeter*'s transporter room had reported that their operations officer, Ensign Thomas Vincent, had transported down a few minutes earlier. *Vesta*'s Ensign Jepel Omar had been part of the survey team for their biodome and had remained there to greet the rest of his team when they arrived. He was already busy unloading Patel's supply crates. Only Lieutenant Lasren had yet to report in.

Patel was just about to call for him over the comm when he hurried into the transporter room.

"Good morning Lieutenant," he greeted her.

"You're late, Lasren."

He handed her a padd. It contained the most detailed scan made to date of their site at the stepwell. Her heart began to race a little in anticipation. Several previously undetected caverns were now visible beneath the water line. She smiled broadly. "How?"

"I stopped by astrometrics a few hours ago and begged Seven for a few minutes on her sensor array," Lasren replied.

"You're forgiven," Patel said as they both stepped up onto the transporter platform.

DK-1116

Ensign Thomas Vincent hadn't felt dirt between his toes in more than a year. As a child, growing up near the equator in Earth's western hemisphere, he'd run wild though the reforested jungles near his home and spent long days in the garden with his grandmother learning how to coax life from soil. Back then, the bottoms of his feet had always been filthy. He didn't realize how much he would miss the simple pleasure, the way it made him feel part of something ancient, until he'd joined Starfleet and traded soft earth for hard deck plating. He'd been tempted more than once to remove his boots and tromp around in the soil of some of *Demeter*'s larger airponics bins but wasn't sure they would have supported his weight. Also, Brill would have had his ass. The creamy packed sand-like substance that bordered the stepwell where he would be spending most of his time on the planet looked like heaven. He was tempted to shed his boots on the spot, but didn't think Patel would approve, and he didn't want to start this mission on the wrong foot.

He'd received Patel's briefing packet and been somewhat annoyed with the specificity of their first assignments. He'd hoped for a more collaborative approach when the mission parameters had first been outlined for the crew by Lieutenant Commander Fife.

Still, he was planetside without an EV suit. He knew the warmth touching his face was only so pleasant because the actual radiant energy of the binary stars was heavily filtered by the biodome field. The air had an odd metallic tang to it, but his tricorder assured him of its breathability. The landscape near the well was flat and dotted all over by gray-green bushy plants he bet Commander O'Donnell would be sampling wherever he had been assigned. They were one of the few types of flora that was common to most of the biodomes.

Analysis of any of these curiosities would have to wait until the gear Patel had requisitioned for their group was unpacked and set up, so he joined Ensign Jepel, his operations counterpart from *Vesta*, with the grunt work while awaiting Patel and Lasren's arrival.

Vincent knew Jepel's voice well enough. Given that they were all alpha shift operations officers for their respective ships, they were each other's first contacts when intership cooperation was required within the fleet. He was actually excited to spend some face time with him.

He couldn't say the same about Patel. She was the ranking officer and a chief science officer aboard *Voyager*. She had already decided that the vast deposits of the unusual element that had brought the fleet to this planet were going to be accessible through the cavern system below. Vincent was less certain, but open to the possibility that she was right. His trepidation came from the fact that she hadn't requested his or anyone else's input when she had prepared their assignments. She outranked him, but he didn't actually report to her. He'd gladly follow any officer that earned his respect, but she seemed to be demanding it without having earned it.

But he was also willing to endure a lot in the name of five days on a pristine world. His position usually required his presence on the bridge, so he was well down the list of potential officers considered for away missions. The last one had been fairly hard labor on the surface of an alien world they had christened Persephone. Its atmosphere had been toxic, and the plants created specifically to thrive there for the amusement of the Children of the Storm had required considerable effort to take root, which had meant long hours sweating inside his EV suit. He intended to enjoy this mission more, assuming Patel left him any time to do so.

"What are these for?" Jepel asked as he opened the second crate with Patel's name on it.

"You mean you didn't read and commit to memory every word of the mission briefings Patel has already provided?" Vincent asked. "I'm pretty sure we're going to be tested on that material when she gets here."

Jepel shrugged. "Then I'm going to fail. I thought this was supposed to be fun."

"It might be, in spite of our fearless leader. We're going to spend a few hours this afternoon exploring the formations under that water," Vincent replied. "Patel doesn't pack light, does she?" Vincent added as he started removing diving rigs and rebreathing units and laying them out on the surface of the long table that would occupy their workspace once the associated tent had been set up.

"Are you planning to stay here once night falls or will you be returning to *Demeter*?" Jepel asked. The young man had clearly coated his face generously with UV protection before transporting down. Some of it remained caked in the ridges above his nose. Vincent also noted that he was wearing a complicated decorative ear piece, despite the fact that most personal accessories were forbidden while in uniform. It must have some special cultural significance to be permitted. Vincent hadn't met many Bajorans in his few years of service, and none served on *Demeter*. He figured he'd find time to ask about its significance once they were better acquainted.

"Not a chance," Vincent replied. "I'm not sure I'll sleep here, but it sounds like dome 10 will be recreation central for the next two weeks, and I plan to take full advantage of that large lake and beach when we're not on duty here."

"I heard Commander Paris was planning to bring down portable replicators to that site," Jepel said with a wide smile.

"I heard someone named Lieutenant Kar is planning on pulling together a gamma-rotation poker tournament in 10, buy-in is a dozen replicator rations or holodeck hours, depending on your rank," Vincent said. "You think they'll let anyone below lieutenant in on that?"

"Kar works security on *Vesta*, and I bet she'll let anyone in with time and rations to lose," Jepel said.

"I think anyone who buys into that game will end up spending the next month alone in their quarters with only water and ration packs for sustenance," a new voice said behind them. They both turned to see Lieutenant Lasren approaching from the beam-in site. Lieutenant Patel followed a few paces behind.

"You play, Lasren?" Vincent asked.

The young lieutenant shook his head good-naturedly. "Wouldn't be fair, would it?"

"Oh, right," Vincent remembered. Lasren was Betazoid

and his natural psionic abilities would likely come in very handy when trying to figure out who was bluffing.

"Good morning, gentlemen," Patel greeted them. "Thanks to Lieutenant Lasren, we've got new sensor scans to study. How about we do that in the comfort of our portable workstation?" she asked cheerfully, grabbing the silver fabric they'd already unpacked and beginning to lay it out on the ground nearby.

It wasn't really an order, but it rubbed Vincent wrong anyway. He would gladly assist his team, but he was struck by the fervent desire to do so on his own terms. Before moving to help Patel, Vincent reached down and removed his left boot and sock. As soon as he had placed his naked foot on what promised to be soft white sand, he cried out in pain. He immediately shifted his weight back to his right foot as he raised his left to examine it. He found, to his surprise, countless shards of white turning red with his blood.

"What's wrong, Vincent?" Jepel asked, hurrying to his side.

Vincent was now hopping on his right foot as the pain of a thousand small cuts began to burn his left.

"The ground," Vincent replied. "It's like broken glass."

Lasren joined Jepel on Vincent's other side and they carefully guided him closer to the crates, where they helped him sit.

"Where's the medkit?" Lasren asked.

"I think I'm sitting on it," Vincent replied. "Just give me a second." He gingerly tried to brush the white sand from his foot, which turned out to be a terrible idea. Rather than remove it, the motion seemed to embed the sharp particles deeper into his foot.

Patel was suddenly standing over him with a water bag. "Hang in there," she said as she began to pour the cool, clear liquid over the blood-soaked area.

It hurt for a few seconds, but soon enough provided the first relief he'd felt.

"Thanks, Lieutenant."

"You want to head back up to *Demeter* and let your doctor take a look?" she asked.

Vincent didn't. "Do our emergency medical supplies include a dermal regenerator?" he asked.

"Do I look like a first-year cadet to you, Ensign?" Patel asked with a trace of a smile. "Of course they do."

"Give me a few minutes to debride this and restore the skin, and I'll be good as new," Vincent assured her.

"Your call."

"Thanks, Lieutenant."

By the time Vincent's foot was repaired and back in his boot, Patel and the others had completed setting up their main tent and donned their diving gear.

"All better?" Patel asked.

"I think so. I'm really sorry, Lieutenant. It never occurred to me that the sand would be a hazard."

"Then you didn't notice the mineral analysis I included in your briefing materials?"

"I did, but . . ."

"This area is largely comprised of a mineral similar to crushed kyanite. It tends toward splintery or blade fractures and isn't compressed enough to show wear around the exposed edges."

"I'm sorry, Lieutenant. I guess I should have paid more attention."

Patel shrugged. "Too much information can be just as

dangerous as too little. I wanted everybody to know ahead of time what we were facing, but details like that probably got buried. Don't worry. The silica around the lake in Biodome 10 is way softer, more like some of the white beaches you find on Earth. Why don't you grab some more samples and run them while we make our way down to the water? You'll be our comm center when we go under. If you lose contact with anyone, alert me at once."

"Will do," Vincent said. "One question?"

"Sure."

"Did all your research suggest anything about the people who created this, or is it simply a natural formation?"

"Best guess: there's nothing natural about it. And all this suggests so far is that anybody who spent much time here either didn't touch the ground, or had much tougher skin than we do."

Vincent nodded. He found himself suddenly grateful that Patel, whatever her other faults, was so ridiculously conscientious. No matter how benign this place looked, like every unknown environment, it could probably kill you fifty different ways. He had forgotten that. She hadn't. She had come here prepared to keep her team alive, and he could respect that.

Being Borg had its moments. Ensign Icheb would never have admitted this aloud to anyone, even Seven, although he believed she would have backed him up given appropriate context.

For the few years Icheb had been Borg, life had held no mysteries. It sounded dull. But dull wasn't automatically a bad thing. Dull freed one from pointless internal unanswerable questions and allowed one to focus their entirety of effort upon whatever task was before them. Never wondering what anyone else around you thought about anything at all had been, in some respects, blissful. Individual Borg did not have thoughts. They had data and directives. There was a constant, low-level hum of information being exchanged unencumbered by emotion. Borg did not feel anything about the work they undertook. They simply performed their duties in calm efficiency until their bodies required regeneration. To regenerate was to cease to exist. Awareness of oneself and the Collective vanished as nanoprobes collected and distributed energy throughout a Borg's organic and technological components. One awakened from this state to absolute harmony of thought and purpose.

Granted, the price of this existence was unacceptably high. To never have the opportunity to think an original thought or to feel anything beyond the Collective's purpose was the purest form of slavery. And, ninety-nine times out of a hundred, the Collective's purpose had been horrific evil perpetrated upon the unsuspecting *or* unwilling.

What it had also been, however, was *easier*.

When Icheb had first found himself disconnected from the hive mind, his collective reduced to a small group of immature drones, he had responded by attempting to re-create the only form of existence he had ever known on a tiny scale. He had succeeded, more or less, until his ship had encountered *Voyager*. Her crew had led him and the other Borg children out of the darkness of their previous existence into the dawn of individuality.

Seven had been instrumental in his personal transformation and had warned him that one of the most difficult adjustments he would be required to make was to live most of his life in silence. The absence of constant input from others had almost driven her mad, at least at first. Icheb had not found this difficult. In fact, the liberation of his own mind and its incessant quest for understanding and meaning might have drowned out the Collective had the two ever been capable of existing simultaneously.

Few things embodied this dissonance as clearly for Icheb as standing in the presence of Lieutenant Phinnegan Bryce on the surface of DK-1116.

As he and Bryce made their way through a patch of dense overgrowth toward the construct at the heart of Biodome 23, dutifully scanning with their tricorders in search of any sign of the biodome's field generator, Icheb's mind was a maelstrom of questions he could not voice. He could not shake the suspicion that his ability to contribute meaningfully to the work at hand was severely diminished by his inability to focus.

Not that Bryce noticed. He was his typical, garrulous self, and as they approached the construct—the easiest landmark and most obvious rendezvous point for their team—he chattered away about any number of trivial matters.

"I swear half of my department has already checked out for the next two weeks. Senigg tried to turn in an end-of-shift report from three days ago, and when I called him on it he admitted he was distracted by trying to figure out what to pack for his downtime on the planet."

How can someone who seems like the most open of books stir so many questions? Icheb wondered.

The first question, of course, was, *Why am I here?* Bryce and Lieutenants Elkins and Benoit were their respective ship's chief engineers. The focus of their efforts for the next five days would be to attempt to locate and understand the technology that generated the biodomes sustaining what life existed on DK-1116. Each of them could probably have completed this work on their own. As a team they would definitely make short work of the problem.

While Icheb knew he had already begun to distinguish himself among his peers, and circumstance had placed him in Bryce's path quite often, there were still dozens of engineers in the fleet who deserved the chance to participate in this mission with the fleet's chiefs more than Icheb did. And yet, Commander Paris had advised him that Icheb had been personally requested by Bryce for this team.

Why?

Icheb was good. But no one was that good. *Were they?*

Their biodome's construct was similar to the others present, although quite a bit larger. One of the tallest of the alien artifacts that had first attracted Seven's attention to this planet burst forth from the overgrowth and rose almost fifty meters in the air. Near its midpoint, it curved in a delicate arch toward the east. Its base was all but buried in dense clusters of wide bluish-black leaves, but his tricorder calculated that it was several meters in diameter. The plaited pattern of the metal was significantly smaller and tighter at the base but seemed to expand as it climbed upward.

"If it were made of anything other than metal, I'd say it grew like this and maybe the energy of the field above it dictated its curvature," Bryce offered as they paused in a relative clearing less than a dozen meters from the base.

"That does not seem likely," Icheb observed as he studied his tricorder intently, wishing only to hide himself and his thoughts from Bryce, which was absurd. Until he had learned of Bryce's request to add Icheb to the team of chief engineers, Icheb had never felt anything but perfect ease in Bryce's company. Phinn's display of confidence in his abilities and a desire for Icheb's contributions to their team should have, if anything, increased his comfort. But it didn't. And that made no sense.

"I'm not detecting any traces of the field generators or the *Sevenofninonium* here, are you?" Bryce asked.

Icheb looked up, aghast. "The what?"

Bryce smiled, a child caught misbehaving. "Hadn't you heard? That's what everybody is calling it."

"You are referring to UI791116PJ4702700001?" Icheb asked.

"You already memorized the temporary designation for Seven's new element?" Bryce asked. "Never mind, of course you did."

"What else is there to call it until the Federation Division of Applied Chemistry gives it a proper name?" Icheb asked.

"Rumor is, Gwyn came up with the placeholder and it stuck. I'm sure she did so out of respect and affection," Bryce added.

"I have not noticed any particular respect for anyone from Ensign Gwyn," Icheb said, still puzzled. "If anything, she appears to treat most of her fellow officers with benign disdain, unless she intends to seduce them."

"Holy wow," Bryce said, clearly shocked. "You realize you said that out loud?"

"Is it inaccurate?"

"No," Bryce said, chuckling, "but if you said it to Gwyn's face she'd probably punch you."

"It wouldn't be the first time one of my female peers has done so," Icheb admitted. "You're suggesting the fault is mine."

"Not at all," Bryce replied. A sort of wistful smile settled on his face as he shook his head gently. "Please don't take offense."

"I have not. But Seven might. The term seems intended to belittle her discovery."

"There isn't a junior officer in this fleet other than you that Seven doesn't intimidate," Bryce noted. "It's a coping mechanism, not an insult, I promise you."

Bryce's words were completely intelligible. The tone suggested kindness, even affection. Any meaning beyond this eluded Icheb.

"I am not detecting any of the . . . ahem . . . element either," Icheb said.

"I have a theory," Bryce said, moving effortlessly to a new topic.

"About what?"

"This," Bryce said, opening his arms to take in the entire area.

"What is it?"

"I'm starting to think the whole planet might be a massive abstract art installation."

Icheb studied Bryce's face. Its lines and contours were at rest, but his bright blue eyes twinkled merrily.

"It would not be the first," Icheb noted. "At the Academy we studied the Inuioda Pardemom. Have you heard of them?"

"No."

"They devoted the majority of their planetary resources to artistic endeavors. Their society collapsed after five centuries when they were invaded by the Belnin."

"Alpha Quadrant?"

"Beta."

"Huh. That sounds like a shame."

"They created some astonishing pieces on scales few have ever matched, none of which have survived. Once they had evolved to prioritize their artistic pursuits, they refused to believe that other species might take advantage of them and ceased creating and sustaining defensive technology," Icheb said. "Their desire for harmony at all costs sowed the seeds of their ultimate downfall."

"Professor Treel?"

"Yes."

"Do you miss it? All those wonderful theoretical discussions?" Bryce asked sincerely.

Icheb almost replied immediately in the affirmative. The part of him that didn't understand what was happening in this moment, but believed it was somehow significant, would have gladly fled to the comfort and safety of academic pursuits. It had been toying only moments before with the relative joys of assimilation.

But the rest of Icheb knew he wouldn't have traded this moment or any other since he had joined the fleet for the façade of security the Academy provided. For all its terror, the present was invigorating. Icheb suspected he was supposed to enjoy the intense and confusing emotions now beginning to overwhelm him. He did not, but wondered if he might eventually.

"You could be correct about the sculpture's purpose," Icheb said.

Bryce smiled. "Wouldn't that be something?"

"It would, but personally, I suspect we will find there is much more to these constructs than evoking subjective responses."

"Any hypotheses yet?"

"No," Icheb replied honestly as Lieutenant Cress Benoit came into view on the opposite side of the construct. As he waved Bryce and Icheb over to his position, the ensign added silently, *Just mysteries.*

Between final adjustments to the crew's planetary rotation teams and schedules, collecting his gear, signing off on all final departmental reports, and officially transferring command to Lieutenant Kim, Captain Chakotay was the last of his group to reach the surface. Upon arriving he found Admiral Janeway, Captain Farkas, and Commander Glenn pacing over what appeared to be a vast metallic deck plate. O'Donnell was scanning some of the native plant life that bordered the plate's north side.

Unlike many of the other constructs, the one native to Biodome 04 was not plaited. It was a perfectly smooth sheet, roughly rectangular, that covered almost five square kilometers and was composed primarily of three stable osmium isotopes. Osmium was one of the least abundant elements of the Earth's crust. Chakotay wondered if he was staring at more of the element in one place than had ever existed on his homeworld. Back in the days when wealth could be accumulated and measured in monetary units, a find like this would have made its discoverers grotesquely rich.

The scene before him filled him with an almost giddy delight. The people responsible for leading the Full Circle Fleet through the Delta Quadrant thus far had faced peril at almost every turn. To see them now, heads bent over their tricorders, moving slowly and purposefully around this scientific anomaly, was to imagine them as they must have been when their careers with Starfleet began. They had become warriors, but once they had been scientists and explorers. It was incredibly satisfying to simply flex those muscles again.

The southern edge of the plate was bordered by a forest of tall blue stalks that spread across several miles, almost to the biodome's edge. Aerial scans confirmed that a number of small but deep pools of water were spaced almost perfectly equidistant from one another across the same area. Chakotay found the spot where the others had discarded their personal duffel bags beside four small crates stocked with survival gear. Barring an unexpected emergency, the admiral intended to spend the next five days and nights on the surface, and Chakotay hoped to do the same. He was also looking forward to a late-night swim, assuming the water was warm enough. He didn't think he'd have too much trouble convincing Kathryn to join him once he'd found an appropriately secluded spot for them.

Dropping his bags and opening his tricorder, he headed toward the others. Janeway looked up as he approached and offered him a smile so wide it nearly stopped him in his tracks.

Even admitting his personal bias, Kathryn had never looked lovelier. Her auburn hair had started to grow long again of late and rather than tame it in the blunt cut that had become her standard over the last year, she'd opted to let it go for a bit. It was coiled loosely at the base of her neck, with a few unruly wisps framing her face and curling in the slight humidity. She'd dispensed with her uniform jacket and wore a simple gray short-sleeved uniform tunic and black pants that hugged the contours of her petite frame. Her eyes were bright blue, reflecting the platinum glow of the surface on which she stood. Her cheeks were flushed with exertion or excitement; it was hard to tell which.

The smile suggested the latter. He hadn't caught her in a moment of such unreserved delight in a very long time, and he knew at once that his choice to bring all of them here had been a good one. Starfleet Command would commend them and likely footnote this part of their mission as significant primarily for Seven's discovery. Chakotay would prize the effect it had had on the fleet's crews far more.

"Chakotay, over here," she said as soon as their eyes met.

The edge of the plate was only a few meters away, and as he stepped up on it, the first thing that struck him was how warm it was. He could feel the heat radiating up through his boots. Had his tricorder not confirmed the plate's composition, and had he not known that osmium's half-life was measured in hundreds of thousands of years, he might have worried about radioactive decay. As it was, he simply marveled along with the others at the strange artifact.

"Have you figured out what it is yet?" he asked when he reached her side.

"Not at all," she said. "But it extends down more than six meters below the surface, like a solid brick."

"I'm surprised you can't cook on it," Chakotay said.

"The temperature beneath the surface is more than thirty degrees cooler," Janeway said, offering him her tricorder, where a rough map of the plate's molecular composition was taking shape. "It mitigates the effect of the ambient radiant energy. But, unless I'm mistaken, the flow of air over the surface is also designed to control temperature."

"We're in an enclosed biodome," Chakotay said. "There are no weather patterns to create air flow."

Janeway shrugged. "I'm not sure how it's done, but I believe the energy field does much more than enclose the space. It also regulates temperature and keeps the atmosphere within circulating."

Captain Farkas and Commander Glenn had paused over a section of the plate and rested on their hands and knees over it. Janeway and Chakotay ambled toward them, curious.

"Yoga?" Chakotay asked when they were within earshot.

"Later, by the lake," Glenn replied with a wink. "We thought we detected some irregularities in the surface, but it was just some sediment that had settled there."

"How do you manufacture something this large and this perfect here?" Farkas asked, sitting back on her knees and brushing the dirt from her hands. "According to my tricorder, the thing is flawless. Even our best industrial replicators have miniscule margins for impurities. Did someone create it somewhere else and just drop it here?"

"I don't see how," O'Donnell said, joining the group. "A ship of the size required to carry this thing couldn't have landed on the surface."

"Maybe they transported it down," Farkas suggested.

"If they did, it was in pieces. And I haven't found a single seam in it yet, have you?" O'Donnell asked.

"No," Farkas replied.

"What have we got on the planet's mineralogy?" Janeway asked. "Is there sufficient osmium in the crust or buried beneath it to have harvested for creating a piece this size?"

"No," O'Donnell replied. "That analysis is still incomplete, but the densest concentrations of metals beneath the surface appear to be significantly heavier."

"They could have been converted," Janeway suggested.

"Using what magical technology?" O'Donnell asked. "There's nothing here except for the results of whatever process formed these things. Work like this requires civilization and science and math, and all of those things tend to leave a mark where they are cultivated."

"Could this have been a piece of something bigger?" Glenn asked. "Or maybe it was intended to be cut into smaller layers and used for building something."

"Like what?" Farkas asked.

"The hull of a ship?" Glenn posited.

"It's too soft for that. But more important, doesn't it feel to you like this thing is in its final form?" O'Donnell asked. "This entire ecosystem has to be balanced for preservation. The plant life around us isn't random or decorative. It exists to process the atmosphere contained within the dome and to maintain a specific chemical composition. I'm not sure how it accomplishes this yet. Our tricorders aren't being terribly helpful this morning. But visual analysis coupled with a lifetime as a botanical geneticist tells me that the growth rate of the organic life here is incredibly slow. I won't be able to confirm this until I can get some samples back to my ship, but I guarantee you when I do, we're going to find intentional arrested development. After four thousand years, one or more of these specimens should have vanquished the others and overrun this biodome. That's what nature does when left to its own devices. It competes and it evolves or it dies. There is nothing about this that is natural."

"What does that suggest about the people who created it?" Chakotay asked.

O'Donnell shook his head. "It's not that we're not capable of the types of genetic manipulation that could create a perfect closed system like this."

"But this isn't how we think," Janeway said. "As a culture

we put intentional limits on the kinds of genetic manipulation we permit. Our mandate is to allow all living things, sentient or otherwise, to develop without interference as much as possible. Yes, we cure disease and improve agricultural yields and harvest the minerals we need to live and build what we require, but always with a sense of sustainability and forward motion. We live for progress."

"And this, whatever it is," O'Donnell added, "is the opposite of progress."

"If whoever made this was trying to tell any explorers who came after them to appreciate stasis, might our presence here disturb that?" Chakotay asked. "Are we altering these perfectly balanced systems just by being here?"

"Not in small numbers," O'Donnell said. "But if we started cutting down trees and digging up minerals, or tried to build permanent settlements here, we certainly could."

"Could all of this be some sort of natural museum?" Glenn suggested.

Chakotay shrugged. "It might be now. But I'm not sure that's how it started. Who the hell did this?"

"I don't know, but I, for one, hope we'll be here long enough to find out," Janeway said.

7

As Lieutenant Harry Kim entered astrometrics, he paused to observe a stunning image on the massive viewscreen that dominated the space. A small star moved through a solar system consisting of seven planets, clearly caught in the gravitational pull of the large star at the system's center. As it progressed, all of the planetary orbits were disrupted. The gravimetric stresses were so intense that each planet lost its orbit and was torn apart in spectacular fashion.

Eventually, the new star settled into an uneven orbit around its larger partner, dancing among the wreckage of an entire system.

"Simulation failed," the computer reported, as if that much weren't painfully obvious.

"What exactly are we trying to simulate?" Kim asked, startling Seven, who turned abruptly to face him.

"The birth of this binary system," she replied.

"Do you get extra points for each planet you destroy in the process?"

Seven smiled wanly. "This isn't a game, *Captain.*"

Kim understood that she was mocking him, but he had to admit, he liked the way that sounded. Nothing else in his life made sense, but Paris had been right about one thing. From the moment he had assumed command of *Voyager* much of the tension he'd been carrying for the last several weeks had diminished. And somehow, just sharing the issues with which he was struggling with Tom had helped.

Kim was lonely without Nancy in his life, but he no longer felt alone. He had work to do, but he also felt like he had room to breathe. And probably most important, his daughter had been born. He hadn't been able to admit to himself, or to Nancy, how much he had wanted her to live. He didn't feel he had the right to force that choice on Nancy, especially with everything else she was facing. Only now that it was done did he understand how much of his anxiety over the last several weeks had centered around that single, unexpressed wish. Absent that crushing pressure, Kim found he once again had the bandwidth to focus on his duties to the ship and the fleet. He also no longer felt the almost constant need to punch something. For better and worse, his priority had been forced to shift from himself to the hundred-plus crew who were now his responsibility. It focused his mind in a way nothing else had since Nancy's diagnosis.

"Then what is it, *Miss Seven?*" Kim shot back, choosing the mode of address only Doctor Sharak ever used sincerely in Seven's presence.

Seven turned her back to him and reset the main viewscreen. Devastation was replaced by the only slightly less chaotic image of the system in which the fleet was now ensconced.

"My initial analysis of the system has yielded several interesting facts," Seven began, "the most significant of which concerns the orbital pattern of the binaries."

Kim stepped up to stand beside Seven at the data panel. "Okay."

"The secondary star's orbit is most irregular. The barycenter is located just within the mass of the primary star, creating a distinct wobble."

"Uh-huh."

Seven looked to Kim, clearly disappointed.

"That's hardly an unprecedented discovery, Seven."

"Not in and of itself," Seven agreed. "But the presence and composition of the small asteroid belt surrounding the B star indicates a cataclysmic event sometime in the last fifty thousand years or so."

"Based upon what assumptions were you able to calculate that number?"

"Based upon an extrapolation of Starfleet's stellar cartographic database."

"We don't have detailed star charts for this area of space going back two decades, let alone fifty thousand years."

"I might have modified them using my recollection of some of the Borg's charts of this area."

"That you pulled from memory?"

"And some of the data nodes that we discovered on the *Raven*."

"You still have those?"

"I integrated them into my personal database several years ago. When I joined the fleet, I made sure those files were added to *Voyager*'s."

Kim had to hand it to her. The woman was nothing if not thorough. "And you think that cataclysm was the arrival of the smaller star?"

"I do."

Kim shook his head in disbelief. "How and from where?"

"That is what I am attempting to extrapolate."

"Seriously?"

Seven looked offended that Kim would even question her sincerity. "Yes."

"We've observed our fair share of rogue comets, planetoids, even planets in our explorations, Seven, but what are the odds a star goes rogue inside our galaxy?"

"One in six thousand trillion, one hundred ninety-two billion—"

Kim cut her off. "So not large?"

"The vast majority of rogue stars exist between galaxies and galactic clusters. But that does not make it impossible," Seven insisted.

"Just improbable. More to the point, why does it matter? At best this is an interesting theory. You're not going to be able to prove beyond any doubt that the secondary star originated outside this system."

"Would you care to wager on that?" Seven asked.

Kim's jaw dropped. "You have officially spent too much time with Tom Paris," he said.

"Is that a *no*?"

Kim crossed his arms. "Okay, I'll bite. How are you going to prove this theory?"

"I'm going to allow this simulation to run continuously until a trajectory can be found that would result in the destruction of enough planets to result in the concentration of asteroids found in the B star's belt and current orbits of the remaining planets. While it does so, I'm going to take a shuttle into that belt and collect some samples. If we are ever going to determine how DK-1116 came to be where and what it is, we are going to have to understand how this system was created."

"Not alone, you aren't."

"Every other member of this crew is either at their post, on the surface, or preparing to go to the surface."

"Take Gwyn."

Seven sighed. "I'd really rather not."

"She's our best pilot short of Tom Paris. She'll get you there and back in no time."

"I expect the mission to collect all we need might take several days. I would hate for Gwyn to miss her rotation on shore leave."

"You can have her for two days. She got pulled from the first away team for medical reasons."

"She's ill?"

"No. Doctor Sharak needed her for something, so we had to rearrange the schedule at the last minute. She's fine. In fact, this will be a nice distraction for her while she's waiting her turn."

"Are there any other pilots available?"

Kim searched his memory. "Gleez."

"If you insist, I'll take Gwyn," Seven said, resigned. "She is intemperate, but competent."

"Gleez is competent."

"As long as we're in orbit."

Kim would have been insulted on poor Gleez's behalf if Seven hadn't had a point. "Perhaps some time alone with you would do him good. He might benefit from a little training while you're out there in the asteroid belt collecting your samples."

"You do realize that you can't order me to take anyone with me."

"That's true. But I can deny your request to use a shuttle."

"You wouldn't."

"But I can. Come on, Seven, it's a safety issue and you know it." Kim's eyes narrowed, daring her to defy him.

"Very well," Seven said, knowing when she was beaten.

"Very well, what?"

Her face lost all traces of amusement. "Very well, *Captain*."

VESTA

Ensign Aytar Gwyn stared at Doctor Sal's face wondering why when the doctor spoke, all she heard was her mother's voice asking the same question.

"The first what?" Gwyn asked.

"What was the first day of your last cycle?" her mother repeated, all the while wearing Sal's face.

A sick pit knotted itself in Gwyn's stomach. It had been a little more than a week. Since then she'd shared her bed twice with Ensign Gary Blond. He was one of the fleet's recent additions—*a stellar cartographer, maybe . . . no, an airponics engineer*—she couldn't honestly remember. Gwyn never chose her partners for their professional skills or conversational abilities. In most cases, all she required was a reasonably satisfying way to pass the time. Both times she had taken appropriate protective measures. Neither encounter had been particularly earth-shattering. For a horrifying moment the rest of her life as Mrs. Ensign Gary Blond played out in slow motion.

She remembered well the first time she'd lived this particular nightmare. Her final year of second-tier studies had just been completed. Three of her best friends had already applied to Starfleet Academy and been accepted. Despite being their intellectual peer, Gwyn had never shown the slightest interest or inclination to pursue that path. She honestly had no idea what she might do with the rest of her life, but on Krios, as on any other Federation world, the only limits placed on possibility were in her imagination.

The only thing she knew for sure was that whatever she ended up doing, it would be in close proximity to Jerrik Laor. She didn't remember a time when they hadn't known each other. She'd been too young to create long-term memories when they'd first started playing together. As they grew, always attending the same local tiers, they'd been more or less close as their emotional and physical development dictated. She had plenty of memories of the awkward years in mid-tier when they'd known they were friends but weren't allowed to show it for fear of merciless teasing from their friends. *Jerrik and Aytar, hand in hand, down by the creek bed kissing in the sand.* She could still hear the singsong torments only children of a certain age found amusing. Finally, when second-tier began, it was suddenly socially acceptable to start pairing off, if not mandatory in order to maintain social status.

And so they had. For three years, off and on, they'd been the closest and most envied couple among their friends. They'd done everything first, including the normal explorations that inevitably led to sex. Everyone knew, especially Aytar and Jerrik, that they were going to spend the rest of their lives together.

That certainty remained until the moment, not long after their commencement ceremonies, while they were both still gripped by the heady intoxication of total freedom absent any real responsibilities, when Aytar realized that she'd missed a cycle. She'd never really bothered to keep track, but it didn't matter. The math hadn't alerted her to the potential problem. Something else had. It was hard to describe, especially to anyone who wasn't Kriosian. It was a sudden awareness, one morning over breakfast, that she wasn't alone in her body. Another presence had joined her in the night. It wasn't exactly frightening. It felt normal, in the most abnormal way possible.

It had also apparently been written all over her face, because the split second her eyes locked with her mother's, Vara Gwyn's face had set in hard lines. Her mother had pulled Aytar into her bedchamber and demanded to know what had been the first day of her last cycle.

There were worlds in the Federation where an event like this wouldn't have meant the end of Aytar's life as she'd always known it. Girls and women her age and older, when confronted with an unplanned pregnancy, might have chosen whether or not to bear the child without fear of social repercussions or familial pressures.

Technically, this was also true on Krios. It was considered a fundamental protection of all Federation citizens. It just didn't matter on Krios. No one blessed with a child on Gwyn's homeworld was permitted to do anything other than bear it and raise it. It was partly an issue of faith in the everlasting plan of the universe and partly a social obligation. Birth rates among Kriosians had plummeted in the last few centuries and healthy children were the only thing standing between these proud people and their demise as a species.

Her mother had asked and Gwyn had known full well that the answer meant that there were no longer any choices about how she would spend the rest of her life. She and Jerrik would be sealed in the local *Degnar* tower, and from that day forward, her life would be forever intertwined with his. Even without the benefit of the rare metamorphic empathy a fraction of Kriosians possessed, society would demand that they become each other's perfect mates and devote themselves entirely to the new life they had created.

And young Aytar Gwyn had known beyond doubt that in that life, she would die of boredom. In an instant, the only person she had ever considered spending the rest of her life with became a densely woven *herrada* cord binding her irrevocably to a life she could not imagine living.

She hadn't needed to share these thoughts with her mother. As with every thought Aytar Gwyn ever had, her mother had read them clearly in her eyes. She'd returned to the kitchen and prepared tea for her. Aytar hadn't been thirsty, but her mother had insisted she drink. For two weeks, the same tea greeted her each morning at breakfast. At dawn, fourteen miserable days later, Aytar had begun to bleed.

Neither she nor her mother had ever spoken of the relief Aytar felt. They had never spoken of the crime against nature Vara had committed in the interest of her only daughter's future happiness or how her mother had known the recipe for ending an unwanted pregnancy. The only comment her mother had made that morning as Aytar lay in her bed, her lower abdomen tensing with the most painful cramps she had ever felt, was, "Never again, my child."

Aytar had understood. This had been a gift of sorts. Her life had been restored to her. But the next time she missed a cycle, she would be expected to fulfill her obligations to her family and her people.

After that, Aytar had become possessed by a single notion. She had to leave Krios. She had to create a life for herself beyond the narrow borders limiting most of those who grew to adulthood on her homeworld. She had to find her own freedom.

The following year she tested for Starfleet Academy and was accepted. When Gwyn left, she'd never looked back.

The experience hadn't soured her on enjoying physical intimacy with anyone except Jerrik. If anything, it had increased her appetites. Freedom from her people's traditions wasn't simply a matter of geography. It was internal as well. She had learned to be careful and as long as she was careful, she could taste of every conceivable physical delight without fear.

The terror of this moment was in realizing with Sal's question that the life she had cherished for the last six years might have just come to an abrupt and irrevocable end. She had no sense that she was not alone in her body, but it might simply be too soon for that.

"Um," Gwyn muttered. "A little over a week, maybe."

"Can you be more specific?"

Gwyn did the mental math. "Twelve days."

Sal released a sigh that sounded like relief. "That explains it."

Gwyn was afraid to ask what *that* was or what it explained. All she could think of were the vials of blood Sal had taken two days prior and the tests she must have performed on them.

"I'm going to need a few more samples of your blood, Ensign," Sal finally said, "if that's all right with you."

"Why?" Gwyn whispered.

"The cells I extracted showed evidence of the genetic sequences I need to cure the patient I told you about. But in the absence of certain hormones, the genes I require remain dormant."

"So, I'm not . . ." Gwyn began.

"Not what?"

"Pregnant," Gwyn asked.

Sal chuckled. The gruff cackle was the most beautiful sound Gwyn had ever heard.

"Of course not. I didn't know that was a concern."

Gwyn shook her head. "It isn't. I just couldn't imagine why you would need to know . . ."

"Apologies," Sal said warmly. "This isn't the first time I've worked with Kriosian tissue. I actually visited your homeworld thirty years ago, well before you were born. I made certain assumptions based on my prior experience, primarily that I could activate the necessary genes by using synthetic hormones to mimic the precise blood chemistry required. It turns out I can't. You're the only one who can do that, but the good news is, your body does it naturally every thirty-six days as you move through a normal cycle. So we have a couple of choices. Assuming you're still willing to help me, we can wait another twelve days until the necessary hormonal changes occur naturally within your body, or I can give you an injection that will induce the changes now, and you can give me another few vials of blood day after tomorrow."

Gwyn considered the alternatives. "Does it matter for your patient?"

Sal nodded somberly. "Actually, it does. Every day that goes by is another day of damage done to her body. I hate to wait, but if you're not comfortable with the idea of the injection, that's okay. It's not unlike some of the synthetic compounds we use for annual injections to repress your cycle. There won't be any side effects beyond shortening the length of this one. It will end a few weeks early. But that happens normally in a woman's body every so often."

"Her?" Gwyn asked.

Sal paused. Her face shut down like a room where the lights have just been turned off.

"It's Lieutenant Conlon, isn't it?" Gwyn asked.

"Does it matter?"

Gwyn turned away. Everyone on *Voyager* knew that Conlon had taken a medical leave. Everyone knew that at roughly the same time, Lieutenant Kim had gone from being one of the more approachable and generous senior officers to busting the balls of anyone who stepped even a hair out of line. Even with her mild and intermittent natural empathic abilities, Gwyn could feel the tense, sick knot he carried in his stomach wherever he went these days. It wasn't hard to connect those dots.

Gwyn didn't need to know the specifics. Sal had been right about one thing. *Voyager*, this fleet, had become a new sort of family to Gwyn. They had replaced the one she'd left behind on Krios. She didn't need it to be a permanent situation; in fact, she knew it wouldn't be. Very few Starfleet careers ended on the same ship where they'd begun. But that didn't change what it was now, or Gwyn's appreciation for the tenuous bonds that bound them all. She thought of Patel and her naked envy of the particular closeness of their ship's senior officers. Gwyn had never felt the same need to share in that unique comradery, but she also took comfort in its existence. Anything that threatened them, threatened the whole ship. It was little enough Gwyn could do to try and make the lives of her fellow officers a little easier.

"It doesn't," Gwyn finally said. "But it's nice to know whom I'm helping."

"I can't confirm," Sal began.

"You don't need to," Gwyn insisted. "I'm scheduled to pilot a shuttle for Seven over the next few days, so go ahead. Let's do this now."

Relief washed over Sal's face. Behind it, something else stirred. Gwyn could not say for certain. She didn't have her mother's deep empathic abilities. Still, Gwyn was suddenly conscious that while everything Sal had just told her was true, there was a great deal the doctor wasn't saying.

DK-1116

Biodome 10 was almost ready to start receiving the first groups of crew members on shore-leave rotations. The *lake*, as Commander Tom Paris had taken to calling the vast still pool of water at its center, was crystal clear and by some unknown mechanism maintained a temperature just below that of a normal human body. It was as close as Paris had come to a natural hot spring since his family had toured Yellowstone when he was twelve. A narrow white beach composed primarily of silica edged the water all around. The floor was a gentle slope that bottomed out around two kilometers. Beyond the beach to the southeast was a wide plain covered with silky grass. To the north the "forest" began. The tall, metallic braided poles branched out like massive oaks near the tops, giving way to wide, flat tendrils, some of which were small enough to look more like platinum leaves. They were warm to the touch, but not too hot. Beneath them, a wider variety of flora bloomed, most in dark blues and grays. Patches of tall white fronds were interspersed. These were the only "hostile" life-form, in that any bits that brushed against a black uniform tended to cling mercilessly to the fabric, becoming quite sticky. Paris had already decided that the pants he'd worn for the first several hours of preparation were unsalvageable and would have to be recycled.

But apart from this incredibly minor inconvenience, the site was perfect. Dozens of replicated beach chairs were set up beneath wide umbrellas. Crates of blankets and towels were ready for sunbathing. Those who intended to stay the night, like Paris, had been told to provide their own camping gear. His family tent was already set up on a small plateau about twenty meters from the water. Out of deference to the carefully controlled ecosystem, no camp fires would be permitted, but Paris had brought down a portable heater with exposed coils that would be perfect for roasting hot dogs and marshmallows, or whatever version of those two delicacies the replicator could manage.

Two large semipermanent structures had been erected to house the provisions that had been sent down. Crates filled with a diverse menu of replicated snacks and ration bars were present with large cisterns of water. Inside the smaller base, Tom had installed a portable replicator, ostensibly for emergency medical needs, but the fifteen extra battery packs B'Elanna had scrounged up from *Vesta*'s stocks ensured that the replicator could and likely would be used to create more exotic food and beverages once the re-creating really began.

Lieutenant Ranson Velth—*Galen*'s chief of security—and Lieutenant Commander Atlee Fife of *Demeter* had assisted Paris for the last several hours in making these preparations. Velth had already traded his uniform for a pair of shorts and a T-shirt and was wading along the water's edge while Fife sat on a nearby beach chair fiddling with a tricorder.

"Gentlemen," Paris said, approaching them, "I believe we're ready to face the hordes."

"I don't know, Paris," Velth said. "I think at least one more security sweep might be in order."

"Of what?" Paris asked.

"Did any of our advance teams check out the water?" Velth asked. He looked serious, but his light tone couldn't quite sell the concern.

"They scanned it, but you're probably right. Someone needs to give it a try."

"Fife," Velth called.

"Yes, Lieutenant?" the gangly young man asked, looking up.

"Can you give me a hand here?"

"Of course," Fife said, setting his tricorder aside and joining Paris at the water's edge.

The next thing Paris knew, Velth had grabbed him under the shoulders and was lifting him from the ground. Without missing a beat, Fife secured his legs.

"You know what they say, Mister Paris?" Velth said good-naturedly.

Paris struggled, knowing full well it was futile. Suddenly, he was eleven again, at a family reunion at Lake Shasta. He'd been a scrawny kid then, no match for his older cousins who had decided to make the admiral's only son the butt of all their jokes and pranks.

"That assaulting a superior officer is a great way to get your shore leave revoked?" Paris asked.

"He's right, Fife," Velth said. "Let him go."

Paris could see Fife's face. "Of course, sir. Apologies. On three?"

They counted together, swinging Paris between them. At their mark, Paris found himself flying through the air.

Paris had never allowed his inner child to wander too far from home. It got a lot of play these days when he was caring for Miral and Michael. It was rare, however, for men closer to his age to give rein to the younger selves, the boys they had been before the Academy and Starfleet service wore down the rough edges. As he hit the water, Paris decided he was going to enjoy making Fife and Velth pay for this.

The water wasn't too deep but as soon as he entered it, Paris felt for the bottom. Letting the last of the air out of his lungs and grasping for the sand, he floated beneath the surface, waiting for the right moment.

It took fifteen seconds for Fife and Velth to begin to worry enough to start wading toward him. Paris darted forward and grabbed Fife around the ankles, dragging him under before breaking the surface to catch his breath. Fife bobbed up quickly and got his feet under him. Velth stood nearby, his hands on his knees, laughing at both of them. A simple look exchanged between Paris and Fife cemented their alliance. Both of them rose from the water, their uniforms soaked and clinging in uncomfortable places, and after a brief game of chase, they had wrestled Velth to the ground and tossed him into the water.

Paris clambered back toward the shore, and as the water receded to about waist-deep, he bent over, breathing heavy. "When the hell did I get this out of shape?" he asked.

Fife and Velth were treading water several meters deeper but both stared with blank faces over Paris's shoulder.

"What's this," a familiar voice asked, "the best two out of three?"

Paris turned to see B'Elanna standing near the water's edge holding Miral by one hand. Michael was strapped to her body in a sling.

"Daddy, you forgot your swimsuit," Miral chastised him.

"I was going to leave these two with you and cover engineering for a few more hours, but now I'm not so sure," Torres said.

It was a struggle for Paris to pull himself and his drenched uniform the last few meters out of the water, but he managed. "No, no," he said. "You go. I've got this."

"Are you sure?"

"Don't I look sure?"

Torres shook her head. "You look like you lost a bet."

Paris started to wrap his dripping arms around her. Then he realized that Michael would get soaked first and opted to simply lean in and kiss his wife tenderly.

"Still love me anyway?"

Torres patted his cheek. "Just keep them alive until I get back. I'll bring dinner."

"Did you pack me a suit?"

"It should be in the tent."

"Give me five minutes to change?"

Torres nodded as Miral began to inch toward the water.

Paris started toward their temporary encampment but turned back as he heard his daughter cry out in delight.

"Mommy, look!"

She stood only ankle deep in the lake, but a few meters beyond her, multicolored lights flashed over the water, forming a small rainbow. A smile bright enough to light the sky lit his daughter's face.

Young Tom Paris had made it his mission in life to taste every delight available from the Federation's most exotic worlds: the fragrant fields of Artan, the soft packed snow on the mountains of Mons Tianus, the pools of tranquility on Sirangai, and an entire menu of delights on Risa. That day, Commander Tom Paris decided that the waters of an unnamed planet in the Delta Quadrant seen through his daughter's eyes put them all to shame.

Kathryn Janeway hadn't felt her mind hum with the heady anticipation of discovery in a long time. *This is the problem with promotions,* she decided. *They never tell you this is what you're sacrificing for the good of Starfleet, because if they did, no one would ever accept the offer.*

After spending a couple of hours walking over the surface of the massive metal plate, the command officers had broken into two groups to explore the areas directly north and south of the construct. Janeway and Chakotay took the southern forest, planning to take samples of the soil and plant life, while O'Donnell, Farkas, and Glenn set off to scout the northern plain.

The temperature dropped slightly inside the blue forest. Janeway had half expected that the opposite would be true. According to her scans, however, despite the presence of several pools scattered ahead and the generally warm temperature, there simply wasn't enough humidity in the atmosphere to create a tropical climate. Instead, the shade of the wide leaves that capped the trees simply blocked some of the ambient heat, creating a comfortably cool interior.

Chakotay had paused to examine an outgrowth of long, thin red fronds that burst forth from the base of a nearby tree.

For her part, Janeway kept turning over O'Donnell's analysis in her mind. *This isn't how nature works. One or more of these species should have conquered the rest and thrown this entire ecosystem out of balance. But they hadn't. Four thousand years later, these life-forms seemed designed to simply maintain the status quo.* But life, at least as she understood it, just didn't do that.

Except when it did.

Watching Chakotay remove small samples of the soil and foliage around the base of the tree, Janeway thought back to the instinctive reluctance she felt a few days earlier when she thought Chakotay might have intended to propose to her. *Where did that come from?* It was fair to say that since their relationship had transformed from platonic to physically intimate, they'd suffered several setbacks. Trust did not seem to come as easily to either of them as their long shared history might suggest it should. That lack was at the heart of all of their recent disagreements. At first she had believed it had to do with their respective positions with the fleet. During the time that she had been presumed deceased, Chakotay had taken ownership of his command. He rightly chafed against any order or decision she made that put them in what he perceived as unnecessary jeopardy. When she'd had his job, she'd been as merciless with the admiralty as he was now. But since she *was* an admiral, and he knew her devotion to be no less than his, she had assumed this was one set of battles they could avoid.

They hadn't. He had fought her at so many steps along the way during her first months leading the fleet. He had made assumptions that wounded her deeply, partially accurate as they might have been. More important, he had either lied directly to her or withheld information that was critical to their mission when he wasn't absolutely certain how she would respond.

And yet, each and every time, they had found their way back to each other's arms. Neither of them had seemed able or willing to upset the status quo. They were moving into the future together, but it was hard to see that motion as forward progress.

Was that what she feared? Were she and Chakotay only able to maintain what they'd built together in an uneasy stasis? Was this the only future she could envision for them?

"I don't think these are living organisms," Chakotay said, startling her from her reverie. "I think they are incredibly well-preserved fossils."

She moved to the base of the tree he was scanning with his tricorder. "Don't they scan as life-forms?"

He shook his head. "Inconclusive. There are traces of what might be remnants of ancient DNA. O'Donnell seemed to think these species were designed to grow incredibly slowly, but I wonder if these are actually dead."

"But he also said that they are critical to maintaining the ecosystem, the conversion of radiant energy and oxygen to carbon dioxide. They couldn't do that if they were dead, could they?"

"Maybe only a small percentage regulate the atmosphere," Chakotay posited.

Janeway moved to the next closest specimen, a thick blue trunk with distinct rings around it spaced roughly ten centimeters apart. She took baseline readings with her tricorder and found the same confusing results Chakotay had described, essentially *lifeless life-form.* Setting her phaser on its lowest setting, she cut a small square segment from the trunk six centimeters deep and placed it in a small vial for later analysis. "We'll see what the microspectrometers back on *Voyager* make of it," she began, but paused when a low crinkling sound met her ears.

"Chakotay, do you have a SIMs beacon handy?" she asked.

He brought her the small light and focused it on the area from which she had extracted the sample. She set the vial aside and again focused her tricorder on the damaged section. Under the bright illumination of the beacon, they watched together as small blue filaments emerged from the heart of the incision, weaving and coiling around one another until, a few minutes later, it was almost impossible to tell that there had been any damage to the organism at all.

Janeway's heart was racing. Without thought, she took

Chakotay's hand. He squeezed hers in return, a small gesture of comfort and commiseration.

"Not dead," she said softly.

"But not living, either," he added.

She lifted her eyes to his, searching for a classification in which to place the minor miracle. "Zombie?" she ventured.

A smile of genuine amusement lit his face. "That would be a new one for us."

"We need to try that again," she said.

They moved through the forest together, taking several more samples of six different strains of plant "life." Each one was obviously a distinct species. None of them scanned as "living" until they were damaged and the repair process began. Once it was complete, they reverted to the strange "indeterminate" readings they generated when inert. Oddly, none of the samples they extracted exhibited the same regenerative properties.

Once their work was done, they set a steady pace back toward the metal plate, brimming with hypotheses and eagerly anticipating the reports of the rest of their team.

When they reached the edge of the "zombie forest," as it would now forever be known, Chakotay retrieved two full canteens and they slaked their thirst gratefully. In the distance, Farkas and Glenn could be seen approaching.

"What do we have," Janeway said once they were met, "and where is Commander O'Donnell?"

"About two clicks north there's a string of low hills," Glenn reported. "He wanted to check several unique plants growing there. Or not growing."

"I can't speak for the rest of you, but I'm not sleeping on the surface of this planet tonight, or ever," Farkas said.

"Why not?" Chakotay asked.

"It's not right," Farkas replied. "I don't know what this place is, but it's just not right."

"Several of the plants we examined have an unusual capacity for regeneration," Glenn said. "It's the most amazing thing."

"I know," Janeway said, grinning.

"You saw it too?" Farkas demanded.

"I'm dying to know what O'Donnell makes of it," Chakotay added.

"Well, you should feel free to ask him," Farkas said. "Myself, I just think it's spooky."

"But it explains so much," Janeway said, her thrill at their discovery not diminished in the slightest by Farkas's fears. "This may very well be an entirely new kind of life-form."

"One we don't have the slightest idea how to communicate with or tame," Farkas said. "To my mind, that makes them dangerous."

"They're just plants, Regina," Glenn insisted. "They can't hurt you."

"How do you know that? How many plants have you seen elsewhere that can repair themselves quicker than you can cut them down?"

"None," Glenn said. "But even on Earth there are many regenerative life-forms: worms, lizards, starfish. This isn't an unprecedented biological phenomenon."

"All those things are definitely *alive*," Farkas countered. "Our tricorders don't even know what to call the grass we're standing on right now. It all reads as inert."

"We're going to get to the bottom of this, Captain," Janeway said gently.

"Excellent. I look forward to reading your report when you do. In the meantime, I'm going to head back to *Vesta* and make sure we've got clear transport locks on all of our away teams. I know we can't cancel shore leave because this place gives me the willies, but I want to make damn sure our people can be pulled out the minute this goes pear shaped."

"A wise precaution," Janeway agreed. "But if O'Donnell is making camp for us, at least come back and join us for dinner in a few hours."

"Is that an order, Admiral?"

"No. A request. Part of the point of this exercise is for us to share our unique perspectives and insights. That will be hard to do from *Vesta*."

Farkas sighed. "Very well. Dinner. But no promises on dessert."

A few moments later, Farkas disappeared in the glowing cascade of the transporter effect.

"It's unusual, isn't it," Glenn said, "to see someone whose career has been as long and storied as hers so affected by a strange natural phenomenon."

"Don't judge her too harshly," Janeway suggested. "We're trained to respect our gut instincts. That's all she's doing."

"You think she's right? Do you believe anything here poses a serious danger to us?" Chakotay asked.

"No," Janeway replied. "Actually, whatever this is, I don't think it is the slightest bit interested in us."

"For now," Chakotay said.

8

The slow and steady march from the edge of the stepwell down to the water had been challenging. Standard-issue wet suits were designed to breathe out of the water and conserve maximum body heat once submerged. Even the newest versions of these marvels were better at the second than the first.

In the past, when suits were worn for extended durations on shore, it was a simple matter to cool down by removing the boots. Even before Ensign Vincent had provided a practical demonstration, Devi Patel understood that wasn't an option. In fact, she had insisted that both Lasren and Jepel also wear their gloves as they made their way down the narrow ledges, just in case they needed to use their hands for balancing as they descended. By the time they came within safe jumping distance, the faces of all three were plastered with sweat and their breathing had become labored.

"Take a minute before you put your masks on to calm your breath," Patel ordered. She understood that her fellow officers were meant to be working as a team. As long as they did so in the manner she required, she would welcome their input. But someone had to take charge in situations like this, and her rank and experience gave her that privilege.

Jepel and Lasren merely nodded, wiped the sheen of sweat from their brows, and collected themselves briefly before donning their portable rebreathing units.

"Vincent, are you reading us?" Patel asked through the mask's comm unit.

"Loud and clear, Lieutenant. I'm showing unsaturated filters on all three units and full tanks. You should be able to descend to a depth of fifty meters for a maximum of half an hour."

"You'll signal us when we hit twenty minutes, right?" Jepel asked.

"Sure thing, Omar," Vincent replied.

"As soon as we're in, check your depth gauges and start your dive clocks," Patel said. "The water is unusually pure, but it will be really dark down there. Activate your lamps now."

Both Lasren and Jepel turned on the bright beacons attached above their masks. They would wait to activate their SIMs beacons until required.

These preparations complete, Patel nodded to Lasren, stepped to the edge of the nearest ledge, and pushed off, easily clearing the remaining steps between her and the water below. She expected to feel the sudden brisk relief of cold water but was surprised to find that the temperature was exceedingly warm.

Two splashes to either side of her alerted her to the arrival of Lasren and Jepel. They took a minute to orient themselves in relation to one another, extended the short fins embedded in the soles of their dive boots, and as a group began their descent.

Fifteen meters down, the steps became wider. This was no surprise. These features had been prominent from the first sensor scans Patel had reviewed. As she made her way along the wall, she searched diligently for any sign of an opening.

"Why is this water so warm?" Jepel asked.

"It doesn't appear to be that deep," Lasren said. Aiming his right hand ahead of him, he pointed out a wide ledge roughly twenty meters below. *"Maybe it retains the heat generated on the surface by the energy fields."*

"That's not the bottom," Patel advised.

"No, but it's unusually large," Lasren said. *"I'm going to check it out."*

"We should remain together and circle the well at this depth for any entrance to the caverns beneath," Patel said.

"We've only got half an hour, Devi," Lasren said. Even through the processing of the comm unit, she could hear the calm certainty of his voice. *"Let's not waste time arguing."*

"It's not possible to be too careful diving in unfamiliar waters," Patel retorted.

"Fine. Jepel, stay with Devi," Lasren said.

Before Patel could argue, Lasren began to swim toward the large ledge. Biting back the urge to dissent, Patel continued to move slowly through the water above him, Jepel following a few meters deeper. They had barely completed their first circuit around the well when Lasren's voice crackled through the comm.

"Holy Rings of Betazed. Devi, get down here."

It only took a few seconds for Patel to see where Lasren waited. His head and wrist beacons guided her and Jepel down to his position. As soon as she reached him, Lasren gestured to the wall just below the large ledge that had been his target. With the light of his beacons playing off it, the otherwise pitch-black surface appeared to glow. A metallic substance braided throughout the silica gleamed back at them like a massive vein of silver or platinum.

Patel swam toward the wall and, securing herself on the

ledge, shined her beacons across the well. Even though the far wall was at least fifty meters away, the faint glimmer told her that at this depth, all of the walls were composed largely of this metallic substance.

"Good work, Lasren," Patel commended him.

"Lieutenant?" Jepel said.

"What?" both Patel and Lasren answered in unison.

Jepel was playing his light over an area ten meters down that looked like a wide oval shadow running along the next step below. It was only easy to see because of the obvious contrast with the otherwise metallic surface. Patel started to swim toward it, but Lasren grabbed her by her left ankle.

"Check your dive gauge, Devi. We're already at fifty meters and seventeen minutes elapsed. We need to allow for a few decompression stops during our ascent."

"If it leads to an internal cavern, we can run more detailed sensor scans while we're back up top. I don't want to waste any time."

"You also don't want to spend the next few days in a recompression chamber," Lasren insisted.

"You guys head back. I'll just be a minute," Patel insisted.

Lasren looked to Jepel, who had already ascended a few meters. *"No way. If we do this, we do it together."*

". . . lieuten . . . an . . . hea . . . Vincent . . . ease . . . ond . . ." came Vincent's voice, crackling through her mask. Clearly the metallic deposits were interfering with their signal.

"Jepel, go ahead and get back to the surface. Report our status to Vincent and make sure he's prepared to request an emergency transport. Lasren, with me."

Patel's dive gauge put her depth at sixty meters when she reached the shadow on the wall. Only it wasn't a shadow. It was an opening, easily wide enough to swim into. At most she had three minutes to explore before she had to begin her ascent or risk decompression sickness. The smart move would have been to follow Lasren's advice and return to this position in an hour.

Patel was tired of playing it safe.

"I'm going in," she said.

"Right behind you, boss," Lasren said.

The cavern was long and wide. Even with her beacons at maximum illumination, she couldn't see an end. The walls practically glowed, so dense were the metallic deposits within. It became harder and harder to shake the illusion that she was swimming through the remains of a massive vessel rather than a natural cave system.

A low warning alarm sounded over Devi's comm channel.

"That's it, Devi, time to go," Lasren said.

Patel checked her gauge. The good news was that despite the fact that she had seemed to be swimming more or less along a flat plane, she had actually begun to slowly ascend. She and Lasren were already at fifty meters. The bad news was that she had less than nine minutes of air remaining and she would need most of them for a safe ascent.

There was a good chance this cavern would end in nothing but a solid wall. Given that, she should definitely head back. But either her gut or her pride insisted that this was the entrance to the cavern system Lasren's latest scans had shown.

"Just a few more meters," Patel said.

She didn't look back to see if Lasren was following her. Somehow, she knew he was. If she ended up being wrong about this, she could easily be killing both of them.

This was the moment. This was the place where officers who never got very far in Starfleet played by the rules and followed orders. People like Seven and Admiral Janeway and Captain Chakotay talked a good game about personal responsibility and security, but Patel knew in her bones that the line between reckless and legendary was damned thin.

She forged ahead. Checking her gauge again, she clocked her continuing ascent. *Thirty-five meters.*

And four minutes of air left. Just enough for a rapid ascent, emergency transport, and a day in a recompression chamber.

Lasren had come up beside her. In a universal signal he pointed upward with his thumb. Patel looked up and saw nothing but blackness above. Despite this, Lasren allowed his feet to float down and began a steady ascent.

Patel followed and, with less than two minutes of breathable air left in her unit, broke the surface of the water.

Lasren pulled a tricorder from his belt and removed it from its watertight case. After a quick scan, he removed his dive mask and rebreathing unit.

Patel did the same.

Playing her wrist beacon around her, she realized that they had entered a massive cavern filled with breathable air.

Twenty meters beyond their position was a shoreline. Side by side, they made haste to claim it.

Once they were seated on the ground, Lasren said, "That's the dumbest thing I've ever done."

"Me too," Patel agreed. "Isn't it great?"

Lieutenant Cress Benoit was tall and exceedingly thin. He towered above Bryce and Icheb. His skin was deep ebony and despite, or perhaps because of, a faintly visible receding hairline, he kept his scalp clean shaven. He was quick to smile and his large brown eyes had a particular intensity that was faintly unnerving to Lieutenant Bryce. When he spoke to you, he often appeared to be searching your face for every possible microgesture's deeper meaning. However long that moment lasted, you had no doubt that you held his full attention.

As *Galen*'s chief engineer, Benoit's duties, apart from maintaining the ship's power and propulsion systems, consisted largely of managing the first generation of specialized engineering holograms. Bryce was fascinated by this new technological marvel and peppered Benoit with question after question while the three of them hiked toward the edge of their biodome, where Elkins awaited them to compare the results of their initial scans. Apparently *Demeter*'s chief was already hard at work directly testing the energy field that sustained the biodome.

"Do they ever complain?" Bryce asked Benoit.

Deep dimples framed Benoit's lips in prelude to his response. "Not so far. They accept any order I give them with the polite deference and enthusiasm you would expect from any junior officer."

"Enthusiasm?"

"Barclay indicated that some of the older Mark Ones had temperament issues that could be misconstrued as disrespectful. He said it was an issue with the template they had tried very hard to correct in each successive generation. I think they were trying to err toward the positive, but the result is a little uncanny. They seem pleasant enough, but it's forced. No one is that happy to retune a magnetic constrictor."

Bryce glanced toward Icheb, whose brow had furrowed despite keeping his eyes locked on his tricorder. "Something you want to add, Icheb?"

"No, sir," he replied stiffly.

Bryce couldn't put his finger on any particular cause, but there was something strained in Icheb's manner since they'd arrived on the planet; that was unusual in Phinn's admittedly limited experience with the ensign. He wondered if Icheb had taken offense at the *Sevenofninonium* thing. Bryce knew well that Seven and the holographic Doctor were two of Icheb's closest confidants. Perhaps he had unintentionally put his friend on the defensive. "*Voyager's* Doctor was a Mark One, wasn't he? You know him better than either of us," Bryce said, hoping to draw Icheb out.

"I think some people confuse competence with unearned superiority. It is true, in my experience, that the Doctor does not suffer fools. But his concern and compassion for his patients is sincere. I believe that when he was first activated, his program was limited by the expectations of his designers. No one imagined that he would be required to take the place of his human counterpart full-time. What I find most impressive about him is that over time, he expanded his knowledge and experiences with the intention of becoming a better doctor. He continues to do so even now. I wonder, Lieutenant Benoit, if you have observed any similar capacity in the holograms you supervise. Have any of them, in your opinion, exceeded their initial programming?"

Benoit seemed to consider the question seriously. "I can't honestly say that they have. I believe it is the hope of Lieutenant Barclay that at some point they will. But I'm not sure even he understands what spark of inspiration led to the evolution you have described in our CMO. We're talking about sentience, yes?"

"Yes," Icheb said.

"Do you honestly believe that *should* be the intention here?" Bryce asked. "Holograms are incredibly powerful tools. But if all of them could be made like your Doctor, to evolve into sentient beings, that's the end of their utility. With sentience comes individual rights. We would require their consent in order to keep them in service."

"What leads you to believe that most of them wouldn't wish to continue their service? The Doctor certainly has," Icheb countered.

"The Doctor is unique. He possesses technology that grants him autonomy. The holograms Chief Benoit uses can only exist within the confines of the *Galen*. Until we master the specs on that mobile emitter, the life of any other sentient hologram would be little more than benign imprisonment."

"There's another issue as well," Benoit added. "While they are extremely competent workers—you've never seen an engine room as meticulously maintained as mine and I'm not taking all the credit for that— they aren't the best companions. I have three full-time organic engineers, and we have to rotate shifts so usually only one of us is on duty at a time. It affects morale. We make sure to grab as many hours off duty together as we can, and to mingle with the rest of the organic crew members. Without that, it would be a pretty lonely job."

"Perhaps if you made more of an effort to get to know them," Icheb suggested.

"Time will tell, Ensign, but I fear that the Doctor may end up being the exception that proves the rule. Holograms are useful but can never replace flesh-and-blood crew."

"And even if they could," Bryce added, "would we want them to? We build these ships so that we can throw ourselves out among the stars. We seek to expand our knowledge, to experience things others never will. If holograms could do that work for us too, who's to say we wouldn't begin to decline as a species?"

Icheb paused in his steps to stare at both of them. Crimson began to creep over his fair face. "I believe in the essential wisdom of the notion of infinite diversity in infinite combinations. The evolution of other species does not have to limit ours. Existence is not a zero-sum equation. For others to gain the self-awareness of the Doctor might also lead us to an expanded understanding of the nature of consciousness. Surely that is a goal as worthy of pursuit as our understanding of the composition of the rest of the universe."

Bryce could see that he had unintentionally wounded Icheb. Thinking before he spoke had never been one of his strengths. He didn't believe his argument was wrong, but he hated to think that Icheb believed he harbored any sort of racist or speciesist tendencies. Before he could think of a way to correct the misconception, Benoit said, "You might be right, Ensign. I'd like to think you are. But don't judge those of us whose understanding is limited by our experiences too harshly. You were Borg once, weren't you?"

"I was."

"You have been granted a perspective few others can ever know. You have lived as an individual and as part of a technologically enhanced collective. I can easily see that your definition of consciousness would be different from mine. That those boundaries I take for granted mean nothing to you. Part of the reason we are here, working together, is to facilitate exchanges like this. But you mustn't take offense at my limitations. Rather, you might help me expand them."

This seemed to mollify Icheb considerably.

"Took the three of you long enough," a gruff voice interrupted.

Lieutenant Elkins, *Demeter*'s chief engineer, trudged toward them over the rocky terrain that edged the biodome. Beyond him, a faint shimmer, like heat rising from the ground, was the only visible sign of the barrier that stood between the officers and the rough and wild surface of the unprotected portions of the planet. A storm raged outside this dome, kicking up swirls of red and gray dust over jagged rocks that burst forth from the soil like the gnarled hands of a giant.

Bryce's many inadequacies slipped to the section of his mind marked "for further study" as the fragility of his existence within the biodome rushed to the forefront.

"Dear gods," Benoit said, a note of awe suffusing his voice, which Bryce echoed silently.

"Chief Elkins will do, Cress," the portly man in his late fifties said cheerfully. His head was covered with thick waves of wiry black and gray hair, and his skin was a rich tan that suggested overexposure to the sun. His hazel eyes were alight with energy. He seemed invigorated by the subject of their inquiry rather than unnerved by it. He shook each of their hands in turn with a meaty fist, then said, "Let me guess. None of you picked up any readings of this field's generator?"

"No, sir," Benoit was the first to reply. Icheb and Bryce quickly added their negatives.

"Do you want to know why?" Elkins asked brightly.

"Absolutely," Bryce said.

"Come here," Elkins said, motioning them over to the edge of the energy field. He then lifted his tricorder so that all three could see the display. The closer the device came to the field, the more intense the energy readings. "Now watch this," he said.

Without warning, Elkins stepped to the edge of the field and then, beyond it.

"Wait," Icheb called out in instinctive fear.

Reason told Bryce that Elkins should already be dead. The unprotected surface of DK-1116 was a toxic wasteland with temperatures well above two hundred degrees Celsius when facing the suns. And that was before you added the exotic radiation pummeling the planet at all times given its relative proximity to the binaries. Never mind the absence of atmosphere.

And yet, miraculously, Elkins stood there, almost two meters beyond the border of the field, in perfect health. The ground beneath his feet was the same rough red as the rest of the unprotected surface, but apparently none of the toxic atmosphere had found its way inside as the field had expanded. Either that or it had somehow been immediately filtered by the field.

"The field expanded to accommodate your presence," Benoit said. "It is aware of you and your movements and is designed to keep you alive."

Elkins smiled broadly. "Yep."

"Could you step back inside please," Icheb asked, his voice tight.

"Join me, Icheb," Elkins suggested instead. "Don't be afraid, son."

It was a challenge and if only to save face, Icheb would swallow his fear and accept. Moving like a man condemned, he did as Elkins had suggested and paused only briefly before stepping beyond the apparent boundary of the field. A faint smile played over his face as it dawned on him that he, too, had survived.

"Now look at this," Elkins said, raising his tricorder for Icheb to see.

"The field strength has intensified along a forty-five-degree axis," Icheb said.

"Do you see?" Elkins asked.

"In order to accommodate this geometry, the field generator must be located several miles below the surface."

"If we think of this not as a dome but as a sphere of energy, its source has to be roughly ten kilometers down beneath the absolute center of the area," Elkins agreed. "Based on the placement of the other domes . . ."

"A single generator creates and sustains all of them," Icheb finished for him.

Elkins clapped the top of Icheb's shoulder. "Brilliant, isn't it?"

"So I guess we're not going to dig it up," Benoit said, clearly disappointed.

Elkins sighed, stepping back inside the normal boundary, Icheb following on his heels. "I'll admit I'd give anything to take it apart. But to do so would be to endanger the entire ecosystem, and I'm not comfortable with that."

"Now that we know where to look, with properly placed sensors in each biodome, we might at least be able to get a schematic of the design and more precise readings of its power distribution," Bryce suggested.

"It will take at least a few days to replicate and place those sensors," Benoit noted.

"You gentlemen have somewhere else you'd rather be?" Elkins asked.

Bryce did, but held his peace. Instead, he shook his head along with Icheb and Benoit. "No, sir."

GALEN

"When Tama was not much older than you are now, he met Drak. They spent their days running wild beneath the *hariar* blossoms and sucking the juice from the *siamate* until their fingers were stained *rahar*. They knew themselves to be brothers. Drak's mother feared that one day she would lose her son to Tama's people because she was not one of them. She decided to return to her home across the ocean. But Tama could not bear to be separated from his brother forever. He wrapped himself in Drak's *ashanyar* and presented himself to Drak's mother, saying, *'I am ready to return to our home as you bid me.'* They journeyed several *setz* across the ocean, and when they finally reached Drak's home, Tama was brought before Drak's family, who stared at him, unable to believe their eyes. *'This cannot be Drak,'* they said. *'How is it possible that you do not know your own son?'* Tama said, *'Your eyes deceive you. Do not trust them. This woman knows the truth.'* Only then did she understand that the differences between her people and Tama's were so insignificant as to be meaningless. The fear that had driven her to separate Tama and Drak was the lie. She fell to her knees before Tama and asked, *'Is there a place for me among your people?'* Tama took her hands in his and said, *'You are my mother as surely as Drak is my brother. There is no place in the world where that is not true.'* She smiled at Tama and begged his forgiveness. Together she and Tama returned across the ocean and were reunited with Drak. She lived among them in peace for the rest of her days and when her eyes closed for the last time, she was still smiling.

"You are truly blessed to be born into a universe where this truth, *Tama and Drak, at Mianna,* is already known by so many, little one," Doctor Sharak said, placing his hands against the gestational incubator where Lieutenant Conlon's child floated.

"What the hell?"

Sharak turned to see Lieutenant Kim hovering in the doorway. He immediately understood the lieutenant's disorientation.

That morning, Sharak had discovered a unique property of the Doctor's medical bay. Several of the treatment rooms, including this one, were also miniholodecks. They were installed to allow patients to access a number of peaceful, scenic environments during recovery.

He had chosen to replace this room's dim lighting with an illusion he found particularly delightful. To anyone entering, it would appear that Sharak and the baby floated among a sea of endless stars.

"I hope you don't mind," Sharak said. "Do come in. I thought she might find a slight adjustment to her environment stimulating."

"She can't hear you, can she, Doc?"

"Not yet," Sharak replied. "But her neural pathways develop daily. I assure you, this will not inhibit that process in any way."

"I didn't think it would," Kim said. "It's actually very cool."

At least once every day, Kim visited both Lieutenant Conlon and the baby. His current responsibilities prohibited lengthy stays, but that only intensified Sharak's respect for Kim. Many in his position might not make the effort at all.

"The vibrations of the world around her are the critical thing at this point. Their presence alerts her developing synapses to the whole of which she is a part. Were she still developing in her mother's womb, the sensations would be constant. As that is no longer possible, I am spending as much time as I can compensating for the deficit and encourage you and Lieutenant Conlon, as soon as she is able, to do the same. It would indeed be tragic, should the child survive the next several months, for her to take her first breath unaware that she already belongs to a thriving community."

Kim moved to stand on the other side of the incubator and placed both hands on its smooth, transparent surface. "Hi, sweetheart," he said. "It's your daddy."

"The processing power will still be insufficient, won't it?" the Doctor's voice sounded from the main medical bay. The Doctor and Lieutenant Barclay had been working for the last several days toward a goal Sharak was not at all sure he understood. They had clearly just returned from the main holodeck, where most of the research was currently centered.

"It depends entirely upon how independent you expect this program to be."

"Ideally, the lieutenant would have access to the entire ship. Confined to sickbay, she would probably run mad in short order."

There was a longish pause while Lieutenant Barclay apparently considered the problem.

"In order to maintain integrity, which will be crucial,

we will have to run this program through its own discrete holographic generator. Linking it to the rest of the ship will produce a noticeable drag on other systems."

"Other holographic systems?"

"All systems," Barclay said. "During normal operations no one would be likely to notice other than ops, but in battle, or if other systems were critically damaged, it might be an issue."

"I won't place her neural patterns in a program that is vulnerable to the whims of Ensign Drur."

Sharak watched Kim's face as he, too, listened to this exchange. At first he seemed confused, trying to grasp the significance of the Doctor's and Barclay's words. In a startling dawning of awareness, Kim hurried into the main bay.

Sharak patted the incubator, gently saying, "I will return shortly," and hurried after Kim.

Lieutenant Kim had placed himself between the Doctor and Barclay. "Whose neural patterns are we placing inside a hologram?" he demanded.

The Doctor seemed peeved at first, but quickly shifted his countenance to one of patient concern. For his part, Barclay simply appeared devastated at the sight of Harry Kim. One of the things about humans that had most heartened Sharak during the few years he had worked among them was the speed and ease with which they assumed one another's burdens.

"We haven't done anything yet," the Doctor assured him.

"But you're talking about Nancy, right?"

The Doctor nodded.

"Please forgive me for dropping eaves, but I do not understand," Sharak admitted.

All three turned their attention to him but it was Barclay

who said, "Technically, it's not eavesdropping if we can all see you standing right here."

"Most appreciated, Lieutenant," Sharak said.

"You want to do the same thing to Nancy that you did to Denara Pel, right?" Kim asked.

"If it becomes necessary," the Doctor said. "We're not there yet. But I want us to be prepared in the event we run out of other options."

"Gentlemen," Sharak said insistently.

The Doctor turned his attention to Sharak. "As you know, Doctor Sharak, Lieutenant Conlon's condition is progressing more rapidly than any of us thought possible."

"What about the stem-cell therapy Doctor Sal was going to try?" Kim asked.

"Although she successfully harvested some cells, there weren't enough for her to create the appropriate therapeutic vectors," the Doctor replied. "I'm sorry, but that possibility no longer exists."

"So this is Plan B?"

"Think of it more like Plan Z," Barclay said. Turning to Sharak, he continued. "We know it is possible to temporarily transfer the neural patterns of an individual into a holomatrix. The Doctor already successfully did so several years ago with a patient named Denara Pel who was suffering from the Phage."

"The Phage?" Sharak asked.

"As degenerative illnesses go, the Phage made Lieutenant Conlon's condition look benign," the Doctor said. "The point is, until we can come up with a way to reverse the damage to her DNA, we need to do all we can to keep her body alive and to slow the progress of the condition. One way to do that is to place her in stasis. By transferring her neural patterns into a holographic matrix, she could continue to exist among us while we work on a more permanent solution."

Sharak looked to Kim, who appeared to take the suggestion quite well.

"How long do you think she could survive in a holomatrix?" Kim asked.

The Doctor shrugged. "That's the issue. A program like that requires an immense amount of free processing space, and *Galen* doesn't have it."

"I'm working on a discreet interface with its own dedicated power source," Barclay said. "The issue now is whether or not to tie it directly into a segregated section of the main computer or keep the entire mechanism separate."

"You trade power for security," Kim said, nodding.

"We'll probably end up opting for the segregated processor," Barclay admitted. "We just have to keep it operational during unexpected power distribution disruptions."

"Do you really think it's going to come to that?" Kim asked.

The Doctor shook his head. "Doctor Sal is working on an alternative theory as we speak. She hasn't yet shared her progress, but we all believe she is the most likely among us to find the mechanism to reverse the damage repair syndrome. Our focus is keeping the lieutenant alive until she succeeds."

"But is that *life*?" Sharak asked.

Again, all three directed their attention toward him. This time, from the looks of confusion between them, Sharak wondered if he had unconsciously briefly lapsed into his native tongue.

"It is not life as you experience it, Doctor Sharak," the

Doctor admitted. "For anyone who has been organic, it would seem like a pale shadow of the existence they once knew."

"But you cannot know," Sharak said. "You have never been anything other than what you are."

"In point of fact, I did once share my consciousness with Seven's. It was a fleeting gift, but during that time I was able to grasp more than you might imagine of what it is to be organic: to taste food, to feel the touch of another." An elemental sadness seemed to momentarily overtake the Doctor, but he quickly shook it off. "While holographic existence cannot compare to the sensations available to an organic being, it is not intolerable and in this case, might be the best way to protect her neural patterns from degrading along with her body."

"You will, of course, give Lieutenant Conlon the option to refuse?" Sharak asked.

"Yes," the Doctor said, "but I doubt she would."

"I doubt she would accept," Sharak said.

The Doctor appeared taken aback, perhaps even insulted. "Why do you say that?" Kim asked.

Sharak sighed deeply. "What you are suggesting might be an effective temporary solution. You might see it as a brief vacation from one's natural state, a short respite. I submit to you, however, that such a radical shift in one's ability to perceive and interact with their environment could be terribly destabilizing."

"It wasn't for Doctor Pel," the Doctor said. "In fact, in the end, she resisted returning to her body, so preferable did she find living as a hologram."

Sharak shook his head. "I cannot speak for this woman," Sharak said. "And perhaps given the alternative, Lieutenant

Conlon might feel the same. But surely part of our role as healers is to prepare those we cannot save for acceptance of their imminent death. To postpone the inevitable, and to do so in such a radical way, seems . . . I am not sure if this is the right word . . . but disrespectful?"

Kim stepped toward Sharak, his face drawn in tight lines. "I can't speak for Nancy either, but should it come to this, I will do everything I can to convince her to attempt this alternative. Death is inevitable for all of us, but as healers, it is your responsibility to put it off as long as possible using every means at your disposal."

Sharak considered Kim. He understood that the young man was unwilling to accept the reality that his beloved and the mother of his child might not survive. He felt immense pity for the lieutenant. But that did not change his belief that this solution, marvelous as it might seem in the abstract, could do more damage to Lieutenant Conlon than the alternative. She had already been forced to contend with one violation of her consciousness by an alien life-form. That act of aggression was responsible for her current medical condition. While he did not doubt the intentions of the Doctor, Barclay, or Kim, he did fear that they were acting more in their own interests than Conlon's. He resolved to keep these fears to himself, but to bring them to the attention of Counselor Cambridge at the earliest opportunity.

"It will, of course, be Lieutenant Conlon's decision," Sharak said. "Now if you will excuse me, I will return to your daughter. Before you go, you should spend some time speaking with Lieutenant Conlon. The same positive effects I described for your child will also apply to her, even in a comatose state."

Kim nodded. "I will. Thank you, Doctor."

Sharak had only lived among the variety of alien species present in the Federation for a few years. He respected them tremendously, particularly their tenacity. But one belief the Children of Tama embraced that he feared these men never could, was the certainty that death was not an end. It was merely a transitional state. To deny it was to deny the preciousness of life itself, and to live in fear of it was to endure constant, unnecessary anxiety. Like them, he hoped Lieutenant Conlon would survive. Unlike them, he knew that either way, she would endure. How she did so mattered. Inflicting intense mental suffering in the name of a few more days or weeks seemed cruel.

Sharak hoped dearly that this option, however well intentioned, would never become reality.

9

W hat about that one?" Ensign Gwyn asked.

"No," Seven replied.

No-o, Gwyn repeated in her head, consciously modulating it to re-create the satisfyingly petulant sass of her five-year-old self when she'd asked to spend a few more minutes splashing in the creek before dinnertime and been refused by her mother.

It had taken them only two hours to reach the asteroid belt surrounding the B star. The rest of Gwyn's life was apparently going to be devoted to finding the most perfect chunk of rock among them for Seven to sample.

"It's almost the right size."

"Size is not the issue."

"Then what is?"

"Adjust your course bearing four-eight mark two-one," Seven requested.

Like everything else in the Federation, courtesy is free. This had been a favorite phrase of Gwyn's *leedi,* Mayla Fui, a dear friend of her mother who had attended every large and small family gathering from Gwyn's birth to her going-away celebration before her departure for the Academy. They still corresponded often. *More often than Vara and I, come to think of it.* As well as Vara knew her daughter, Mayla's insight into her favorite "daughter of the heart" was uncanny. Often she didn't even need to see Aytar to know something was up. She'd just happen to knock on the door the day before a big test or the day after a fight with a close friend. There would be long walks and hot *soria* cakes and somehow everything would look different, better than it had before she'd come.

When she'd been a girl, Gwyn had often feared her mother. She missed Vara, but on her worst days, ached for Mayla's company.

Inside, Gwyn was cursing Seven's obliviousness. Mayla would have remonstrated Gwyn for allowing her impatience to fester. It cost Seven nothing to be courteous when suggesting a heading, especially as she was a mission specialist with no rank and technically couldn't *order* Gwyn to do anything. But Gwyn was not obligated to take offense. That was a choice. To allow the whims of others to determine one's own internal state was to cede power. If Gwyn was going to give hers up so cheaply, she deserved the pain and frustration that accompanied the sensation of weakness.

"Course altered."

Seven did not respond.

You're welcome.

Though the asteroid belt was relatively dense, they were navigating an area free of the smaller rocks that made traversing such fields so hazardous. Seven had her sights set on a fragment large enough to land the shuttle on and with enough gravity to allow both of them to take an EV walk without running the risk of flying off the surface.

They'd already passed six such sites for reasons Gwyn could only guess at. Apparently Seven didn't feel the need to confide in anyone else. Of course, for most of her life, she'd had no choice about that. Being Borg meant your thoughts were never your own. *Maybe she's overcorrected her course,* Gwyn thought. It might be too generous. Seven could just feel so superior to everyone else that no one else's ideas were worthy of consideration. But placing Seven's actions in a context that suggested a less insulting reading made Gwyn feel marginally better.

Gwyn smiled gently at the realization that Mayla would have been pleased.

Focusing her attention on the asteroid they were now approaching, Gwyn could see that the surface conditions were visibly different from the others Seven had rejected. Most of the asteroids were boring variations of red, brown, and gray. This one sported several wide veins of metal circling it. A glance at Seven's sensor panel showed massive deposits of several common and a few unusual minerals.

"You're looking for more of the element we discovered back on the planet, aren't you?" Gwyn ventured.

"Not precisely."

"Which part did I get wrong?"

"I am looking for a fragment that most closely matches the planet's geological makeup," Seven replied. "I do not expect to find substantial levels of the *Sevenofninonium* anywhere in this field."

Gwyn swallowed the anxiety that immediately welled within her at Seven's casual use of a term she had intended as a joke.

"I'm sorry about that, Seven. I hope you didn't take offense."

For the first time since their mission had begun, Seven turned to face Gwyn, her features a complacent mask revealing nothing. *What I wouldn't give to be able to do that,* Gwyn thought.

"I did not," Seven said with unexpected sincerity. "But I would question its accuracy as a designation."

"Well, yeah. It's kind of a silly word," Gwyn agreed. "But

it's not unprecedented. We've also got Einsteinium, Curium, Californium."

"Each of those designations was assigned to acknowledge significant scientific contributions of the individuals they were named for," Seven said. "While I detected the unusual properties of the new element, I could not have done so without the tools Starfleet has put at my disposal or the efforts of the crews of our fleet's various vessels. Perhaps *Starfleetium* or *Fullcirclium* would be more appropriate."

Her face was still a mask but a new, faint light flickered from Seven's eyes at this. She might have been teasing Gwyn.

For the first time since they'd met, Gwyn felt as if she was conversing with Seven rather than simply doing her bidding. It was a heady sensation. She'd never appreciated Patel's longing to be included among the closer senior staff. Tasting that acceptance, as Patel surely had in the past, it made significantly more sense.

"I think I see a safe spot to land, if this one looks promising," Gwyn said, bringing the shuttle closer to the thickly veined asteroid. Much of the surface was composed of jagged peaks and narrow, deep valleys, inhospitable but not entirely unmanageable for a pilot with Gwyn's skills. The shuttle's short-range sensors directed her attention to a high plain roughly three kilometers wide, which would do nicely as a base of operations for their rock collecting.

"I will transmit our coordinates and intention to land back to *Voyager*," Seven said. "Take us in, Ensign."

"Adjusting course and matching speed to bring us within the asteroid's gravitational field," Gwyn said. Within half an hour she had brought them safely to the surface. After two hours of essential EV safety preparations, their explorations began.

DK-1116

The first priority once Patel and Lasren had caught their breath and assured themselves that they could survive indefinitely in the cavern was to make contact with Vincent. Devi didn't doubt for a moment that Jepel had returned to the surface as she'd ordered, and that he and Vincent were likely having kittens at the moment. Had she been in their shoes she would have contacted *Voyager* and requested a targeted sensor scan to confirm her and Lasren's life signs beneath the surface. It was likely that the heavy metals surrounding them might disrupt sensors, but a skilled enough operator—and Lasren's replacement, Vanessa Waters, was certainly one—would be able to find their signals.

Both she and Lasren had carried spare air tanks. They couldn't have traded them out while underwater, but they would use them when they returned to the surface. If Vincent didn't hear from them and *Voyager* was able to get a clear transporter lock, they'd be transported out before their explorations could begin.

Refusing to give in to dismal speculation, Patel opened her comm link. "Patel to Vincent, do you read me? Vincent, are you there?"

A sharp burst of static pierced her eardrum.

"Ow," Patel said, pulling her mask away from her ear. Lasren had removed his as well and was tinkering with it with a tiny metal tool. "What are you doing?" she asked.

"Switching to our main emergency band," Lasren replied. "Our ship's communications array is a little larger than Vincent's remote unit." Seconds later, he lifted the unit to his ear and said, "Lasren to *Voyager*, do you copy?"

"Hey, Kenth." The warm voice of Waters reverberated

through the cavern. *"Vincent just made contact reporting that you and Patel were probably dead. I told him we'd run a few more scans before notifying your next of kin. What happened?"*

"We found our way into an underground cavern. It's got atmosphere, and we've got spare tanks and plenty of power left in our lights. We're going to do some looking around. Is there any chance you can get a transporter lock on us?"

"Affirmative. We've got you."

"Don't pull us out without our authorization. And tell Vincent not to worry. Have him switch his comm signal to this band and await further instructions. We'll be in touch."

"Understood. Good hunting."

"Lasren out."

"That was quick thinking," Patel commended him.

Lasren shrugged. "Emergency comm protocol 101."

"I knew there was a reason I wanted to be on your team," Patel said.

"Don't worry, I won't let it go to my head," Lasren teased. Playing his light over the cavern walls, he continued, "What do you think this place is?"

Patel had been formulating hypotheses from the moment they'd surfaced. Checking her tricorder, she was thrilled to see new geological data populating her screen. "I have a theory," she admitted, stepping past him and focusing her hand beacon on a large metallic deposit twenty meters beyond their position. The ledge between her and the area wasn't wide, but she stepped carefully to avoid slipping back into the water. "Your scans confirmed lots of large caverns in this direction. Many of them read as being filled with water, but obviously some of them aren't. Beyond them, a little deeper, are a number of sensor holes. They could indicate anything."

"So you're telling me that when you risked our lives getting here, you did it on a solid hunch that this cavern was here?"

Patel turned to face Lasren. She knew lying to a Betazoid was pointless, but even if that hadn't been true, he deserved the truth. "I knew it was possible."

"Fifty-fifty?"

"More like eighty-twenty."

Lasren shook his head. "I understand wanting to make your mark and get ahead. But the next time you pull a stunt like that, you're doing it alone."

Patel nodded. "Understood."

They continued along the edge of the water for twenty more meters until the shore widened at a vast wall composed largely of the same metallic ore that had marked the entrance to the cavern.

"These deposits share certain characteristics with the osmium constructs in other biodomes," Lasren noted. "But they are significantly denser and more varied."

Patel stepped forward and ran her gloved hand along the nearest metal band. "I wonder if this was the source of the materials used to construct them."

"Without analyzing all of them, I couldn't say. But I don't think so. There's none of Seven's element here."

"But our scans detected large amounts of it in this area."

"Those deposits aren't anywhere near here," Lasren said, shrugging.

Patel continued studying the wall, stepping gingerly along the shore. Suddenly her breath caught in her throat.

"Devi?"

She had turned her body to face the wall and was wiping both hands over it. "This is smooth. There's a door here," she said.

Lasren joined her, brushing away several layers of dirt until large sections of a perfectly smooth circular door were revealed.

"Should we knock?" Lasren asked.

"Because there's someone back there four thousand years later who can answer?" Patel asked.

"I was kidding."

"There's no handle or hinges or visible activation panel," she said.

"Perhaps it only opens from the other side."

Patel stepped back, playing her light around the edges of the door. "Do you see anything that looks like a manual override?"

Lasren studied the rest of the wall but found nothing. Stepping forward he said, "I'm going to try something." Placing both hands on the door, he closed his eyes and slowed his breath. He seemed to be listening really hard, but the only sound was the faint lapping of the water at the shoreline. After a few minutes like this, he opened his eyes.

"There's something here."

Patel's eyes widened. "Could you possibly be more specific?"

Lasren shook his head. "I'm not getting a person, individual consciousness per se. But there is something that feels like life; something pretty big."

Patel swallowed hard. Her heart rate accelerated and she felt her extremities begin to tremble. To steady them, she reached again for her tricorder. "I'm not reading any life signs."

"It's not life like we're life, Devi. It's powerful, but not terribly organized, if that makes sense."

Lasren removed one of his diving gloves and ran his hand over the surface of the door. Near the center of it, he paused, resting his hand there.

"What is it?"

"I think it's getting warmer here."

Suddenly, the door was illuminated by a bright blue light. It looked like an energy field had snapped into existence, but it carried no current. Patel quickly removed both her gloves and placed her hands next to his. "It could be bio-sensitive," she suggested.

They waited there for almost a minute until the light vanished.

Patel emitted a frustrated huff. "What are we doing wrong?"

"It's automated. It sensed our presence but maybe it recognized us as someone who isn't allowed to access this area."

"Or maybe it needs more data," Patel posited.

"What kind of data?"

Patel squared her shoulders and placed her hands on the door once again. "I am Lieutenant Devi Patel, of the Federation *Starship Voyager*. I am human and my planet of origin is approximately fifty thousand light-years from our present position. We come in peace and seek only to better understand this world and those who inhabited it."

Both waited tensely for a few moments for any response. When none came Lasren added, "Devi is an Aries and in her spare time enjoys calculating black-hole densities and kayaking."

The blue light returned, but this time only in a small circle near the center of the door. Patel inhaled sharply. She moved her right hand so that it rested within the lit area and immediately noted a difference.

"It's not solid anymore," she said. "It's softer, squishier." Seconds later, Patel cried out and pulled her hand back in alarm.

"What happened?"

"It cut me," she said, holding her hand under Lasren's light. A circle of shallow pricks could clearly be seen on her palm. They weren't deep, but small drops of blood bloomed and pooled in her palm.

"I've got a small medkit," Lasren said, shrugging out of his shoulder pack.

"Don't worry about it," Patel said, wiping her hand on her dive suit and staring at the door, transfixed.

Lasren followed her gaze and watched as the brightness at the center of the door expanded again. It grew so intense that both of them had to look away, shielding their eyes.

When they looked back, the door was gone. Beyond it, darkness beckoned.

SURFACE OF UNNAMED ASTEROID

Seven was not at all certain what she expected to find on this asteroid. *A clue as to the composition of the other bodies that were once part of this solar system?*

Possibly.

But in her heart, she was also seeking the answer to an absurd question that had nonetheless plagued her from the moment she'd begun to study the binaries.

Where did the B star come from?

It was an absurd question because most often binary stars were simply formed when the disc of gas and dust surrounding a new star fragmented and a second star was created. Gravitational capture of a second star by the first was not impossible, just highly unlikely and required a third body with sufficient gravity to account for the required conservation of mass. But as Admiral Janeway had noted during their first briefing, the size and composition of the

B star's asteroid belt suggested the fairly recent destruction of one or more terrestrial bodies.

For her, this was the essential mystery of this system and might actually hold the key to understanding the alien species that had created the biodomes on DK-1116. If the asteroids were composed primarily of the same material as the surviving planet, that would argue for normal binary formation with possible orbit loss resulting in destruction of one or more former planets. If the asteroids contained significant amounts of material that was quite different, her belief that the binaries had been formed by a rare instance of gravitational capture would gain credence.

"There is a significant deposit of a composite metal just ahead," Gwyn's voice sounded through the comm system of Seven's EV suit.

Seven adjusted her tricorder, directing it toward the site Gwyn had indicated.

"There are trace heavy metals, iron, iridium, chromium, but the largest concentrations appear to be unique alloys," Seven said as the list before her continued to expand.

"That's kind of weird, isn't it?" Gwyn asked.

"Could you state your query more precisely, Ensign?" Seven asked.

After a brief pause during which Ensign Gwyn was probably biting back her first few responses, she said, *"What I mean is, aren't relatively few alloys naturally occurring?"*

"Did you not study basic mineralogy, chemistry, and molecular geology at the Academy?"

"I did. I passed those classes but never excelled at them. I always knew I was going to fly and figured I could leave the study of the worlds we were flying toward to everybody else on the ship," Gwyn replied with a level of honesty Seven

found strangely endearing. Most Starfleet officers considered themselves to be the best of the best. Competition among them was fierce in order to gain admission to the Academy and only intensified from there. Few individuals Seven had served with would have been as eager to admit to their shortcomings as Ensign Gwyn. It was true that in her case, her skill as a pilot so thoroughly dwarfed most of the other pilots Seven had known, short of Commander Paris, that her choice to focus her efforts there had certainly borne fruit.

"They are," Seven replied, "but that does not necessarily rule out natural formation here. More interesting are the traces of significantly less common elements, many with brief half-lives and unstable isotopes."

"So that's weird."

"Yes, Ensign."

"Does it mean anything?"

"It suggests several hypotheses, none of which we are going to be able to confirm until we extract samples and return to *Voyager*."

"So, I should just shut up and start digging?"

In the bulky EV suit it was difficult to simply turn one's head and see another's facial expressions. Seven made the effort, turning her entire torso around to face Gwyn. Despite her words, the ensign was smiling.

"We will both start digging," Seven said.

Pointing out the nearest deposit, a massive reflective vein running through a large rock directly ahead, Seven said, "Begin here. Extract ten discrete small samples. Try and get as many unique alloys as possible. I will do the same from our secondary site."

"Yes, ma'am," Gwyn said cheerfully enough as she dropped

her tool pack to the ground and began rummaging around in it for her phaser.

Seven moved off to study another formation roughly a hundred meters down a gentle slope that burst from the surface of the asteroid in an unusual spiked shape. She retrieved her phaser and set it at the lowest possible strength for cutting. A tight, steady beam was emitted, and Seven began to extract extremely fine slices from the odd deposit.

"So is one of your hypotheses that this asteroid used to be part of another planet in this system?" Gwyn asked.

"Most stars have planets, usually more than one," Seven said patiently. "It is possible that the secondary star of this binary pair entered this system after it was formed and in doing so destroyed any other terrestrial worlds that might have existed prior to its arrival."

"How does taking samples of these deposits help you confirm that?"

"Are you asking for your own edification, Ensign?"

"Actually, I'm pretty sure that once we get back, Devi is going to test me on every single aspect of this mission and I want to be prepared to answer her questions."

"Lieutenant Patel is welcome to read the reports I will file once our mission is complete."

"Oh, she'll definitely read them. She'll probably commit them to memory. It's not the data she'll be interested in."

That didn't make much sense to Seven. As chief science officer, Lieutenant Patel should concern herself with all of *Voyager*'s scientific discoveries. "I do not understand," Seven admitted.

"Devi's really smart."

"I do not disagree."

A light chuckle echoed through the comm system. *"But*

she tends to think about problems the way we were taught at the Academy. Every situation is a test she thinks she might fail. So she plays things safe. She never wants to do anything wrong."

"Some errors are essential to discovery," Seven said, slicing another shard and depositing it in her pack.

"That's probably true, but it doesn't mean that it feels good to make them. You make connections that Devi can't seem to find. She lives inside the box. For you, it's like there is no box. She might eventually reach the same conclusions you do, but she won't get there the same way. There will be lots more trial and a lot less error and she won't ever go out on a limb with a fringe theory unless she's sure she can prove it. What she's looking for in your reports is the train of thought that led you to any particular discovery. She thinks you're better at this than she is, so she wants to be more like you. I keep telling her she needs to relax. She's her own worst enemy, if that makes sense."

"It does. But Lieutenant Patel should not compare herself to me or anyone else in the fleet. Each of us has a unique role to play and many ways in which we can contribute to the fleet's work."

"Forgive me, Seven, but that's easy to say when everyone already knows you're brilliant."

"All of Lieutenant Patel's superior officers believe her to be a valued member of our crew," Seven said.

"Have they ever told her that?" Gwyn asked.

"I do not know. I have never participated in the crew review process."

"What the . . . ?"

"Ensign? Is something wrong?"

Gwyn's voice was faint and the comm now carried a strange crackling sound to Seven's ears. It sounded like something was interfering with her signal.

"None of these metals are supposed to be in liquid form, are they?" Gwyn asked.

"You should limit your samples to those available on the surface. At greater depths, it is possible . . ."

". . . I don't understand. The tricorder isn't making any sense of . . . what the hell is that?"

The fear in Gwyn's voice made Seven drop her tools on the spot and move immediately back toward Gwyn's position.

"Ow . . . that's really . . . ouch, what the . . . ? Seven? No . . . no . . . Seven?"

EV suits weren't designed to allow running, but Seven pushed herself, taking large, bounding steps to move as quickly as possible.

"Calm yourself, Ensign."

A loud screech sounded over the comm that resolved into steady white noise.

"Ensign? Ensign Gwyn, please respond," Seven said.

A few meters farther and she gained the top of the rise that led back to Gwyn's position. The sight that met her eyes was horrifying.

Gwyn's had fallen to her knees, holding her right arm out in front of her, waving it wildly. Her right hand and forearm were covered in a thick, viscous black fluid. It moved of its own accord past her elbow, toward her shoulder. With the comm channel malfunctioning, Seven could not hear anything, but as soon as she reached Gwyn's position she could see that within her suit, Gwyn was screaming.

Seven moved to grasp Gwyn's left arm and studied her display panel. It was flashing bright red and indicated multiple breaches. Her oxygen supply was rapidly depleting, and the suit was detecting unacceptably high levels of radiation.

The black fluid was still moving. Seven searched the

ground and quickly retrieved Gwyn's phaser. She adjusted the setting to stun and aimed it directly at the strange black substance. A quick burst and the fluid seemed to solidify. Gwyn fell to the ground, limp and unconscious. Whatever the substance was, it was obviously corrosive and possibly toxic, but there was no way to get Gwyn back to the shuttle without the protection the rest of her suit still provided.

Careful not to touch the substance herself, Seven grabbed a rock and used it to try and remove a little of the black goo that had solidified upon contact with the phaser beam. It fell from Gwyn's suit in dry flakes.

"Hang on, Ensign," Seven ordered as she lifted Gwyn over her shoulder and carried her back to the shuttle.

DK-1116

Lieutenant Patel started forward into the darkness.

"Whoa," Lasren said sharply, grabbing her by the back of her wet suit and tugging.

"What?" Patel demanded.

"We're not going in there alone."

Patel looked around the cavern. "There's no one else here, and I'm not going to wait for Jepel and Vincent to risk the dive."

Lasren shook his head. "You're so intent on finding whatever is back there, you're not thinking straight. We don't have to wait for them to dive down here. *Voyager*'s transporter room has a lock on our position."

"Oh, right," Patel said, chagrined.

"Plus, don't you think we should share this with the rest of our team? Isn't that part of the point of this exercise . . . all of us working together?"

Patel activated her combadge. "Patel to *Voyager*."

Waters responded. *"Go ahead, Devi."*

A few minutes later, Jepel and Vincent materialized in the cavern a few meters from the open doorway.

"Wow," Vincent said, playing his light all around him. "This is amazing."

"You know what I bet is even more amazing?" Patel asked.

"What?"

"Whatever is back here behind the hidden door Lasren and I found. Let's move."

Jepel was quiet, simply studying his tricorder readings. Lasren could sense unspoken anger studiously controlled.

"Omar?" Lasren said softly, stepping close to him.

The young Bajoran lifted his dark brown eyes to meet Kenth's. *Not now*, they demanded.

Much as Lasren wanted to respect Jepel's wishes, he wasn't about to enter an alien environment with a team member harboring resentment toward one or more of the rest of them.

"Look," he began. "I don't know what we're going to find down here, but I do know that if it's problematic, the only way we're going to survive it is by trusting one another."

Lasren could see Jepel's jaw clenching.

"Whatever you have to say, you should say it," Lasren continued.

Some of the tension Jepel was holding seemed to release. Turning to Patel, he said, "Lieutenant Patel, a word?"

"What is it?"

Jepel stared at her for a long moment, then shook his head. "What you just did, endangering all of us in hopes of discovering this, was bullshit. I know you fancy yourself the leader of this mission, but I will not follow anyone who is careless about my safety or their own."

Patel absorbed this, then stepped closer to him. "I apologize," she said coldly. "It was a risk, but a calculated one. I didn't have time to explain it, but the odds were good, based on my readings of our most recent scans, that this cavern was here. You don't have to like following me. But I am the senior officer, so if that doesn't work for you, speak now and you can transport back to the surface. I'm sure there's time to assign you to another team, maybe one that's planning a little flower gathering or sunbathing."

Lasren didn't like where this was going one bit, but he also knew Patel was the only one who could solve it, were she the least bit inclined to do so.

"Devi?" Lasren said.

"What?"

"The only operative words there were the first two you spoke. The rest only added insult to injury."

"We don't have time for this."

"*This* is the reason we're all down here. We're the next generation of Starfleet's finest. Most of our current commanding officers have been at this for decades. They weren't handed their jobs. They earned them. And if we expect to take their place, this is how we demonstrate our readiness. You made a mistake. None of us care that it panned out. It was still wrong. We need to know that this was a momentary lapse, not a character flaw. Acknowledge that, or we'll be forced to conclude that we might be dealing with a reckless officer and act accordingly."

"You know why I did it, Kenth," Patel said. "You know how hard I worked preparing for this. On any other mission, a find like this would be given to more senior officers. Together, we're all about to prove that we're every bit as capable as they are of contributing to our work in a meaningful way."

"I've never questioned my ability to contribute to this fleet's missions," Jepel said. "My status as a junior officer is a simple function of lack of experience."

"Exactly. And this is how we fix that," Patel insisted.

"Not entirely," Lasren corrected her. "You have a choice to make here, Devi. You can be the officer who made this discovery at the expense of your credibility, or the one who realized in a critical moment that leadership isn't about being smart or being right. It's about protecting those you lead and making sure they understand what you're asking them to risk and why."

"Captain Chakotay doesn't explain every command decision he makes to us," Patel pointed out.

"He doesn't have to. There isn't a single officer serving on *Voyager* who doubts his commitment to our safety. You think his choice to send the most experienced officers he has on missions like this is a judgment on your lack of ability. It isn't. It's about assessing risks and setting realistic expectations. We all get our chances to show we're ready for more responsibility. This is yours and we all want to see you succeed. So please stop screwing it up."

Patel's face flushed. A bevy of conflicting emotions swelled within her. Lasren couldn't help but empathize. He could only hope that she would accept the life preserver he was offering.

Finally she said, "You're right. I'm sorry. Jepel, Vincent, I sincerely apologize for frightening you both. It was careless. I was only thinking of myself and that's unacceptable. Can you forgive me?"

Lasren, Vincent, and Jepel exchanged glances and nodded.

"Thank you, Lieutenant," Jepel said. "That's all I needed to hear."

"Guys?" Vincent asked.

"Yes?" Patel replied.

"Was that light always there?"

All three turned to peer down the hallway, where a faint blue light now lit what appeared to be a long corridor.

"No, it wasn't," Patel said. "Tricorders, please."

All four began to scan the hallway ahead.

"A new power source has been activated," Patel noted.

"Something knows we're here," Lasren said.

"Is that your empathic abilities talking?" Jepel asked.

"Yes, as well as the fact that we had to endure a weird and invasive identification protocol to get the door to open," Lasren said.

"Do you sense hostility?" Patel asked.

Lasren shook his head. "No. It's still just a sense of presence, nothing more."

Patel removed a phaser from her pack. "I'll feel better if we all arm ourselves," she said.

"Agreed," Jepel said.

"I'll take point. Lasren, will you bring up the rear?"

"Yes, Lieutenant."

"We'll go slow and take as many detailed scans as possible. We can analyze the data later. Let's just focus on collection for now."

"Understood," Lasren said.

The first hundred meters of the corridor were traversed with an overwhelming sense of tense expectation. The walls were bare, seamless metal plates composed largely of iron, copper, and aluminum. There were no visible doors or junctions. They followed a gentle downward slope until they reached the source of the light.

At the end of the corridor stood another open doorway. It was circular, similar to but larger than the one at the entrance. Patel entered first, and Lasren could hear her catch her breath in what felt to him like awe. Vincent and Jepel hurried in after her. By the time Lasren passed over the threshold, the other three had reached the center of the room. They faced outward, staring openmouthed at the walls of the vast space.

Lasren joined them, moving to Patel's side. The entire room was lined with tiny alcoves carved into the walls. Each alcove contained a small sphere, roughly a dozen centimeters in diameter. Each sphere was illuminated from within with a pale blue light. Although the effect was similar to a massive collection of lightbulbs, Lasren did not for a moment believe that the spheres' purpose was as a light source.

Lasren's heart began to race. The sight was beautiful and mysterious, but fascinating as it was, nothing in this room felt like the presence he continued to sense.

"What is this?" Jepel asked for all of them.

"My tricorder isn't giving me anything," Patel said. "It's like they don't exist."

"There could be a scattering field of some kind. Whatever is powering them wasn't detectable from the surface. Maybe there is an automated security program," Vincent offered.

The spheres were too high to reach. Lasren tore his eyes from them and began to search the rest of the room. That's when he noticed the other three circular doors spaced evenly about the walls. He appreciated the symmetry. If nothing else, it gave him the distinct sense of purposeful construction.

"I want to try something," Patel said. "Each of you go and stand by one of the doors. Don't touch them. I just want to see if they react to proximity."

Lasren, Vincent, and Jepel did as they had been instructed. Nothing happened.

Patel moved along the outer circumference of the room, walking slowly, tricorder in hand.

"There are faint electromagnetic waves emanating from the center," she said, looking to Lasren. With a shrug and a nod, he urged her on.

She carefully stepped back toward dead center of the room. When she reached it, a blue pillar of light blinked into existence. It was impossible to tell if it came from above or below her position.

"Are you okay, Devi?" Lasren asked.

Bathed in the incandescent glow, she smiled and nodded. "You have to see this," she said, motioning them to step closer. As they did, Lasren realized that within the pillar, strange glowing symbols floated.

"Is that a control interface?" Jepel asked.

"I think so," Patel said. "But since I can't translate any of them, I don't want to touch anything."

"Step out for a second," Lasren suggested.

She did so and the blue pillar vanished.

"That's amazing," Vincent said.

"Let's test the doors," Lasren suggested.

Patel nodded. "One at a time."

Together they moved to the door directly across from the open entrance. As she had done before, Patel placed a hand in the center and said, "I am Lieutenant Devi Patel . . ."

Before she could finish introducing herself, the walls all around her began to scream.

10

Liam O'Donnell did not believe in impossible things. He operated best in quantifiable domains. His entire career had been an exercise in pushing the limits of life-forms. Things that on the surface seemed difficult or impossible, with enough time, patience, and scrutiny, eventually revealed their secrets and became the clay in his hands from which he created new, unique things.

In some ways, this entire planet felt like a similar exercise. But he had not designed this system. Someone else, someone he suspected was infinitely more capable than he, had set all of this in motion and then brought it to a screeching halt. As of yet, he had no idea how they had accomplished this miracle. He was an outsider, and its tantalizing mysteries had slowly transmuted from interesting to annoying.

Impossible, O'Donnell thought for the hundredth time since he began sampling the wide variety of plant life that populated the biodome.

"I'm curious to know what you make of all of this, Commander," Admiral Janeway called from over his shoulder. So intent had he been on observing the regeneration of a single blade of tall white grass, O'Donnell hadn't registered her soft footfalls as she approached his position.

Tearing his eyes away from the magnificent, improbable spectacle, he rose to face her. "Have you reached any conclusions, Admiral?"

A mischievous smile played across her lips. "Chakotay and I believe we might be dealing with zombies."

O'Donnell laughed aloud at this. "The living dead. I suppose that's as good a description as any."

"Commander Glenn found a lovely spot for stargazing on the top of one of those hills back there. We thought we'd make camp and have dinner. She and Chakotay are setting things up. I was hoping you'd join us. There's not much light left. Walk with me?"

The commander collected his tools and specimens and joined the admiral as she led him to their evening campsite.

"What about Regina?" he asked as soon as they were under way.

"She finds this place disturbing. She'll be back shortly, but she's left the analysis to us for the time being."

"She's not the only one," O'Donnell said. "Everything here that looks like life is something else. It's not exactly artificial. The limited cellular analysis I have been able to do shows trace nucleic acids. But they only seem to activate under certain circumstances. The gene regulators involved are more complex by several orders of magnitude than anything governing most life-forms, which, as you know, are already insanely complex."

Janeway slowed her pace as they reached another patch of the tall white fronds. "Do you think it's something we could replicate?"

O'Donnell shrugged, carving his own path alongside the admiral's. "Our tools can give us accurate readings at the subatomic level. But just because we can see something and understand its purpose, doesn't mean we can re-create it ourselves, let alone build upon progress like this."

"Like Seven's catoms?"

"Exactly. In some ways this seems like a variation on programmable matter. It's the fossilized helix and trace nucleic acids that make this more difficult. But catoms are matter designed to *sustain* life. They are not, in and of themselves, living things. These are."

"Sometimes."

"Exactly. Sometimes."

"If it weren't for the fact that it doesn't seem like anyone has been here for a few thousand years, I would say that what we are witnessing here is a grand experiment," the admiral said. "Whoever left these biodomes here didn't secure them. They didn't make them inaccessible. And given the level of mastery of both technology and biology we've already found, my guess is that if they'd wanted to, they could have."

"You think they left them here as a challenge? *'See what we did and let us know if you think you can do better'?*" O'Donnell asked.

Janeway smiled at the thought. "I feel like if they had intended for anyone to follow in their footsteps, they would have left instructions, a message, *something* to help guide those who came after them."

"Maybe they didn't think anyone would. Most of the space around this area used to belong to the Borg. That might not have been the case when these biodomes were erected. And it's really interesting to me that the Borg never seemed to have come here."

"It's easy to get the wrong idea about the Borg, to give them far more credit than they deserve. Advanced, efficient, and destructive as they were, they weren't gods. They were not capable of mastering anything they couldn't assimilate and nothing here would have responded to assimilation, nor are the natural resources that unique."

"The *Sevenofninonium* is."

The admiral turned on him with her most withering glare. "We're not calling it that."

"*I am.* I think it's a perfect designation."

"Yes, well, we will never know how many interesting anomalies and good ideas the Borg failed to notice along the way," Janeway said.

"I'm kind of glad they never came this way or wrote it off. This kind of technology isn't really safe in anyone's hands, least of all theirs."

"What about ours?"

O'Donnell paused his steps and crossed his arms, considering the admiral. "I have plenty of faith in the essential goodness of our people, especially now that I have a much broader basis for comparison."

"One of these days you're going to have to let go of your anger with the Confederacy of the Worlds of the First Quadrant."

"Maybe. But not today. And I wasn't actually thinking about them. I was thinking about the Krenim."

Janeway inhaled deeply and exhaled very slowly, clearly purging her own complicated emotions on that subject.

"What I find most worrisome about anyone who would turn to time manipulation to accomplish political ends is their stunning lack of faith in themselves," O'Donnell said.

Janeway smiled in spite of herself, resuming her previous meandering pace. "It's hard to equate arrogance like that with insecurity."

"Tell me I'm wrong."

"You aren't. I just never thought of it that way."

"All of these incredibly powerful civilizations have one thing in common. The Federation, the Borg, the Caeliar, the Confederacy, and the Krenim, they all develop unique tools in the name of progress. They each set lofty goals for themselves and harness those tools in the service of reaching those goals. But of all of them, ours seems to be the only one still confused about our ultimate purpose."

"Confused? I don't believe that's true. Our goal is to learn as much as we can about the universe we inhabit and all of those with whom we share it."

"And if, along the way, we find others whose purpose conflicts with our own?"

"We prioritize our survival while doing all we can to forward the notion of peaceful coexistence."

"But how devoted are we to that peaceful coexistence thing? How devoted can we be when our existence is threatened so frequently by species who will never give us the same respect we are willing to extend to them? We kill others to preserve ourselves and our way of life."

"As a last resort."

"But still, it's always there. We don't send ships out to explore without arming them."

"Are you, of all people, arguing for greater pacifism from us?"

"No. Not at all. I like living and I intend to continue doing it for as long as possible. I'm saying a little more humility on all our parts might be in order."

"Humility?"

"Even the Caeliar weren't above making horrific mistakes. They knew their technology to be beyond that of most of their spacefaring contemporaries and responded by hiding themselves as best they could from the rest of the universe. Whoever created this is playing at the same level, but they left their work here for anyone passing by to visit and study. This construct is meant to outlive us all. And I think you're wrong about them not leaving instructions. Everything we need to understand this technology and its purpose is right here. But it's only meant for the taking by those wise enough, advanced enough, and humble enough to see it for what it is."

"What is it?"

"I'm starting to think we're not ready to find out."

Janeway smiled. "Patience and faith, Commander. Those two things have taken me a lot further than humility."

"Patience and faith? Two qualities I have never managed to cultivate."

"Stick around long enough and they might just rub off on you."

In the distance, O'Donnell spotted the shadowed figures of Chakotay and Glenn moving around a small, stationary light source.

"I hope not," he said.

"Should I be insulted by that?" Janeway asked semi-seriously.

The commander shook his head. "I don't know. Personally, I've never seen the point in polite contrivances created to justify our natural tendency to waste time."

O'Donnell had almost reached the top of the low hill where the rest of the team waited when he realized that the admiral had stopped several meters behind him. Turning, he saw her silhouette outlined in the fading light.

"Admiral?"

She walked toward him slowly. When their eyes met, he could see, even in the dimness, that something hard had replaced the clear blue pools that he normally characterized as vivacious.

"I'm sorry, Admiral, if I said something to offend."

"Not at all, Commander. As usual, you've given me a great deal to think about. Let's not keep the others waiting any longer."

VESTA

On the rack before Doctor El'nor Sal's eyes sat twelve vials. Each vial contained a vector—a perfectly prepared, genetically modified virus awaiting its final instructions. By this time tomorrow, segments of Ensign Aytar Gwyn's DNA, including the metamorphic regulators Sal required to overwrite Nancy Conlon's malfunctioning ones, would be added to the vectors. Several hours in a centrifuge later, they would be ready. After enduring weeks of hopelessness, Sal was going to bring to her team and those nearest and dearest to Conlon the best news they'd had since she was diagnosed.

Nancy Conlon was going to live.

"Got a minute?"

Sal turned on her stool to see Captain Regina Farkas standing in the doorway to the medical lab. Her arms were crossed at her chest and the fine lines around her eyes had grown deeper.

"Weren't you supposed to be enjoying shore leave today?" Sal asked.

"I was. I did. It was awful."

"I guess that explains why you look like hell."

"Compliments will get you nowhere, Doctor Sal."

Sal rose and grabbed her medical tricorder. Aiming it toward Regina, she said, "Were your fellow commanding officers not working and playing well with others?"

"I have no complaints about the company."

"You didn't drink enough water today, Regina. You're dehydrated."

"I'll live."

"So what happened?"

Farkas shook her head as she crossed to Sal's stool and took the lab's only seat. "We need to get the hell out of here."

Sal was justifiably intrigued. Regina was many things, but faint of heart had never been one of them. "We've got another week and a half in orbit, don't we?"

"Not if I can help it. But it's going to be a heavy lift to convince anyone else that I'm not just getting too old for this shit."

"Analysis of the fecal matter?"

"That's not a planet down there. It's a damned freak show."

"Until now, I wasn't upset that my work was going to keep me up here. Do I need to see this?" Sal asked.

"It looks so peaceful, so intriguing. But you scratch the surface and nothing makes sense. All those weird metal sculptures with no purpose. The plants look like plants but if you cut them, they grow right back before your very eyes."

"Like earthworms?"

"Earthworms are alive. Our tricorders can't even tell us what these things are."

"Huh."

"It's wrong. Everything about it is just wrong. It's like we're children, stumbling around in a mad scientist's lab. We don't know what to touch, what not to touch. We don't understand the first thing about the people who built this or what they intended to do with it. If we're not careful, best-case scenario we're going to get some of our people killed. And so far, we're not being careful. Half the fleet's crew is down there right now having a picnic by a vast body of water they're calling a lake, but unlike most lakes, it has no discernable source."

"Regina, calm down. You love a good mystery as much as every other insanely curious girl who decided to give her best years to Starfleet. How exactly is this different from the way we blunder into every strange new situation we've ever encountered?"

The captain sighed, rising to her feet and beginning to pace fitfully. "We've all seen some pretty weird things, I will grant you that."

"Part of the job."

"Yes. But sometimes our job is to look dispassionately at what we find and say, 'Nope. We're not ready for this.' Right now, all I want to do is recall every single person on that planet, tuck our tails, and run."

"Does anybody else feel this way?"

"Hell, no. It's all awe and wonder and *isn't this amazing* down there."

"Have you told the admiral how you feel?"

"There's no evidence that I'm not just losing my mind. I feel like Cassandra. And I'm never that girl."

Sal smiled wearily. "I know the feeling."

Farkas paused, staring at Sal as if she suddenly remembered something important. "How's your thing coming along?"

"Better than I could have hoped. I'm almost there."

"That half Kriosian helped you out?"

"She did. Not a problem at all."

"Well, that's a relief. Congratulations."

"Too soon for that by a few days. But I'll let you know when to start popping the champagne."

"I have to get down there," Farkas said miserably.

"Why?"

"Dinner with my fellow commanding officers."

"Don't hold back, Regina. You and I both know where not listening to our instincts leads. Tell them how you feel. Maybe you're not the only one who's worried but no one wants to be the first to say something."

"I hope you're right."

"I'm always right."

"Priority message for Doctor Sal from Doctor Sharak," the computer called over the comm.

Sal sighed wearily as she opened the channel. "Go ahead."

The face of Doctor Sharak appeared on the screen before her. Everything about him was tense. For the life of her, Sal couldn't remember ever having seen Sharak sweat before, but a bright sheen covered his high forehead and scalp. *"El'nor, are you available to transport over immediately?"*

"I am. What's the problem?"

The words "Ensign Gwyn" had barely escaped his lips when Sal rose saying, "I'll be right there. Sal out."

"What is it?"

Sal saw the fear in her face reflected in Regina's eyes.

"My half Kriosian," Sal said.

"Go."

Sal did.

DK-1116

Now this is a party, Commander B'Elanna Torres decided as soon as she materialized not far from her family's campsite near the lake. She couldn't count the number of bodies milling in and out of the large tents, cavorting along the shoreline, or playing in the water beneath dozens of portable lights that thoroughly illuminated the area while still creating the feeling of nighttime on the beach. Someone had brought an amplifier, and loud music with a heavy beat beneath stirring strings set Torres's pace as she moved among the throngs toward the spot where she hoped to find her husband and children.

"Evening, Commander!" several cheery voices greeted her as she passed. She caught a few familiar faces in the crowd, mostly her engineers, and returned the smiles they offered. As much of a logistical nightmare as this leave rotation had been, it was well worth it to see so many letting loose and truly enjoying themselves.

Chakotay was right. We needed this.

Several people were munching on finger foods or holding brightly colored beverages. For the first time it crossed her mind that cleanup in this biodome was going to require special attention. Torres didn't mind folks enjoying themselves, but when it was time to go, they were going to leave this place exactly as they'd found it, no matter how loud the complaints were. She took note of several strategically placed recyclers and hoped everyone was making use of them. She decided that a carefully worded memo to all officers in their morning briefings would be in order, just to remind everyone to clean up after themselves. Otherwise, their last days here were going to be more work than play.

Her pace quickened as she reached the ridge leading to her family tent. Voices could be heard above, laughing and chatting. The music was less oppressive this far from its source. As she reached the top she saw Tom holding a sleeping Michael in a backpack he normally used for family hikes on the holodeck. Miral was next to him, her eyes glued to a gooey, melting white blob at the end of a wooden stick she knew her husband had replicated just for this occasion. Several others, including Fife, Velth, Icheb, and Bryce, were roasting their own over a small heating element Tom had packed with this purpose in mind.

"Mommy!" Miral cried in delight as soon as she caught sight of Torres.

"Evening all," Torres greeted the group as she stepped clear of the circle to catch Miral in a tight embrace.

"Mommy, Mommy, this is the most beautiful place," Miral said, her words tripping over one another in her haste to get them out. "I found a birdhouse and it's big enough for all of us and Michael, and I think there are enough for everybody, and we should live here now. Mommy, do you want a marshmallow?"

"Hang on," Torres said as Miral grabbed the nearest stick from Icheb, who surrendered it graciously, and thrust it at her mother. "Yes, honey, thank you."

Tom's smile could have lit the whole biodome as Torres stuffed the molten sugar into her mouth and did her best to swallow it gracefully.

"It sounds like you all had quite a day," Torres said as she took Miral by the hand and led her back to Tom's side.

"Hello, gorgeous," Tom said, kissing her without restraint as she settled herself beside him and took Miral into her lap.

"Tell me about this birdhouse," Torres continued, wrapping her arms around her daughter and taking a moment to revel in the sweet smells that would always mean "Miral" to her. Among them was a faint tinny fragrance Torres didn't recognize.

"I climbed the trees, Mommy," Miral said jubilantly. "All by myself."

"You're getting to be such a big girl," Torres said, smiling. Miral beamed at the compliment.

"It's actually a significant find," Fife said. "Your daughter is a natural explorer."

"What was it?"

Tom picked up the story. "It looks like there might have been an avian species here at one time. Most of those metal trees back there have hollow spaces that lead to flat surfaces. There weren't any archeological remains, but the architecture is pretty compelling. Whatever those things are, there's room in most of them for several of us to make a home."

"That's amazing."

"That's not the half of it," Bryce said.

"What did your team do today?" Torres asked.

"It took Elkins all of ten minutes to figure out that these biodomes are enclosed by fields generated from a single source," Bryce reported.

"Did you find it?"

"We're constructing a surface sensor array to get the most precise measurements possible," Icheb replied. "Some of us are, anyway."

"Elkins and Benoit have it covered. Benoit has actually got a team of holographic engineers working around the clock so we can start placing them tomorrow," Bryce interjected. "He let us go a little early so we could join the party, but we'll be back at work first thing, so Icheb can start enjoying himself again."

Torres looked to the ensign and noted signs of embarrassment. Normally he took Bryce's gentle ribbing in stride, but it seemed to sting tonight in a way it never had before.

Before Torres could inquire further, Miral said, "Mommy, I don't want to go back to the ship. I like it here."

"Really?" Torres asked.

Miral nodded solemnly, which was hard with bits of marshmallow glued to her cheeks.

"We live on *Voyager*, honey," Tom said.

"We used to live on *Voyager*," Miral corrected him. "But now we can live here."

"We really can't, sweetheart," Torres said gently. "This isn't our world. We're just here exploring. When we're done, we're going to find other worlds to study. That's what Starfleet does."

"But I like this world," Miral said.

"Miral," Fife spoke up, "do you know the difference between a ship and a planet?"

"Ships are small," Miral said.

"They are smaller than planets, yes," Fife agreed. "But they both move through space."

"We're not moving here," Miral insisted.

"Can you feel it when you are on a ship and it's moving?" Miral's slightly ridged brow furrowed.

"Sometimes."

"Only when you see the stars moving past your window, right?"

Miral nodded.

"Even though you can't feel it, or see it, this planet is moving through space almost as fast as our ships move at low impulse."

"It is?" Miral asked dubiously.

Fife nodded, smiling.

Torres was struck by the thought that she had never before seen Fife interact with her child. He came by it so naturally, she wondered if he had children of his own somewhere, or perhaps much younger siblings.

"But the planet only moves in a circle, more or less, around its stars. Our ship can do that too, but it can also move between stars and planets. The two places aren't that different. One of them feels larger, but the other can take you so much farther."

"Why don't we make the planet move like our ship?"

All of the adults chuckled at this.

"You know what, sweetie?" Tom said. "We've encountered alien species that could almost do that. Their ships are huge compared to ours."

"Can we live with them?"

"Miral," Torres said, her stomach suddenly turning, "aren't you happy living on *Voyager*?"

A distinct lull fell over the group as all eyes turned toward the girl.

"I don't remember home," Miral finally said. "I know you show me on the holodeck, but it's not the same. It doesn't smell the same. It doesn't feel the same. I want to see home again."

Torres embraced her daughter tightly.

"We will," Tom said. "It'll be another few years, but we'll go home again. And until then, home is wherever you and your brother and mommy and I are."

"How about first thing in the morning, you show me one of these birdhouses," Torres suggested.

"Okay. You will love it."

"I love you."

Miral snuggled into her, resting her head. "I love you, too, Mommy."

"I think somebody's ready for bed," Tom said.

Torres nodded and the others began to extricate themselves from the makeshift "campfire." Miral was already drowsing as Torres carried her into their tent and settled her in her sleeping bag. Once Tom had placed Michael in a low pocket that extended from the tent wall like a bassinet, he came to B'Elanna and pulled her into his arms.

They remained like that for a long time, neither of them speaking. They didn't need to in order to know that they were sharing the same thought. Their devotion to Starfleet was such that it had never really occurred to them to consider a different kind of life for their children. Every obstacle life in space had thrown at them, they had found a way to counter and manage. Miral's health, her education, even companionship were all accounted for. *But she still didn't think she was home.*

Torres didn't feel the tears coming until they were wetting her cheeks. Tom gently nuzzled her, whispering, "Shh, shh, it's going to be okay."

Both of them knew better than to have this conversation now. They also knew they'd be having it sooner rather than later.

As Icheb watched Fife and Velth disappear into the crowd, he turned to see Bryce staring at him.

"Are you going back to *Voyager* tonight?" Bryce asked.

"I am. You?"

"I don't know. I don't feel like being in the middle of all that," Bryce said, motioning toward the milling throngs, "but I'm still too—I don't know—there are so many things running through my head, I know I won't sleep yet."

Icheb nodded but did not offer a solution. He felt the

same, though he doubted the thoughts plaguing Bryce were the same as those that would keep him up later.

"I would like to see those birdhouses," Icheb offered.

Bryce smiled broadly in something that looked like relief. "Let's check them out."

They moved together, side by side, toward the tree line. Icheb was grateful that there was enough ambient light to make hand beacons unnecessary, although he didn't think climbing any trees made sense after dark. His survival teachers would have definitely taken off points for needlessly courting hazards.

"She's a cute kid," Bryce finally offered, as much to break the silence that had descended between them as anything else, Icheb thought.

"It is a shame she does not appreciate the tremendous gift she has been given by her parents," Icheb noted.

"Give her time. She's what, five?"

"Almost," Icheb said. "By the time I was five, I had already been assimilated."

Bryce paused. "You've never really talked about what that was like."

"I don't honestly remember it," Icheb admitted. "I was simply Borg, until I wasn't."

"Did you like being Borg?"

"I didn't know there was another option. Afterwards, I didn't like knowing what my parents had done."

"Your parents?"

Icheb turned to face Bryce. Other students at the Academy had asked questions from time to time, always with a morbid curiosity. He didn't sense that from Bryce. Instead, he saw real compassion in his bright blue eyes.

"I was a tool they created to destroy the Borg. A pathogen was placed in my body, and I was sent by them to be assimilated. The Borg had devastated our planet and my parents believed that was the only way to free themselves from the constant attacks."

Bryce looked stunned, then angry. "They what?" he said in obvious disbelief.

"They were just trying to protect themselves," Icheb said automatically. He'd repeated this justification to himself and others so many times it was almost a reflex, but for the first time, Bryce's absolute horror triggered something new in Icheb. His mouth went dry as he saw himself and his parents through Bryce's eyes.

"You don't believe that, do you?"

Icheb turned away.

"I did. For a very long time, that's what I told myself."

"Did it work?"

"When I was finally released from my maturation chamber, the pathogen killed all of the drones on the vessel that assimilated me, but the ship was separated from the Collective to prevent further infection."

"Not the pathogen. What you *told yourself* about them. Do you still believe that? Do you think what they did was okay because they were just trying to protect themselves?"

A cascade of impossible emotions raced through Icheb. He'd never felt most of them before, so it was difficult to choose one, let alone connect it to a belief.

Bryce stepped closer to Icheb, placing his hands on Icheb's upper arms and squeezing gently.

"I'm so sorry, Icheb," he said with quiet intensity that brought more new questions to the forefront of his consciousness. He wanted to pull away almost as much as he wanted to step closer.

The next thing he knew, Bryce had moved near enough for Icheb to feel the heat of his body. He took Icheb in a gentle embrace. Without thought, Icheb lifted his arms in kind and wound them around Bryce.

"Why did you bring me here?" Icheb heard himself ask. It was the one thing he'd wanted to know more than anything else all day. Why he'd blurted it out now, he didn't know, but there was relief in giving voice to the question.

Bryce pulled back, still touching Icheb's arms as casually as if this were a normal physical vocabulary they shared. "You didn't want to come?"

"I did. I just . . . there are so many more qualified engineers that could have joined your team."

Icheb could see Bryce's mind start to race. A lengthy explanation filled with jarring segues and run-on sentences was about to begin. Icheb almost smiled in anticipation of it. But then, a new look came over Phinn's face, as if he had just decided something important. "I didn't want them. I wanted you," Bryce said simply.

"But why?"

Bryce swallowed as a tentative fear flashed over his face. His struggle was brief. Taking a deep breath he placed both his hands on Icheb's cheeks and brought Icheb's lips to his.

Icheb knew what he was supposed to feel. He understood the intensity of physical intimacy. Part of him also understood that every moment he had spent with Bryce from the first day they'd met until now had been leading to this. In his mind, an argument he'd been having with himself was settled. Bryce *liked* him. He was seeking more than a mutually beneficial professional relationship with him. Icheb shared that desire. He'd never known anyone else like Bryce. When they were together, he was at his best and when they were apart, he spent an inordinate amount of time wondering when they would see each other again.

Bryce lingered in the kiss. Icheb tried to respond. His mind wanted this, but for reasons he could not fathom, his body remained unmoved.

When they finally separated, Bryce looked at him almost apologetically. "I'm sorry. I've wanted to do that for such a long time."

"I am glad you did," Icheb said automatically. *He was.* But he was also more confused now than he'd ever been.

In Admiral Janeway's brief absence to retrieve Commander O'Donnell, Chakotay had set up low chairs in a circle around a small portable replicator and light source. As soon as she arrived, Janeway looked at the restricted menu, selected pasta and tea, then settled herself beside Chakotay, who seemed to be enjoying what looked like a vegetable stew with a chunk of bread.

The night was more pleasant than the day had been. The air was slightly cooler and unusual light fragrances of floral and spice—always with faint metallic undertones—were carried on the light breeze.

Commander Glenn had begun to pepper O'Donnell with questions the moment he'd taken his seat on the other side of Janeway. *Had he detected the same unusual regenerative properties of the plant life? Was it even life? Was he able to find any DNA? Did he still believe the plants could be responsible for regulating the environment?*

O'Donnell fielded them cordially enough. "All I can really

say is that a day later, we know less about this planet than we did before we came here."

"What I find amazing is the complete absence of any archeological remains to hint at the identity of the people who built all this," Chakotay said.

"I'm beginning to think that was the point," O'Donnell said. "You know the old saying—*the medium is the message*? It might best apply here."

"How so?"

"If the architects of this world wanted to leave anything more specific than they did, they certainly could have. The fact that they didn't means everything we need to understand this place is here. Anyone lacking the ability to see it for what it is might not be ready to know more."

"You believe our knowledge and technology aren't up to the task of unraveling this mystery?" Chakotay asked, not offended but pushing a little.

"They aren't so far," O'Donnell said.

"We're just getting started," Chakotay countered. "Maybe we should wait to hear the reports from our other teams before we give up."

"Give up? Are we giving up? Because if so, I'm in," Farkas said, stepping into the circle.

"Good evening, Regina," Janeway greeted her.

"Admiral."

Farkas took the remaining seat between Chakotay and O'Donnell.

"Something to eat?" Chakotay asked.

"No, I'm good," Farkas replied.

"Have any problems been reported today to *Vesta*?" Janeway asked.

"Nope," Farkas said. "But give it time."

"I'm sorry, Regina, but what exactly are you afraid of here?" Janeway asked. "I'm genuinely curious."

Farkas shrugged. "It's a gut instinct, Admiral. Nothing more."

"Yes, but even those are informed by observations," Chakotay said.

"Well, my first observation is that the only reason we're all sitting here is by the grace of ancient alien technology we don't understand. The strange behavior of the pseudo-life-forms might have been designed to maintain stasis, as Commander O'Donnell posited earlier, or their regenerative abilities might have been created to counter a periodic dropping of these energy fields. If this field fell right now, we'd all die within seconds. Nothing else here would change dramatically, and any damage done would repair itself almost as soon as the fields went back up."

Janeway looked to Chakotay, whose face clearly indicated that until now, he hadn't considered this possibility.

"That's not entirely true," O'Donnell said. "The loss of atmosphere would take quite a while to restore, and I'm not sure even these strange plants would be capable of regenerating without it. More to the point, the water would disappear immediately, and with no internal sources to replenish it, I don't know how you ever get that back. The plants are strange, I agree. But the presence of the water tells me these fields have remained in place since the planet was abandoned."

"Fair point," Farkas said.

"Do you know what I like about this place?" Glenn said.

"What?" Janeway asked.

"It's uncomfortable."

"It is that," Farkas agreed.

"What I mean is it's been a long time since humans were at the shallow end of the comprehension pool. Thousands of years ago, our ancestors on Earth lived with mysteries all around them. They sat beside campfires, *real ones*, and they cooked whatever meat they could catch or whatever vegetables they could grow. They had little to no control over the most basic and essential needs for survival. At night, they sat under stars like these and couldn't begin to imagine what they were really seeing.

"Tonight, here on this world thousands of light-years from Earth, we're like them. This planet operates under rules different from ours. Those rules were created by unknown hands who may or may not have had anyone else's best interests at heart. *If they even had hearts.* I'd like to think that we haven't lost the drive that led our ancestors out of their ignorance and into the light of the scientific discoveries and allowed us to reach the stars. And I don't think it's a bad thing to be forced to recognize once in a while that, advanced as we may be, we still have a long way to go. I think this planet might have been a gift left for those curious enough to push themselves to understand that which on its surface is incomprehensible."

"It's a nice thought," Chakotay said. "But you're forgetting an essential part of humanity's march of progress. Our ancestors, sitting around those fires, staring at those stars, needed to understand their place in the world and their universe. Even without knowing how or why, they felt themselves to be connected to creation."

"Usually they decided they were the center of it," Farkas noted.

"They did," Chakotay agreed with a smile. "They looked up and told themselves stories about the stars and the miraculous beings that inhabited them: gods, demons, angels, and monsters. They poured their hopes and dreams, their fears and desires, into creatures of unimaginable power and then decided that those creatures cared about them enough to interact with them from time to time."

"And then science came along and took all that away from them," O'Donnell said.

"Did it?" Chakotay asked. "There are still plenty of human experiences that are beyond our science."

"Name one," O'Donnell said.

Chakotay paused, then said quietly, "Love."

"Come on, Captain," O'Donnell said. "The biochemical reactions of our neural pathways coupled with a basic survival instinct drive us to form relationships that will allow us to procreate and bind us to our offspring."

"That's true," Chakotay said. "But I don't honestly believe it accounts for all of the various aspects of what we call love, do you? Why do people stay together once those instincts are quiet?"

O'Donnell seemed to seriously consider the question. He glanced away from the group for a moment, and a look of longing crossed his face. Finally he said, "I concede the point."

"That's love," Glenn said, pointing to the sky.

Janeway followed her gaze. "The stars?" she asked.

"That particular formation, do you see it?" Glenn asked. "Those two galaxies up there and the bridge of stars between them?"

"The bridge of stars?" Janeway asked.

"Uh-huh," Glenn said, nodding. "I can't remember the whole story. Two galaxies were one but over time, the natural expansion of the universe separated them. Still, they couldn't bear to be torn apart, so each of them sacrificed a few of their stars to leave a bridge between them so that no matter how far apart they drifted, they could never truly be separated."

"That's beautiful," Chakotay said, glancing toward Janeway with a gentle smile.

She felt herself smiling back at him.

"Yes, but obviously not true," Farkas said.

"How do you know, Regina?" O'Donnell asked.

"Because just like you, I understand the forces of gravity and the movement of stars and galaxies," Farkas replied.

"You understand how they work most of the time," Janeway agreed. "But if this planet teaches us anything, it is that there are sizeable gaps in our knowledge yet to be filled and until we can fill them with facts, perhaps it does no harm to fill them with comforting mysteries."

"There might have been a time when I found mysteries comforting," Farkas said. "But not that long ago, I lost hundreds of people to a mystery, and I'm not sure to this day I really comprehend why. The stakes are very real here. They are measured in the lives of those we command. We have a responsibility not to lead them into a false sense of security or complacency."

"We all do," Janeway said. "But we also have a responsibility to expose them to the mysteries and challenges that they will have to conquer as we progress in our understanding of the universe."

"I know it's scary, Regina," Glenn said. "And for those of us with fresh wounds, it must seem like the height of arrogance to rush headlong into a situation as risky as this one."

"What I'm feeling about this place isn't post-traumatic stress, *Doctor* Glenn," Farkas said.

Janeway bristled at Regina's use of Glenn's other title. To lead *Galen*, Starfleet's newest specialized medical vessel, they had selected one of the few ranking officers who had completed both her medical studies and her command training.

"I wasn't positing a diagnosis, Captain. Forgive me. I would never presume. But it does occur to me that the five of us, as the leaders of this fleet, probably don't take enough time to share our unique perspectives and challenges with one another—the only people around us who can truly appreciate our particular stresses and struggles." Turning to Chakotay she continued, "Thank you, Captain, for leading us to this moment. I am truly grateful for it."

Janeway turned to Farkas. Her eyes seemed to glisten in the light cast by the vast panoply of stars overhead.

"I suppose I am too," Farkas said.

Chakotay looked at each of them in turn. "The greatest value I have found in this life I chose has been sharing it with men and women like you," he said simply. "For me it will always be worth the risks."

11

Doctor Sal entered the medical bay and found a small crowd hovering outside a level-ten force field separating a single biobed at the rear from the rest of the room. Acting Captain Harry Kim, Doctor Sharak, Counselor Cambridge, Seven, and two nurses stood watching the holographic Doctor as he tended to the unconscious Ensign Gwyn. Her right arm looked like it had recently passed through a meat grinder. The rest of her body that was exposed, her shoulders and face, showed obvious evidence of radiation burns.

"What happened?" Sal demanded as she joined the group.

Seven quickly briefed her on the events at the asteroid and the strange, toxic sludge that had assaulted Gwyn. "I was able to get us back to the shuttle, and as soon as we were in transporter range I signaled *Voyager* for an emergency beam out."

"Do you know what the substance was?" Sal asked.

Seven shook her head. "I did not take the time for analysis. When Gwyn was transported back, the biofilters removed any traces of it from her body."

"I'll send a team out right away to retrieve the shuttle," Kim said. "We'll enforce standard biohazard protocols in handling the substance on Gwyn's EV suit."

"It changed when I fired on it," Seven said. "The molecular structure of the original substance will no longer be intact."

"Can we retrieve any of the original for study?" Sal asked.

"Is that really necessary?" Cambridge interjected. "Why court further disaster?"

"Because I need to understand how whatever it was did whatever it did to her," Sal replied.

"It ate through her suit very quickly," Seven noted. "This wasn't an instance of the ensign touching something she shouldn't have touched. Once it made contact with her, it moved up her arm. It continued to move until I stunned it, at which point it appeared to lose its liquid properties."

Sal moved past the group and addressed the Doctor. "Do you have a prognosis yet?"

The Doctor continued to work without looking up as he replied. "She suffered level-eight radiation exposure. She's going to require immediate antiproton therapy to reverse the damage. The burns and other cosmetic damage will be relatively easy to repair, but I won't begin full dermal regeneration until the radiation protocol is complete."

"Have you taken any samples of her blood?"

At this, the Doctor did look up. "The bio-scanner is taking constant readings. Is that not sufficient?"

"I really do need a few vials, if it's not too much trouble, Doctor," Sal said.

"Why?"

Sal paused to look at all those assembled. Her gaze settled on Captain Kim. "I need the room for a few minutes," she said. "Cambridge and Sharak can stay."

Kim seemed to do a quick analysis and nodded. "Okay. I want a full report whenever you have settled on a course of action and can update me on Gwyn's prognosis. Seven, with me."

Cambridge followed them as far as the door and after

a brief, private exchange with Seven returned to Sal's side. Another glance from Sal was enough to send the two nurses out of earshot.

"The floor is yours, El'nor," Cambridge said.

"Ensign Gwyn is the key to Nancy Conlon's cure," Sal said simply. "You can't initiate the antiproton therapy yet."

"If I don't initiate the therapy right away, it is very likely Ensign Gwyn will die from the radiation exposure."

"Then we have a problem," Sal said.

The Doctor moved through the emergency force field, a disquieting sight even though it was one of the advantages of his holographic form, and gestured for Sharak, Sal, and Cambridge to follow him into Sharak's private office.

Once they were all settled and the door shut, Sal continued. "Ensign Gwyn's body contains cells I require to create Conlon's gene-therapy regimen. I've already prepared the vectors. I just need the cells. Shortly before she went on that damned away mission, I gave Gwyn a hormonal booster to initiate the optimal cellular conditions. By now, they should be perfect, unless whatever did this to her, or your anti proton therapy, causes them to revert or did some other damage of which we are yet unaware."

The Doctor crossed his arms at his chest, his high, balding pate furrowing intensely. "What particular advantage do Ensign Gwyn's cells possess? There's nothing in her medical file that indicates any unusual biochemical processes."

Sal had been hoping this conversation might never be necessary. As it was, she still might be able to get through this without betraying the depth of the ethical dilemma in which she had mired them all.

"I'm not surprised you missed it, Doctor," Sal said amiably. "The technique I am utilizing has only been shown to be effective in a handful of cases, most recently by a specialist who is no longer working with the Federation Health Institute."

"My reading interests are wide and varied," the Doctor said.

"Doctor Dorothy Chen-Minatta?"

The doctor paused, as if thinking. He was actually probably searching his program's medical database. He seemed slightly alarmed when the proper file wasn't located. "I haven't heard of her work."

"Like I said, the applications aren't that wide," Sal said, knowing full well that they would be were it not for the politicians on Krios.

"Is there any danger in taking some of her blood?" Sharak asked. He seemed impatient for this conference to end, undoubtedly thinking only of Gwyn's immediate needs.

"Ensign Gwyn is well aware that I would be requiring more samples of her blood when she returned from her mission," Sal said. "I suggest you allow me to take them and then begin the antiproton therapy. The results won't matter if she dies now. Assuming she survives we can try again as soon as she's able."

"I will collect the samples for you," the Doctor said. Sharak followed him out. Sal was about to do the same when Cambridge cleared his throat.

"The most obvious genetic factor unique to Ensign Gwyn is her partial Kriosian heritage," he began thoughtfully. "And Doctor Dorothy Chen-Minatta's most recent medical miracle also involved a patient from Krios, as I recall."

"Very good, Counselor. You get an A-plus for reading comprehension and analysis," Sal said.

"Typically, Kriosians are unwilling to act as blood or

organ donors to any other species," Cambridge continued. "I'm curious to know how you convinced Ensign Gwyn to break with that tradition."

"I told her what was at stake, while protecting Conlon's privacy, of course. Turns out she's a little more open-minded than most of her people."

"And that hormonal therapy? That's unusual, isn't it?"

"We've already had this conversation, Counselor."

"Yes, pushing ethical boundaries, I remember."

"Then I should get back to work."

"Is our next conversation going to be about unintended consequences?" Cambridge asked.

Sal paused. "I sincerely hope not."

"But you can't be sure?"

"Not until I get a look at her blood."

Cambridge nodded slowly. "You'll let me know as soon as you do."

"I'm curious about your interest, beyond the health and welfare of Lieutenant Conlon."

"As a crew member on *Voyager*, Ensign Gwyn's psychological needs are also my responsibility."

"I'm sure she'll seek you out if any of the trauma she experienced on that asteroid becomes too much to bear," Sal suggested.

"One more thing you should know, Doctor."

"Really?"

"When this little working group was formed a few weeks ago, I took the time to read everything in our databases about you, Doctor Sharak, and the Doctor. It was my intention to make sure I was prepared to handle any internal conflicts that might arise among us. You spent some time on Krios many years ago, did you not?"

"I did. It's been so long I hardly remember."

"That's odd. I would imagine those ghosts might be more talkative than most, especially considering the fate of Kataly Norol. You don't fail often, Doctor, but when you do . . ."

"I do so spectacularly," Sal finished for him. "Do us both a favor, Counselor. Let the dead lie, and let's focus our efforts where they can still do some good."

"I will if you will," Cambridge replied.

Sal nodded and returned to the medical bay, where three vials of blood awaited her. Sharak and the Doctor stood just outside the force field. The area contained within had been dimmed, and soft golden waves already targeted Gwyn's body in short, computer-controlled bursts.

As Sal collected the vials she feared she was now carrying the fate of two women in her hands. One word repeated itself over and over in her head, more a prayer than a mantra.

Please, please, please, please, please . . .

DK-1116

Lieutenant Patel instinctively retreated from the door as she lifted her hands to her ears to dim the shrieking that now filled the chamber. Lieutenant Lasren did the same as they all moved back toward the center of the room, though he was careful to avoid the spot where the interface light was activated.

"What the hell is that?" Jepel shouted.

Patel shook her head. "Are you getting anything, Kenth?"

Lasren closed his eyes, obviously trying to concentrate, but after a moment gave up.

"Anger," he said. "Rage."

Patel was about to order everyone back to the relative safety of the cavern when the sound ceased as abruptly as it had begun. Everyone paused, waiting for another round. When it didn't come, she said, "So let's avoid that door for now."

"Works for me," Vincent agreed.

Slowly, Patel crossed to the second unopened door. Taking a deep breath, she lifted her hand to its center and introduced herself. "I am Lieutenant Devi Patel of the Federation *Starship* . . . ouch."

Just as before, her hand was pierced and after a few moments, the door vanished and a foul, dank stench wafted from the opening. Beyond it, a large space, more utilitarian than the sphere room, was filled with tall, internally illuminated white columns spaced every few meters. Checking her tricorder, she said, "The oxygen-nitrogen balance in this room is being adjusted. I think whatever controls this place is making it more comfortable for us."

"How thoughtful of it," Lasren said.

"Anything?" Patel asked.

The lieutenant shook his head. "Not here."

"Okay, let's take a look."

All four entered the room. It soon became clear that the columns were also demarcations, separating various equal-sized square spaces. Several contained tables of varying heights. All had been cleared of any tools, and the surfaces of the tables were coated with heavy layers of dust.

In the back of each space, a small alcove had been carved into the wall. None of them contained spheres, but each alcove appeared to be an appropriate size to house one.

"Thoughts, gentlemen?" Patel asked when they had regrouped in the central aisle that extended from the doorway to the far end of the room.

"It feels like a work space, several of them," Lasren said. "Whatever equipment was used is long gone, but I can imagine people standing in each of these squares doing something."

"Performing experiments?" Vincent ventured.

"Hard to tell," Jepel said.

Patel moved to examine the nearest column more closely with her tricorder, then wandered about for a bit, following the readings. "There's a ton of energy running through these columns, but I can't pinpoint a source."

Lasren stepped to her side and reached for the column. The moment his hand touched it, a face emerged from the bright white glow.

Both Patel and Lasren leaped back, startled, as Jepel and Vincent exclaimed in unison, "Whoa."

All shared the momentary adrenaline rush, quick breaths, and racing hearts, then Patel said, "Was that thing inside the pillar?"

"I actually don't think so," Lasren said. "If I'm wrong, you guys get ready to run," he added with a wink.

Vincent took a few steps closer to the door as Lasren again approached the column. The moment he touched it the face appeared, attached to a body. The face itself was no more or less startling than many aliens Lasren had encountered. It had an angular shape, fourteen deep-set sockets covered by solid black lenses. A central opening below them housed a set of sharp-looking pincers. Wide indentations rose from a point at the bottom running along the sides in a V shape. A long, wormlike body extended from the face, undulating back and forth. It was thick and ropy and covered with small, fine cilia. Four longer tendrils were attached to the body, ending in triangular-shaped "hands" that looked more like articulated spades.

"This is like a viewscreen," Lasren finally said.

"So he's not in there?" Patel asked.

"No. It's an image."

Several of the same alien glyphs Patel had seen in the blue pillar of light were scrolling above the top of the pillar, just above the alien's head.

"I wish we could translate those," Patel said.

"Looks like his name is Glorf Malorfovitch to me," Jepel said, clearly hoping to cut the tension a bit.

"Let's check the others," Patel suggested.

They did so, and by the time they were done, the physical parameters for sixty previously unidentified species had been added to their tricorders' databases, many of which were humanoid. Several, however, including one with bat-like wings and three heads, and a dozen that had between four and sixteen legs, were more exotic.

In each case, a series of alien characters unique to the species accompanied the image. When their cataloguing was complete, Patel wanted to return to the blue pillar and see if she could find the same series of characters in the light.

Lasren was anxious to see what was behind the other door that did not scream at them when they approached. Patel activated it, and when it vanished another metal hallway, similar to the one they had used to first access the sphere room, appeared.

"There's a staircase at the end of this one," Lasren reported.

"Up or down?" Patel asked.

"Way down," Lasren replied.

"Why don't you three check it out?"

"Are you sure you'll be okay here alone?" Jepel asked.

"I'm not planning on doing anything more dangerous

than playing with this interface, and it's going to take me a while," Patel replied. "Keep your comms open. Get back in twenty minutes."

"You're the boss," Lasren said with a smile Patel found somewhat patronizing.

Once she was alone, Patel stepped back into the blue pillar of light. She studied her tricorder display of the characters that designated the first alien they had found. She then searched the characters streaming all around her for a match. It took several minutes of patient study before the glyphs began to make a little sense to her.

"Glorf Malorfovitch," she said aloud when she finally identified the correct string. She took a moment to check her surroundings once again before reaching up and touching the matching characters.

The response was instantaneous. A single blue sphere was ejected from its alcove and came to rest directly before her.

The rush of accomplishment was almost overwhelming.

Putting her tricorder back in her pouch, Patel reached for the sphere. It was incredibly light, almost as if it had no substance at all, but with her fingers wrapped around it, it moved with her as she stepped out of the pillar.

Patel carried the sphere back into the room of columns. She entered the first work space to the left of Glorf's column and lifted the sphere into the alcove above the table.

Immediately, a new interface was activated before her eyes. It was a three-dimensional, holographic rendering of what appeared to be one of the biodomes. But unlike any of the domes they had scanned, this one was teeming with lifeforms, all of which looked like Glorf. The scene appeared to move in a time lapse, rushing forward and covering several days if not weeks in moments. Patel risked reaching her hand into the display and when she did so, it paused. She soon realized that her hand gestures within the display could alter her view, enlarging certain areas or collapsing others. It was incredibly intuitive, and she simply played with it for a bit, mastering the controls.

She eventually discovered that one of the controls, a small set of blue dots superimposed on the playback, was for volume. Once it was activated, she could hear the communications of the creatures depicted as long as she slowed the replay to something close to real time. The problem was that the universal translator couldn't parse the strange shushes, clicks, and whistles of Glorf's species. Deciding there would be time later to try and synch her translator with this system, she disengaged the audio.

Ultimately, she realized that the majority of the scenes were covering the same area of the biodome. Within a grove of tall blue trees, one of the metal constructs that had first caught Seven's eye was in the process of being built. *No, not built*, she realized. *Grown.*

Patel's breath caught in her chest as understanding struck her. The planet had once been some sort of working scientific lab. This room appeared to be its library. Given enough time, she could learn all the secrets of those who had once inhabited DK-1116.

Patel was anxious to examine some of the other spheres, but allowed Glorf's record to play through to completion. Eventually, the number of life-forms diminished until all that was left was the metallic sculpture they had cultivated in their biodome.

When the playback was done, Patel lifted the sphere from the workstation alcove and returned to the sphere room. She released it and it floated back to its waiting alcove.

Patel was about to step back into the blue pillar when she stopped dead in her tracks. The fourth door, the one that had screamed at them the first time they had approached it, had vanished.

Patel considered this new reality as calmly as she could, despite the fact that her heart was now pounding so intensely she could feel it in her toes. Perhaps the screaming had simply been some sort of alarm. Perhaps her ability to interface with the system had deactivated the security protocols.

She stepped closer to the open doorway. The area beyond it was dark. In the distance a few small patches of faint blue light were present. A sick sense held her at the entrance. Curious as she was, she had no desire to explore this area alone. Instead, she tapped her combadge.

"Patel to Lasren, do you copy?"

She waited through ten full seconds of silence before trying again.

"Patel to Lasren. Kenth, can you hear me?"

Nothing.

Patel stepped back from the doorway. As she did so, the clear sound of metal scratching against metal met her ears.

Something was down there. Something *angry*, if Lasren's empathic abilities were to be trusted. And there was no longer anything separating it from Patel.

Worse, she had lost contact with her team.

For the first time since this adventure had begun, Patel wished she weren't the senior officer present. She had no idea what to do next.

"I don't know, I think I might have been too hard on her," Jepel said as he, Lasren, and Vincent made their way down the hall toward the wide metal staircase at its end.

"I think she got the message," Vincent said. "She seemed genuinely sorry."

"She's putting herself under a lot of pressure," Lasren said. "You need to understand that it's different on *Voyager*. When you guys shipped out on *Vesta* and *Demeter*, you were part of their first crews. *Voyager* has history. Devi and I are part of it now, but the most important part, that's shared by a select group and it's hard to feel like you're not spending all your time playing catch-up."

"Do the senior officers make you feel that way?" Jepel asked.

"Not intentionally," Lasren replied. "And after the first couple of years on board, I think most of us felt like we'd earned our places. Except Devi. She was more or less replaced when Seven joined the crew."

"How come she didn't just request a transfer?" Vincent asked.

Lasren considered the question. "I'm not sure. If I had to guess, I'd say it was because Devi would have considered that a failure and she has a hard time accepting those."

They reached the steps, and Lasren noted that each tread was considerably longer than would be comfortable for a standard humanoid's stride. For each step that you took, another short step was required before you could descend again.

They continued down for about fifty meters before ending abruptly at another circular door.

"Any takers?" Lasren asked.

The naked fear in Vincent's eyes and clear trepidation in Jepel's settled the matter. Stepping forward, Lasren took a deep breath and placed his hand at the door's center. Nothing happened.

"Huh," Lasren said. "I was sure that would work."

"I'll try," Jepel said, stepping up. Again, the door remained stubbornly closed.

Vincent shrugged. "I guess it's my turn." Following the example of Lasren and Jepel, Vincent placed his hand near the center of the door.

"Ow!" he cried out. When he pulled his hand away, a ring of punctures was centered on his palm. "How much blood am I going to have to lose on this planet?"

"Why did it react to him and not to us?" Jepel asked.

Lasren considered the question. "Both Vincent and Patel are humans," he said. "Maybe that matters."

The door opened. As soon as it did, Vincent gasped.

Lasren and Jepel crowded in behind him. "By the Prophets," Jepel said softly.

"What the . . . ?" was all Vincent could manage.

Beyond the door lay a vast cavern, several kilometers deep and extending so far into the distance it was impossible to see the far end.

Staircases like the one on which they stood ran along the walls in every direction, with long catwalks between them and several large visible landings. The walls themselves were hard, brown stone studded throughout with long veins of silver and black metal.

This was the least interesting sight that met their eyes.

Continuing down the staircase directly in front of them and crossing several wide landings, they came to a vast, circular plate. In the center of it stood a wide metal box covered with bright white panels that reminded Lasren of the same technology as the columns they had seen in the upper chambers. Behind it, extending up from the base, was a series of mechanical arms. They were dozens of meters long, and each was articulated with at least two joints. At the end of each was a three-pronged extension, two that looked like pincers and the third that was a simple tube. At rest, the contraption looked like a gigantic spider resting on its back with its legs in the air.

Crisscrossing the vast open interior of the cavern were thick ropes of silver and black metal, as if the stone surrounding similar veins running through the walls had been chipped away, leaving only the ore. The twisted deposits were similar to the constructs found on the surface with two notable exceptions. First, all of the long, dense veins were illuminated from within, a bright white light source dazzling the silver and only slightly muted by the interwoven blackness of the metal. The light burned from the center and played in dazzling patterns all over the cavern walls. Second, the veins were in constant motion, gyrating and undulating like massive living snakes.

Finally Lasren thought to remove his tricorder and begin to scan. The first thing he noted was the presence of vast quantities of the *Sevenofninonium*. "Well that's one mystery solved," he said softly.

Vincent and Jepel had also conquered their awe and were moving around the center platform taking their own readings.

"Um . . . guys," Vincent said.

Lasren turned toward Vincent and saw several meters beyond him, a gigantic waterfall of sorts. Flowing over a tall, smooth stone was a viscous black liquid. Several thin cords hung above it, each one extending from one of the moving veins above. Every so often, a single drop of the black liquid fell from above and was added to the fall. It was impossible to see how far down the fall extended. Past a few hundred meters, even the light from the undulating metal did not illuminate the bottom of the cavern.

"Any idea what that is?" Lasren asked.

"Nope. The tricorder can't even figure out its molecular structure," Vincent replied. "Should I try to take a sample?"

"Let's not touch anything just yet," Lasren suggested. "Why don't we head back? It's going to take more people than us to unravel all of this. We should signal for one of the engineering teams to join us as soon as possible."

"Do you think Devi will agree to that?" Jepel asked.

Lasren shrugged. "Our rotation is only five days. We could spend ten times that down here and not make a dent. I think we can convince her to share."

"One second," Jepel said. "What is that?" he asked, pointing to another circular platform high overhead and a good half a kilometer in the distance.

Its construction was similar to the platform on which they stood, but without the giant spider. Instead, a single large white sphere rested in its center with dozens of white pipes extending from its center and terminating all throughout the cavern at different points. There were also a dozen or so pipes of dull gray, perhaps no longer functioning.

"I have no idea," Lasren said. "But there's plenty of time to figure it out. Let's get back to Devi before she starts to worry."

Nods from Jepel and Vincent settled the matter. Together they retreated to the doorway and began their ascent.

VOYAGER

Icheb didn't even remember how he had bid farewell for the evening to Phinn. Something about an early start in the morning. It had been lame and awkward. Phinn's face, even in the dimness, had betrayed his confusion. But Icheb couldn't think about that right now. He had a bigger problem. As soon as he'd returned to the ship, he'd tried to contact the Doctor and been told he was tending to a patient aboard *Voyager*. Icheb had considered waiting until morning, but with the Doctor so near, his anxiety got the better of him.

When he entered sickbay, the lights were low. At the far end of the bay he saw a patient resting on a biobed behind a force field. Curious, he stepped closer and recognized Ensign Gwyn.

"May I help you, Ensign Icheb?" the warm, melodious voice of Doctor Sharak asked.

Icheb turned. "I was looking for the Doctor, the EMH. I was told he was here."

"Of course," Sharak said, gesturing toward his office.

Inside, the Doctor sat at Sharak's desk studying the screen before him intently.

"Excuse me, Doctor."

The Doctor looked up. "Icheb, are you okay?"

"I am," Icheb said. "I had . . . that is to say . . . I have a personal matter I need to discuss with you."

"Oh," the Doctor said, glancing toward Sharak, who hovered just behind Icheb.

Icheb turned to see Sharak nod sagely before returning to his duties in the main bay.

"I did not mean to insult Doctor Sharak," Icheb said as soon as he and the Doctor were alone.

"I don't think you did. Have you come to me with a medical question?" the Doctor asked kindly.

"I don't know," Icheb replied honestly. "Would you prefer I discuss this with Doctor Sharak?"

"Sharak is an excellent physician, and as a member of *Voyager*'s crew, your health needs fall within his purview. But I am your friend, and will be happy to address any concerns you might have in that capacity."

Icheb nodded. "Thank you."

The Doctor perched himself on the front of Sharak's desk and said, "Take a seat."

Icheb felt his face growing warm. He looked at the empty chairs situated before the desk and shook his head. "I . . . that is . . ."

The Doctor leaned forward, his concern obvious. "What's wrong, Icheb?"

"I experienced something I do not understand tonight. I'm afraid it might be evidence of a problem."

"That sounds serious," the Doctor said.

"I have never," Icheb began, "I mean, there have been very few times in my life when I have interacted with others in an intimate way."

Some of the Doctor's initial concern seemed to give way to relief. "That can be a very intense experience. Do you have questions?"

"No," Icheb assured him. "I am well aware of the particulars of sexual intimacy."

The Doctor nodded. "Of course."

"It's just that, when intimate contact was initiated, I did not feel what I believe it is normal to feel under those circumstances."

The Doctor looked away briefly, clearly processing this information. When he turned back to face Icheb, he said, "I do not wish to pry, Ensign, but can you be more specific as to the nature of the contact and your expectations?"

"It was just a kiss," Icheb said. "It surprised me, but it

was not unwelcome. In fact, it was a relief. Many concerns and questions I'd had up to that moment were answered."

The Doctor smiled. "That sounds about right."

"But it wasn't. I wanted to respond. I knew in my mind that this was a good thing. But I didn't *feel* anything."

"What did you expect to feel?"

"Connection . . . excitement . . ." Icheb ventured.

The Doctor nodded for him to continue.

"My body seemed to grow cold, to shut down," Icheb said haltingly. "It was the opposite of what I knew I should be feeling."

"Perhaps, as much as you might have wanted the contact, you have certain reservations of which your body was making you aware."

Icheb shook his head. "I am intensely attracted in every way imaginable to Phinn."

"Lieutenant Bryce?"

"Yes. We have spent a great deal of time together since I joined the fleet. I consider him a good friend, and he made it clear to me tonight that he would like our rela tionship to proceed beyond that. I want that too. But I don't understand my physical response. Why didn't I feel anything?"

The Doctor rose and moved closer to Icheb. "There could be many reasons." He hesitated for a moment, then said, "I hope you will not take this question the wrong way, but is this the first time you have engaged in intimate contact with another man?"

"Yes. Does that matter?"

"Not unless there is any hesitation on your part to en gage in a same-sex relationship."

Icheb shook his head. "It's not something I've thought

about in those terms. I've always believed that attraction was attraction. I would have been open to finding a partner of either gender. Since I've known Phinn, however, it's become clear to me that *he* is my preference."

"Okay. Then, I assume you have come to me to rule out any physical disorders that might account for what you experienced?"

Icheb nodded. "Yes."

The Doctor smiled reassuringly. "That should be very simple. We'll perform a quick physical and a few tests and if, as I assume they will, they show no causes for concern, I will suggest that you discuss this further with Counselor Cambridge."

Icheb shook his head. "I don't believe I am suffering from a psychological disorder."

"I don't think you are either, Icheb. But new experiences can be difficult to process. If the issue is not physical, the counselor is the best person qualified to address any underlying psychological challenges."

Icheb nodded. "I have never discussed anything with him. But I know Seven regards him highly."

"I would prefer you not share this with him, but so do I," the Doctor admitted. "He can be maddening, and I find his overall approach a little brusque. But he is an excellent counselor. I would not suggest you speak to him otherwise."

"Okay."

"But, first things first. Do you have any objections to allowing Doctor Sharak to perform the necessary tests?"

"No," Icheb said. "Seven also holds him in the highest esteem."

"With good reason. Shall we begin?"

Icheb felt something that had been coiled tightly around his chest release just a bit. "Yes, please."

DK-1116

Shortly after Tom Paris's head had hit the pillow attached to his sleeping bag, he had begun to snore softly. B'Elanna had found sleep more elusive. At first, she had chalked it up to a combination of Miral's unexpected revelation, and the ambient noise from the party still in progress by the lake. But within a few hours the noise outside had died down.

Finally, sick of tossing and turning, Torres decided a little air might clear her head. Stepping outside the tent, she realized that the vast majority of officers who had been there earlier had gone back to their respective vessels for the night. She expected this pattern to repeat itself every night of the fleet's stay in orbit.

She considered walking toward the trees, but decided to wait to share those explorations with Miral in the morning. Instead, she directed her steps toward the shoreline. As the water's edge came into view, she immediately understood the odd quiet of those still present that were now assembled in small groups along the beach staring at the lake. Over the water, gorgeous lights—green, purples, and blues—cascaded in a spectacle of vibrant beauty that was truly stunning.

"Oh, my," she said softly.

Natural phenomena like this one weren't all that rare, but that didn't make them any less worthy of wonder and awe. Not unlike the aurora borealis on Earth, the rich, pulsing colors were the simple result of the interplay between electrically charged particles released by the binaries hitting the gasses present in the atmosphere. She did think it was odd, however, that the particles weren't blocked by the bio-dome's energy field. Of course, for all she knew, the charged particles were part of the atmosphere being held within and this was just an unusual side effect.

Something about this was unsettling, but she wasn't able to put her finger on it right away. Instead, she wrestled with the choice of whether or not to wake Tom and Miral. She knew that when they heard about it in the morning, they would both be sorry to have missed the sight.

"It's weird, isn't it, Commander?" a soft voice said behind her.

Turning, she saw Lieutenant Bryce gazing out at the same thing that had transfixed her.

"What are you still doing here, Lieutenant?"

Bryce shrugged. "Who knows when any of us will have a chance to walk by a lake again."

Torres nodded, wondering why the garrulous Bryce seemed so somber. Of course, it had been a long day for both of them.

"Why do you think it's weird?" Torres asked, looking back to the unusual lights in the sky.

"I could understand the presence of charged particles around some of the constructs. They're primarily metal. But all of the water sources in the biodomes are pure," Bryce replied.

This was news to Torres. "They are?"

Bryce nodded. "I don't know that any of the teams have been focusing on the water sources, but in looking at the energy fields and searching for the conductive pathways, we had to rule out the water. Every sample that has been taken has shown the same property. It is absolutely pure and therefore, not conductive."

"No standing water is that pure," Torres said. "Particles from the surrounding lake bed or ground would provide for at least minimal impurities."

"Not here," Bryce said. "I haven't analyzed the ground at this site, but in our biodome, the area around the water was silica based. It's like it was designed to keep the water sources pure."

"What would be the purpose of that?" Torres wondered aloud.

Bryce shrugged. "Who knows? It might not have been intentional."

"But what if it was?"

"Yeah," Bryce said, looking back to the sky. "Either way, it doesn't matter now. There's no way that lake is a pure water source after a couple hundred of us swam in it today. And beautiful as that sky is, I don't like it."

Torres didn't either.

12

The first sensation of which Ensign Aytar Gwyn was aware upon waking was hunger. This was unusual. But everything was unusual.

This wasn't her bed. The lights around her were dim, so it was difficult to determine where she was. She tried to turn on her side, and immediately her right arm protested, sending shocks of icy pain shooting up her arm, side, and neck.

That sparked a memory: her right arm and excruciating pain. An instinct to flee took hold of her at once and despite the pain, she forced herself to a sitting position. Tightness across her chest and a sense of something ripping were her reward for the abrupt motion.

A man approached her. *An alien.* His face was dark brown and spotted. His hairless scalp had a ridge in its center, leading down to a wide nose. His eyes were incredibly kind. She focused her attention on them.

So lonely, she thought at once. *He is lost here, but seeks understanding. He misses the stars of his home. He does not believe he will ever see them again.*

She wanted to comfort him. No, she *needed* to comfort him. She would not be whole until his suffering had ended. What's more, she knew she could make it end. For him she could become the thing that filled his emptiness and made him whole at the same time.

But she was so hungry. Her stomach rumbled greedily. The absence at the center of her being was agony. Food would help temporarily. But not forever.

She had become a creature defined by need.

"Ensign?" The alien with the kind eyes spoke to her.

Her mouth was a desert. She swallowed, trying to force moisture into barrenness.

"Where am I?" she asked.

"You are in sickbay, Ensign. You were attacked on your last away mission. We have treated most of your injuries and radiation exposure, but you still need to heal. You require rest."

"Hungry," she said.

"It is too soon for food. I can get some water for you, but you must lie down."

She obeyed without question.

She knew him. He was familiar to her. But she had never seen him as clearly as she did now. All of the new information flooding her senses replaced her previous knowledge, pushing it beyond her grasp.

When he returned he gently lifted her head and helped her sip from a glass of water.

"Better?" he asked so kindly.

She reached for his hand. "Who are you?"

He smiled, confused. He was studying her as much as caring for her. He had a new concern. He was worried about her.

"I am Doctor Sharak. Do you know who you are?"

"I am Aytar Gwyn," she replied.

"That's right. Do you know where you are?"

She looked around before pulling the answer from his mind. As soon as she found it there, she realized she had known, but been unable to find the answer in the wilds of her new mind.

"Sickbay. *Voyager*."

His relief became hers.

"That's right. Very good."

He started to turn away. She reached for his hand.

"Don't go," she said. "I am for you, Doctor Sharak."

He patted her hand as he would that of a child. This was not what she wanted, but what she wanted did not matter. All that mattered was what he wanted.

"I am here for you as well, Ensign. Just rest. You are going to feel better soon."

Until the hunger was filled, there would be no better. She knew that. She also knew he did not understand.

He would. In time, she would help him understand.

A soft hiss at her neck and some of the pain in her arm and chest diminished. A wave of weariness washed over her. She did not wish to leave him, but she had no choice.

All she could see in her mind's eye was his face drifting farther and farther away from her. She reached for him. Did he sense it? He turned back, touching her forehead with his warm hand.

He did.

He would be hers.

She would be his.

The hunger would end.

DK-1116

Captain Farkas had long since returned to *Vesta*. O'Donnell and Glenn had each pitched tents around their makeshift campsite and bid the admiral good-night. Chakotay had busied himself setting up the tent in which he and Kathryn would sleep beside O'Donnell's. Admiral Janeway could hear Commander O'Donnell speaking softly to his XO, reporting some of the day's finds and discussing personnel issues that had come up on *Demeter* in his absence.

Despite her weariness, Janeway felt certain that sleep was not going to come easy to her tonight. When she had first imagined this time, she had been warmed by the thought of sharing several uninterrupted days and nights with Chakotay. Now she wondered if she might not prefer a little solitude.

Chakotay placed a gentle hand on her shoulder. "Ready for bed?"

She turned her head to look up at him. His face was as it had ever been: a perfect balance of care-worn determination and mischievous idealism. "I don't think so."

"I was hoping you'd say that," he said with a soft smile. "Would you care to take a walk?"

Janeway nodded as he helped her rise from her chair. He carried a soft bag over his shoulder as they made their way down the hill and back toward the zombie trees.

"It seems you have a destination in mind," Janeway observed.

"I do."

They continued on for a bit in companionable silence. Roughly a hundred meters into the "forest" they came upon a pool of water, too small for a lake, but much larger than a pond.

Chakotay knelt beside the water, testing it with his hand. A wide smile crossed his lips. "I remember well your fondness for baths. Will this do?"

Despite the misgivings that had complicated her feelings since she arrived, she had to admit that the thought of a midnight swim in calm, warm water sounded like heaven.

Chakotay had thought ahead. He removed large towels from his bag and laid them out in preparation for their return to the shore. In pleasant silence they helped each other out of their uniforms and entered the pool together.

For a time, they simply swam about. The pool was probably a dozen meters deep at its center, but near the shore, they could easily stand submerged up to their necks.

Eventually he reached his hands out to her and she allowed him to envelop her in an embrace. He kissed her tenderly and, for a time, all thoughts beyond the comfort and pleasure they gave each other were forgotten.

Finally, they emerged from the pool, wrapping themselves in the towels and relaxing in the breeze.

When they had settled themselves on the ground, their feet intertwined, Chakotay said, "I hoped coming here would grant you a little peace. Was I wrong?"

"No," she said. "It's wonderful."

"Then why aren't you happy?"

"I am."

His head cocked to the side. He knew her better than that.

Janeway considered her next words carefully. After a moment she said, "Do you think we're wasting our time?"

Chakotay's brow furrowed, puzzled. "You mean taking so many days for shore leave?"

She shook her head. "Not here. I mean us. Are we just wasting our time together?"

"I'm not," he replied. "But I can't speak for you."

She reached her hands out and took his. "We have two more years out here. Two more years of exploring and discovering . . ."

"And occasionally fighting for our lives," he finished for her.

"If history is any guide," she agreed. "You said once that this was all you needed. This is home. Do you still feel that way?"

"I do."

"But in all the time we've had since we found each other again, we haven't really talked about the future beyond those two years."

"Do we need to?"

Janeway shuddered. "I think maybe I do."

"Okay. Where do you want to go when this mission is done? Are you ready to retire? The work we do will never be complete, but are you starting to feel that it's time to allow others to carry these burdens?"

She released his hands and placed hers under her chin, elbows on her knees for support. "I've never imagined this coming to an end. I've never wanted to."

Chakotay nodded. "So when we're done here, we take whatever Command offers next."

"What if they want to separate us?"

"That's not going to work for me."

Janeway smiled. It was a simple statement of fact.

"I turned my back on Starfleet a long time ago," he continued. "You brought me back, and since then I've gone where they asked, when they asked, and done my best to keep those I've led alive. But the days of either of us going where we're told if it can't accommodate our relationship are past, at least for me."

"Starfleet might be more willing to acknowledge that if we did, officially, I mean," Janeway said.

Chakotay's eyes grew wide. "Why, Admiral Janeway, is that a proposal?"

Twice in her life, Janeway had been engaged. Neither

one had ended in marriage. Both times she had believed they were forever. Both times, fate had intervened and taken that away from her. Was it possible that her fear now had nothing to do with Chakotay? Was she simply afraid to believe again?

"It's an observation," she finally replied.

To her surprise, he didn't seem wounded.

"If marriage is what you want, Kathryn, then we will marry. As far as I'm concerned, the only thing we haven't done is legalize our union. But the absence of that doesn't change anything for me. To be honest, I haven't been sure that you even wanted to marry."

"You haven't?" she said in genuine surprise.

"If I had any doubts, one look at your face when you thought I was offering you a ring took care of that."

She felt her cheeks warming. *Of course he had noticed.* "I was just taken off guard by the timing," she offered.

"No, you weren't."

"All right, I wasn't. I was momentarily terrified. But not because I don't want to be with you."

"You're content with where we are now," he said. "So am I. Maybe we don't have to know anything else right now."

"I am content. But I'm also afraid. I'm not sure I trust this. At times like this everything seems so clear. But then something always seems to come between us."

"That's not going to change because we get married," he said. "You and I have been together too long and seen too much to ever lie to each other about that. Set aside the reality that every long-term relationship that has ever been is subject to disagreements, tragedies, and unforeseeable events that can do great damage to its foundation. Forget the fact that all relationships live and die not by any single choice but by the countless daily choices they contain, the myriad moments where kindness, patience, and understanding prevail over our most base drives of selfishness and self-preservation. The deepest personal betrayals bear within them the seeds of grace and forgiveness. I don't care if we ever marry. For me, nothing can change the fact that your happiness is indistinguishable from mine."

Staring into his dark eyes, she felt the doubts she had nurtured slipping away on a single breath. She reached out to him again, pulling him toward her. Their bodies met, two galaxies subject to the inexorable outward pull of the universe, both determined to remain connected, if only by a bridge of stars.

Lieutenant Devi Patel took a deep breath. She stepped back slowly from the door, wishing she knew how to close it. Every other door they had managed to open remained that way. Perhaps leaving the sphere chamber the way they had come would seal all of them. But she couldn't attempt this without the rest of her team. Much as she wanted to explore more of the spheres, she also couldn't do that as long as this eerie chamber was open and whatever waited in the darkness might be on its way out right now ready to rip her arms from their sockets and beat her to death with them.

Get a hold of yourself. You're a Starfleet officer. You've spent your entire adult life preparing for this moment. Whatever is back there has been there for thousands of years. Just because it sounds scary doesn't mean it's dangerous.

Reasoning things out helped a little. Tempted as she was to flee down the same hallway Lasren and the others had taken, she knew that she would lose whatever remaining shreds of credibility she had with them if she showed her fear. Also, the thing in the dark might follow and she would have led it to three other potential victims.

Just take it slow, she decided. Every instinct she possessed practically screamed otherwise, but she refused to allow fear to start running this show.

She prepared carefully. First, she lit the beacon around her wrist. In the same hand, she held her tricorder. It hadn't done a great job thus far interpreting the data of this strange architecture, but she had to try to collect whatever she could. In her other hand, she held her phaser, set to kill. Nothing could possibly be alive back there, but the feel of her hand around the grip was reassuring.

Ready as she would ever be, she stepped into the new space. Her beacon illuminated the walls, which appeared to be simple brown stone. Here, alone, the metallic ore that had led them to the cavern was absent.

The shriek of metal against metal met her ears again. It wasn't as piercing as the alarm that had sounded when they first tried the door, but it remained unsettling. Friction suggested movement. Lasren's empathic abilities had sensed disorganized life and rage. She tried not to imagine what those two things might look like conjoined.

Roughly twenty meters in, she discovered the source of the strange blue light. All along the walls, more blue spheres were embedded within alcoves above circular openings. They were dimmer than their counterparts in the main room. Many glowed with a barely perceptible grayish hue. She was struck by the random notion that compared to the data spheres, these seemed to be dying.

The first opening wasn't covered by a door. Instead, a faint trembling of the light indicated a force field. Focusing

her beacon into the space beyond, she saw a small form resting on the floor of the otherwise empty cell. It was vaguely
spherical, less than a meter in diameter, and mostly metal, a
strange hybrid of the silver and black they had found everywhere. Draped all around the object were long, rusty brown
tentacles. They seemed to extend from within the metal but
they appeared to be organic. *Whatever this thing is, it's not
alive.* She comforted herself with this thought until the moment the light from her beacon found a tentacle that extended out from the metal all the way to the far wall of the
cell. It appeared to be taut. As she played her light over it,
the tentacle snapped toward her, hitting the force field with
a slap of electric energy.

She stumbled back, her heart racing.

"It can't hurt you from in there," she said aloud. She
didn't honestly believe that, but she sure as hell hoped it
was true.

Lifting her hand, she used the beacon to illuminate as
much of the rest of the corridor of cells as she could. Shadows remained in the far distance, but between her and them
were several more cells—and the metal screeching didn't
sound that far off as it occasionally bounced off the walls
toward her.

Emboldened, she continued forward. Each cell contained a variation on the same theme as the first; chunks
of metal in varying shapes, all with visible organic components. By far the most disturbing was one that appeared at
first to be a large, relatively flat metal plane, smooth except
for every few meters where soft tissue resembling lips pro-
truded. They opened and closed as if trying to breathe or
gasp, or suck or wail. A few of the mouth-like openings
even contained small metallic teeth.

As she passed and noted the contents of each cell, her terror was transmuted into horrified fascination. *What was this place?* If the spheres and workstations were a library of data, this felt more like a zoo.

One potential answer to her question lay near the end of the cavern in a cell whose sphere glowed more intensely than the others.

Patel steeled herself as she stepped toward the force field. Here, the screeching sound reached a pitch almost as deafening as the "screams" that had sounded the first time Lasren had approached the door to this chamber of horrors. There was no doubt in her mind that this was the source of the sound.

The cell was darker than the others. The object within had no reflective surfaces. It was not solid metal. At first it looked like a blob of black viscous liquid a little more than two meters long end to end, lying in the center of the cell. Where the other figures had small features that moved, this one was in constant motion. It writhed in apparent agony as distinct shapes undulated into being briefly, only to lose cohesion and dissolve back into an unformed mass.

Patel watched the spectacle, a sick pit growing in her stomach as some of the emerging shapes became more coherent: an arm, a leg, a torso. Her mind rejected what she was seeing. It was impossible. *You are simply trying to make sense of this*, a calm, rational voice insisted. But that explanation lost credibility when one end of the black mass seemed to push itself up into being, a head above a torso and two arms emerging clearly. As soon as the head turned to face her, shrieks of unutterable pain reverberating all around her, Patel glimpsed the features of the face. It was like looking into a mirror. The shape of the face was hers. Morbid fascination held her there for a few seconds as the shape of the face distorted and then settled again into something recognizable as herself.

The things in the other cells, those were finished works. This thing was in the process of becoming, and whatever else it was, part of it was *her*.

Patel retreated a few steps, trying desperately to calm herself. As she did so, the form seemed to briefly solidify. She stared at a grotesque mirror image, where her flesh was black fluid and her uniform was twisted metal.

Its lips moved, not simply opening in a cry, but with greater precision, although the noise was still a shriek. From above, however—*the sphere*, Patel quickly realized—a more familiar sound reverberated.

"Interlocutor complete. Is this interface acceptable?"

No, Patel wanted to scream. If watching the thing taking shape had been alarming, hearing it speak to her was a vision that was going to populate her nightmares for years to come.

The creature repeated the question. *"Is this interface acceptable?"*

"I understand you, if that's what you're asking," Patel replied.

"Interface established."

There were a million questions running through Patel's mind, but she found it difficult to settle on just one. The obvious was the first she uttered. "What are you?" she asked.

"Interface for Species 196.2," the thing replied.

Suddenly Patel was struck by a thought. Looking at her punctured palm, she asked, "Did you create yourself using my blood?"

"Biological sampling is mandatory for all species."

That sounded like a *yes*.

"What is the purpose of the creation of this interface?"

"Interface is required for proper data retrieval and classification. Species 196.2 has been detected in twelve experimental stations. Environmental modifications for all inhabited stations complete."

"You altered the atmosphere within the biodomes to accommodate us?"

"Environmental modifications for all inhabited stations complete."

Whatever this thing was, there were obviously limits to its linguistic parameters.

"What is this place?" Patel asked.

"Sector four data storage and retrieval."

"No, not this room, this planet," Patel said, growing impatient.

"Imprecise query."

"Okay," Patel said, not really understanding why this was a hard question. She tried another tack. "Are you responsible for the creation and maintenance of the environmental systems operating in sector four?"

"Interlocutor interface required for data storage and retrieval."

That sounded like a *no*.

"Who created this system?"

"Species 001."

"Does Species 001 have a name?"

A high-pitched tone followed by several clicks and a wheeze was the answer to this question. Clearly whatever the name of Species 001 was, there wasn't a word for it in Patel's language.

"Are any representatives of Species 001 present now?"

"Negative."

"For what purpose did Species 001 create the system?"

"Evaluation and propagation of the Edrehmaia."

Edrehmaia? That wasn't a word this thing could have pulled from whatever limited exposure it had to Patel's knowledge.

"What is the Edrehmaia?"

"Object of inquiry."

This was as frustrating as it was illuminating. "What is the current status of the operating system?"

"Containment system modifications detected. These modifications will result in system termination and closure."

That didn't sound good. In fact, that sounded like something Patel's commanding officers needed to know immediately.

"How long until system closure is complete?"

"At current penetration rates, system will be terminated in eleven hours, sixteen minutes, nine seconds."

"Can you reverse the modifications?"

"Negative."

"What happens when the system termination and closure is complete?"

"Insufficient data."

"It's your system. You don't know?"

"Containment created to delay system termination in order to determine intent of Edrehmaia. Insufficient data present to determine intent."

Pieces of this puzzle were starting to fall into place in Patel's mind.

"You are saying that Species 001 came here and created this system in order to evaluate the intention of the Edrehmaia and to propagate it if possible?"

"Affirmative."

"But they never gathered enough data to determine intent or to re-create the Edrehmaia?"

"Affirmative."

"And the actions of Species 196.2 have broken system containment?"

"Affirmative."

"Will this containment failure and system closure effect the data stored here?"

"Do you wish to secure sector four data storage?"

"Absolutely. Yes," Patel replied automatically.

"Security protocol enabled."

"Good. Thank you," Patel said.

There were so many more questions to be asked. But before she could do so, the form began to undulate again, as if it was losing cohesion.

"Wait, where are you going?"

"All available power required for security maintenance. Interface system will be terminated."

"No," Patel cried out. "Wait, please."

The light above the alcove flickered and dimmed. Her doppelganger melted to the floor, where it remained, a torso of metal, melted arms, and a face of black goo tipped forward as if it had suddenly decided to take a nap.

Considering the occupants of the other cells, it occurred to Patel that this interface would continue to exist, probably in this form, for as long as the sector for data retrieval and storage system remained intact. It was as comforting as it was horrifying. Lasren had sensed "life" and "anger" from the inhabitants of these cells. Given how long some of them had been here, she understood the anger. The *life* was harder to quantify but equally unmistakable.

Patel bolted back down the corridor, running headlong into a solid form that grabbed her firmly.

"Devi?"

The arms that held her were Lasren's. Behind him, Vincent and Jepel stared at her in wide-eyed alarm.

"Go," was all she could manage.

"Devi, calm down," Lasren pleaded. He was just this side of trying to shake some sense into her. It was much too late for that. Patel pushed him forward, hurrying the team back down the corridor.

When they reached the sphere room again, Devi took a second to orient herself. Three of the four doors that accessed the sphere room were still open. One of them was the entrance to the cavern of horrors she had just escaped. The other two led to the staircase Lasren had just descended and the column room.

The door directly across from her, however—the door that led out of the chamber and back to the cavern from which they could request emergency transport and inform the fleet of all she had just learned—had closed while she was otherwise engaged by the interface that seemed to share her DNA.

Patel and her team were trapped.

VOYAGER

Acting Captain Harry Kim stared at the bridge's main viewscreen trying desperately to process the information his eyes and the ship's scanners were providing. The screen was set at its highest magnification. Centered on it was the *Van Cise*, the shuttle Gwyn and Seven had taken on their ill-fated journey to collect rock samples from the B star's asteroid belt.

Only it wasn't really a shuttle anymore.

Somehow in the five hours since Seven and Gwyn had requested emergency transport and left the shuttle at station keeping, the black, viscous substance that had attacked Gwyn had recovered from the blast of Seven's phaser and begun to consume the shuttle.

The bow, the point farthest from the airlock in which Gwyn's suit and the unknown matter had been sealed, was the only part of the shuttle that was still visibly intact. How long that would remain true was anyone's guess, but likely not long.

The rest of the ship no longer held its former shape. Instead, an area roughly the size of the shuttle writhed and gyrated as the alien substance seemed to remake every section of the ship it touched. Long, whiplike tentacles shot forth randomly, striking out wildly. Despite its pitch-black coloring, the light of the binaries illuminated the spectacle, giving the matter a silver-blue tint.

"Can anybody tell me what that is or what it's doing, apart from the obvious?" Kim asked.

Waters was the first to offer a response from ops. "It's eating the ship, sir."

Kim turned on her. "It's alive?"

Waters studied her display for a few more seconds. "At this distance, our sensor readings are inconclusive, but they suggest organic and inorganic properties."

"Making it what?" Kim asked.

"Living technology," Waters ventured.

"How do you figure that?"

"The matter that was once the shuttle is being consumed,

but as that happens, it is being transformed. It is being utilized as this thing remakes it into something else. Whatever the alien matter once was, it is no longer a discrete entity. What we are seeing is a new thing, a combination of the alien substance and our technology."

Kim shook his head. "What the hell could do that?"

Waters shrugged. "To answer that, we need to get closer."

The part of Kim that lived for a new scientific mystery agreed. The part of him that had command of *Voyager* protested vehemently.

"How close can we safely get?" Kim asked.

"The range of those tentacles is almost half a kilometer and growing longer every second. By the time we could break orbit and position ourselves to take better scans, they might be able to reach *Voyager*'s hull. That is assuming they continue to grow at a constant rate."

"It's also closing on our position, Captain," Aubrey advised from tactical. "It is moving toward us at a speed close to one-quarter impulse."

"Why would it do that?" Gleez asked from the helm.

"It's had a taste of our tech and perhaps it senses that another meal is within range," Kim replied. "Can we break orbit and get just a little closer?" he asked.

"Aye, sir," Waters said, "but you should be advised that Patel's away team is now half an hour overdue for their check-in, and I've lost my lock on their life signs."

"When did that happen?"

"Three minutes ago, sir."

So breaking orbit was out of the question.

Kim hated to give the order he was about to give. But under the circumstances, it was the right one. There was no way to perfectly categorize the spectacle they were witnessing, and the sensor data they had received thus far might yield more information on closer study than was possible at this moment. Should his superior officers take issue with the order, it was likely that there was more of the original substance on the asteroid where Seven and Gwyn had landed. A safer means of sampling and studying it might yet be devised. But for now, his choices were limited to one.

"Ensign Gleez, adjust our orbit to provide the widest possible angle of visibility for our targeting sensors. Lieutenant Aubrey, assuming the entity out there doesn't alter course or speed, the moment it is within weapons' range, target it and vaporize it. I want it reduced to its subatomic essence. I don't want a stray atom of that matter to remain. Are we clear?"

"Perfectly, sir," Aubrey replied.

"In the meantime, Waters, I need you to locate our lost away team."

"Already on it, sir," Waters replied. "It's not like they could have gone far."

"You have no idea how far they might have gone," Kim snapped. "What we have already seen of this planet presents us with technological mysteries that we are nowhere near understanding, let along mastering. Assume nothing. Imagine the most ridiculous possibilities and eliminate each of them before you report any conclusions to me. Understood?"

Waters nodded, appropriately chagrined. "Aye, Captain."

"Astrometrics to the bridge," Seven's voice rang out clearly over the comm.

"What is it, Seven?" Kim asked.

"Please report here immediately."

Kim fought briefly for the strength to be courteous. When he had won that battle he replied, "We've got our hands full up here, Seven. Can it wait?"

"If it could, I would have sent you a report, Captain. As I haven't, you should assume that it cannot."

This was the job Kim wanted. Nothing in his training or eleven years of personal observation had ever suggested to Kim that it would be easy. Still, it was hard to believe that what was supposed to be a simple and restorative exploratory mission was so quickly devolving into chaos.

"Stand by, Seven," Kim ordered. "Aubrey, estimate to weapons' lock?"

"Twenty minutes, sir."

Kim could be back by then. He hoped.

"Aubrey, maintain your station, but for the next few minutes, the bridge is yours."

"Aye, Captain," the tactical officer acknowledged.

Kim entered the astrometrics lab expecting to see the program running its ten thousandth simulation. Instead, the program appeared to be frozen. Seven stood at the data console simply observing the image before her. Stepping toward the interface station, he studied the image on the massive screen and found it eerily similar to the existing images of the system he'd been looking at off and on all day.

"I could have sworn I ordered you to get some sleep," Kim noted.

"I simply stopped by to check the simulation's progress on the way to my quarters," Seven said. "To my surprise, it has yielded an unexpected result."

Seven ordered the computer to rerun its last simulation and yawned as the program loaded. Seconds later, Kim was staring at a system with a single star orbited by six planets.

As he watched, a large terrestrial body came within range of the system. It was too big to be a comet or asteroid. Its dimensions placed it closer to the category of rogue planetoid. Moments later, another body entered the system, apparently guided by the planetoid: a small star.

His jaw slack, Kim watched as the two bodies moved through the system, their presence causing catastrophic destruction of every planet present. Eventually both bodies were caught in the gravity of the star and the planetoid was destroyed while the star settled into a stable orbit.

A binary system was born, out of nearly impossible circumstances.

"That rogue planet was dragging a star behind it," Kim said softly.

"Yes," Seven agreed.

"Meaning it couldn't possibly have been a planet. It had to be a ship of some sort."

"Having just completed a survey of dozens of fragments of that planet and discovering several more unusual mineral formations, including a toxic substance that nearly ate Ensign Gwyn, I must contradict that assessment," Seven said evenly.

"That's impossible. It had to have propulsion, not to mention one hell of a tractor mechanism to keep hold of a star that size. I can't even imagine the gravitational geometry required to attempt such a thing, let alone believe that it occurred naturally."

"I am all but certain it did not," Seven said. "But that is not the most interesting part of this simulation."

"What is?"

"Note the final result," Seven suggested.

Kim tore his eyes from the binaries and studied the debris field. It was massive and in constant motion. It would take thousands of years to settle into the configuration of the current system.

Then it hit him.

"Where is DK-1116?" Kim asked.

"It's not there," Seven said. "None of the previous planetary bodies could have survived the transit of the planetoid or the star as they moved through the system."

"Then where did the planet our people are currently studying come from?" Kim demanded.

"An excellent question," Seven said.

As Kim pondered the possible answers, Seven switched the view on the screen to the last image taken by the long-range sensors of the system and its surrounding asteroid belt. A faint bleep sounded on her panel, alerting her to a new reading.

"Hmm," Seven said.

"Hmm?" Kim asked.

"Approximately six hours ago, a faint but perceptible EM energy wave was detected from an asteroid in the outer belt. It is focused on the planet and has increased in intensity by fractional amounts every hour since it was first identified."

"Source?"

Seven shrugged. "We need to take a closer look to confirm, but at this range, there is no sign of technology anywhere in the asteroid field."

Kim nodded. "I think it's time to make contact with our commanding officers."

13

U nable to accept the reality now before her, Devi Patel stepped toward the sphere room's only known exit to the surface. Placing her hand in its center, she waited for the familiar pinpricks to her palm required to activate the cavern's entrance doors.

Nothing happened. Resisting the urge to panic, she ran both of her hands over its surface.

Again, nothing.

"Devi, what is going on?" Lasren demanded.

"Why is that door closed?" Jepel asked, noticeably panicked.

"I don't know," Patel snapped back at him. As she stood before the metal surface now standing between her and a long, productive life, she forced herself to take slow, regular breaths and consider the question.

Suddenly she did know. She knew exactly why that door was closed.

It was her fault.

Tapping her combadge she said, "Patel to *Voyager*. *Voyager*, do you read me?"

Silence answered. Not even static.

"*Voyager*, please respond."

She tried again several times before accepting the obvious. Her comm signal had been blocked when she tried to reach Lasren and the others when they were separated. Something down here inhibited them.

Turning back to her team, she lifted her chin slightly and said, "We have a number of problems."

"Is one of them that closed door?" Jepel asked.

"Yes, but it may not be the biggest one."

Lasren stepped forward. "Explain," he requested in a tone that reminded Patel annoyingly of Seven.

"Remember the screaming sound?" she asked.

Lasren and the others nodded.

"That sound was the formation of an interface that was created using my DNA in order to interact with us. It is located in a cell in that room," she added, pointing to the entrance directly behind Vincent, "and it is no longer operative."

As she continued, Vincent looked toward that chamber nervously and stepped closer to the others.

"The interface told me that containment on the surface has been breached by the actions of our crews."

"How?" Jepel demanded.

"It didn't say."

"You didn't ask?"

"You know what?" Patel said. "The next time the four of us are working together, I'm going to let you take charge, Jepel. That way you can witness the birth of a monster bearing your face and try to have a conversation with it. And when you do better than I did at getting all of our questions answered, you can start criticizing me."

Jepel's face fell. "I'm sorry," he said immediately. "I didn't mean . . ."

"I know," Patel said more gently. "It's a lot to take in all at once."

"Do you have any idea what it meant when it said that we had breached containment?" Lasren asked.

"No," Patel replied, "but there is a definite possibility it might include the failure of the biodomes in which our people are currently exploring and enjoying shore leave. It said the system would fail in a little over eleven hours, so it's not something that is an immediate threat. I have to hope that there are signs on the surface of the impending system failure and that all of our people will get off the surface in time. But if there aren't, we need to find a way to warn them."

"Those biodomes have stood for thousands of years. We've been here a little more than a day and we already found a way to break them?" Vincent asked, aghast.

"Not that long ago, we almost broke the entire multiverse," Lasren reminded him. "We're good."

"That still doesn't seem possible," Vincent said, clearly turning the prospect over and over in his mind.

"The species that built all of this was identified as Species 001. Every other species that has come here is also numbered. We are 196.2."

"Point two?" Jepel asked.

"Really?" Patel shot back. "You're standing in the middle of *this* and the decimal point is what's throwing you?"

Jepel shook his head.

"I'm guessing that the other species explored this place under the supervision of Species 001, so they probably had access to rules and regulations we don't. This whole world is one gigantic science lab built to evaluate and if possible propagate something called the Edrehmaia." She held up her hand to forestall more questions as she continued. "I don't know what that is exactly, but I'm guessing it is whatever substance, including the *Sevenofninonium*, all of those structures on the surface are made out of."

"You might be right about that," Lasren said. "You need to see the cavern down below."

"What's down there?" she asked.

"The mother lode of impossible things," he replied. "It's going to take several teams of our best people working for weeks to crack that code."

"Noted," Patel said. "Now here's the part you're not going to like."

"You mean the *other* part we're not going to like?" Vincent asked. "Because seriously, Devi, there isn't a single part of this yet that I'm actually liking."

Patel sighed. "When the interface told me that system failure was imminent, it asked if I wanted to secure this data storage and retrieval station. I didn't think. I just said 'yes.'"

A look of understanding came over Lasren's face. "Oh, no," he said.

Patel nodded. "I think so. I think I inadvertently locked us all into this area. That door isn't going to open on its own."

"So we need to find a way through it," Jepel said.

"Stand back," Patel said. When they had obliged her, she doubled-checked that her phaser was at its maximum setting, lifted it, and pointed it directly at the door. The beam caused the door to glow an angry crimson for a few moments, but did nothing to destroy it.

"So that's not an option," Patel said, finally lowering the weapon in defeat.

"And that can't be our focus now anyway, can it?" Lasren asked.

Patel met his eyes and shook her head slowly.

"We have to find a way to reestablish communications with the surface," Lasren continued. "That is our only priority. We have to warn them, just in case there are no obvious signs of system failure."

"And if possible, we need to give them access to as much of the data as we have found here. This is what we came here for and it would be wrong for them to depart without learning it," Patel added.

Lasren nodded his understanding. Even if Jepel and Vincent hadn't figured it out yet, he and Devi knew the truth. There might not be time to figure out how to reestablish communications *and* escape the chambers. It was highly likely that all four of them were going to die down there.

VOYAGER

Ensign Icheb was due to return to the surface of the planet within the hour to begin placing some of the newly replicated sensors for Lieutenant Elkins. He had received three messages from Bryce since he departed the surface, but thus far hadn't responded to any of them. Until he knew exactly what he wanted to say, he couldn't bring himself to speak with Phinn, even via the comm.

The tests Doctor Sharak had run the previous evening had been quick and painless. Icheb wasn't sure what to expect but had begun to believe as the hours wore on that this was going to end with him and Counselor Cambridge engaged in several lengthy conversations.

When he entered sickbay at Sharak's request and found Cambridge waiting in the doctor's office, this suspicion seemed to be confirmed. The Doctor was also present, and though he offered Icheb a reassuring smile when their eyes met, the ensign could tell that something was troubling the hologram.

Sharak, however, took charge as soon as the door to his office closed behind Icheb.

"Good morning, Ensign," Sharak greeted him. "I have completed my analysis of your scans and asked both the Doctor and counselor to join us while we discuss the results."

"Then there is something wrong with me," Icheb said, not sure if he was more relieved or troubled by this development.

Sharak released a deep breath. "There is something different about you, but whether or not it is *wrong* is unclear."

"What does that mean?" Icheb asked, looking automatically to the Doctor for more information.

Sharak continued. "Brunali physiology is similar in many respects to that of humans. However, we lack sufficient Brunali genetic samples against which to compare your test results. Again, I would like to stress that what we have found might be within normal ranges for other members of your species."

"But it might not," Cambridge interjected.

"As you say," Sharak agreed.

"What did you find?" Icheb demanded.

"The issue at hand was your lack of physical response to an emotionally and sexually charged encounter," Sharak said simply. "Normally, humans in similar situations experience the feelings I believe you anticipated as a result of the interplay between a multitude of sensory and neural receptors and the brain properly identifying the sensory input. Hormones are released that increase respiration and heart rates but in addition, they heighten the experience, often creating the perception of physical and emotional pleasure."

Icheb nodded for Sharak to continue. Thus far, nothing he had said contradicted anything he understood of basic anatomy and physiology.

"In your case, your sensory receptors have been artificially blocked by an unusual gene regulatory sequence on your sixth chromosome. As I said, this might be perfectly normal for Brunali. However, it is also possible that the sequence in question was placed there on purpose."

"Why?" Icheb asked.

The Doctor stepped forward. "As you know, you were genetically altered as a child to carry a virus to the Borg. I believe that the sequence in question was also created so that when you were assimilated, you would not experience any undue suffering."

"While it is difficult to credit your parents with anything approaching affection for you, given their actions," Cambridge added, "it does make sense that they would have wanted to make your assimilation as easy as possible. They expected you to destroy the Borg following your assimilation. They did not anticipate that you would survive that process, or that their little gift to you would complicate your life once you reached physical and sexual maturity."

"But if the sequence is designed to inhibit my sensory experiences of pain, why would they also affect my experiences of pleasure?"

"The same receptors are involved," Sharak said kindly. "All signals are blocked, regardless of their origin."

Icheb shook his head. "But I do experience pain from time to time."

"For example?" Cambridge asked.

"When someone I care about is suffering," Icheb offered.

"Emotional stress is different from physical stress,"

Cambridge said. "Situations that evoke compassion or sadness are based upon a mental process; your empathy, for instance, would not be blocked in the same way. Unfortunately, your physical receptors are critical in the normal expression of sexual instincts. While in time you might be able to convince your brain to order the proper responses, with no stimuli to engage your mind, it would be a wholly mental process."

Icheb remained still as he processed this information. Finally he asked, "Can you fix it?"

Sharak shook his head. "Not until we know for certain that the sequence in question is not vital for other normal physical processes. We will run the necessary models, but it will be some time before we can determine if a gene therapy would be appropriate for you."

Icheb felt his face beginning to burn. It was decidedly unpleasant. Understanding that the source of his discomfort was emotional— embarrassment and fear—did not diminish the intensity.

"There might be an alternative," Cambridge said quickly.

"What?" Icheb asked.

"A version of behavior modification. The goal would be to train your mind to respond to various physical stimuli in the absence of other sensory input. As powerful as our bodies are, at the end of the day, our minds are infinitely more powerful. With patience and time, you might learn responses that are currently denied you."

Icheb shook his head. "I will, of course, engage in any therapy you believe would be helpful. But I doubt its effectiveness. I have never felt as strongly about anyone as I do for Phinn. The appropriate mental triggers are present. But my body simply betrays me."

"We're not going to give up, Icheb," the Doctor insisted. "The first step in finding any cure is identifying the problem. That much we've done. While we search for alternative solutions, you should continue to engage in any behavior you believe will strengthen your emotional bond to Lieutenant Bryce."

"You should also be honest with him," Cambridge suggested. "If he truly cares about you, as I suspect he does, he would want to understand what is happening to you."

"But can our feelings for each other overcome my genetic destiny?" Icheb asked.

Cambridge shrugged. "We've never seen anything like this before, so none of us can say to any degree of certainty what the outcome will be. The alternative, however, is unthinkable. You cannot allow this to warp the development of normal, healthy relationships going forward. It is something to be fought and defeated, not something to which you should simply submit."

Icheb nodded.

Doctor Sal approached the unconscious form of Ensign Gwyn with miserable trepidation. It had been a little more than a day since she had briefly tasted the potential for victory over the disease ravaging Nancy Conlon's body.

So damned close.

If she was right—and she was certain she was—that victory was, at the very least, a few steps further away; steps that would now be denied her by the specific language written by a group of cowardly, sanctimonious assholes into the admittance charter that granted the planet Krios membership in the Federation.

That was a problem. The bigger problem by far was Ensign Gwyn herself. She was no longer a donor. She was now a patient.

The blood tests had been conclusive. The metamorphic cells Sal required to rewrite Conlon's genetic code had been present. But the radiation exposure Gwyn had suffered when her EV suit was breached by whatever the hell had attacked her on that asteroid had damaged too many of the metamorphic cells for them to be safely used. Sal would need new samples. But if her gut was right, those samples would now be impossible to come by honestly.

Sal ran a medical tricorder over Gwyn's still form and immediately checked the results. The things the device could confirm only fortified Sal's frustration. Hormone levels were radically altered. Neural activity was off the charts. Her body's natural defenses had been busy trying to adjust to the one-two punch of exotic radiation and antiproton therapy. It was doing what it knew how to do to cure her. It was changing. It was reverting to its most basic, ancient programming to save itself.

The metamorphosis had begun.

Sal had seen similar data once before, on Krios. The woman who had provided it, Kataly Norol, had died before Sal could help her. The most likely scenario here was that Gwyn would join her shortly.

Unless Sal could find a miracle that had eluded her many years ago.

After confirming that Gwyn's vital signs were as stable as they were likely to get, Sal took a hypo filled with a mild stimulant and pressed it gently to the young woman's neck.

Gwyn's eyes fluttered open. They passed over Sal as she tried to sit up, scanning the rest of the room.

"Where is he?" she demanded.

"Where is who?" Sal asked.

"Sharak."

Sal inhaled deeply and released the breath in a huff. Clearly Gwyn had already begun the process of imprinting upon her "perfect mate." That needed to stop.

"Ensign Gwyn, I need you to focus and to listen to me very carefully," Sal said.

Gwyn pushed herself upright and brought her legs down over the side of the biobed. "I'm sorry, Doctor, but I need to see Sharak."

"I'm sure he's around here somewhere," Sal assured her. "I'll call for him in a moment."

"Doctor Sharak," Gwyn cried loudly to the otherwise empty sickbay.

"Gwyn, focus on me," Sal said more intently. "There was an accident. You were attacked by some sort of organic compound you discovered on that asteroid."

Gwyn looked away, searching her memory. "I . . . what? Does that matter now?"

"It does. It's part of the reason you feel the way you do. Let me guess: in addition to craving the presence of Doctor Sharak the same way you require air to breathe, you're also starving and uncomfortably warm."

Gwyn seemed to do a quick internal physical check. "That's true," she said, staring up at Sal in wonder. "How do you know that?"

"Because I know what's happening to you."

"Nothing is happening to me. I need Doctor Sharak. I am for him."

Sal repressed the violent urge to shake some sense into the ensign. "Prior to awakening in sickbay, have you ever even spoken to Doctor Sharak for more than a few moments?"

"No."

"Then does it make any sense to you that he has suddenly become vital to your continued survival? Does your desire for him track with any experiences you actually remember?"

Gwyn started to speak but paused abruptly, again searching her interior landscape for a handhold. Finally she said, "What did you do to me?"

Sal wished she could respond truthfully that she had done nothing. In fact, the hormone therapy she had provided to coax Gwyn's limited metamorphic cells into increasing their number, as they did normally every month during her regular cycle, was likely at least partially responsible for Gwyn's current state. The accompanying radiation exposure and antiproton therapy had undoubtedly exacerbated the problem, but it might not have happened at all were it not for Sal's initial intervention.

"Ensign Gwyn, you have entered a state of heightened physical development unique to your species. You know what the *finiis'ral* is, don't you?"

Gwyn shook her head petulantly. "We've already had this discussion, Doctor. I am not an empathic metamorph."

"You are now," Sal said simply.

Gwyn pushed herself off the biobed and began to make her way toward the main door.

"I'm going to find Doctor Sharak," she said.

"Computer, seal main sickbay door," Sal ordered. "Authorization Sal beta lambda."

With a series of chirps, the computer complied.

At the same time, Sharak poked his head out of his private office. "What's going on out here?" he asked.

"Doctor Sharak," Gwyn said, moving toward him and throwing her arms around him. "Please help me. I am for you."

Sharak looked to Sal in alarm as he tried to gently disentangle himself from Gwyn's embrace.

As he did so, both the Doctor and Cambridge stepped outside the office on Sharak's heels.

"Ensign Gwyn," the Doctor said, slightly appalled at the spectacle, "what are you doing? You need to get back in bed."

"I need Sharak," Gwyn insisted with feral intensity.

Cambridge looked to Sal. "Unintended consequences?" he asked.

"Later," Sal insisted, crossing to Gwyn and taking her by both arms as she pulled her away from Sharak. She spoke softly in Gwyn's ear. "Look at them. Look at each of them. Tell me what you feel."

Gwyn tried to shake herself free, but Sal held her tightly. With serious effort, she pulled her eyes from the wide, mottled face of Sharak and looked at the Doctor. After a moment, she recoiled.

"What was that?" Sal asked.

"He's not there," she said.

"Very good. And the counselor?"

Gwyn focused her attention on him briefly. After a few moments, a new lightness came into her eyes. "A challenge."

"Could you also be for him?" Sal asked.

"What is the meaning of this?" the Doctor demanded.

"A moment, please," Sal requested. "Ensign?"

After a moment, Gwyn nodded. "Absolutely."

Cambridge seemed intrigued by the implied compliment but remained silent.

"That's good news," Sal said, gently leading Gwyn back toward the biobed.

As she approached the biobed again, Gwyn placed both

her hands on its side, rejecting the attempt to be forced back into it.

Icheb suddenly emerged from the office. He took the scene in briefly before heading toward the main doors, which did not open for him.

As he moved across the room, Gwyn's eyes followed him curiously. For a moment, they lost their heat.

"Icheb," she croaked. Reaching out a hand to him, she beckoned him closer.

"It's all right, Ensign," Sal said. "Computer, unlock the main door."

Icheb stared at Gwyn. Despite his clear desire not to intrude upon whatever was happening, he seemed to sense the raw need in Gwyn's voice.

"You can go, Ensign Icheb," Sal said.

"No, please," Gwyn said. "Icheb."

He stepped closer to her.

Freeing herself from Sal's grasp, she moved toward him, stared at him intently for a few moments, and relaxed almost imperceptibly.

"I remember the asteroid," she said quite calmly. "I remember the black substance and the pain. I remember," she said, staring quizzically at Sal. "When I focus on the others, all I can sense is them. What they need from me. What I must do and be. But with Icheb . . ." She shook her head, searching for words.

"Go on," Sal suggested gently.

"I feel more like myself," she said softly.

Sal looked at Icheb with new eyes. She had no idea why this young man was different from any other when it came to Gwyn's unnatural instincts, but at this moment, she was simply grateful.

"We need to talk," Sal said to the other physicians.

"You think?" Cambridge asked.

"In the meantime, Ensign Icheb, would you please remain here with Gwyn? Just for a few minutes?"

Icheb nodded. "Of course," he said. Addressing Gwyn, he continued, "I believe the doctors would like you to rest."

Gwyn nodded mutely as Icheb moved closer to her and helped her back onto the biobed.

"Just keep her company," Sal said. "If she tries to leave the room again . . ."

"I won't," Gwyn said, tears beginning to glisten in her eyes.

Sal knew Gwyn was beginning to understand her predicament. What Sal did not know was if she was going to be able to fix it.

Admiral Janeway entered *Voyager*'s conference room to find Lieutenant Kim, Commanders Paris and Torres, Captain Farkas, and Seven waiting. Captain Chakotay and Commanders Glenn and O'Donnell, all of whom had just returned from the surface with Janeway, entered the room behind her and the group quickly seated themselves at the table.

"You have a report for us, Mister Kim," the admiral said with a tight smile.

"I do," Kim replied. "And I'm sorry to pull all of you away from your various research efforts."

"No apology is necessary," Chakotay said. "We trust your judgment."

"Thank you, Captain," Kim said. "There have been a number of developments related to our investigations here that have occurred in the last few hours. The most significant is the loss of contact with one of our away teams."

"Which one?" Janeway asked.

"Lieutenants Lasren and Patel with Ensigns Vincent and Jepel."

"How long have they been out of contact?" Chakotay demanded.

"A little over three hours," Kim replied. "Comms aren't functioning, so we have already dispatched a rescue team to their last-known transport coordinates. They report finding a sealed door that our tricorders and ship's sensors are having trouble penetrating. We believe Patel's team might have found a way to open it and became trapped on the other side."

"So cut the damn thing open," Farkas suggested.

Kim sighed. The look on his face clearly said, *Can she possibly think we haven't tried that already?*

"We have made several attempts. Our phasers are unable to damage it, even on their highest settings. To be more precise, any damage we are able to inflict repairs itself almost immediately. Although the door is a metal alloy, it has previously undiscovered regenerative properties."

"That sounds familiar," O'Donnell noted ominously.

"What about the walls surrounding the door?" Chakotay asked. "If you can't get through it, how about removing it from its housing?"

"Apparently the walls of the cavern are densely striated with a plaited metallic substance that is equally resistant to our weapons. At this point, the only solution left might be to detonate a small amount of explosives."

"In an underground cavern?" Janeway asked dubiously.

"I know," Kim said. "We could bring the whole thing down on top of them if we aren't very careful."

"Am I to understand that this is one of several problems we are now facing?" Janeway asked.

"Yes, Admiral," Seven chimed in. "There are traces within

the plaiting that are similar to an unusual substance I discovered with Ensign Gwyn while attempting to take samples of some of these unusual metals from one of the asteroids within the inner belt of the system. That substance essentially attacked Gwyn and ate through her EV suit before I was able to stun it with my phaser."

Janeway simply shook her head in disbelief.

"I cannot tell you if any of that substance might be released should we try to breach the walls around the door, but should that happen, the dangers posed would be immense," Seven added.

"It ate through her suit?" O'Donnell asked.

"Seven stunned it and by doing so was able to bring Ensign Gwyn back aboard her shuttle," Kim reported. "But once they transported to *Voyager* the substance seemed to recover. It continued to expand, transforming the shuttle into some sort of new biological entity that I destroyed two and a half hours ago. It was approaching the ship and I felt the risks posed by its presence far outweighed the possibilities for scientific discovery."

Janeway started to speak, but held her peace. It was Kim's call to make and that had to be the end of it. Second-guessing anyone now wasn't going to help.

"I think you should be aware, Admiral, that I have also completed a simulation of the formation of the binary system that suggests that the B star was pulled into orbit of the A star by a terrestrial body. Its remains, along with those of the planets that once made up this star system, formed the B star's asteroid belt," Seven said.

"By what possible mechanism does a planet pull a star into this system?" Janeway asked.

"Unknown," Seven replied.

"But you're sure that's how this system was formed?" Chakotay asked.

"As certain as I can be without going back in time to witness the event myself," Seven assured him. "The planet we have named DK-1116 was also formed by unknown means after the binaries settled into their orbit."

Janeway nodded as she began to prioritize the issues before her. "Anything else?"

Torres took the floor. "The biodome we had reserved for recreational purposes is showing a significant change. The water source our people were swimming in yesterday was apparently once pure. That is no longer the case, and as a result, there are a number of newly scanned metallic formations growing beneath the water."

"Let me guess," O'Donnell posited. "They are densely plaited, similar to the formations located in the walls of the cavern where we lost our away team."

Torres nodded. "They are the same."

"Why does it matter that the water used to be pure?" Farkas asked. "How pure could it have been?"

"We only knew to go looking for the formations because of the presence of charged particles interacting with the gasses in the atmosphere. It was gorgeous to witness, but as Lieutenant Bryce pointed out to me, given the purity of the water, that reaction shouldn't have been possible," Torres said. Turning to Farkas, she continued, "Pure water isn't conductive. It is possible that the purity was the only thing preventing those metallic formations from encroaching into the water. By disrupting that, we may have thrown the entire ecosystem out of balance."

"Where is our most recent geological survey of the planet?" Janeway asked.

Seven handed Janeway a padd and rose to the room's small display located on a wall behind the table. Everyone turned to give her their full attention.

"As you will note, the metallic substance in question forms a little more than fifty percent of the planet. It runs beneath the surface in an intricate pattern, seemingly disrupted within the various biodomes by the water sources. In two places, the biodome where Commander Torres discovered the growths, and in the stepwell where we lost our away team, new growths are prominently visible."

"Does it pose any danger to us?" Chakotay asked.

"Impossible to know at this point," Seven said. "But if the water sources were strategically placed on the surface to disrupt further growth, we might theorize that those who created the planet had good reason for designing it the way they did."

"There's one more thing, Admiral," Kim said.

Janeway turned to face him.

"We've been running continuous scans of all electromagnetic wave patterns within the system since we arrived. In the last several hours, a new concentration has been detected, emanating from the system's outer asteroid belt focused on the planet."

"Suggesting what?" Janeway asked.

"That we got someone or something's attention," Kim said.

Janeway sighed.

"First things first," Farkas said. "Shore leave is over, right?"

Janeway considered the question briefly, noting the disappointment on Chakotay's face, before she said, "It is."

14

D octor Sal paced the small office fitfully as Sharak, Cambridge, and the EMH seated themselves, Sharak at his desk and the other two on opposite outer edges of it.

"Well, El'nor?" Cambridge encouraged her. Alone, he suspected, among his companions, he believed he already knew some of the relevant facts Sal was about to deliver. As her story began, however, he quickly realized he had seriously underestimated the dimensions of the catastrophe she had created.

"Roughly thirty years ago, Regina and I—"

"Captain Farkas?" Sharak asked.

"Yes. Captain Farkas, who was then commanding the *Thetis*, and I found ourselves facing a nightmare. While attending a diplomatic reception on Krios, several of our officers were bitten by an insect that on that planet is considered little more than a nuisance. That insect carried a virus, Vega Nine, to which the Kriosians are naturally immune. Our people, however, were not, and within days they began to fall victim to the ravages of a DNA damage repair syndrome much more aggressive than the one currently plaguing Lieutenant Conlon.

"As soon as the infection was detected, we returned to Krios to ask the local medical authorities for any assistance they could provide. They were unusually reticent to help us, citing the passages in their Federation admittance charter permitting them to hide much of their medical science behind *culturally specific observances*."

"They had religious objections to offering medical assistance?" the Doctor asked, aghast.

"They had religious objections to allowing anyone to study their genome, wherein the key to their immunity to Vega Nine would have been easily detected and which ultimately might have saved twenty-three of our officers," Sal replied. "All they were willing to do was confirm that the insect population carrying the virus had been completely eliminated."

Her eyes grew cold and distant as she continued. Cambridge immediately recognized the signs of long-buried trauma.

"I was watching our people deteriorate at a rapid pace, with only the resources of a small *Miranda*-class sickbay at my disposal."

"Sounds like hell," Cambridge noted.

"It was," she assured him. "A diplomatic aide, a young Kriosian woman named Kataly Norol, took pity on us. She began her career as a historian and had been privately attempting to reconstruct the century surrounding the Kriosian Dawn, their first contact with the Vulcans, as it happens, which ultimately led them to a wider understanding of their place in the universe. She had become aware of certain facts about her people that every administration since the Dawn had worked diligently to erase from the historical record.

"No doubt you are all aware of the Kriosian empathic metamorphs," she continued.

"I am not," Sharak interrupted her gently.

The Doctor obliged him with a quick response. "Into

each generation of Kriosians, a small number of individuals are born that possess a unique genetic anomaly. All Kriosians are empathic to some degree, but these metamorphs possess the ability to bond with others, including aliens, in an unusual way. During a period of heightened hormonal activity known as the *finiis'ral*, these individuals are introduced to their mates and, through a process we do not entirely understand, take on the characteristics those mates will find most pleasing. They literally become another's perfect mate, while simultaneously sacrificing their own identity to the bonding process."

"That sounds horrifying," Sharak said. "What of the rights of these individuals? Are they not protected from this loss of personal freedom and identity? Have the Kriosians not found a cure for this condition?"

"You would have thought, wouldn't you?" Cambridge agreed.

"The empathic metamorphs are highly prized among the Kriosians. They are identified as infants and kept secluded from the rest of the population. Most often their mates are chosen for political or personal gain for their families. Many of them have been used to seal diplomatic relations with other cultures. They are considered priceless gifts," Sal said.

"And the Federation allows them to be members while continuing this practice?" Sharak asked, bemused.

"The issue was debated hotly when they were considered for membership. They are a rich and enlightened culture, for the most part, ideal candidates for an organization like the Federation," Cambridge said. "Given that there are so few of these empaths born, and the Kriosians' genetic analysis suggested that over time this variation will likely become extinct, it was decided to make an exception, on the understanding that all metamorphs entering into bonded relationships sign official waivers indicating that they are doing so of their own free will."

"They raise the metamorphs to believe that they are special and are under obligation to their society. When the time comes, none of them would dare refuse the honor," Sal said. "But believe it or not, that isn't the worst part of all of this."

All three men facing Sal grew silent as she continued.

"Kataly was able to provide me with limited genetic data going back centuries. That data showed that almost all Kriosian females are born with the metamorphic variation. A smaller population of the men are also affected, but Kriosian society prior to the Dawn took very different views of their male and female metamorphs. Essentially the women were born into biological servitude. All were meant to become the perfect mates of their eventual male counterparts. It wasn't a problem until they began to encounter other species who didn't share their particular patriarchal fetish."

"After the Dawn, Kriosian women, en masse, began to revolt against their society's customs. It was a time of great civil unrest. Many of them found a way around their genetic destiny," Sal continued.

"How?" Cambridge demanded.

"If I knew, I'd tell the Federation to go to hell and make sure the entire universe was told," Sal replied. "But I don't. No one does. This was hundreds of years, forty generations ago. What we do know is that over that period, the rate of metamorph births declined sharply, dwindling to something resembling its present reported numbers. Kataly allowed me to sample her genome, against her people's cultural taboos, and to my surprise, she possessed the variation.

Her body had the ability to make metamorphic cells, but it only occurred during specific times of her monthly cycle.

"Those metamorphic cells are extraordinary, especially when it comes to battling genetic illnesses. She agreed to allow me to use her cells to attempt to cure Vega Nine."

At this Sal trailed off, momentarily overwhelmed by the memory. "Before I could extract the cells, her so-called *treason* was discovered. She was forbidden further contact with us. Regina petitioned anyone she could get to listen, but the Kriosians formed an impenetrable bureaucratic circle around her and the Federation Council was unwilling to press them further.

"I was forced to pursue other avenues of curing Vega Nine, and ultimately I succeeded. We lost twenty-three of the original thirty-seven victims. Shortly thereafter, I convinced Regina to allow me to submit my cure to the Kriosian medical authorities. A few days after that submission, Kataly got us a message out. She was frantic. Terrified. She had been examined following our work, and it was determined that she was, in fact, an empathic metamorph. They were in the process of selecting a mate for her. She had refused to sign the waiver and was requesting political asylum."

Sal paused again, collecting her thoughts.

"By the time we had received permission from Starfleet to respond to her request, she was dead. I don't actually know if she was killed, or if her newly discovered 'condition' caused her to take her own life. Either way, it was made clear to Regina and me that the matter was considered closed and we were forbidden to investigate further."

Cambridge was the first to break the silence that followed this revelation. "A fascinating and tragic story, Doctor Sal, but how does it explain Ensign Gwyn's current condition?"

"When the potential for a stem-cell therapy was gone, I determined that the quickest and most certain way to cure Lieutenant Conlon was to use metamorphic cells."

"Ensign Gwyn is half Kriosian," Sharak said, suddenly understanding.

Sal nodded. "There was a chance she didn't possess the mutation, but the first blood samples I took showed the presence of the cells I required. I did not coerce Gwyn into parting with those cells, nor did I share with her the unofficial history of her people. I simply asked her to consider whether or not a cultural restriction she never understood meant more to her than the possibility of saving a life. She agreed to every step of this process."

"One cannot consent to a medical procedure when they are not provided all of the relevant facts about that procedure, as you well know, El'nor," Cambridge noted.

"A minor detail given the circumstances," Sal shot back. "I artificially induced the necessary hormonal levels just prior to her mission to that damned asteroid. My concern when she returned was that exposure to the radiation might have damaged the cells. It appears now that they actually increased their number. The cells have surged within her body, probably in response to the antiproton therapy, and have induced the *finiis'ral*. She is now under a biological imperative to find and bond with her perfect mate. I was concerned she had settled on you, Doctor Sharak, but her response to Cambridge suggests that it is still early in the process."

"Can we reverse this?" the Doctor asked.

"I don't think so," Sal said. "I can't imagine sentencing that poor girl to a life as anyone's perfect mate, but I have no idea how to stop it. I also have no idea why her reaction to Ensign Icheb was so different."

"We can help you there," Cambridge said. "Icheb possesses a unique genetic variation as well, repressing his sensory receptors. If the hormones emitted as part of this empathic bonding require a detectable response from the intended mate, he is biologically incapable of providing them."

"She can't bond with Icheb," the Doctor said.

"Obviously not," Sal said. "She can't be allowed to bond with anyone. But perhaps Icheb's presence is calming in a way no one else's can be. Since she can't bond with him, she is better able to retain her own sense of identity when she is with him."

"Can we seclude her until this passes? Surely the hormonal levels can't remain at their heightened levels forever," Sharak suggested.

"The only medical fact the Kriosians ever shared about empathic metamorphs with the Federation, the one that I think eventually convinced them to allow the practice to continue, was the reality that metamorphs who are prevented from bonding die. Once the process has begun, it must be completed," Sal said.

"But you said that generations of Kriosian women found another solution," Cambridge interjected. "So there has to be a way. Perhaps we could reach out to the Kriosian authorities and explain Gwyn's condition."

"Unless diplomatic progress of which I am unaware has occurred in the last thirty years, she'd be brought home immediately, most likely just assigned a mate by her people, and forced to complete the bonding," Sal said.

"We can't allow that," Sharak insisted.

"And we're not going to let her to die," the Doctor added.

"I'm open to alternative suggestions," Sal admitted.

"May I make one?" Sharak asked.

"Of course," Sal replied.

"The Doctor's presence does not appear to affect her, to activate this need to bond. Perhaps we should transport her to an environment where neither I nor many other humans will be available to further torment her."

Sal smiled. "An excellent suggestion. Doctor?"

The EMH nodded. "I'll arrange for transport to the *Galen* immediately."

"In the meantime, I think one of us owes Ensign Gwyn an explanation," Cambridge said pointedly.

"By *one of us* you mean me, right?" Sal asked.

DK-1116

Patel and Lasren stood in the lower chamber, doing their best to make sense of the room's various alien technologies. Vincent and Jepel had agreed to remain in the column room and to download the data from as many spheres as they could into their tricorders. The library of data was large and their tricorders had limited storage space, but all had agreed that as much usable data as possible would be transmitted to the fleet as soon as communications were reopened.

"Thoughts?" Lasren asked.

Patel shook her head and sighed. Apart from limited, unsurprising molecular structures and various ranges of power readings, their tricorders were useless in terms of explaining what the various pieces of this puzzle were and how they fit together. The science officer was reduced to hypothesizing based on observation and what little data she'd been able to synthesize from the initial scans of the planet and all she'd seen beneath its surface.

Lifting a hand and pointing toward the illuminated snakes writhing all about the cavern, she said, "I'm calling that pure, unrefined Edrehmaia. That's the base from which all of the experiments on the surface begin."

Lasren nodded. "Seems plausible. This stuff runs throughout the entire planet. It forms the veins of ore in the walls of all of the caverns. But down here it has different properties. The luminescence, the tiny amounts of that black liquid that is extracted from it at a fairly steady rate and then cycled through that system over there," he said, indicating the waterfall and the staging platform nearby with the spider legs.

"That's the biological portion of it," Patel said. "That's the stuff that was used to form the thing I spoke to. But it was mingled with my DNA, so, at its most basic level, it has the capability to replicate and transfer genetic material and build from there. It is clearly critical to the experiments the other species were running here."

"Like a virus?"

"Sure. Just a billion times more complicated."

"So what we are looking at is a sort of living technology base," Lasren surmised.

Patel nodded thoughtfully. "The potential applications of this are mind boggling."

"As in?" Lasren asked.

"If you could properly control and modify something like this, you could grow any number of energy storage-and-release devices, everything from simple light sources to phasers or warheads with exponentially higher destructive capabilities than even our antimatter torpedoes."

"Hull plating for starships?" Lasren asked. "That could repair itself if damaged?"

Patel nodded. "There is really no end to the possibilities."

"Why is growing these things better than just building them?" Lasren asked.

"For us, it isn't," Patel replied. "We've found other solutions to those problems using the elements that were plentiful on our worlds. But if your species had bigger goals, more powerful enemies you were facing, or shortages of resources on your own world, a discovery like this is a game changer, comparable to humanity's discovery of fire."

"Only way more potentially destructive," Lasren noted.

"And creative," Patel countered.

"The volume of exotic radiant molecules here is most likely the thing that is jamming our communications," Lasren offered. "I'm guessing our problem is simply our proximity to this stuff."

"I agree," Patel said. "Even a few kilometers away in the first cavern, we had comm and transport abilities."

"But that door is literally closed to us now."

Patel was searching the cavern above the living ore. Her eyes landed on the large white sphere with the spokes radiating out from its center, some of which were clearly no longer active.

"One of the things we know this substance does is release energy. It's basically an unlimited and seemingly perpetual supply. It makes sense that you'd need something like that to sustain the energy fields creating the biodomes on the surface," Patel said.

"Those could be the hard lines shunting power to the field generators," Lasren said.

"And that thing could be the field generator," Patel suggested.

"Does that help us?" Lasren asked.

"It might," Patel replied. "Up for a little climbing?"

"If it means we get to live longer, absolutely."

Together Patel and Lasren started up the staircases and down the catwalks that led closest to the sphere. It took the better part of half an hour to get as close as possible, and both were breathless when they had reached their goal. The first thing Patel did was open her tricorder and begin to scan.

"It's definitely a massive power generator," she finally said.

Lasren's eyes were fixed on the nearest gray spoke that clearly no longer had power running through it. Finally he said, "Not that I'm actually anxious to get any closer to the massive ball of glowing death, but I wonder something."

"What?"

"If these are hard lines and some of them are no longer functioning, doesn't that suggest that these might still reach the surface or close enough that we might get a signal out?"

A wide smile spread over Patel's lips. "We should try to open a channel."

Lasren took out his tricorder and used it to search for patterns of transmission. The first few bands he accessed nearly blew out the tricorder and were accompanied by a shrill, screeching sound that nearly deafened both of them as it bounced around the cavern.

Finally, he found one that did not. Reconfiguring the communicator in his badge took another few minutes. When it was done, he handed the badge to Devi.

"Do the honors, Lieutenant?"

"It's your creation," Patel said.

"You're the commanding officer of this team," Lasren reminded her. "It should be you."

It was a simple gesture of confidence and respect. It moved Patel more than anything she had discovered on the planet. Nodding, she accepted the badge and tapped it gently.

"Patel to *Voyager*. Do you read?"

A few heartbreaking moments of silence were quickly followed by faint static.

Patel repeated her hail. "Patel to *Voyager*. Please come in."

"Patel? This is Waters. Where the hell are you?"

Lasren's eyes met Patel's in this shared small victory.

"Never mind that, Vanessa. I need to speak to the captain. And you have to get everyone off this planet immediately."

Waters's response was comforting. *"Way ahead of you, Devi. Keep talking to help me refine this signal while I get Chakotay for you."*

DEMETER

Lieutenant Elkins was seated over a data terminal in his ship's main engineering section when Lieutenant Bryce reported as ordered. Lieutenant Benoit was staring at the terminal over Elkins's shoulder.

"Morning, Chief," Bryce said. "Cress."

"Where's Icheb?" Elkins asked.

Bryce was stung by the question. *Not returning any of my messages* was the truth, but he didn't think this was the time or the place for that discussion. He settled for "I haven't heard from him since he returned to *Voyager* last night."

Elkins sighed. "I really wanted him to see this, but I don't think it can wait." Indicating the schematic of the planet before him with a stubby finger, he said, "We've been running continuous scans of the planet for several days, but starting last night I narrowed the focus to the areas where we intended to plant those sensors to determine the precise geometry and location of the field generator."

Bryce studied the display and one thing smacked him squarely in the face.

"The power distributed along the angles we believe are linked to the field generator have remained constant, but in the last thirteen hours, new, significantly larger power readings are being detected planet-wide," Bryce said.

"Right," Elkins said with a satisfied nod.

"Why, and what does it mean?" Benoit asked.

Elkins shrugged. "I don't know. What I do know is that the largest concentrations of increases have occurred in these six locations."

The graphic shifted to show magnified scans of several of the biodomes.

"That's where the water was contaminated," Bryce realized immediately.

"Yes. And in those areas, new deposits of the planet's native ore are growing at an incredible rate."

"It's like they're making new connections," Benoit said.

"If we think of these deposits more like conduits than raw elements, the structure of this system, of this entire planet, becomes something quite different, doesn't it?" Elkins asked.

Bryce nodded as the horrific potentials began to play out in his head.

"Depending upon how many water sources we disrupted, we're looking at power surges that will continue to increase exponentially," Bryce said.

"But toward what end?" Benoit asked. "What device requires that much energy? It's way more than the biodomes require to function. They're remaining stable."

"But if the biodomes have nothing to do with this planet's true purpose, then we have to ignore that and consider other possibilities," Elkins said. "To my mind, this planet only looks like one thing."

"A bomb," Bryce said.

Elkins turned to stare at him. "Not necessarily."

"Then what's your theory?" Bryce asked.

"An immediate release of all of the energy moving through this system would be catastrophic to the planet, that's certain," Elkins said, "but also pointless. Why create something like this if all you intended to do when it reached its maximum capacity was destroy it? But properly focused along these natural vectors here, it might serve a different purpose."

"A weapon," Bryce realized. "But something that powerful could knock another planet out of orbit, and there aren't any other planets in the system. So why build this and leave it here?"

"I honestly can't answer that," Elkins said. "But whatever the purpose was of whoever built this, I have a feeling we're a few hours away from witnessing it."

"We need to get out of this star system immediately," Benoit said.

"We're still getting away teams off the surface," Bryce said. "Even if we finished that now and started away at maximum warp, we might not escape the blast radius or shockwave."

"And we can't bring the slipstream drives online until we have cleared the outer asteroid field," Elkins reminded him.

"We need to go now," Bryce said.

"If my math is right, we needed to leave about four hours ago," Elkins said.

GALEN

Since she had arrived on *Galen*, Ensign Aytar Gwyn had eaten almost two days' worth of calories. And still she felt famished. Doctor Sal had filled in the gaps in her understanding about empathic metamorphs and the *finiis'ral* before she transported to *Galen*. While she couldn't deny that everything she was feeling and all of her medical scans tracked with the diagnosis, she still found it impossible to believe that very soon she was either going to become the perfect mate of one of her fellow officers, or die. She was less clear on *why* this was happening to her. The odds of her injury on the asteroid and the life-saving radiation she had received resulting in this condition had to be impossibly long. But then, math unrelated to navigation and speed had never been Gwyn's strongest suit.

"I hope whoever becomes my perfect mate likes their women curvy," she said miserably.

"What would happen if they didn't?" Ensign Icheb asked.

Gwyn stared at him openmouthed for a moment. *Is he trying to make this worse?* It was nice that she didn't simply know the answer to that question. Unlike every other individual Gwyn had come within a few meters of since she had awakened, to her Icheb remained a cipher. With him, there was no urgency, no need to *become*. With him she felt almost normal.

Except for the constant hunger.

She decided he was asking out of simple curiosity and

ascribed no other motives to the question. Clearly he cared enough to accompany her here, despite the fact that helping her remain sane was not among his many duties. She had embarrassed herself enough already when she was told she was being transferred to the *Galen* and practically got down on her knees and begged him not to leave her alone.

Now that she was here, she understood the wisdom of the move. There were so few organic people on this ship, and none in the medical bay other than herself, Icheb, and Lieutenant Conlon, who remained comatose. The constant humming pressure she had felt on *Voyager*, the physical possibility of connection with every individual she encountered, had diminished significantly. She was simply left with an aching emptiness in the center of her being that had to be filled and could only be filled by giving herself completely to another.

Her prolonged silence seemed to trouble Icheb, who suddenly said, "I'm sorry, Ensign. Did I offend you?"

"No. Not at all. I mean, yes, but it's okay."

The confusion on his face was almost funny. He hadn't been with the fleet long, but now she wondered why she had never sought out his company. She'd made a point of getting to know every eligible male she served with since the day she boarded. But even before this madness had seized her, she'd never thought to give him the time of day.

He's just so young, she decided, though she was all of four years older than he.

"I don't know all that much about the bonding process," she finally admitted. "It's not something we talk about. So few Kriosians are born metamorphs that really, they're the only ones trained to deal with this." After a pause, she added, "I guess if the person I ultimately choose really had a thing for skinny partners, I'd stop eating for them. I mean, I'd eat enough to live. But I wouldn't *want* to be anything other than what they wanted me to be."

"The Doctor will find a way to reverse this condition," Icheb said gently.

"Why were you here?" she suddenly thought to ask. "I mean, on *Voyager*? Why did you come to see him? Are you sick?"

Icheb's face paled as he shook his head. "I am fine."

"Icheb, you are a terrible liar."

"It's a personal matter, Ensign," he insisted.

"A personal matter?" she demanded. "Are you kidding me? More personal than your entire life being turned upside down by a ticking genetic time bomb you weren't even aware was inside you? In the last few hours, Icheb, you've learned more about my personal life than my mother ever knew. I don't have a choice right now. I'm an open book to you. Would it kill you to return the favor?"

Icheb appeared stung. She was being too hard on him. He was trying to help her, and he didn't deserve her temper or her prying.

"I'm sorry," she said.

"No. I'm sorry," he said. "You are right. And oddly enough, my reason for visiting the Doctor was not entirely different from yours."

Now she was intrigued.

He went on to explain quickly the broad strokes of his own genetic time bomb. When he had finished, she said, "That's why you're not a problem for me. You are physically incapable of bonding in the way my body requires."

"I realize that this cannot be a permanent solution,"

Icheb said, "but I will gladly keep you company until this is resolved if you find it helpful."

Gwyn felt herself smiling in gratitude. "You're one of the good guys, Icheb. I know what Phinn sees in you."

Icheb shook his head. "Even if he does see whatever that is, how likely is it that we will be able to have anything resembling a normal relationship if I am physically incapable of responding to him?"

"Look," she said simply. "I'm not going to pretend that sex isn't a great thing or an important part of an intimate relationship. But I've had plenty of it, enough to know that while pleasant, it has very little to do with sustaining a relationship. You can easily have sex without a relationship. And there are plenty of relationships that never include sex. There are a million other things that attract us to a person and keep us around, long after the physical desire fades. Those are the things you want to cultivate if you really like him and want something deeper."

Icheb nodded. "I understand, in theory. But I would be lying if I said I wasn't looking forward to enjoying a physical relationship with him. Now that it seems possible, even though I guess it isn't, it's almost all I can think about."

Gwyn laughed aloud. "That makes you normal, Icheb. And who knows? If you're so certain they're going to be able to help me, what makes you think they won't be able to help you too?"

Icheb shrugged. "Nothing about my life has ever been normal. But until now, I never wished that it had been different. I thought I had escaped my parents and what they did to me long ago. Now it seems like no matter how far I get away from them, what they intended will always take precedence over what I want."

"I know what you mean. I had to leave Krios to get away from everyone's expectations. I never really felt free until I joined Starfleet. I remember worrying that I would miss them so much, all the people I left behind. A few months after I entered the Academy, I had a dream that I was back home with all of my friends and I was panicked. I never wanted to be there again. But that didn't make sense because it was the only life I'd ever known. I didn't calm down until I woke up and heard my roommate snoring. It was the most beautiful sound. It meant I was still free. I think all those years I was there, I was holding my breath and it wasn't until I got out that I realized what it really was to breathe."

"You don't miss them at all?" Icheb asked.

Gwyn shook her head. "I miss my *leedi*, sometimes. Mayla."

"*Leedi?*"

"She's like a member of my family. But we're not related. She and my mom have always been friends, since before I was born. I've known her forever. Her face is one of my first memories. I always felt like she knew me, but not in the same judgmental way my mom did. I could tell her anything." Tears began to well in Gwyn's eyes. "I'd give anything for her to be here right now. She'd know what I need to do."

Gwyn pushed herself off the biobed that was going to be her home for the foreseeable future and began to pace the main medical bay. Clearly sensing her anguish, Icheb remained in the chair beside her bed, giving her what passed for solitude.

There were several private rooms down the main hall that broke off the rear of the bay. Gwyn wandered down, pausing at the door to Nancy Conlon's room. The lieutenant looked so peaceful. Gwyn knew that was a lie. She understood that some of what she was enduring was the result of her desire to help Conlon, and even though she might have justifiably been angry and blamed Conlon for her current condition, she didn't. Everything she was suffering paled in comparison to Conlon's troubles. At least there were ways for Gwyn to survive this. That might not be one of Conlon's options.

Fresh tears threatened, so Gwyn moved on. A few doors down, a warmly lit bio-chamber sat in an otherwise darkened room. Something small floated inside the chamber.

"Icheb?" she called. Moments later he was by her side.

"Are you all right?"

"I am. What's that?" she asked, pointing to the chamber.

Icheb shook his head. "I don't know."

Gwyn entered the room and checked the chamber's display.

"That's a child," she said, in awe. "That's Lieutenant Kim and Lieutenant Conlon's baby. But what is it doing here?"

Icheb had remained in the doorway. "I'm not sure, but I don't think we should be in here."

Suddenly the urgency of Sal's requests for her aid made more sense. There had always been more to this than Conlon's life. She had been pregnant. They might have been trying to save more than her life with Gwyn's cells.

Gwyn lifted her hand and placed it on the chamber. The being floating inside was so tiny, so fragile. An instinct Gwyn had never before known she possessed rose within her. She wanted to protect this tiny creature. She wanted it to live and thrive. She didn't know it. She couldn't. The same empathic senses that drew her so powerfully to the individuals that were potential mates also connected her to this tiny living being. But there was a difference. She didn't need to be anything other than what she was for this child. It had no needs or desires of her other than protection and devotion. For a moment no longer than a breath, she was fascinated, standing on the edge of a cliff. It would be the easiest thing in the world to step off and fall.

"Gwyn," Icheb said more forcefully, pulling her from her reverie.

She turned to him, as if seeing him for the first time.

"I need to talk to my mother."

15

The large conference room, built to hold most of the command staffs for the entire fleet, was full. Captain Chakotay entered and immediately searched the room for Admiral Janeway.

The conference tables were surrounded by officers, although none of them sat. Each featured small holographic displays, and each table was configured to study one of the many problems the fleet was currently facing.

At the far end of the room, Seven, Glenn, and Elkins were staring at a hologram of the planet upon which Chakotay had placed so many hopes not that long ago. *A good old-fashioned mystery. A chance to be explorers again.* It had all sounded so promising at the time. And maybe a little over a day of that kind of tranquility was enough. Whether it was or wasn't no longer mattered. It was going to have to be.

Even from this distance, Chakotay could see that the veins of ore that composed so much of DK-1116 were highlighted on the model. No doubt these three had been tasked with determining exactly what would happen when the new veins that had begun to grow roughly fifteen hours earlier completed that process. Most of the hypotheses being floated thus far included the destruction of the planet and the fleet.

Another station, where Lieutenants Kim and Bryce stood, displayed a section of the outer, spherical asteroid field surrounding the binaries and traced the patterns of the strange new energy waves originating from one of the larger rocks out there directed toward the planet. In the last few hours they, too, had increased in strength but also seemed to be growing more focused on one of the planet's polar regions at regular rotations governed by the motion of both the asteroids and the planet.

A third group, which included Commander O'Donnell and Lieutenants Velth and Benoit, was analyzing the sensor feeds of the alien substance that had first attacked Ensign Gwyn and later the shuttlecraft *Van Cise*. Chakotay hadn't had a chance to review that footage in detail yet, but even at this distance, it was no mystery to him why Kim had ordered it destroyed.

Commander Torres stood at the largest table with Admiral Janeway and Commander Fife. Their display featured a close view of the landing site where Lieutenants Patel and Lasren and Ensigns Jepel and Vincent had been lost, side by side with one of the planet's exposed, desolate plains. The team's comm feed had been patched to *Vesta* shortly after it had been recovered. It was unsurprising to Chakotay that this was Kathryn's focus—making sure all of her people made it off this planet alive.

Chakotay took a brief moment to realize that what he had hoped most to gain from this mission, true synthesis among the members of the fleet's different vessels, was happening before his eyes. It didn't matter that they were no longer on the surface of DK-1116. They were all working together as one.

As Chakotay took this in, Captain Farkas entered the room and made a beeline toward Admiral Janeway. Pulled from his thoughts, he quickly followed.

"All of the away teams, except the one, have been retrieved, Admiral," Farkas said with palpable relief.

"Excellent," Janeway said, then turned her attention to Chakotay. "Do we have an estimate?"

Chakotay nodded. "Commander Paris has done the calculations and assuming whatever happens out there falls within the range of our current models, if *Vesta*, *Galen*, and *Demeter* depart the system at full impulse and activate their slipstream drives once they are beyond the outer asteroid field, they will most likely survive any cataclysmic blast."

"What happens to the numbers if they fail to make it through the outer field in time?"

"Their odds of survival fall to the high sixty percent range."

"What about *Voyager*?" Farkas asked.

"Assuming *Voyager* departs now, she'll reach the outer asteroid field easily at maximum warp. But we can't do that, can we?"

"*Voyager* can't depart for at least two more hours," Janeway replied.

"Why not?" Farkas asked.

"B'Elanna?" the admiral said, bringing her fleet chief into the circle.

"We think we can use the same open line Patel used to reestablish communications to embed a transporter beam and bring her team to the surface."

"How long can that possibly take?" Chakotay asked.

"We can't do it from orbit," Torres said. "We have to send a shuttle down with at least two officers, a pilot, and a transporter specialist. Honestly, I'd like to fill that role," she added.

"Why?" Chakotay asked.

"We have to land on the surface at the precise location

where that hard line terminates, excavate it, and establish a transporter link there. In addition to some specialized soil displacement devices Commander Fife has provided us, we'll need pattern enhancers, a portable force-field generator and transporter, and an atmospheric processor. There's no active biodome in that area, so we'll be working in EV suits, and when we transport them up, we'll have to bring them to the surface one at a time into the area protected by the force field and filled with atmosphere. It's the only way we're going to be able to get them. I won't risk bringing up their gear, given that I'll be manually adjusting their patterns every step of the way. I don't want to add any unnecessary complications to the buffering sequence. As soon as they materialize, we will need to relay their signals immediately to *Voyager*'s transporter room to get them safely back on the ship. The force field protecting them from the exposed surface will have to be dropped the moment the transport beam is activated. The timing will be tricky. It will take a few minutes to reset the system for each of them, but once we have them, the pilot and I can transport back to *Voyager* directly from the surface."

"And then we run?" Janeway asked.

"Yes, Admiral," Torres replied.

"Let's get started," Chakotay said. "Have you selected a pilot?"

"I was hoping to use Gwyn," Torres said. "I think Tom should take *Voyager*'s helm."

"Gwyn is not going to be able to help us this time," Chakotay said. "She's still recovering from her previous injuries."

Torres shook her head. "Damn it."

"B'Elanna, this fleet is filled with capable pilots," Janeway chided her.

318 ■ KIRSTEN BEYER

"The build-up of energy on the surface is increasing every second we stand here talking," Torres said. "I don't think it will be a problem on site, but there is a chance that as it increases, it will interfere with our transports from the surface. We might all end up needing to pile back into the shuttle to escape. I don't want a capable pilot. I want *the best*," Torres said.

"That's Tom," Chakotay said.

Torres nodded. "I wish I didn't agree with you about that."

"If things get tough, I can take *Voyager*'s helm," Chakotay added, "but if you'd rather both of you weren't on the away team, I'll take the shuttle controls."

Torres shook her head. "No. We've got this."

"How long do you need to prepare before you launch?" Janeway asked.

"An hour," Torres replied.

"As quickly as possible, please," Janeway ordered.

"Understood," Torres said, and hurried out of the room.

Lifting her voice, the admiral said, "Attention, everyone." Within seconds the ambient bustle fell to silence.

"We have officially overstayed our welcome in this system. Commanders Glenn and O'Donnell, return to your ships and prepare to set course out of the system. Commander Paris will forward each of you your flight plans and rendezvous coordinates. Captain Farkas, as soon as *Voyager*'s officers are transported back, you will set course out of the system as well. Train all of your available sensors on the planet. Whatever happens here, assuming we survive, we'll want to get the best possible images of the spectacle. *Voyager* will follow you as soon as we have retrieved our last away team."

"You're staying behind, Admiral?" Farkas asked dubiously.

A tight smile flashed over Janeway's face. "We're going to make it, Captain. *All of us.*"

Chakotay wasn't sure that Farkas understood, but he did. There were fifty moving parts to Torres's plan and at some point it was highly likely that someone was going to have to decide who made it off the surface and who didn't. Chakotay would do it if he had to, but Kathryn wasn't going to let him. She was going to take full responsibility for any deaths this day brought, even if that included Tom and B'Elanna.

"Okay," Farkas said. "We'll see you on the other side."

"Go," Janeway ordered.

Captain Farkas left the conference room quickly, already formulating the dozens of orders that still needed giving before they could set course.

"Farkas to Doctor Sal," she said, tapping her combadge. To her surprise, the computer responded for her.

"Doctor Sal is not on board."

"Where the hell is she?"

"Doctor Sal transported to the Galen *sixteen minutes ago."*

Shaking her head, Farkas called to Roach.

"Malcolm?"

"Go ahead, Captain."

"We've got a number of passengers who will be on their way back to *Voyager* in the next few minutes. Contact Commander Paris and confirm our course and prepare to break orbit as soon as we're cleared.

"Yes, Captain."

"Oh, and Malcolm. Contact Doctor Sal on the *Galen* and tell her to get her ass back here immediately. I want her on board when we depart."

"Understood."

GALEN

Ensign Aytar Gwyn slapped the side of the comm panel before her to improve the quality of the sound of Devi Patel's voice. It kept breaking into static with periodic harsh buzzing noises. She had no idea why Patel wanted to speak to her now. The timing couldn't have been worse. But when the call had come through, the Doctor had brought her to one of the medical bay's private rooms and then returned to his lab, where he was conferring with Doctor Sal and Counselor Cambridge. Icheb waited just outside the room, her only tether to sanity. But the obvious stress in Devi's voice served to focus Gwyn even better than the presence of Icheb.

"Gwyn . . . can you hear me?"

"I'm here, Devi. What's wrong?"

Gwyn slapped the panel again and finally the buzzing ceased. It was still distorted. Devi sounded like she was speaking from the far end of a distant tunnel, but at least her words were relatively clear.

"Nothing. Everything's fine. I just wanted to . . . that is . . . I heard you were injured in a shuttle accident."

Devi was lying about being fine. Even had her empathic abilities not been on maximum overload at the moment, Gwyn would have been able to sense that.

"Devi, cut the crap. What the hell is happening to you?"

"We don't have a lot of time. My survey team got ourselves into a bit of trouble on the planet. A rescue team is on its way, so I asked them to give us a short comm window while we wait."

"A rescue team? Why can't they just transport you up?"

"We're beneath the surface. There's a lot of interference. Lasren helped me rig this comm channel. They're going to use it to piggyback a transporter signal."

That sounded terrifying, but Gwyn had witnessed enough Starfleet technological miracles to understand that if they were trying it, it would most likely work.

"Good," Gwyn said, hoping some false bravado would reach and inspire her friend. "I'm sure you'll be fine."

Patel paused for a moment. Gwyn wasn't sure if the feed was degrading again or not.

"Devi?"

"I'm here. We found so much down here. It'll take years of analysis just to categorize the alien species we discovered. And the technology the Edrehmaia left behind is incredible. The Sevenofninonium was just the tip of the iceberg. It's a legacy to be proud of."

Gwyn smiled in understanding even though she didn't have the first clue what or who the Edrehmaia were. Devi was getting cold feet as the moment of rescue approached and wanted to make sure someone would be able to acknowledge her achievement in case things went south.

"Just make sure I'm there when you give the captain your report. And Seven. I want to see the look on their faces," Gwyn said.

Patel's next words came out in a rush. *"The thing is, they can't prioritize transport of our technology. Our tricorders, our data, it's all going to be lost. I can't begin to re-create it from memory. And it's too important. Starfleet needs to know what we found down here."*

A knot began to twist itself into being in Gwyn's stomach.

"So transport the data now over the comm line, while you're waiting for your rescue," Gwyn said.

"We can't. No one is sure how long this channel will remain stable, and they're not willing to risk a potential overload with a data dump."

Gwyn's pulse began to race. It might have been the hormones raging through her body, but she doubted it.

"Devi, listen to me," Gwyn insisted. "If they can't bring up the data, don't worry about it. We'll find another way to get it. You come first. Do you hear me?"

"I'm sorry about that day on the shuttle. I was mad at you, but that was dumb. You know that, right?"

"I do. Of course I do. None of that matters now. All that matters is that you come home."

The signal began to break up again.

"Gwyn . . . Gwyn?"

"I lied, Devi, when I said I was okay. I'm not. Me, the girl who doesn't believe in lying, even to spare people's feelings, I was giving it a try because you sound like you have more than enough to deal with right now. But I can't do it. There's something terribly wrong with me. I'm going to need your help. You have to come home. You have to help me."

"Gwyn . . . sorry . . . that last . . . what?"

"Devi? Devi!"

"Gwyn? If you can hear me . . . the others, they won't understand. You have to make them understand. Okay?"

A loud burst of static interrupted. Gwyn rose from her seat at the terminal and slammed the station hard enough to free it from its brackets.

This time it didn't work. The connection was lost.

A new urgency welled within Aytar Gwyn that had nothing to do with a perfect mate. It had to do with a loss that was much more immediate. There was no reasoning with Devi at this point. She was about to do something incredibly stupid and somebody needed to stop her.

But Gwyn couldn't do that unless she could prove that she was fit to return to duty. And there was only one way to make that happen. She had to complete the *finiis'ral*.

DK-1116

Once the comm channel was lost, most likely due to *Galen*'s less than optimal orbital position, Devi Patel switched Lasren's tricorder out of transmission mode and into receiving mode. Vincent and Jepel had joined her and Lasren at the top of the catwalk, nearest to the field generator. They were as close as they could physically get to the hard line Commander Torres was about to turn into a transport conduit.

The relief of the rest of her team was palpable. Until the comm line had been successfully established and Torres had concocted her rescue plan, they had begun to resign themselves to the inevitable. It had made Vincent cranky and Jepel a little manic, but Lasren had begun to retreat into himself. Only now, with rescue a few minutes away, was he smiling again. He was focused with great intensity on making sure they had done all they could on their end to ensure a successful transport.

The clock on the system failure had wound down to less than six hours. They'd been advised that all personnel had been safely recovered from the surface, so there was no longer any fear that anyone would die when the energy fields fell. But Patel knew there were other problems. She didn't know what they were, but the tone of her interactions with Captain Chakotay and Commander Torres and the specifics of the rescue mission had given her pause. The energy build-

324 ■ KIRSTEN BEYER

up on the surface might be connected to the failure of the fields, but she doubted it. Something else had gone wrong, but no one was going to tell Patel or her team, most likely because there was nothing they could possibly do about it.

She had been ordered to abandon all of the data she had collected, to simply commit as much as she could to memory. Which meant there was no way another team would be sent later to retrieve what was about to be lost. But Vincent and Jepel had managed to fill every bit of memory in their tricorders with the data on dozens of species that had experimented with the Edrehmaia on the planet. Patel had filled hers with data collected from the cavern and its many moving parts.

Devi Patel was not one to refuse a direct order. It went against everything she believed about her role as a Starfleet officer and every instinct she had developed during her years at the Academy and in service.

But this one needed to be refused. She searched her heart over and over as she created the link between the three data-filled tricorders and added the one piece of additional information that would allow her to put her plan into action. She wanted to believe her motives were pure, that this was a sacrifice made on the altar of gathering knowledge, Starfleet's core mission.

Fame, glory, these had never interested her. They were fleeting illusions at best. The action she was about to take wasn't going to lead to either of those. Time and again during the last few years as she had wilted in the shadows cast by Seven and the other senior staff, Patel had wondered what she had to do to prove herself. It seemed like there were a million tiny things she should have done differently.

What she realized as she stood in the cavern surrounded

by scientific mysteries and data that would keep the Federation's brightest minds pushing new boundaries for decades to come was that sometimes it wasn't all the little things. Sometimes, the difference between being a good officer and a great one came down to a single choice.

The fleet's commanding officers had decided that if the choice was between rescuing her team and securing the knowledge they had accumulated on this mission, the team came first. Patel disagreed, but there was no time to convince them of that and had she pushed any harder than she already had, it might have raised suspicion. Patel knew that being part of a team meant subsuming one's personal needs to the greater good. The Vulcans had a pithy saying for it—*the needs of the many outweigh the needs of the few.* In seeking to stand out among her peers, Devi had been seeking acknowledgment of her abilities. What she saw now with perfect clarity was that there was nothing for her to gain in this moment or any day that would follow that could compare to the secrets she had helped uncover. This treasure trove of data was more important to Starfleet than Patel would ever be.

And she was going to make damn sure they received it.

GALEN

Doctor Sal was at a complete loss. She stared openmouthed at the terminal filled with Ensign Gwyn's biological data and, for the first time in her life, wondered if she needed to reconsider her general tendency to dismiss miracles as the purview of fanciful minds.

The Doctor updated the readings once again to make sure what they were witnessing was accurate. He shook his head as he did so, no doubt filled with the same misgivings that were currently accosting Sal.

"According to these readings, Ensign, your hormone levels have returned to normal and the metamorphic cells within your body have fallen below one percent."

Gwyn smiled with absolute confidence. "I told you Doctor, a few minutes ago, something changed. The need, the hunger, they simply went away. I started to feel like myself again."

The Doctor turned to Sal. "Could this be some sort of temporary reprieve, a natural fluctuation in the process of the *finiis'ral*?"

"I have no idea," Sal said. "I suppose. It's also possible that since this change was brought about by unnatural circumstances, her body is reverting to its normal levels. She might have been experiencing a false metamorphosis, in the same way sometimes pregnancy tests result in false positives."

"The metamorphic cells have all but vanished from her system."

"I can see that, Doctor."

"I need to return to *Voyager*," Gwyn insisted. "I need to get back to my post."

"We'll clear you for duty soon enough, Ensign," the Doctor said, "but we're going to want to make sure we're seeing a permanent stabilization."

Gwyn sat up and swung her legs over the side of the biobed.

"I *know* this crisis has passed. Personally, I think Icheb deserves a lot of the credit. He helped me hold on to myself through the worst of it. I'm sure I could never have recovered without his help."

Counselor Cambridge stood a few paces back beside Icheb, who stared at Gwyn with faint disbelief. Sal didn't know what the look on the ensign's face meant, but it was one of several pieces of the puzzle before her that wasn't fitting easily into place.

The Doctor placed a reassuring hand on Gwyn's shoulder. "You can't return to *Voyager* at the moment. Our ship is about to depart the system. Admiral's orders. But by the time we have regrouped with the rest of the fleet, I'm sure we'll be able to get you back on duty."

"May I speak with you, Doctor?" Icheb asked, passing meaningful glances to both Sal and Cambridge in the process.

"Of course. Rest, Ensign Gwyn. We'll be back in a few moments."

Sal spared one last glance at Gwyn before following the others into the Doctor's private office. Whatever had happened to Gwyn should have felt like a reprieve. She had no idea why it didn't.

As soon as the door to the Doctor's office slid shut behind him, Icheb released a torrent of words he had clearly been biting back during Gwyn's exam.

"She's not lying, exactly. But the *finiis'ral* didn't just end. She ended it. I don't know how exactly, but she did."

"What are you talking about, Icheb?" the Doctor asked.

"Gwyn. She was speaking to Lieutenant Patel. She was upset, but I don't know why."

"Lieutenant Patel is one of four officers still trapped on the planet, Ensign," Cambridge advised him. "I believe a team will be dispatched to rescue them shortly."

"When her conversation with Patel was over, Gwyn wouldn't talk to me," Icheb continued. "She had the strangest look on her face, like she had decided something. Then she went back to look at the baby again and when she came out, she was herself again."

"The baby?" Sal said, suddenly concerned.

The Doctor pulled up a new set of readings on his display. "I've been monitoring her life signs constantly, Doctor Sal. There is no cause for worry. She's fine. See?"

Sal studied the various readings of the embryonic monitor for a moment. They were, just as the Doctor said, all well within normal limits.

"How did you and Ensign Gwyn find out about our youngest patient?" the Doctor asked Icheb, his disappointment clear.

"Gwyn was restless, wandering around, poking her head into the private rooms, and we found the incubator. I'm sorry, Doctor. I won't tell anyone, of course. And I'm sure Gwyn won't either. But it was so strange, the look on her face when she saw the baby. And then she said something about wanting to talk to her mother. Of course, that's impossible right now."

A sudden shot of adrenaline began at the base of Sal's neck and poured down her torso and limbs.

The baby.

A smile began to play over her lips as a new idea burst into her brain. Five hundred years ago the women of Krios had decided to take their genetic destiny in their own hands. They had refused en masse to continue bonding with the men of their society, and yet, they hadn't died, at least most of them hadn't.

Dear gods, she thought. *How did I never think of it before?*

The period of unrest following the Dawn on Krios should have resulted in plague-like death tolls with entire populations refusing bonding, but there was nothing like that in the records she'd seen so many decades earlier. So they didn't die. They bonded with someone . . . *just not their perfect mates.*

An embryo, an infant who had yet to develop a personality or any preferences beyond the most basic survival instincts, had been the one creature with whom the completion of the finiis'ral *did not have to result in the concurrent death of one's own identity.* And Sal could easily see the pregnant women of Krios deciding to give this gift to their suffering sisters in the name of creating a better future for all of them.

"I know what she did," Sal said softly before hurrying toward the office door.

As it slid open, Sal called, "Ensign, I must . . ."

But she paused when she realized that the room was empty.

Cambridge was right behind her. He immediately called out, "Computer, locate Ensign Gwyn."

"Ensign Gwyn is not on board."

16

Commander Tom Paris worked as quickly as the bulky gloves of his EV suit would permit. The shuttle flight to the surface had been more challenging than he had anticipated. The energy build-up on the planet was altering its gravitational pull. The last readings he'd seen suggested that the rate of rotation of the planet was also increasing. Paris understood, of course, that planets didn't do that, but the more Seven and Harry had told him about DK-1116, the less convinced he was that this truly was a planet.

All he wanted was to complete this rescue mission and feel the firm deck plating of *Voyager* beneath his feet once again. To do that, he had six minutes to get the pattern enhancers appropriately calibrated and to fill the small force field he had activated around them with breathable atmosphere.

It felt like a lifetime ago that he had been splashing in the lake with his daughter and roasting marshmallows. In truth, it had been less than fifteen hours. Once this was over, he and the rest of the fleet's senior officers were going to spend a great deal of time figuring out how a simple exploratory mission had gone to hell so quickly, and he would work as hard as any of them, assuming he lived long enough to see it. He refused to think about Miral and Michael and the fact that both of their parents were currently involved in a life-threatening emergency situation. Every time he did, his hands started to shake and that wasn't helpful. He'd barely had time to kiss them quickly before leaving them in the care of Kula. He was going to see them again. There was no acceptable alternative.

"Are the enhancers stable?" B'Elanna asked.

"Working on it."

"I'm going to make final contact with Patel's team before I cut the comm channel completely."

"I'm guessing they couldn't be more ready to get off this rock."

"They're not the only ones. Just stabilize that field. We'll be back home before you know it."

"I love you."

"I love you more."

The heat in the main cavern had gone from pleasant to oppressive in the last few hours. Lieutenant Kenth Lasren felt the layer of sweat covering his skin, even though the fabric of his uniform was designed to minimize perspiration. He wondered idly if the slight increase in radiant intensity he perceived from the living ore all around him was his imagination. There was no longer any way to check. His tricorder was being used to maintain their comm signal and Patel had confiscated the others. She seemed to be studying the data on them the way she had probably prepared for every test she had taken in her life. It was a shame the data was going to have to stay behind for now, but he had no doubt that Captain Chakotay would prioritize returning to this chamber and taking even more detailed readings as soon as they could figure out how to do it safely. They were still at the beginning of weeks of exploration, after all. Even without the protective energy fields, there was still much to study on the surface of the planet. This was simply a hiccup in what was going to prove to be an incredibly productive mission.

Vincent and Jepel had seated themselves on the landing nearby with their backs to the cave wall. Both of them looked weary. He understood. There wasn't much either of them could do at the moment but wait. He wished Devi could relax. This part was going to be over soon enough, and the recognition she so desperately craved when this mission began was sure to be hers.

Looking at her now, her head bent over, sweat dripping from her forehead, he wondered if she was ever going to see herself the way others saw her. She was an excellent officer among a team of outstanding ones, and a Starfleet career could last decades. She had plenty of time to make her mark, she just didn't realize it.

"Torres to away team, do you copy?"

"We're here and standing by to transport," Lasren said.

"I'm going to kill the comm line in a second. Each of you needs to position yourself as close as you can to where Lasren is standing right now. Without the channel, I won't be able to confirm each transport. Just hang in there. It will be a few minutes between each one. But we'll get you all out of there."

"We'll be ready, Commander," Lasren said.

"Commander Torres," Patel interjected at the last second, "my team goes first."

"Understood. See you soon. Torres out."

Lasren exchanged a glance between Vincent and Jepel. Both of them rose to their feet. He knew that both of them wanted to ask why Patel had insisted that they be rescued first, but neither of them argued. He didn't want to tell them the answer, if they hadn't guessed it already. This was an untested transporter protocol. It was less than one hundred percent guaranteed to succeed. The first would be the riskiest because it had never been done before. By the time they got to Patel, they'd either have the process down to a science or have abandoned it as impossible. It looked like a small act of bravado on Patel's part. In truth, it might have been the most selfish thing she had done since this mission began.

He was not a pessimist by nature. He decided that, right now, that was a good thing. Handing his tricorder to Devi, he stood still and closed his eyes. If these were the last few moments of his life, he preferred to spend them in silent contemplation of all the things that had brought him joy. He focused inward and thought of home, his family, and his dearest friends.

The next thing he knew, the tingle of the transporter beam took him.

VOYAGER

"What do you mean Ensign Gwyn is on a runabout headed for the surface?!" Harry Kim demanded.

Lieutenant Waters shrugged her shoulders. "You think I would make that up at a time like this?"

Kim looked to Chakotay, who remained, as ever, the calm at the center of the storm. Admiral Janeway stood beside him, but moved closer to operations at Waters's response.

"We'll recover Ensign Gwyn and the runabout," Chakotay said more evenly than Kim could have managed.

"Do we know what precipitated this?" Janeway asked.

Doctor Sal's voice sounded throughout the bridge. *"She was in brief contact with Lieutenant Patel. Ensign Icheb believes that she is concerned about Patel's safety."*

"Is she physically able to fly?" Chakotay asked. "Her last medical report indicated she was off duty until further notice."

"*Her physical health seems fine. I can't say the same for her mental health,*" Commander Cambridge reported.

Chakotay turned to Janeway, who said, "*Demeter* has already left the system. *Galen* is to do so at once, as is *Vesta*. Don't worry about transporting back to your respective ships now. We'll deal with that once the fleet is safe."

Affirmative responses came quickly from each of the two remaining ships. Chakotay then ordered a channel open to Gwyn's stolen ship.

RUNABOUT *OKINAWA*

"*Ensign Gwyn, this is Captain Chakotay, please respond.*"

Gwyn considered maintaining comm silence, but thought better of it. She didn't think they would shoot her down, but she had technically stolen a ship, so the option was on the table.

"Gwyn here, Captain."

"*Alter your course and make for* Voyager *immediately. We have officers on the surface in the process of rescuing Lieutenant Patel and her team. They do not require your assistance. The moment the rescue is complete,* Voyager *will be setting course out of the system at maximum speed. The longer you delay our departure, the greater the risk that no one on the ship will survive. Do you understand?*"

Gwyn did, all too well. Even the runabout's scanners were humming and nearly overloading with the amount of data the planet was kicking off. A massive build-up of energy was occurring. As best Gwyn could tell, it wasn't localized to any particular area. It was coming from the entire planet. Shifts in gravity and the planet's rotation were playing hell with her navigational controls. She hadn't even reached the atmosphere yet, and already the ship was roughly buffeted by gravimetric distortions. At best, this was going to be one of the roughest rides of her life.

She maintained course anyway as she responded. "I'm sorry, Captain. But I can't alter course just yet. I am moving into position to rescue Lieutenant Patel."

"I gave you an order, Ensign," Chakotay barked. *"Refuse and you subject yourself to disciplinary action and a possible court-martial."*

"I understand, Captain, and am more than willing to face the consequences of my actions, just as soon as this mission is complete."

"This mission is unnecessary, Ensign. Lieutenant Patel will be back on board Voyager *in the next few minutes. The best way to preserve her life and yours is to be back here when she arrives."*

Gwyn thought before she spoke again. There was always a chance she was wrong and if so, Devi shouldn't suffer for Gwyn's misguided hubris, but neither should *Voyager*'s entire crew. "Captain, it is not my intention to risk anyone's life but mine. Should Patel return in the next few minutes as you have indicated she will, set course out of the system and I will do my best to rendezvous with you. Don't wait on me."

The next voice to sound through the comm wasn't Chakotay's. It was the admiral's.

"Ensign Gwyn, why are you refusing a direct order from your commanding officer?"

Because I know when my friends are lying to me didn't feel like an appropriate response, or one that would move Admiral Janeway.

"I'm sorry, Admiral. I have reason to believe that Lieutenant Patel will require means of rescue beyond those you have put in motion."

An alert blared from her console. *Voyager* had just activated her tractor beam and was attempting to lock on to the runabout. Evading the beam required altering to a more treacherous angle of atmospheric entry, but she executed the maneuver with relative ease.

Damn it, Devi, she thought furiously. The conversation they were going to have when this was over was going to be incredibly unpleasant. Gwyn looked forward to it.

DK-1116

Commander Torres's heart pounded but her hands remained steady as the first transport cycle of her hastily rigged mechanism was completed. Lieutenant Lasren stood within the force field smiling with obvious relief.

Before he had a chance to offer his thanks, Torres signaled *Voyager* and he disappeared again in a cascade of light.

One down. Three to go.

She had barely begun resetting the system when the ground beneath her feet began to shake.

VOYAGER

"What's happening?" Admiral Janeway asked.

Seven stood at the bridge's rear science station and was the first to respond. "Several of the growths we detected on the surface have completed new circuits with existing deposits of ore. Their presence has increased the speed of the build-up of energy exponentially. Our initial estimate of five additional hours of stability is no longer accurate. Two of the existing biodome fields have fallen, and the others will follow within the next half hour.

"*Transporter room to the bridge. Lieutenant Lasren has arrived safely.*"

"Acknowledged," Chakotay responded.

"Large areas of the surface, including the location of our away team, are experiencing tremors," Seven added.

"Chakotay to Torres. B'Elanna, you're going to need to hurry."

DK-1116

Commander Paris fell to his knees as the ground beneath his feet shifted. The pattern enhancers had been planted several feet into the surface as a precaution using the same excavation tech they had brought to expose the hard line. For the moment, they held position, but Paris didn't think that was going to be the case in another few minutes.

"Honey?"

"*Relax,*" Torres advised him. "*The signal has a wider capacity than I thought. I'm going to bring Vincent and Jepel up together.*"

"That sounds like a great idea."

Tom waited, the seconds stretching out into lifetimes as he monitored the force field's stability around the enhancers. Twenty meters beyond his wife, their shuttle sat on a desolate plain. Behind it, the sky, which was already a dusty brown, was darkening.

Paris wasn't sure he wanted to know, but he aimed his

tricorder at the horizon anyway. It confirmed that a large, electrically charged dust storm had formed a few dozen kilometers from their position and was heading their way. It shouldn't interfere with their return to *Voyager*, but it would hamper any effort to leave the surface via their shuttle, should that prove necessary.

He didn't want to scare B'Elanna. She needed to focus on what she was doing. He was scared enough for both of them anyway.

Lieutenant Patel watched as Vincent and Jepel vanished in a flutter of transporter energy simultaneously. If Torres was risking a double transport, that meant conditions on the surface were likely getting worse.

As much as she had anticipated this moment over the last hour, now that it had come, she faltered momentarily. She didn't want to die, especially alone on an alien planet. And maybe there would be another way to retrieve the data she had collected.

As she began to shake, Gwyn's voice rose in her mind. *"You know if you get your ass out there and discover a brand-new element yourself, maybe that'll change."*

Patel's response now was the same as it had been only a few days earlier.

"No, it won't," she said aloud.

There were likely only seconds left to her. She detached her combadge and placed it on the tricorder, activating the final program she would ever create as a Starfleet officer, a quick bit of code that made the device transmit her life signs, and placed the linked tricorders on the ground Torres would target with her transporter beam. Patel then turned and moved quickly back down the catwalk, away from rescue, away from life, and toward her final few hours of existence.

As she did, she felt certainty mingled with remorse. She didn't allow herself to turn back, even as she heard the sound of the transporter beam activate and take what had become her life's work back to the surface of the planet.

Commander Paris stared inside the force field dumbstruck. It had grown darker in the last few minutes, but all he could focus on were the three small tricorders B'Elanna had just transported up.

"What the hell?" Tom asked.

Tom dropped the field and collected the tricorders. Shaking his head, he held up a combadge.

"I don't think she's coming back, B'Elanna."

Torres shook her head as Paris dropped the tricorders into one of his suit's outer pockets.

"Reactivate the force field. I'm going to try one more time."

Paris did as he had been instructed.

"Chakotay to away team. What's the hold-up? Where is Lieutenant Patel?"

"Patel sent up her data, sir," Paris replied. "We're attempting to establish another lock on her."

"It's not working," B'Elanna cried. *"I've got nothing."*

As Paris struggled to accept this unacceptable proposition, the ground shuddered again as a wide crack opened, tipping the shuttle forward into it. Seconds later, the gray sky turned black.

Tom stumbled to B'Elanna and grabbed both her wrists.

"It's over," he said. "We're done here."

"I have enough power for one more transport. I'm not leaving her behind."

"B'Elanna, she wanted you to leave her behind."

"Chakotay . . . away . . . can't acquire transporter lock. Stand . . ."

Paris was pretty sure the end of that message was "by." Their odds of success when they had accepted this mission had been long, and were moving rapidly into impossible territory.

"If they can't transport us up, we have to get back to the shuttle, now."

He could barely see his wife's face through their helmets, but he could easily imagine her stricken expression. B'Elanna sucked at failing. She took every loss personally. But that didn't change reality.

"Give me one second."

Tom watched as B'Elanna initiated the final transport. Seconds later, the area inside the force field was still empty and the power cells for the portable transporter faded to blackness.

"Damn it!" Torres said.

"It's now or never, B'Elanna," Tom reminded her.

Side by side, linked at the elbows, Tom Paris and B'Elanna Torres struggled for every step as they made their way back to the shuttle. Tom wasn't sure how its systems had been affected by that last quake or how he was going to get it fired up. He just knew if he didn't, he and his wife were going to die on this planet.

VOYAGER

"Gwyn was right," Admiral Janeway said softly. "Patel intentionally sabotaged her own rescue."

"Where is Ensign Gwyn's runabout now?" Chakotay asked.

Kim had resumed his position at the tactical station and replied, "She is headed for the coordinates where Patel's team first transported down. That biodome field fell a few minutes ago and all of the water has evaporated from the surface. She won't be able to land safely, much less mount a rescue on foot now."

"We don't need her to land," Chakotay said. "Open a channel."

OKINAWA

Gwyn was having trouble making sense of the new surface readings that were populating her display screens. The surface of DK-1116 looked nothing like it had the first time she'd seen it and barely resembled the landscape recorded in the fleet's database on the biodome Patel's team had been assigned to study. All she could see below was a massive hole at the bottom of what looked like a giant staircase.

She was in the process of focusing her transporter's scanners on any detectable human life signs when Chakotay's voice came over the comm.

"Okinawa, this is Chakotay. You have to alter course."

"Not yet, Captain," Gwyn replied, marveling at her reckless bravado. She had always nurtured a rebellious streak, but her actions now were so far beyond any acceptable boundaries, she almost didn't recognize herself.

It had something to do with the bonding. Terrifying as the prospect had been, the absolute contentment and resolve that had washed over her when she had opened herself up to the tiny life that would someday become Nancy Conlon and Harry Kim's daughter had altered her forever.

Until that moment, nothing in Gwyn's world had been

as important to her as her own life. Her determination to rescue Patel had been an instinct driven as much by avoiding loss for herself as ensuring Devi's survival.

The few times her mother and her *leedi* had spoken to her about the empathic metamorphs, they had told her that the process, while difficult to contemplate and horrific in its way, was said to be a positive one for those who accepted it. The stability of their lives post bonding was well documented, as was their productivity and general well-being. They spoke of living for their mates and usually their lives ended not long after those they bonded with. It was impossible to imagine for those who never experienced it, and most agreed that the sacrifice of one's identity was much too high a price to pay, but now Gwyn could acknowledge from personal experience that what might have been lost paled in comparison in some ways to what had been gained.

Gwyn's life had a new purpose. Her love and devotion to a being not yet fully formed was absolute. It went so far beyond anything she had ever wanted for herself, including her career, that she wondered how she had ever found the will to live until she had known what it was to live for another.

That broadened perspective made her commitment to Patel's rescue equally intense. She knew what she had to do. She understood what it truly was to be of service to another. Her priorities were in perfect synch with her deepest self and the sense of empowerment that calm, still certainty at the center of her being brought dimmed any fears she might have for the consequences of her current course.

"Ensign Gwyn, listen to me very carefully," Chakotay continued. *"Commanders Torres and Paris are still on the surface not far from your position and in need of emergency transport.*

We can't get a lock from orbit. The interference is scrambling our transporter signals."

"What about Devi?" Gwyn asked.

"Lieutenant Patel sabotaged her own rescue. If you can retrieve her, do so, but Tom and B'Elanna are also in danger. I am sending you their last coordinates now. We will await your return as long as possible."

That her mission had just become harder did not alter Gwyn's certainty. As the new coordinates appeared on her navigation panel, she replied, "Understood, Captain. I'm on my way."

DK-1116

Devi Patel stumbled and pitched forward onto the catwalk as a deafening crack sounded from somewhere overhead.

"What the hell was that?"

Her words echoed around her as the cavern grew brighter and dust descended from above like gentle rain. She grabbed the nearest railing and felt it vibrating in concert with the movement within the planet.

Looking down, she watched as the bright conduits of dancing ore began to move less randomly. The slack that had been present and created the illusion of undulating snakes decreased as the heavy lines seemed to tense and shorten.

Her teeth began to ache as a distinct hum, emanating from below, moved through her.

For a moment she wished for her lost tricorder. She couldn't make sense of what she was seeing and doubted it would help, but the instinct to understand was apparently going to remain with her until she breathed her last.

Far down, she could see the giant spider's legs moving

with precision as they altered large strands of ore, connecting them in new patterns whose purpose Patel couldn't begin to guess.

Whatever was happening, she did not doubt for a moment that it was intended by whoever created this place. Despite the desire of those who had come here before seeking understanding, she saw now how futile their efforts had been.

"We're not ready to harness power like this," she said. She doubted their predecessors had been either. But one thing was certain. She alone, of all of them, would see the frightful design of the Edrehmaia in all of its glory. It wasn't all she might have hoped for, but it was hers. If there was anything eternal in a human life, she paused to hope that what she had gained here would go with her into whatever infinity held.

Tom and B'Elanna could barely see more than a few inches in front of them. Their only confirmation that they were headed for their shuttlecraft came from the display panels in the arms of their suits that were keyed to the shuttle's transponder.

"Where is it?" B'Elanna demanded.

"According to this, we're practically on top of it," Tom replied.

Tom reached forward and felt nothing. Only then did he realize that in the storm, the shuttle had fallen farther into the crevice created by the shifting ground.

There wasn't time to think about how stupid his next move was. He simply sat down on the ground and began to inch forward until he legs fell over the side of the new hole that had claimed his only way off of this rock.

Swinging his legs back, he oriented himself onto his stomach and pulled himself to the point where he could see over the edge.

There was nothing to see but inky darkness, but his display confirmed that the shuttle was resting ten meters below.

"I'm going to try to activate the shuttle's emergency transporter," B'Elanna said.

"You'll never get a lock in this mess."

"You'd rather jump for it?"

"I'd probably break both my legs when I landed."

"Forget your legs. You'll shatter your spine."

"I could use a little positive thinking right about now," Tom said.

B'Elanna didn't answer. Tom pulled back and looked up. B'Elanna had lifted her arm and was pointing it at the heavens above.

"What are you doing?"

"There's something up there."

"How do you know?"

Before she could answer, a sick sensation hit Tom's gut as the lights of B'Elanna's EV suit vanished.

OKINAWA

The next thing Tom Paris knew, someone was pushing him forward.

What the . . . ?

The grime on his faceplate was so heavy that he had missed the moment when he had been transported aboard what appeared at first to be his shuttle.

He quickly removed his helmet only to hear Ensign Gwyn shouting at him.

346 ■ KIRSTEN BEYER

"Clear the pad!" she ordered.

B'Elanna had already stepped into the forward section of the runabout and removed her helmet and gloves. She pushed Tom into the nearest seat and took the one opposite him.

"What are you doing here, Ensign?" Paris asked. "Not that I'm complaining, mind you."

"Can one of you, sirs, get up here and take the tactical controls?" Gwyn asked.

Torres stood and moved quickly into the seat beside Gwyn. "What are we doing?" she asked as she did so.

"We're going to make that hole down there a little bigger," Gwyn said. "The only thing I can get a lock on is your shuttle. Target it and fire phasers at ten percent."

"Why are we destroying our shuttle?" Paris asked.

"I need to make that hole around it bigger."

Paris looked to Torres. He didn't need to speak for her to read his mind. *You're okay with this?*

She nodded. "You're going to try to transport Devi, right?"

The runabout shook and dipped to the left, sending Paris careening into the bulkhead.

"There's a good chance she dies if the cavern down there collapses all around her," Gwyn said. "We're talking about a window that is only a few seconds long."

"But if we can get direct access to it at all, I should be able to lock on to any human life signs," Torres said.

"Don't wait," Gwyn said. "We're only going to get one shot at this."

"I know."

Tom made his way forward until he was hovering over Gwyn's shoulder. "Adjust attitudinal control by three percent," he said.

Gwyn had been about to do so anyway. Normally she hated for anyone to second-guess her flying. Tom Paris was one of the few people alive who had that right. She'd been forced to loop back around in order to target the shuttle.

"We're in range, B'Elanna."

"I see it," Torres said. "Firing."

As the phasers lit the darkness, Gwyn shunted power from the warp engines to the shields. It still felt like they'd been hit by a small torpedo. A cracking boom sounded all around them as Gwyn struggled to gain a little more altitude for their final pass.

"Anything?" Paris asked Torres. She was focused with quiet intensity over the runabout's transporter controls.

"There she is," Torres said softly and passed her fingers gently over the controls.

Paris looked back to the transporter pad automatically. A figure was trying to coalesce into being, but kept fading in and out.

"I'm taking power from environmental controls," Torres said.

"Sure. Breathing is overrated anyway," Gwyn teased.

The transporter beam sputtered again, until finally resolving into the still form of Devi Patel, lying on her side.

"Take us up, Gwyn, fast as you can," Paris said as he hurried to Patel. She was a mess. She was bleeding from a nasty gash on the side of her head, and her breathing was shallow. She had broken her right arm, both legs, and several ribs. He was glad she was unconscious because otherwise the pain would have been unbearable.

"Is she alive?" Gwyn called from the conn.

"Barely. We need to get her to sickbay as soon as possible."

"We'll be back on *Voyager* in five minutes, assuming we can get out of the atmosphere," Gwyn said.

Torres turned to Gwyn and placed a hand on her shoulder. "Thank you for coming after us."

"I didn't actually," Gwyn said. "I came for her."

Off Torres's deeply furrowed brow, she added, "But you're still welcome, Commander."

"Do you have any idea why she did this?" Paris asked.

Gwyn didn't reply.

"Ensign?"

"She thought the data she recovered on the planet was more important than her life," Gwyn finally replied.

"She should know better than that," Torres said.

Gwyn cast a glance toward her. "She didn't. And as her commanding officers, you should take the time to figure out why. My guess is, she's not the only member of our crew that could make that mistake."

17

Seconds after runabout *Okinawa* had docked, *Voyager* had broken orbit and set course out of the system. Ten minutes later, Tom Paris had reported to the bridge and at Chakotay's request had taken over for Gleez at the conn. The captain had then left the bridge to his first officer and joined Admiral Janeway and Seven in astrometrics. Best guess was that the planet was going to tear itself apart in the next three hours and *Voyager* was going to be the best place in the universe from which to view the spectacle, right up until the shockwave from the destruction of DK-1116 hit them and destroyed the ship.

Paris had devised two short warp maneuvers that had bought them a few more minutes of life. But there was no warping through the asteroid field they were currently traversing at full impulse. At least the other three fleet vessels had almost cleared it. Odds were good that *Demeter* was going to manage a slipstream jump in time. *Vesta* and *Galen* would be cutting it close, but their chances were significantly better than *Voyager*'s.

It was a uniquely frustrating moment for Harry Kim. He was proud of the bridge crew. Lasren had returned to duty in order to relieve Waters. He, Aubrey, and Paris were Kim's only company on the bridge. Everyone else was either off duty, or relieved and spending their last few hours composing final personal logs or transmitting messages home. They wouldn't reach the Alpha Quadrant for a few days, even with the aid of the communications relays the fleet had dropped when they first returned to the Delta Quadrant. By the time their family and friends learned their fate it would all be over.

Had it been possible, Kim would have spent this time with Nancy and their daughter. Last he'd heard before the fleet broke up, both were doing well. The Doctor thought it would be safe to revive Nancy in the next couple of days. Kim hated to think that the first thing she might hear was that he was dead.

They had passed the time listening to Lasren's report on his team's discoveries on the planet. Now that its architects had a name, the Edrehmaia, and it was understood that their fleet had been the last in a long line of explorers to visit DK-1116 and try to unravel its mysteries, Kim was overwhelmed with frustration.

"Would it have killed them to leave instructions for those who came after, so we could have avoided all of this?" Kim had asked of Lasren.

"They did, sir," Lasren had replied. "I never saw the interface Devi found, but it tried to help us. It gave us plenty of warning about the system failure we triggered. It wasn't Devi's fault that she inadvertently locked down the command station. She was trying to preserve the records there."

Patel had almost died to make sure she wasn't the only one who learned all that Species 001 had done to further the understanding of many sentient species.

Lieutenant Devi Patel was still in surgery. No one knew yet if she was going to survive, and while Kim understood that both she and Gwyn were going to face disciplinary action for their choices, his inclination as a commanding officer would have been to reward both of them for their selflessness and devotion to duty. Kim wondered if the admiral and captain were going to make the same call.

If nothing else, Aytar Gwyn had saved the lives of Kim's best friends. That was going to grant her a great deal of leeway going forward, at least in Kim's book.

Three hours and six minutes after *Voyager* had broken orbit, Tom Paris called out from the conn, "Eyes forward, everyone. I think the floorshow is about to begin."

Admiral Kathryn Janeway stood between Seven and Chakotay at the astrometrics lab's control panel. Behind them, dozens of crew members had assembled to watch whatever was about to happen with their commanding officers.

While fully conscious of the danger in which they found themselves, part of Kathryn Janeway felt like a child preparing to open a birthday present. For days, she had wondered at the purpose of this small world in the Delta Quadrant. For better or worse, her curiosity was about to be satisfied.

Why? she still wondered as she stared at the distant rock, now lit by its own internal, infernal light. It looked more like a tiny sun than a world on which she had walked less than a day earlier. The strange substance that contained the only known source in the universe of the element that would, it seemed, forever be known to her crew as *Sevenofninonium,* had been storing potential energy for thousands of years. That energy was about to be released. The most likely result would be the cataclysmic destruction of the planet. But somehow, Janeway believed that wasn't going to be the only thing her crew was about to witness.

Janeway had asked that Commander Torres join them to

observe the spectacle, but B'Elanna had demurred, preferring to watch from her quarters with her children. The admiral didn't fault her for that. But she had shared so much of her life with B'Elanna. If it was truly about to end, a tiny, selfish part of her wanted to do it together, as one, in the same way they had faced so many dangers in the past.

"Admiral," Seven said suddenly.

Janeway felt Chakotay take her hand and give it a gentle squeeze.

Seconds later, Lieutenant Kim's voice sounded. *"Seven, are you seeing this?"*

"We are, Lieutenant."

"Keep this channel open," Janeway ordered.

For a moment, the planet on the screen grew brighter. Then, quite suddenly, it rotated almost ninety degrees on its axis and a single, massive beam of radiant energy shot forth from what had once been its southern pole.

The light seemed like a living thing as it flew from the planet.

"Does it have a target?" Janeway asked.

"It is on course to impact the B star, Admiral," Seven said.

At any other time in Janeway's life, that response would have been met with confusion. As it was, thanks to Seven's simulations, the admiral now believed she understood precisely what the purpose of the planet's strange design actually was.

The moment the energy from the planet impacted the star, it began to move gently out of its orbit.

"Gods of my fathers," Janeway heard Chakotay whisper.

Indeed, she thought. *Who but a god would intentionally alter the orbital path of a star?*

The first gravimetric waves to impact *Voyager* were still a few minutes away. You didn't rip apart a solar system without radically altering the flow of energy moving through it. The asteroid field through which they were now traveling would be the first noticeable casualty. Millions of small pieces of rock would soon find their courses violently shifted. Most of them would be smashed into dust, but those that weren't would eventually settle into a new orbit.

"The star has now been pushed twenty-six kilometers out of its standard orbit. Its speed is increasing," Seven reported.

Horrifying as it was, watching a star move at the behest of an object designed specifically to free it of any stronger gravitational pull was one of the most majestic, awe-inspiring things Kathryn Janeway had ever seen.

"Seven, I'm reading three hundred discrete subspace waves targeting the B star," Lieutenant Kim reported from the bridge. *"Their intensity is increasing."*

Janeway had been so focused on the star's movement that she hadn't noticed the new readings that were now scrolling across the screen before her.

"They are emanating from the outer asteroid ring," Seven said.

"To what purpose?" Chakotay asked.

Seven was hurriedly requesting information from the ship's sensors, tapping at her control panel and shaking her head as the results began to appear on the screen.

"The subspace waves appear to be altering the geometry of space around the B star," Seven said.

"It's like they are carving a path for it, guiding it out of the system," Janeway added.

"And simultaneously minimizing the normal distortions created by the star's movement," Seven said.

"Remarkable," Chakotay observed.

They learned, Janeway thought. *The Edrehmaia, or whoever did this the first time—or maybe the thousandth, who knows—they destroyed the system when the star entered it. They didn't want that to happen again, so they found a solution.*

"*The intensity of the beam from the planet is starting to diminish,*" Kim reported from the bridge.

Janeway held her breath, waiting for the planet's explosive death throes.

They never came.

Instead, the inner light of the planet dimmed to nothing, its energy spent. But to everyone's amazement, it remained intact.

"Admiral," Seven said, "the B star has broken from its orbit and is departing from the system heading zero-eight-one mark six."

"*That guidance system had to be designed by the same species that constructed the planet,*" Harry Kim said. "*What were they called again?*"

"*The Edrehmaia,*" Lieutenant Lasren responded.

"It's a hell of a thing they created," Chakotay said. "It sent that star on its way while containing the destructive potential of its release."

"*So we're all going to live?*" Paris asked.

"For now," Seven replied.

"*But what use is a rogue star?*" Lasren asked.

"To us, nothing more than scientific curiosity," Janeway replied. "But I'd give a great deal to learn what use the Edrehmaia might have for one."

"Are we going to go looking?" Chakotay asked.

Janeway grinned. "Commander Paris, take us out of the

asteroid field, recall the rest of the fleet, and keep long-range sensors active. I don't want to lose track of that star."

"Aye, Admiral," Paris responded.

Ensign Aytar Gwyn sat beside the still form of Lieutenant Devi Patel. Low trills and beeps sounded constantly, the only sign that Devi was still alive.

Doctor Sharak had worked patiently for hours attempting to put her broken body back together. Gwyn suspected that wasn't going to be the hardest part to fix.

Sharak had allowed Gwyn to remain in sickbay while he worked. As soon as he had completed the surgery, he asked, despite his obvious exhaustion, to examine her.

She agreed, and added her profuse apologies for her behavior toward him while in the midst of the *finiis'ral*.

"Why would you apologize, Ensign, for something over which you had no control?" he asked kindly.

"I don't know," she replied. "To be polite?"

"Your desire for me was a biochemically induced imperative driven by a collection of powerful cellular processes. You could not have resisted it had you tried."

"But it must have been embarrassing," Gwyn said.

"I have never once been embarrassed by the desires of another," Sharak said. "I am pleased that your body found a way to subdue the metamorphic transition. Given what little I understand of the condition, it was an unexpected and entirely welcome development."

"It was," Gwyn agreed.

The doors to sickbay swished open and Lieutenant Kim entered. Gwyn pushed off the biobed and stood beside it.

"How is she doing?" Kim asked immediately of Doctor Sharak.

"Lieutenant Patel has survived a massive trauma. She will be monitored constantly for the next several hours," Sharak replied.

Turning his attention to Gwyn, Kim said, "I'm headed over to *Galen*. She just got back. Doctor Sal is still there and asked me to bring you over with me."

"I'm awfully tired, Lieutenant Kim. And Doctor Sharak just gave me a clean bill of health. Can it wait?"

Kim shrugged. "I hate to disappoint her, but given all you just went through, I'm sure she'll understand. Why don't you head to your quarters and get some rest. I'll take the heat for disappointing Sal."

"Thank you," Gwyn said, incredibly relieved.

"Thank you for bringing our friends home."

Something small and angry within the ensign suddenly reared its head.

"It shouldn't have been necessary," Gwyn said softly.

"I beg your pardon?"

"When you made contact with Devi's team and told them they would have to leave the data they had acquired behind, did she argue with you?"

Kim seemed taken aback by the question. "I don't remember," he said. "We were dealing with a number of emergency situations at the time. Our focus was on making sure that all of our crew members made it off the surface alive."

"Of course it was," Gwyn said, "but *think* for minute. Did she tell you how important what she had learned was?"

Kim searched his memory. "She requested permission to transmit the data over the comm line we had established. Commander Torres refused to allow the attempt. None of us were sure how stable that line was, and it was our only possible conduit for the remote transporter that Torres was creating."

Gwyn's spine stiffened. "If it had been Seven on the planet and she had been the one to insist that her data was every bit as important as the lives of those who had gathered it, would you have done the same?"

Kim did her the courtesy of seriously considering the question. Finally he said, "I don't honestly know. Seven has a way of making everyone around here feel like we're working for her. If she'd put her foot down, we might have spent a few more minutes trying to devise a work-around."

Gwyn turned to look at Patel's sickly pale face.

"And because you didn't, Devi made a call all of us are prepared to make, but none of us should have to," Gwyn said. "Ask yourself why Seven's insistence would have mattered more than hers. Devi graduated near the top of her class from the Academy and she has served this ship for four years. She's a Starfleet officer, not as experienced as you or the rest of our commanders, but every bit as bright.

"You didn't have any idea that she would risk her life to make sure you learned what she had down there. It never occurred to you that she would do anything but accept your decision, because no matter what, you know better."

"That's what being in command is, Gwyn. We don't always make the right call, but we live with whatever call we make. And I would have much preferred for that planet's secrets to have remained hidden forever than for her to have suffered as she obviously did."

"She knew better. She knew how valuable that data was. You dismissed her, as you do many of us who are newer to this ship and this fleet. And your lack of respect for her told her everything she needed to know about the value of her own life to this fleet."

Kim paled slightly. "You don't have to tell me about serving in the shadows of great men and women, Ensign," he said. "I did it every day for seven years before I was even acknowledged with a promotion. When we sign up to serve Starfleet, we do it where and how we are needed most. It isn't about us as individuals. It is about the greater good for the most people at any given time.

"I understand the choice she made better than you can possibly imagine," Kim continued. "And I understand why you did what you did as well. Had it gone any other way, you might be dead or your career might be over and that would have been a tremendous loss to us."

"I thought the point of this mission was for all of us to get a chance to show what we can do. But the minute things got tough you and the rest of our commanding officers reverted to business as usual. The point, Lieutenant Kim, is that *you don't know.* You haven't taken the time to get to know those of us who weren't with you for seven years. You don't know what we're capable of and every time you pass over us or silence us, you're missing out on valuable perspectives.

"This mission was cut short, but please, don't let the idea behind it, the belief that everyone here has a contribution to make beyond keeping their head down and following orders, end too. You need to set a better example for your fellow commanding officers and for the child you have brought into this universe."

Kim stepped back. "How did you . . ."

"I'm . . . I'm sorry," Gwyn said, backtracking quickly. "I was undergoing medical evaluation on the *Galen* and I saw her there. I have no intention of sharing that information with anyone else. You and Lieutenant Conlon are her parents, and any and all decisions regarding her are yours to make."

And by the way, I just suffered the torments of the damned in an attempt to save Lieutenant Conlon's life, almost followed that statement, but Gwyn bit it back.

"Thank you for understanding, and respecting our situation," Kim said.

Gwyn couldn't have done otherwise. It was possible that in the days and years to come, no one other than her parents would ever love that child more. But the truth of the choice Gwyn had made was that she would forever after be the one person in the universe who knew the child best. Even now, if she brought the baby to mind, she could feel the fluttering heart and a sensation of warm weightlessness.

Finally, Gwyn understood what her *leedi* truly was and had always been. Sharing that truth with Gwyn's mother had obviously been a great comfort to her. Gwyn had thousands of memories of the two of them chatting quietly over *triaka* tea. She used to wonder what they were talking about. She didn't wonder any longer.

Gwyn would be denied that. She had no idea how Kim or Conlon would react to what she had done and, for now, she had no intention of finding out. It didn't matter. If it did in the future, Gwyn would cross that bridge and set it aflame if necessary, to make sure that this tiny human, who was now and forever part of her body and soul, had everything she needed to be happy and healthy.

"I appreciate what you've said, Gwyn," Kim finally admitted. "You've given me a lot to think about."

"Good."

Ensign Icheb hadn't been back on *Voyager* for half an hour after *Galen* entered transporter range when there was a chime at his door.

Lieutenant Bryce didn't bother to ask permission to enter. He simply did, as soon as the door opened enough to grant him access.

"Phinn, I . . ." Icheb began.

"I'm so glad you're okay," Bryce said. "I mean, I'm glad we're all okay, obviously. I spent most of the last several hours contemplating my life ending. Well, honestly much of that time was devoted to analyzing our shield geometries to see how far I could push them when it came to surviving the death of a star system and a spherical asteroid belt that was about to become a galactic blender, and by the way, I have a few theories I need to run by you. But honestly, the thought of me dying didn't bother me nearly as much as the thought of other people's lives ending. Especially people who were traveling on vessels that are too small to integrate multivector subspace minivariables into deflector control and who lack the personnel to attempt those modifications. Frankly, I don't know if you or I should spend very much time in the future aboard the *Galen*. She's pretty, but she's a death trap in a lot of ways and not at all equipped to handle what we were just facing. I know your people put her survival in the sixty percentile range, but my numbers were in the low twenties and I think my math was better."

Icheb stared in silence, waiting for a moment to interject and sensing it would be some time coming.

"But that's not why I had to see you right away. I need you to know . . ." At this, Bryce's breath seemed to fail him and he took several quick inhalations to steady himself.

"I need you to know that I'm sorry. Obviously that kiss was a mistake. I didn't mean to push you. You're clearly not ready. Hell, I don't even know if I'm ready. But either way, it's not worth it, if it means I freaked you out so badly that you don't even want to return my messages. Sorry about that, by the way. Six was probably too many. Two was probably too many."

As Bryce considered the fingers of his hands, likely replaying the contents of each of his messages as he did so, Icheb stepped toward him and took both of Phinn's hands in his.

"Phinn," he said. "Stop it."

The physical contact had its desired effect, at least on Bryce. He swallowed whatever he had been about to add and simply stared in terror at Icheb.

"I'm sorry I didn't respond to your messages. There was a lot going on. Some of which I can't even tell you about. The part that I can will take some explaining. But you didn't do anything wrong."

With this, Icheb pulled Phinn close and kissed him gently.

When they both stepped back, Phinn's face was flushed, but he was smiling.

"Oh. Well, then. Good," he said.

It was a strange sensation, their second kiss. It didn't come close to activating the sensory pleasure it should have for Icheb, but there was still something in it. A small happiness that probably had more to do with Icheb's newfound certainty that no matter what his body told him, the rest of him was fully committed to whatever it was that was happening between the two of them.

"Do you have a few minutes?"

"No," Phinn admitted. His smile was frustrated and his eyes glistened brightly. "I'll probably end up on report if the captain finds out I'm here now."

"As soon as you have more time, let me know. And I promise, I'll tell you everything I can."

"Deal," Phinn said.

Commander Tom Paris had never been so happy to see the inside of his quarters as he was when he finally ended his bridge duty and entered to find B'Elanna holding Michael in one hand and caressing the sleeping head of their daughter with the other.

The three were sprawled on the family's sofa, B'Elanna with her feet up.

"Is there room for one more?" Tom asked.

B'Elanna smiled sleepily. "Always."

Tom sat down on the side opposite Miral and put his arm around his wife. She gently transferred her son to Tom and adjusted her position, sending a pleasant-sounding crack up her spine.

"Thank you. That's so much better," B'Elanna said.

"Did you see any of it?"

"Nope," B'Elanna said. "I heard what happened. Seven's already burying me under reports and requests for engineering to put together new teams to examine the remains of the planet. It will be difficult without the biodomes, but we'll figure something out."

"You didn't want to watch?"

"I've seen death coming for us enough times to know that the only thing I want in my mind's eye when that moment comes are the three faces here with me right now," B'Elanna replied.

Tom nodded.

After a long silence he said, "We cut it too close down

there. If Gwyn hadn't broken every rule in the book and stolen that runabout, neither of us would have survived that mission."

"Shhh," B'Elanna whispered. "Not now."

"When?" Tom asked. "When is it going to be the right time for us to talk about this? I love our lives here. I couldn't ask for a better ship or a better crew. But apparently Miral doesn't know what her home is. She thinks we left it somewhere behind in the Alpha Quadrant. What if she was right?"

B'Elanna sighed as she turned to stare into her husband's eyes. "Miral is a child, Tom. She knows what we teach her. If she's confused about what a home is, or how many ways there are to make a life in this universe, it's only because we haven't taught her yet how many valid possibilities there are, or how grateful she should be to have a chance to live out here. We keep shielding her from what we do every day. I think it's time we started to include her more."

Tom was surprised. He didn't disagree, but his own recent fears had been so huge, he marveled that hers hadn't led her to the same uncomfortable place in which he found himself mired.

"As I sat here for the last several hours contemplating the fact that we all might not survive this time, I realized that the only things I really regret in this life are the chances I didn't take because I was afraid. I didn't want to risk my father's indifference, so I missed out on a lot of love he wanted to give me. I was so angry with my mother for so many years, I almost lost the chance to show her that it wasn't being Klingon that was the problem; it was not understanding what being Klingon really *meant*.

"Miral and Michael don't need parents who abandoned their life's work to keep them safe. They need parents who will show them every day how to survive in a universe that doesn't truly care who lives and who dies. Someday they will be old enough to decide for themselves what kind of life they want to lead. Until then, we're going to show them how good a life spent in service and exploration can be."

"Okay," Tom said. "But maybe next time we don't both go down to the planet that's about to explode."

"We saved the lives of four people who would have died otherwise. We were the best people for that mission. We go where we are needed."

"And make sure Gwyn is always standing by?"

"You're first officer. You hand out the duty assignments. If that makes you feel better, have at it," B'Elanna said, smiling.

To see B'Elanna this introspective and forgiving was a rare thing in Tom's experience. He decided it was time to risk a little more honesty.

"There's something I've wanted to tell you for days," Tom said. "I didn't because Harry asked me not to. I'm sure he wanted to do it himself in his own time."

B'Elanna turned to face him and searched his eyes for a long moment. "Then don't," she finally said softly.

Tom knew the surprise on his face was obvious to her. She laughed lightly as she continued, "Harry is your best friend. If he wants you to keep his secrets, you need to do that. It's no more than I asked of you once."

"Yeah, and Harry was furious."

"I'm never going to put you in that position again, my love. Life is too short."

For the millionth time since B'Elanna had agreed to be his wife, Tom Paris marveled at his good fortune. "You are amazing," he said, kissing her tenderly.

"I really am."

Seven sat in her quarters reviewing the data Devi Patel had recovered from DK-1116. It was nothing short of astonishing.

She only recognized six of the species that had at one time or another visited the planet and attempted to manipulate the Edrehmaia substance. She had never heard of the Edrehmaia, which was a little disturbing. Whoever that species was, they had advanced beyond the Borg, beyond Starfleet, beyond the Caeliar, beyond perhaps any species of which Seven was aware short of the Q.

There were no visual records of the Edrehmaia, only all they had left behind and all that Species 001—another species that had apparently successfully eluded the Borg—had created around it in an attempt to master it.

Her station chirped, indicating an incoming transmission from *Demeter*. Seven opened the channel. A few moments later, the face of Commander O'Donnell appeared before her.

"It's incredible, isn't it?" he asked without preamble.

"How did you get your hands on information that has yet to be integrated into our fleet-wide database?" Seven asked.

"The planet didn't explode. It wasn't a bomb. It moved a goddamned star out of orbit and sent it off into the galaxy toward parts unknown. And apparently one of your junior science officers had the presence of mind to make sure that the only

knowledge we will ever get about the species that performed that miracle survived. She's not even a member of my crew and I've already put in for a commendation for her.

"It's living technology, Seven. Not some organic-synthetic hybrid. Not programmable matter that mimics flesh and blood so thoroughly that you forget the difference. We didn't even know what we were looking at when we were down there. Humans have yet to conceive of a merging of biology and inorganic matter at the atomic level. Sadly, our experience of life-forms like the Borg will probably limit our desire to even explore that avenue of research for centuries to come.

"But these people, these Edrehmaia? They don't share our fears. They're busy reordering the universe to suit their needs. To them, we're savages painting on cave walls. How much sleep do you think I'm going to be getting over the next few days?"

"I am planning to put together a team to study whatever is left down there as soon as we are certain it is safe."

"We also need to consider sending teams to find and study the technology in the outer asteroid belt that kept the rest of the system intact."

"I will add that to the list."

"Thank you."

Once she had signed off, Seven set her station to record one more personal message before signing off for the night.

Kenth Lasren, Jepel Omar, and Thomas Vincent sat beside Devi Patel's biobed into the wee hours of the night. Furtive whispers had passed between them. *How could she do that? Why didn't she say anything? What was she thinking?*

Jepel and Vincent seemed genuinely flummoxed by Patel's choice.

Lasren was not. He was, however, kicking himself for

having failed her so thoroughly and for his final, entirely inaccurate characterization of her last orders as their team leader. *She wasn't sacrificing the rest of us. She only ever intended to sacrifice herself.*

He alone had known how seriously Patel was taking this mission. And he alone could have accessed her emotions, especially in those final moments, and done *something* to prevent her from taking the course she had chosen.

He hadn't because he had been blind to the depth of Devi Patel's transformation during their mission and because he had been so concerned for his own safety at the end that he had consciously chosen to focus only on himself.

That's the difference, he decided, *between leaders and followers*. No matter what, leaders put themselves last. The windows he had peered through that had allowed him to see Devi Patel's demons had shown him a young woman driven by a need to achieve. But that was hardly a unique thing among Starfleet officers. More important, they had shown him a young woman trying to do that in a place that might never make room for her voice or her accomplishments. They lived in a world with no outward significers of achievement. The accumulation of personal wealth or commodities meant nothing among their peers. Respect and acknowledgment were the Federation's only currency.

This made it easy for those who weren't driven by a desire to excel. A Federation citizen, a Starfleet officer, could live a lifetime of comfort, adventure, and dedicated effort without risking much of anything, should they so desire.

But those who wanted more often found themselves faced with the prospect of a future that provided no certain path to silencing the demons that had driven them to Starfleet in the first place.

There was nothing wrong with Devi Patel wanting more. And while she had taken a few risks he found unacceptable during their time on the planet, in the end she had decided that she alone would bear the greatest risk and make the ultimate sacrifice in the name of safeguarding her team and honoring what they had all achieved together. A lot of people might think what she had done was foolish, or the result of an insufficient sense of personal regard.

Lasren believed that he had witnessed, without even realizing it at the time, the moment when one of his fellow voyagers grew beyond their limitations and fears and became that which they had always desired to be. Her last act had not been meant to secure her own glory. One needed to be alive for that to mean anything. Her choice had been a statement of selflessness, something he had not credited her with possessing. And it had never once occurred to him. He hadn't given a second thought to the knowledge they had acquired. His only concern had been surviving.

This truth made him feel small. He knew it wasn't meant to. It merely signified that while he and Devi were only a few years apart in age, they were light-years apart in other ways.

Devi stirred. Her eyes fluttered open.

Lasren and the others instantly rose to their feet.

"Hey, Devi. How are you feeling?"

"Do you need anything? Does anything hurt?"

It took her a few more moments to realize where she was.

Instantly, Lasren found himself standing in the cavern once again. He saw through her eyes the last moments she had witnessed, the consummation of the purpose of the planet and its technology. He felt her fear, but he also felt her exultation.

"Give her some air, guys," Lasren chided the others.

"I'm alive?" Patel croaked.

Lasren took her hand and nodded. "You are."

"How?"

"Gwyn."

"Huh," Patel said, as if this thought confused her. "Is she okay?"

"Yep."

"That's good."

"You have about a million messages from the rest of the fleet," Vincent said. "Everybody has already heard about what you did and is pulling for you."

"That's nice," Patel said softly.

"Why don't you guys go tell Doctor Sharak that his patient is awake?" Lasren suggested.

Jepel and Vincent nodded in understanding and stepped away.

"Don't be angry," Patel said as soon as they were alone.

"I'm not. I'm in awe."

"I don't think I deserve that either."

"Maybe not. But you're going to get it anyway, so get used to it." After a moment, he added, "I'm sorry."

"For what?"

"For abandoning you at the end."

"I didn't give you a choice."

"And why was that?"

Patel closed her eyes. When she opened them again, they were glistening. "I didn't get it before—the reason I had never managed to stand out here. I thought it was because I wasn't given the same chances as everyone else. What I finally figured out was that I wasn't doing enough with the chances I was given. There really are things worth dying for. But I couldn't make that call for anyone but myself."

"If you had asked, we might have found another way."

"If I had asked, you would have talked me out of it."

"I would have tried."

The panel above Patel's head pinged softly.

"You have another message. From Seven," he said in surprise.

Patel inhaled deeply. "Great."

"Don't you want to hear it?"

"Not right now."

"You just faced down death. You think this could be worse than that?"

Patel shook her head. "Fine. Just play it."

Lasren retrieved the message and Seven's voice sounded softly around them.

"Lieutenant Patel. I have begun an analysis of the data you recovered from the planet. I understand you were seriously injured and I hope that your recovery is swift. As soon as you are able, we will be assembling several teams to continue our study of the Edrehmaia's technology. Your leadership will be essential to our success. Please let me know as soon as you are able to return to duty."

Lasren felt his chest tighten. When he looked back at Devi, she was weeping freely.

VESTA

The moment Doctor Sal returned to *Vesta* she was ordered to report to Captain Farkas's ready room. When she arrived, Counselor Cambridge was already there.

Sal had waited an extra hour after *Galen* had rejoined the fleet in hopes that Ensign Gwyn would return. Instead Lieutenant Kim had reported that Gwyn had requested time to rest. Sal had to admit that the poor woman had earned it. The fleet's reprieve meant that there would be plenty of time ahead to determine whether or not Sal's suspicions about the termination of Gwyn's *finiis'ral* were true.

She could see from Regina's face, however, that a different kind of reckoning was at hand. She had known that face for most of her life, and Regina was no good at poker. She was beyond furious, which meant that Cambridge had been telling tales out of school.

"Should I sit?" Sal asked wearily.

"This won't take long," Farkas replied. "After discussing your actions over the last several days regarding the care of your patients Lieutenant Conlon and Ensign Gwyn, I have decided to restrict you from further participation in their cases."

Sal was over eighty years old, so she was often cold, no matter what the ambient temperature was. The ice pouring through her veins now had nothing to do with her age.

"You don't mean that."

"Oh, yes, El'nor, I do. You should be glad I'm not adding official disciplinary actions and a report to the board of Starfleet Medical as well."

"Ensign Gwyn," Sal began softly.

"Ensign Gwyn was the worst of it, but hardly all of it," Farkas said. "Before you even got to Gwyn, you pushed Lieutenant Kim to approve a medical procedure for his child that you knew full well its mother did not want. What the hell were you thinking?"

"This was your doing?" Sal demanded of Cambridge.

"Priorities are tricky things," Cambridge admitted. "On the one hand, your previous experience with Vega Nine makes you the ideal doctor to take the lead in curing Nancy

Conlon. On the other, almost every choice you have made regarding Nancy Conlon, up to and including your willingness to endanger another life to save hers, suggests that you lack appropriate perspective to remain on either case."

"You promised me," Regina hissed. "You swore to me that you knew exactly what to do and that Ensign Gwyn was risking nothing more than a blood draw."

"I could not have foreseen the series of events that caused Ensign Gwyn's metamorphic cells to assert themselves the way they did."

"You artificially enhanced them," Farkas said, her voice rising.

"And had she not been forced to undergo antiproton therapy, that wouldn't have been a problem. Did the counselor also tell you that her body apparently reverted to its normal state without further intervention?"

"He did. But before that happened she suffered a great deal, did she not?"

"It was not my intention," Sal began.

"I don't give a good goddamn about your intentions, El'nor. *I know what drove you here*. You've been carrying a grudge against the Kriosian elders for decades now. You want to humiliate them, to punish them for what they did to that poor woman. Nancy Conlon's condition gave you cover.

"But neither you nor I will ever be in a position to extract the kind of vengeance you are seeking, nor will exposing them to the Federation at large do anything other than divide our people at a time when we are still trying to recover from our near extinction at the hands of the Borg."

"Spare me your sanctimonious platitudes, Regina. This isn't about Kataly Norol or the fact that she was murdered by her government to ensure her silence. We're talking about a civilization that condoned the violent repression of half of their population for thousands of years. The people of Krios will never be free of that until they understand their history and confront the darkness of their own instincts."

"Maybe," Farkas agreed. "But who the hell put you in charge of deciding which civilizations are worthy of Federation membership? The thousands of years our people spent doing worse by most of the human race, male and female, isn't exactly a sterling recommendation for our membership either."

"We moved beyond that kind of thinking."

"So have most of them."

"As long as metamorphs are used as pawns for political gain, I am forced to disagree with that assessment, Captain."

The air between them was thick with righteous indignation.

"You realize, of course, the problem is that you're both right," Cambridge interjected at his peril. This had the effect of temporarily silencing both of them as they directed their attention toward the counselor.

"There is not a single race in our Federation, probably not in the entire universe, that can claim a perfect record when it comes to its social development. The good news is none of them have ever claimed otherwise.

"The Federation is an organization of individuals, but it is also an idea. It is a framework, a set of agreed-upon principles that guide civilizations as they continue to develop. It is a commitment to the attempt to do better, to *become* a more perfect union.

"We don't get there by forgetting our past, but nor do we get there by holding current generations responsible for that past as long as they have unraveled the systemic injustices that held them back, or are working diligently to do so.

"The good captain sees our universe as it is. The good doctor demands that the universe do better. But in this instance, you both erred in almost exactly the same way. Neither of you saw fit to bring Doctor Sal's deeply held convictions to the attention of her colleagues. Had you done so, we might have been able to mitigate some of the more unfortunate consequences of her actions before they endangered Ensign Gwyn's life. You chose silence, Captain, because you did not want to believe the worst of your friend. You kept your intentions secret, Doctor, because you knew that dragged out under the harsh light of day, they would have been found to be ethically suspect at best."

Farkas crossed to stand directly in front of Sal. "Not that long ago, El'nor, you and I sat in this office discussing the moral lapses of Commander Jefferson Briggs. Apart from the body count, explain to me the difference between his actions and yours."

Sal felt the strike as if it had landed across her face.

"This is why we make rules. Because even the best of us, when faced with high enough stakes, can justify almost anything in the name of a potential solution. You crossed the line, El'nor. You know you did. I wouldn't be your friend, or your captain, if I didn't drag you back to the other side."

"You just sentenced Nancy Conlon to death."

"No, I didn't. I don't know exactly whom to blame for her current condition, but it isn't me. And there are dozens of dedicated physicians in this fleet who will step in and do what they can to save her. Your actions were not those of a dedicated physician. They were those of someone who has run out of ideas."

Sal squared her shoulders. "Am I dismissed, Captain?"

"Yes."

Epilogue

When Harry Kim finally entered the medical bay, he could see through the transparent window into Nancy's suite that her bed was empty.

"Doctor?" he called out urgently.

"In here, Mister Kim," the Doctor's voice replied.

Kim followed it and found Nancy seated upright in a chair beside the incubator in which their daughter floated. She lifted her face to his, and for a few moments it looked as if she didn't recognize him.

"Nancy?"

"Hi, Harry," she said softly.

"We brought the lieutenant out of her coma a few hours ago and since then have been bringing her up to date on some of the more significant developments of the last several days," the Doctor reported.

"How is she?" Kim asked.

"*She's* right here," Conlon replied a little tersely.

"I'm sorry, I didn't mean . . ."

"I am pleased to say that her neurological functions are once again within normal limits and that she does not appear to have suffered any long-term damage from the rupture," the Doctor said.

Kim pulled up a chair to sit beside Conlon and reached out, taking her nearer hand in his. "That's great news, isn't it?"

Conlon nodded.

"I'm sure you both have a great deal to discuss," the Doctor said. "If you need me, I'll be in my office."

"Thank you, Doctor," Conlon said.

"Yeah, thanks, Doc."

To prevent a prolonged silence from becoming unbearable Kim said, "I guess the Doctor told you what happened with the baby."

"He did. The last thing I remember I was standing in the most beautiful forest. The next thing I know, I'm a mother."

"What forest?" Kim asked.

Conlon chuckled in spite of herself. "Really? You want to know all about the quaking aspens?"

"I want to know everything there is to know about you," he replied honestly.

Conlon looked away. "I was actually okay. I had finally made peace with the fact that I couldn't use this child's cells to cure me if I was unwilling to commit to raising her as best I could. I was content with that choice."

"I know," Kim said. "And if that's still your choice, I'm okay with that. I will make sure that our daughter is taken care of. It doesn't have to be your problem."

Conlon stared at him for a moment as if he were a completely unidentifiable alien species. "That choice no longer exists, Harry. She's here now. She's ours. And we are hers."

Kim knew she could see the relief wash over his face.

"Why didn't you tell me?" she asked softly.

"Tell you what?"

"How much you wanted the baby?"

Kim shrugged. "I just couldn't. I couldn't do one more thing to make your life harder."

"And I didn't give you much of a chance, did I?"

"No."

"I'm sorry. I was so scared. I still am. But everything is different now." After a pause, she continued. "The quaking aspens are a unique tree. From a single seed, thousands of interwoven roots give rise to tens of thousands of trees. From a distance it looks like countless individuals. The less obvious truth is that all of them are one.

"You and I and her are like that, Harry. We look like three, but we're really one."

Conlon gave his hand a gentle squeeze. "You know how sometimes when you turn a problem over and over in your head, you get stuck. No matter how you try to find new ways of thinking about it, you just keep falling into the same old patterns of thought that lead nowhere productive?"

"I guess. Sure," Kim said.

"That's where I was. That's what I went looking for before my brain decided to start bleeding out. I needed a new way to think about all of this. A new perspective."

"Did you find it?"

Conlon turned her head to stare at the gestational incubator.

"No. I can't lie about this, Harry. Not to myself and not to either of you. The odds are really good that I'm not going to be functioning very well by this time next year, even if the doctors can keep me alive after I start to develop all of the other conditions that will result from my DNA's inability to repair itself."

"I'm not saying the problem is going to be easy to solve. But I do believe the doctors will find a way to solve it eventually," Kim insisted.

"They might. But they might not. It just might not be possible."

"We do impossible things out here every damn day. That's pretty much Starfleet's unwritten mission statement."

"You're not helping," Conlon said softly. "I understand what you're trying to do. You don't want me to lose hope. You want me to fight, for myself and for all of us. But I don't want to spend what time I have left at war with myself or you. I want to enjoy it as best I can. And that means accepting that there are limits to it. There are things I'm just never going to get to do."

"You don't know that," Kim said, his voice rising. "You have no idea what the future might hold and neither do I. It's one thing to live every day as if it might be your last. It's another to *decide* it will be, to just give up."

"I'm not giving up. I'm trying to deal with reality."

Kim stared at her, the pale skin, the wide brown eyes and the dark circles beneath them. There was so much fear in them.

"To hell with reality," he said as he rose from his chair and moved to the data panel at the doorway. "I want you to see something," he said, calling up Doctor Sharak's program. Seconds later, the room vanished and Harry found himself standing with only Nancy and the baby in a sea of stars. He heard Conlon inhale sharply.

"Give it a second. You'll get used to it," he said.

"What is this?"

"A new perspective," he said. "I had no idea until a few days ago that several areas of this medical bay are simply holodecks. Doctor Sharak created this for the baby. He thought she would find it soothing."

"Space without an EV suit. Why did I never think to do this before?" she asked.

"Because it's impossible."

"It's absurd."

"You want me to turn it off?"

Conlon considered for a moment. "Never," she finally replied.

Kim stepped closer to her. "For weeks, I haven't been able to breathe. Every time I think about the future my mind just locks up."

"I know the feeling."

"It's fear."

"Fear is a rational response right now."

"It's also useless. We've both been so busy trying to accept the unacceptable we forgot that together, we can do anything. That ends here and now."

"Harry."

"Hear me out. I don't care anymore how we got here. I only care about where we go from this point forward."

Kim took both her hands in his and continued. "As far as I'm concerned, you and I are in this together, for better or worse, in sickness and health, forsaking all others until we are parted by death."

"And if that last part comes sooner rather than later?"

Kim sighed deeply. "I don't care."

Conlon took both his hands and used them to pull herself up. She lifted her face to his and kissed him tenderly.

"Neither do I," she said.

In that moment beneath the naked stars, something that had until then seemed impossible, suddenly felt possible.

VOYAGER

Admiral Janeway sat beside Captain Chakotay on the low sofa under the long port in what had once been her ready room. She wasn't certain anymore how long they had gone without rest. But the events of the last several hours left her pondering far too many things to consider sleep an option now. Beside her, Chakotay had just finished reading her first communique from Agent Gariff Lucsly.

"He can't be serious," Chakotay said as he handed the padd back to her.

"Have you ever met him?"

"No."

"He is, quite possibly, the most serious individual I have ever met."

"He wants us to begin preparations to return to Krenim space and open diplomatic negotiations."

"Yes, he does."

"We're in the middle of a discovery that might very well change everything Starfleet thinks it knows about the laws of the universe."

"He won't care."

"Never mind the fact that you promised Agent Dayne that we would stay out of Krenim affairs for the foreseeable future."

Janeway sighed. "Lucsly's not wrong that our current détente is likely unsustainable. We are once again a variable in their equations, and there is no way to be certain that they will ignore that. The best way forward with the Krenim is to make them our friends rather than allow them to go on believing us to be their enemies."

"If he thinks it's going to be that easy, tell him to get his ass out here and handle that contact himself," Chakotay said.

Janeway tossed him a sidelong glance. "Don't even think it," she said.

"So what are you going to do?"

"For now? Nothing."

"Aren't you required to follow his directives regarding the Krenim going forward?"

"Am I?" she asked.

Chakotay smiled.

"I recall promising to take them under advisement. Before I can possibly undertake a mission of such import, I'm going to have to give the matter serious thought. It would be unwise to rush in unprepared."

"Obviously."

"And I'm afraid our work here has only just begun."

"Agreed."

"By the way, what are you going to do with Ensign Gwyn?"

"I thought I might give Cambridge a chance to make a recommendation before I did anything."

"You should talk to her and Lieutenant Patel."

Chakotay scratched the back of his head. "Patel has always been one of my most capable and steady officers. I still can't believe she did what she did."

"Chakotay, you and I have been setting examples for the entire crew far too long now for that to be the case. I've never been a parent, but 'Do as I say, not as I do' has never struck me as a particularly good form of discipline."

"You think they were both just doing what we would have done in their situation?"

Janeway nodded. "You have a better explanation?"

Chakotay shrugged. "Not tonight. But what kind of commanding officers does that make us?"

"Apparently, terribly predictable ones."

"Do you think Lucsly is aware of that?"

"Oh, trust me. He knows."

"We're going to need a few days to perform repairs and scan the new landscape of this system. And we're not going to let that star fall off our long-range sensors in the process. Now that it's free, do you think there's a chance those who did it might come looking for it?"

"A girl can dream," Janeway said with a mischievous twinkle in her eye.

Captain to the bridge.

Chakotay rose abruptly. "On my way."

Janeway followed him out as he started toward his chair. Both paused as they took in the image on the main viewscreen.

"What the hell is that?" Chakotay asked.

Hanging before them was a large black sphere only visible by the reflected light of the system's single star.

"Unknown, sir," Aubrey reported. "Sensors didn't pick it up incoming. We started reading some sort of displacement field, and then it was just suddenly there."

"Does it match anything in our databases?" Janeway asked.

"Actually, it does," Waters reported from ops.

"What?"

"It shares several key characteristics with that thing Lieutenant Kim destroyed yesterday. The thing that attacked Gwyn and ate our shuttle," Waters said. "Only it is considerably more stable than its predecessor."

"Yellow alert," Chakotay said as he took his seat and Janeway settled herself in the one to his left.

"Hail them," Chakotay ordered.

After a few moments Waters reported, "No response, sir."

Chakotay looked to Janeway.

"Open a channel," the admiral ordered. "This is Admiral Kathryn Janeway of the United Federation of Planets. Please identify yourselves."

"You think it's the Edrehmaia?"

"I think it could be."

The next thing either of them knew, they were picking themselves up off the deck. The bridge was bathed in darkness, illuminated faintly by weak crimson lights. The other officers on duty were doing the same.

"Report," Chakotay ordered.

Waters was the first to do so. "The alien vessel is gone, sir."

"Damage report?"

"None, sir."

"Did they attack us?"

"We have sensor logs for the last eleven minutes," Waters said.

"We've been out for eleven minutes?"

"I think so, sir."

"Play the sensor log onscreen," Janeway requested.

Together Chakotay and Janeway watched as the strange black object altered its shape into a long rectangular configuration. Immediately following that, brightly colored lights all across the visible spectrum began to flash from it.

"What are those?" Chakotay asked.

"I don't know, sir," Waters said.

As this continued, the other fleet vessels could be seen moving in to surround the object.

Chakotay almost ordered them off before he remembered that everything he was seeing had already happened.

The lights dimmed and went out. Several seconds passed, and then a single white beam shot forth from the object in the direction of the *Galen*. Its shields held for less than fifteen seconds before a massive explosion ripped through her.

Chakotay felt his gorge rise as Janeway placed a hand on his arm to steady herself. He couldn't believe what he had just seen. He didn't want to.

"Waters, scan for the *Galen*."

"Yes, sir."

As she did so, several chirps sounded from her station. *Vesta* and *Demeter* were reporting in.

"I'm sorry, Captain," Waters finally said, her voice shaking. "She's gone. The *Galen* has been destroyed."

ACKNOWLEDGMENTS

Once upon a time, a girl who loved to tell stories saw a TV show on which a bunch of humans and a particularly fascinating alien with pointed ears flew around space in a gorgeous white ship discovering all sorts of weird and scary and thrilling things. Her older brother, Matt, was the person who made her watch that show, and later her younger brother, Paul, would fall in love with it too. Her parents, Fred and Patricia, made sure as she grew up that she always had access to all the things she needed to keep telling stories: books, dolls, games, puzzles, more books, and an education at a school where her seventh-grade teacher helped her write her very first novel. (Don't ask. It was terrible.)

By the time that girl was a young woman, she had decided that the last thing in the world she wanted to do was write her stories down. And then she saw another TV show on which an incredibly capable and interesting woman led a crew of humans and more aliens on a harrowing mission to get home after being flung to the far side of the galaxy. This show made her realize that writing her stories down was an interesting challenge, and that writing stories for *this show* was something she really, really wanted to do.

By then she had married David, who—and this is critical—absolutely believed that she could do any damn thing she set her mind to. So she started writing her stories down. At first, they were not very good. But the more she wrote, the better they got. She found another woman who loved this universe as much as she did, and they started trying to create stories together. Her name was Heather Jarman, and shortly thereafter, Heather was invited to start writing books about that universe because she is awesome.

Then the young woman got a little impatient. How exactly was she supposed to become a member of the very small club of people who get to tell these stories professionally? So she wrote to Jeri Taylor, the executive producer of the show with the cool female captain, and asked that question. (Actually, she advised Ms. Taylor in no uncertain terms that she was *supposed* to be working for her.) Because Ms. Taylor is a mensch, she invited the young woman in to pitch her stories.

The first person the young woman ever pitched her stories to was a young man named Bryan Fuller. Because Bryan was kind and thoughtful and very encouraging, the young woman kept at it.

Years went by. The show with the female captain ended, and the woman was no closer to reaching her goal of writing professional stories for that universe she loved so much. But she went ahead and kept writing other things. Shortly thereafter, Heather Jarman introduced her to Marco Palmieri, and Marco invited her to write her very first professional short story and novel.

Once Marco made her that offer, she decided she needed to find an agent to represent her for that deal, and she found Maura Teitelbaum. They've been best friends ever since because Maura has a keen eye for talent. (Not really. I mean, she *does*, but they are best friends because Maura always believed in her ability to do anything she wanted and opened doors that needed opening to make that happen.)

At the same event where she met Marco for the first time, a total stranger who was also writing books in that universe, named Kevin Dilmore, crossed a crowded room to shake her hand and introduce himself, because Kevin is one of the kindest and best people who's ever lived. Kevin introduced her to his writing partner, Dayton Ward, and the woman's belief that the coolest people in the world shared her love of this universe was cemented.

The first couple of books led to more, which is how she started working with Margaret Clark. The woman would eventually dedicate the book you've just read to Margaret, on account of Margaret also being a mensch and saving her literary ass more times than the woman could ever count.

The woman also met Ed Schlesinger, who very kindly offered to keep publishing her stories as long as she agreed to keep writing them.

More years. More books. More new friends. David Mack came along, and although she immediately respected his writing ability, she also hated him a little at first because he was so very talented. That happens sometimes. She got over it. Then she met Christopher Bennett, who knows everything there is to know about science, so more jealousy to overcome. Then she met Una McCormack and James Swallow and Dave Galanter and Keith DeCandido and Bill Leisner and Michael A. Martin and Bob Greenberger and Michael Jan Friedman and Aaron Rosenberg and Scott Pearson and John Van Citters and finally, finally, finally, David R. George and his amazing wife, Karen. By that time she was too used to being awed by the talent of these nice people to be envious, so she just skipped that part and went straight to the being-great-friends-and-colleagues part, which is a much better way to live.

And somewhere in the middle of all that, Anorah was born. Anorah is by far the best thing this woman has ever had a hand in creating and is the reason the woman has anything at all to say about anything. Being a mom focuses the mind and breaks open the heart, and all the words just come pouring out after that. Trust me.

Then the woman met Heather Kadin. When Heather learned that the woman had written all these books about this amazing universe and because Heather was also interested in telling stories in the same universe—and was, in fact, about to create a new TV show about that universe—she invited the woman to meet her good friends Aaron Baiers and Bryan Fuller (of course, the woman already knew Bryan because life is so very strange sometimes it almost seems like someone is planning this shit). And Bryan agreed that the woman should, in fact, not only get to keep telling stories about their old friends on *Voyager*, she should also get to tell stories about their new friends on something called *Discovery*.

Which was a TV show.

Which was the woman's dream way back in the beginning when she decided she wanted to write her stories down.

Which was also the moment that the woman realized that *Full Circle* was not just the title of one of the most challenging stories she had ever told, but also, apparently, the title of her life.

And then she met Gretchen and Aaron and Alex and Jesse and Aron and Nick and Joe and Kemp and Loretta and

Tyler and Chris and Brandon and Melissa and Anthony and Akiva and Craig and Ted and Boey and Erika and Lisa and Jordan and got to work with them all day every day telling *Star Trek* stories.

Which sounds like the end of the story but, as it turns out, is really just the middle, and the end is nowhere in sight.

Dreams come true, my dear readers. They really do. It may take years and it will require you to give the best you have to offer every time you touch them, but they will rise to meet you when and where you least expect to find them.

If I had written this story, a very wise editor like Margaret would probably have told me that while the characters were certainly compelling and the action had plenty of complications, that last bit was just too neat. No one would believe it.

Which is why I'm so glad I'm getting to live this story instead of just telling it.

To each and every person mentioned above and especially the readers who've waited so patiently for me to finish this book while my life was exploding all around me, as well as the countless loves of my life whom I've had to leave out so that this acknowledgments section would not be longer than the novel itself, I can only say: Thank you from the bottom of my heart. Without you, I would not be me.

ABOUT THE AUTHOR

Please see the previous page.
Also, for the record, Kirsten Beyer still has no complaints.